Through the mists of nightmare she saw figures moving, weaving in a peculiar dance. In a clear space a woman stood, a great white Russian wolfhound at her feet. The woman was the one in Sebastian's painting. Adrienne desperately wanted to scream, but though she felt her lips move, no sound emerged.

"Adrienne." The woman smiled, extending a hand. "There is nothing to fear. You are welcome here."

Adrienne saw that the twisting, weaving figures in the background were the other women in Sebastian's paintings, all of them watching her intently while their lips curved in unreadable smiles.

"You will never grow old, Adrienne," the woman was saying. "Forever young, Adrienne. Forever and ever and ever . . ."

"No! No!"

R. R. WALTERS

A TOM DOHERTY ASSOCIATES BOOK

This is a work of fiction. All the characters and events portrayed in this book are fictional, and any resemblance to real people or incidents is purely coincidental.

LADIES IN WAITING

First printing: September 1986

A TOR Book

Published by Tom Doherty Associates, Inc.
49 West 24 Street
New York, N.Y. 10010

ISBN: 0-812-52700-3
CAN. ED.: 0-812-52701-1

Printed in the United States

0 9 8 7 6 5 4 3 2 1

Acknowledgment

Thanks to Patti, in whose dreams
the first portraits were painted,
and to the ladies at Tor who
helped to make the dreams reality.

CHAPTER

The sign was all but invisible amid the untrimmed crotons and twisted peppertrees which formed a ragged barrier between the county road and the property. Adrienne Lewis very nearly missed it, only catching a glimpse of the wooden panel from the corner of her eye as she passed. She muttered irritably under her breath, glanced in the rearview mirror to check for following traffic and brought the Toyota to a slow stop, then backed up slowly, drifting the car to the edge of the macadam, going beyond the sign so she could read it through the windshield.

Neatly burned on the shellacked oak board, cut into the shape of a palette, were the words "Ned Anderson, Photography and Art, Geoffrey Clements, Ceramics." With a little sigh, Adrienne inched the car toward the driveway entrance, feeling she had already accomplished a great deal in just finding the place.

In the driveway, she stopped again, this time to look at the house, set in the ruins of what had obviously been manicured lawns and a formal garden. Compared with the straight, uninterrupted lines of today's tract development buildings, the house looked overweight and awkward. Its wide verandah gave it a middle-aged spread, dormer windows bulged plumply and the steamboat Gothic fretwork was a little unkempt. The house sagged, too, as if the inner structures, like old muscles, had grown tired and stretched, no longer able to hold their tone. A trifle more than half the house was such a clean, sterile white that the newly applied paint appeared still wet, while the remaining portion of it was inflicted with that peculiar muddied hue old paint assumes when the elements have had their way with it for too long. Two ladders, one tall, one short, leaned against the front side at the demarcation between the old and new paint, forgotten along with the monotonous task they represented. Shadows from the dozen or so oaks and pines growing in the yard dappled the house with tremulous shadows, creating an illusion of a constantly changing perspective, bits and pieces of the building appearing to either advance or recede in unending movement. Yet, in spite of its plumpness and weariness, there was a durability about the building unduplicated by modern architecture. Admitting to herself she was not delighted with what she saw, Adrienne nevertheless liked the place. She drove slowly up the driveway.

At the rear of the house, under the branches of an exceptionally large and twisted peppertree, weed stubble dotted a gravel parking area large enough for three cars. Beyond was a carriage house. A Chevrolet station wagon sat in the peppertree's shade.

The carriage house was further along in restoration than the main house. A new paint job was completed, and if there had been any slouching of the outside staircase or sagging of window casements, it had been corrected. What had been the carriage doors were permanently closed to form three arching sections of the wall, with a blooming herbal bed running along their base. In several places, young ivy vines were starting exploratory climbs up the walls.

Adrienne parked the car and got out. A little puff of breeze blew a wisp of black hair into her eye. She brushed it away with a forefinger. Not bothering to close the car window, she stepped several feet away from the vehicle to look around. There was a soft, easy tranquillity about the area, almost like a physical warmth flushing her skin, giving her a feeling of reassurance and comfort, while at the same time she received the impression this was a place where life moved in a slow, rhythmic cadence. The old house and the shadow-dappled lawn around it were an anachronism, she thought, existing in a time before the world had telescoped days into hours, before diodes and microchips controlled everything, uncomprehended except by a small cadre of minds. Here, under the ripe summer leaves, creativity could be a way of life, not a frenzied allocation of time sandwiched into odd moments between tumult and confusion.

She turned slowly, feeling excitement stirring within her. It was a dangerous spur-of-the-moment reaction, a symbol, she tried to tell herself, of weakening emotional strength. She drew a deep breath, reminding herself that what she wanted to do required careful planning. Yet already she was deciding to rent the advertised rooms in the house, without even seeing them.

"Hi!"

Adrienne looked over the top of the car. A tall, statuesque woman in jeans and T-shirt was approaching with long, athletic strides from the house. Sunlight tangled itself in a flare of red hair so the woman's head was ringed with a nimbus of flame. Watching her, Adrienne received the impression of strength and driving needs. Adrienne walked around the car.

"I'm Katie Clements." The woman held out a hand. She was, Adrienne judged, in her late twenties.

"I'm Adrienne Lewis." Adrienne took the proffered hand. "I'm here concerning the studio rooms advertised in the *Sentinel.*"

"Oh, fine." The woman smiled. It touched her eyes and danced in them. It was a good smile, Adrienne thought, full of genuine warmth and interest. "The guys have gone into town for supplies, but I'll show you around. What type of work do you do?"

"The art world calls it crafts, but some interior decorators refer to it as decorative accents, and gift shops sell them as, well . . . as gifts." Adrienne shrugged. "Silk flowers and wreaths, corn husk flowers, vines and stuffed dolls. Those kinds of things. It started as a hobby, but now it's a business. I supply gift shops and decorators and fill mail-order requests." She knew she had said enough, that, in fact, she was talking too much, but the interest on the other woman's face made her continue. "It's reached the stage I either get a bigger working space or give my entire apartment over to work and sleep out in the yard. I haven't had a meal off my dining table in weeks, and I'm on the threshold of a first-class case of claustrophobia from boxes of supplies towering over my bed."

"Lucky you, to be so busy." They came to steps leading up to a side stoop. "Let's go in here. The rooms are just down the hall to the right."

Although the interior, like the outside, hinted at years of neglect and was still in the process of renovation, the high-ceilinged coolness carried a pleasant trace of pine scent. Adrienne wondered if it was natural, from the trees outside the open windows, or synthetic, poured from a bottle. Whichever, it was agreeable.

The two rooms opened off the same hallway and were connected by a door. The largest one had two north windows running from floor to ceiling through which summer brilliance flooded in a crescendo of light. The walls were crisply clean, recently painted a misty blue, and the hardwood floor was scrubbed and shined to a TV-commercial brilliance. Adrienne estimated the room to be perhaps twenty by twenty-five feet. The second room was smaller, with smaller windows, a touch on the gloomy side, but the same shade of blue reflected the light from the walls so it was by no means dreary. It was approximately sixteen by sixteen feet.

"I don't know how much equipment you have to squeeze in," Katie Clements said, "but it can't be too much, can it?"

"No." Adrienne paced off the larger room. She was enthralled with the sunlight cascading through the tall windows, grateful the verandah was on the opposite side of the house. "Actually, the only piece of machinery I use is a sewing machine. Everything else is cut, glue and paste."

Katie laughed. The laugh was as good and graciously warm as her smile. "This is where I'm supposed to go into a fast-talking sales pitch, isn't it?"

Adrienne laughed in answer. She was attracted to this big red-haired woman with her magnificent smile and laugh, sensing that behind the green eyes existed a free spirit which refused to participate in any form of monotonous regularity.

"Can I ask a couple of questions?" she asked.

"Of course."

"Well . . . the rent is sixty dollars a month?"

"Yes. We aren't sure if that's too high or too low, but it seems right to us since it includes electricity and heat and, I guess, anything else you want, including use of the kitchen."

"It's a very fair rent. But I'd like to build two long tables in this bigger room. Would that be all right?"

"I can't see why not. In fact, I bet Ned would probably help you install them. He's not at all good with his hands, but he likes to try." She shook her head. "I've seen him more excited over putting in a light switch than turning out a beautiful bridal portrait."

From her position by the windows, Adrienne looked once

more around the big room, mentally placing the worktables and sewing machine, seeing the straw and wire and grapevines on one of the tables, dried flowers and silk and pinecones on the other. She went again to the door of the smaller room and looked in to satisfy herself there was more than enough space in it to store her supplies.

"You're not going to have to go into a sales pitch," she said, smiling. "I'd like to rent them."

"Great! I was hoping you would. There are times I need an ally of the feminine gender around here, and you'll make a great one, I just know. How much time do you have to spend here now?"

"The rest of the afternoon."

"Well, then, let me show you around. If you're going to be a part of our little haven here, you ought to see it all."

As she followed Katie through the rooms, Adrienne discovered that the house was larger than she had realized. It rambled, one room opening off another, then leading to the next almost spontaneously, as if the builder had constructed the house by compulsion rather than planning.

The short hallway, upon which the two rooms she planned to rent opened, led to a spacious room running the entire width of the front. It could have been nothing else but a parlor, Adrienne decided. As in the bigger room she planned to rent, tall ceiling-to-floor windows poured north light into the area, and two windows with built-in seats opened onto the front lawn. Beyond the room's south windows was the verandah and the vague outlines of the ruined garden she had seen from the driveway. Though now it was a tangle of nettles and brambles, hints of elaborateness could be distinguished along the sides of a path meandering among nearly lost shapes of flower beds.

For a long moment, Adrienne stood looking out at the patch of ruin. There was a terrible, sad desolation out there clinging to the sun-browned weeds and wild grass: a brilliance gone, a dreaded intrusion of death which rattled the dry stalks so they whispered of life's brief time. A green dragonfly darted onto the verandah, fluttered, then settled on the railing to pulse against the faded white. She watched it, and as she did a dark shadow of melancholy touched her, then fled so rapidly she was only partially conscious of it. Yet it left a residue in her mind like an undefined sadness. A little chilled, she turned away from the window.

Photographic equipment was pushed against the room's inner wall, a set of studio strobes, several camera cases, two tripods, three rolls of background paper and many items Adrienne did not recognize. Near the tall north windows, an empty artist's easel stood not too far from a taboret, with stretched but empty canvases leaning against it. A wooden bench, which Adrienne supposed was for posing, was pushed next to the wall between the windows.

"This is Ned's bailiwick," Katie said. "As you can see, he doesn't exactly have it in shape yet."

"It looks like it has great possibilities for his work, doesn't it?"

"That's what he says, but so far we've been so busy trying to get the house put in shape he hasn't had the time to work much on getting it straightened out. Geoff and I've managed to shape up the carriage house—we live in an upstairs apartment, but we have two pairs of hands."

Adrienne nodded absently as she walked around the room once more. Her heels clicked loudly on the hardwood floor, the echoes bounced from wall to wall, sounding as if the space in which they traveled was far larger than the room itself. The atmosphere was not heavy, but neither was it buoyant, and as Adrienne moved, it closed around her, alien and strange. Deep inside her grew a vague awareness of sorrow and pain and hate.

She wandered to one of the front windows with its built-in seat and stood looking down at it, not knowing what had drawn her to it. She noticed it was constructed to open, with a ring embedded in the wood so a finger could be looped through it to lift the seat and reveal the storage compartment beneath.

The seat intrigued her, much like the curiosity of a very young child looking at an unopened box of Cracker Jacks, knowing there was something to be discovered in it. But she felt a dark side to the curiosity, a nagging suspicion that what appeared normal to her at this moment was not quite what it seemed to be. She wanted to hook her finger in the metal loop and pull the white-painted seat up.

Behind her Katie said, "Ned says he's going to pry those open someday. They seem to be swollen shut or stuck with old paint. He thinks they'd give him additional storage space when he gets into business."

Adrienne walked slowly back across the room, disturbed at the effect the window seat had had on her, yet certain she was not overreacting. She had a feeling that whatever had reached for her from the garden and then the window seat was better left undisturbed.

The remainder of the first floor consisted of an empty dining room, a small square cubicle which might once have been a sewing room, a foyer with an outside door to the verandah and stairs leading to the second floor, a pantry and finally the kitchen. Adrienne decided the two rooms she was about to rent were probably a bedroom and accompanying dressing room.

"There's four bedrooms upstairs," Katie said, "and, I'm sorry to say, the only bathroom. Since he owns the place, Ned's laid claim to the master bedroom up there."

"Do you think he'll approve of me renting the rooms? If he's the landlord, he might want to make the choice of the tenant."

"He'll agree. We're a far cry from the flower children of the sixties, but we run somewhat of a three-person commune around here—maybe more of a cooperative. You've got my vote, and that's one third of the shareholders." She winked. "Besides, they respect my judgment."

They were in the kitchen. It was the only completely renovated and furnished room Adrienne had seen. It was painted in what some decorator magazines describe as "a cheerful yellow," with the cabinet doors newly stripped and restained. A brick-patterned lay-it-yourself tile covered the floor. There was no breakfast nook, but an Early American table and four chairs sat beneath a white-curtained window looking out over the parking area. Two store-shiny new appliances, an electric stove and a refrigerator, covered only two thirds of the inside wall against which they were placed, and a stainless-steel sink and Formica drainboards spread under the south window. All in all, Adrienne thought, it was a pleasant room, but as yet it had not assumed the warmth of being worked in, nor did it give any personal indications of the people who used it.

"How about something cool?" Katie asked, going to the refrigerator.

"I don't want to impose."

"You're not."

Adrienne felt somewhat overwhelmed by the big red-haired woman. Katie seemed to enjoy breaking down people's barriers. She was a healthy woman who knew she was valuable to herself and to her husband and made the assumption that other people should also be held in high esteem. Adjusted to her own code, she was an outsider to the rigid structure of society. It made her a unique individual . . . and she made Adrienne feel embarrassingly prissy. Adrienne was also aware that if she was nervous about this new relationship, the blame could not be placed on Katie. She could not discount her own reluctance to become too closely involved with another person. Dear, sweet Andrew had bestowed that self-preserving fear on her. Dear, sweet Andrew, who had not cared a damn how badly he messed up her life just so long as he could hightail it to his Clairol blonde's bed.

"Well . . ." Katie looked at Adrienne over her shoulder. "We've got a big choice: either Miller Lite or Pepsi—and not the diet kind."

"I'll take a Pepsi."

"You don't mind if I have a beer?"

"Of course not." Was she really giving the impression of being as puritanical as she felt?

Katie opened the bottle of Pepsi and the can of beer, poured the contents into glasses, which she set on the table, and said, "Sit. The boys should be back in a half an hour or so. Before you commit yourself all the way, you really should meet the other two thirds of us."

For a little while neither of them spoke. Adrienne had not realized how warm she was until she swallowed a sip of the drink and experienced a tiny shock at its coolness in her throat.

"You know, I'm surprised at myself." She spoke slowly, wondering why she was saying what she was. "Lately I've had all kinds of hesitations when it came to making major decisions and, believe me, this is a major decision. I usually list endless combinations of dos and don'ts, but today I don't have that problem at all. The instant I stepped out of the car I felt at home here, and even before you came to meet me, I knew I was going to rent the rooms." She smiled self-consciously and looked out the window.

Katie held her beer up to the window light and very carefully studied the clear amber fluid shimmering in the glass. "Do you want to know something, Adrienne? I knew when I saw you standing beside your car you were going to rent the rooms. And do you know something else? I wanted you to rent them. You were so neat in your trim slacks and fitted blouse, a contrast to the untrimmed shrubbery. And when I got close to you, I saw the expression on your face. Do you know what it was? It was enchantment. Pure enchantment. So I knew you were going to rent the rooms, and at the same time my woman's intuition told me I was going to make a friend." She set the glass on the table and smiled embarrassedly. "You seem to think you have a problem, but I don't think you do. You're just afflicted with an orderly mind."

Adrienne laughed. "It's a curse inherited from an overly organized father who wouldn't hang a picture without measuring from ceiling to floor and wall to opposite wall."

"It's not really an affliction—I was joking. But, to be truthful, it's a capacity we can use a lot of around here. Both Geoff and Ned are unequaled in their respective fields of art, no one can say otherwise, but neither of them is very effective when it comes to practical considerations . . . you know, handyman capabilities."

Touched, Adrienne looked down at the glass of Pepsi. Katie had found a crack in the emotional ramparts she had erected with such care when Andrew, totally immersed in his quest for female earthiness, had trotted away. But behind those walls, her vulnerability still huddled, still susceptible to being torn and shredded, leaving her humiliated and contemptuous of herself all over again. This was a time to be very careful, but in spite of the danger, she was not going to shut and bar the opening Katie had made. Even if it was with reluctance, she was going to permit some intrusion into her isolation. She wanted to say something spontaneous, but all she could manage was, "Katie, thank you."

Wisdom shone in the green eyes. "I think you deserved what I said."

A few silent minutes passed. Adrienne, for the first time in a long time, felt her individuality returning.

Finally she asked, "Did Ned Anderson just recently buy this property?"

"No. He inherited it."

"How lucky!"

"It is that, but it's also kind of a mystery, to tell the truth.

Neither he nor the lawyers are really certain who in his family actually owned the place.''

''Someone must have. Those kinds of records are usually pretty well kept. You know, county governments and courts.''

Katie smiled. ''And they tangle things up, too. But in this case, I admit, they didn't, though I think some of the tangles were ignored. The property is old, over a hundred and fifty years; so a local historical society assisted. They wanted to see the house and grounds restored, and, of course, the county wanted someone to pay the taxes on it. A lawyer who's a member of the society donated his services and cut a swath through the red tape, so in just a little over two months after Ned received the letter informing him of the inheritance, we were patching and painting on two very dilapidated old buildings.''

Adrienne looked around the kitchen, then out the window. ''And no one is really bottom-line sure why it's his?''

''No.'' Katie swallowed the last of her beer. ''Oh, on the surface everyone is sure; you know, all the legal details and who lived here before and the possibility of that person's relationship to Ned. But the records are a lot of conjecture on who the former inhabitant actually was.''

''Well, is there any doubt he owns the house?''

''No, no. None at all. Believe me, Geoff and I wouldn't have uprooted ourselves and come here if there was the slightest doubt. No, it's very certain, very legally entered in all the records. Ned Anderson owns the property.''

''But it's a mystery how?''

''Like I said, under the surface, yes.'' She tilted her head and grinned. ''This is kind of boring. How did we get off on it?''

''My nosiness, I guess. But now you've got to tell me more. My entire afternoon will go down the tubes if you don't, because I'll spend it trying to make up endings.''

Katie laughed her good laugh. ''Okay, but I'll have to take

it slow. The telling isn't really long, but it's been a while since we went through it and I'll have to shift memory around.

"It began back sometime in the 1880s with a woman named Sabra and an artist named Sebastian. This Sebastian owned the house, having bought it from a family by the name of—uh—oh, hell, I can't remember. Supposedly he was a great man with the brushes, magnificent landscapes and an occasional absolutely stunning portrait.

"Well, he and Sabra married after he moved here . . . and this is where the story gets a little chilling, because just over a year after their wedding they were killed out there in what was, at that time, the garden. According to sketchy notes in the historical society's archives, they were mutilated as if a wild beast had torn them apart.

"So the house stood empty for years. Then in 1924 a man claiming to be their son appeared on the scene, wanting to take possession of it. Apparently he proved to the satisfaction of the locals that he was Sabra and Sebastian's offspring; so his name, Spencer Longtree, was put on the deed. Don't ask me why his name wasn't Sebastian—I think it had something to do with the family who adopted him when his parents were killed.

"Anyway, it seems Spencer was quite a man with the ladies and had all the local belles swooning. There's nothing in the records saying what he did for a living, though a couple of old-timers Geoff and Ned talked to vaguely remembered him as 'playing with art.' Most people think he was living off an inheritance from a fund Sebastian had cached away in another part of the country.

"Anyway, one of his affairs produced an illegitimate daughter, who was sent to live with relatives up North. Not long after that, Spencer got some bad homemade gin and died.

"Now, this illegitimate girl—and I don't remember her name, either—grew up and married a guy named Roy Anderson. She had no children, and after a few years became widowed. About a year ago, she was killed in an automobile accident. In her safe-deposit box there was an elementary genealogy chart which indicated she was a second, or maybe third, cousin of Ned's father.

"Ned's father had died when Ned was still a child, so that left Ned and his mother owning the place . . . and she wasn't at all interested in it. She has a lot going for her in Atlanta, and I can't say I'd want to move to a place you have to draw a map to find, even if it is only four miles outside of Orlando. Ned and Geoff drove down here one weekend from Atlanta to look the place over and came back as excited as two kids playing hooky from school. His mother signed her rights over to Ned, and a couple of weeks later we were moved in and making like construction engineers."

Adrienne drew a deep breath. Around her she was suddenly aware of the enigma of the house's background, almost feeling it shift like a physical power within the rooms. During that moment, it seemed to her the history of the house was a dweller within the vacant rooms, an inhabitant who had never left. Katie's story was a succession of unlikely events, long periods of silent emptiness within the house and then times of overwhelming passion . . . and, she thought, unnatural deaths. More than ever now, she felt she had truly been a trespasser in the old parlor.

She heard Katie saying, "You know, you didn't appear bored once during that ordeal."

"It wasn't an ordeal. You're a good storyteller."

Katie laughed and stood up, picking up the empty beer glass and looking at it. "I could use another one of these, but I'd better hold off. My fat tissues don't know there's thirty percent fewer calories in it per serving." She crossed the kitchen and put the glass in the sink. "Do you want another Pepsi?"

"No, thanks." Adrienne wished the two men would return. She wanted to write a check to Ned Anderson to tie down the rooms. Impulse was giving way to calculation, and although the excitement still lingered, it was becoming tempered with a suspicion she did not need the extra overhead represented by the monthly rent, so she wanted to write a check before she discovered reasons for not taking the rooms.

Katie sat back down at the table. She leaned forward on her elbows. "Do you live far from here?"

"On the south side of town, down on Seminole. I've a small apartment in the Villager."

A momentary embarrassment showed in Katie's eyes. She straightened and leaned against the chair back. "If I'm getting nosy, tell me. Geoff says I'm worse than a bag full of cats with my curiosity."

"You're not." For a moment, Adrienne thought of the cramped apartment she had moved into when Andrew left—and the loneliness coexisting in it with her. Fleeting sequences of the occurrences which had led to her sitting here spun haphazardly through her mind. She felt the urge to tell the red-haired woman of the things that had not gone right these past two years, of the shock and the fear and the bitterness. She wanted company. She wanted an intrusion. But she said only, "I've been divorced for a little more than a year."

"I'm sorry."

"Don't be, please. Continuing the arrangement called for more flexibility and resourcefulness than I could muster. It had become rather shopworn and very untidy."

"It happens," Katie said softly. "It just seems such a shame and waste, though."

Adrienne nodded, but made no comment. Though she might want company, she knew it was too soon to tell her new friend of an orphaned childhood spent without a family, without a real home, of the years during which she was shuffled from foster home to foster home—and the dream accompanying that young girl, the dream to eventually meet the man with whom she could have a family of her own, tightly bound by love and security. Someday she would tell Katie of the anger and confusion which had turned the world into a place of gray shadows from which mocking faces leered at her. Maybe she might mention the terrible feelings of inadequacy which still haunted her. But for now, she would say nothing of Andrew Lewis, the man who had shattered all her fragile young dreams with his reality, the handsome electronics engineer who, after the marriage, insisted on waiting until it was financially feasible before having children, then spent both their salaries on material possessions. She would never, she knew, be able to tell Katie of how frantically she had struggled to make her dream come true as the marriage became only an abstract notion to Andrew, no more than a convenient arrangement for sleeping and eating, and how very quickly her hopes and ideals had turned into leftover principles from an archaic time. So, for now, she would allow the ghosts, with their leering faces, to recede into the shadows.

She smiled. She hoped it was light-looking, but the muscles around her mouth felt tight. "I'm going to be nosy one more time. Why do you want to rent the two rooms?"

Katie answered her smile with one of her own. "You're not nosy, just inquisitive. Me—I'm nosy. We've got more than enough room, but not more than enough capital. The move down from Atlanta wasn't exactly cheap, and the cost of renovation is unbelievable. But Geoff and I are getting back into production, so that should help some. We've made the ground floor of the carriage house into our workshop and studio, and last week we fired up the kiln for the first time to turn out an order of unicorns for our Atlanta dealer. But, as you saw, Ned has a lot of work facing him before he can open his photo studio." She paused, then shrugged. "He was an artist before he went into photography, and a damn good one in both commercial and fine art. Since we came here, he seems to be going back to it more and more, doing sketches, buying a few tubes of paint, stretching canvases . . ."

"Why should he do that? Was his photographic business doing well?"

"Very well. In fact, he's brought several commercial accounts with him. He says it's compulsion, and I guess that's as good as any reason in this business."

"Artists are a breed of searchers, I understand."

Katie nodded and grinned. "Tell me about it. Sometimes I feel Geoff and I are a latter-day Lewis and Clark the way we've wandered from project to project."

"But you liked it?"

"Loved every hungry minute of it."

The sound of a car engine came from the driveway, and Katie got up, saying, "The foragers have returned. I wonder what they forgot."

Adrienne looked quizzically at her.

"Both Ned and Geoff insist it's cheating to make out a shopping list. Their theory is that any normal mind can remember what's needed from the store."

"And . . . ?"

"And both Geoff and Ned forget things."

Adrienne laughed. The shadows were gone from her thoughts. She was going to like it here.

A dusty Jeep pulled into the parking area beside her Toyota. Watching through the window, she saw the two men in it look at her car before getting out to begin unloading shopping bags from the rear seat.

Both men were in their early thirties. The one who had been driving was tall with wavy blond hair and a medium-long beard. He was dressed in khakis, the bottoms of his pants stuffed into ankle-high boots. Although he gave the impression of being rangy, Adrienne suspected his six-foot-plus frame was layered with developed muscles covered with solidly compacted flesh. Watching him approach across the parking area with surprisingly graceful movements, she guessed he was Katie's husband, Geoffrey Clements.

Several inches shorter, with a thick shock of black hair, the other man was dark-hued, so substantial as to look stocky, and did not give the impression of a person involved in the arts. Rather, she would have guessed him to be, of all things, a manufacturer's representative or, maybe, an engineer in one of the more prosaic fields. He was wearing a blue print sports shirt, blue slacks and blue sneakers, so it would seem a good guess, she thought, that blue was his favorite color. He came toward the house with a certainty in his walk.

When they had deposited their sacks on the kitchen table, Katie introduced them. After the first few moments, Adrienne knew that her misgivings about Ned were uncalled-for. The tension building in her subsided, leaving her feeling ashamed of herself, like a person who has believed a whisper of derogatory gossip then found it to be untrue. As of this afternoon she was crossing the threshold of a new life, and she had better damn well regroup her emotions and show some strength.

She became aware of Ned standing at the sink with a glass of water in his hand, looking at her from under a brow raised into a sharp arch. He smiled. "I've been doing some very deep thinking, Mrs. Lewis, and I've come to the conclusion we have to be compatible. You see, you are black-haired, and I am black-haired. You have blue eyes, and I have blue eyes. It's foreordained that we are well matched."

Adrienne laughed. "I can't think of any more important reason. And, please . . . call me Adrienne."

"There are none. Absolutely none, Adrienne." He was making it sound so serious.

"Then I can assume you accept me as a tenant?"

"There's no assumption to it. As of this minute, the rooms are yours."

"I'll write you a check for the first month's rent."

He made a negative wave with his hand. "Wait until the first of the month. It's just a week away, and you should be moved in by then. Otherwise I'd feel you were paying for space you weren't using."

It was a nice gesture. "Thank you."

A short time after that, it was agreed she should start moving in the following day, and whatever help she required, they would provide: hauling, packing, arranging of supplies in the small room. While Katie winked, Ned told her he would build the tables she required.

That evening she ate a tuna salad sandwich and a bowl of soup off the drainboard in the apartment's kitchen. More than once, she had looked smugly into the dining room, thinking that the next days, or at least the following night, she would be eating a civilized meal in there. But like an undercurrent beneath the excitement of returning niceties, she was aware of just how dreary the last fourteen months had been, of the mental numbness and despondency which had threatened to wash over her. Trembling, she looked around at what she could see of the apartment, seeing how thin the nighttime shadows had become, and knew that the darkness which had encircled her, which had hid the keening phantoms, was being pushed back.

When she was finished with the meal, she continued to sit on the kitchen stool and lit a cigarette, one of the six she permitted herself each day.

She puffed slowly, allowing the smoke to drift up before her eyes in a wavering veil. Her mind turned inward, curling upon itself in much the same way the smoke curled in front of her eyes, and she found herself picking bits and pieces of memory from the hidden chambers in the back of her mind where she had stored them. She could examine them now, because the cruelty they illustrated had begun to lose its hold on her.

When Andrew had moved out finally to live with the blonde from the company's typing pool, something within her had shriveled, all the fine thoughts and plans and dreams revealed as the dumb, implausible wishes of a little girl, destroyed by an adult's broken promises. Pride, self-esteem, dignity—all had crumbled, turned to qualities only other people possessed, leaving her with the feeling she was merely tolerated by those around her. She had always felt that others, from the foster homes to the friends she had so desperately tried to make with Andrew, had turned their backs on her. The women knew the secrets she did not know of holding a man; the men knew she lacked knowledge of things which pleased a man. Smiles from them all, into which she read pity bordering too close to contempt. Long months of hurt during which she was a danger to herself.

She drew deep on the cigarette and plumed the smoke ceilingward, watching it fade into the bright light of the kitchen. The emotional exhaustion was over; only memories remained which were fading away like the cigarette smoke. Her body and her mind were rebuilding. Blood tingled through her. She felt a revitalization coming. It had begun this afternoon at the old house northeast of town, and she had felt it continuing on the drive home. The anticipation of the pleasantries awaiting her in the coming days had ridden beside her in the front seat. There had been about the old place and its surrounding grounds a power to restore faith. It had seeped into her, grappled with the self-misery and cast it out.

Still, after she showered, turned the thermostat down to seventy degrees and pulled the sheet over her in bed, worries crept into her mind. They came like aftershocks, like crackles of static in the electric charges of her brain waves, distorting the pleasantries, twisting the old memories and the new ones.

At the time it had been a tale of high interest, but now

Adrienne decided the deed had followed a strangely circuitous route until reaching Ned's hands, a route along which convenient deaths seemed to guide it. Some of the warmth left her body as it had at the parlor window when the unsettling force out in the garden reached for her with its depression. What was it out there in the dead flower shrubs and the rattling grass that had sent a portion of itself through the window to stroke her with its cold fingers? Closing her eyes tight, she managed to push away any horrible suppositions before they were born. But there was nothing which could be pushed away concerning the window seat. She had been lured to it, she knew, by a haunting, but undeveloped, knowledge that within the compartment beneath the seat something waited, that something strange and powerful lay in the darkness under the swollen, paint-stuck lid.

CHAPTER

A high overcast diffused the morning sun. It added an undertone of gray to the young June colors of the hibiscus, bougainvillea and canna lilies spotting the small landscaped area of the Villager Apartments. Inside the second-floor apartment, the watery light creeping through the windows dulled the yellow paint above the wainscoting on the walls in the dining area and reduced the furniture shadows to dingy little splotches that took on the look of patches of soil. What noise came through the thermal panes from outside was muted and blurred, misty reproductions of the original sound.

Adrienne had cleared a space on the dining table large enough to accommodate a coffee mug and ashtray. Dressed in an old blue housecoat, she sat slouched at the table staring into the mug, waiting for the day to pull itself into perspective. This was her second cup of instant Nescafé, one more cup than usual, and her second Benson & Hedges, permitting her only four more cigarettes for the remainder of the day. A cheap and inadequate try at home therapy, she thought. But she felt frayed, as if her nerve ends were splitting, deadening her response mechanisms, leaving her with the uncanny feeling she was sitting somewhere between what was real and what was make-believe.

From down the hallway she heard the thermostat click quietly and listened as the air conditioner began to whir softly, compounding the unnatural coolness in the room. A curl of sleep-tumbled hair trembled in the chilled draft to tickle her forehead like insect feet scurrying across her brow. As she pushed the hair back, she noticed how cold her fingertips were against her face. She took a sip of the black coffee.

Dreams, the remembered ones, were a rarity with her. Only a few times a year did a dream accompany her when she awakened, but they were usually without dimension, vaguely recalled like half-remembered sequences of an old television show, sequences of irrelevant occurrences to be mused over and smiled at while the smoke of the first cigarette of the day bit into the throat membranes and the first cup of coffee jolted the stomach. But the thing which had entered her mind during the night was not fanciful imagining. While she slept, it had led her to a place where loneliness and fear sobbed with a woman's voice, where terror stood as an unseen figure in the darkness.

The sounds of her footsteps echoing in a high-ceilinged room still haunted her memory. Around her the darkness had been absolute, thick with summer humidity and charged with the distant lightning. There was a clean, but heavy, scent around her, cloying, filling her nostrils, which at first she could not recognize, but finally identified as lilac. All of her senses assured her she was alone in the room, but a primeval instinct whispered that the darkness held another being, a being silently watching her, examining her as it would study a creature in a cage for behavioral response-and-movement coordination. Terror brushed her, and under the garment she wore her flesh chilled and rose in gooseflesh as the night breeze entering the windows turned into a cold wind.

Frantically she tried to find a corner of the room in which to huddle away from the coldness, but could find nowhere in which to cower. Turning around and around in a dream-slowed pirouette, she sought a passage through the darkness, certain that once she heard the thing in the room chuckle. But when she concentrated, she could detect no sound from the mass of blackness at the end of the room where she knew it stood. Instead she heard a woman weeping. The crying was an echo of all the sadness and despair mankind had suffered, grieving sobs of fear and weariness and hope long gone. The voice drove into her brain with such a terrible force she had finally covered her ears and screamed.

Adrienne drew a deep breath and snuffed out her cigarette. She took another sip of the coffee, discovered the air-conditioning was cooling it off too fast and drank what remained in one gulp. She grimaced at its bitterness.

She got up, went to the window to stand gazing down at the neatly trimmed lawn accentuated with surgically shaped bushes in the courtyard between her apartment unit and the one to the north. She did not like the view. It was like looking down on the immaculate grooming of a public park rather than a private living area, nothing like the homey feeling of yesterday at the house where lawn care was a task apparently performed as an afterthought.

She turned away from the window to look through the dining area into the gloom of the living room beyond it. This morning she was faced with a decision. No matter how she phrased it, there was a question she must bluntly put to herself and honestly answer. The house, with all its anachronistic charm offering lush tranquillity, had had a disturbing effect on her that left a residue of apprehension, although this admission irritated her more than it troubled her, mostly because she could not shove it away as being inconsequential.

Should she reconsider renting the rooms?

"No!" The answer came quickly. She almost shouted it aloud. "Dammit, no!"

She was doing it again. This time she was deliberately trying to terrify herself with grotesque fantasies. She was doing her damnedest to seek justifications that would prohibit her escape. One degree of vacillation now would be the start of the swing away from the only chance to regain the Adrienne Lewis who had become lost.

She snatched the coffee mug from the table to take to the sink where she ran hot water into it. She was done with thinking. Whenever she tried it in recent months, her mind twisted in upon itself, turning into a tight cocoon that squeezed off rational functions.

There was a knock at the door.

She knew who it was and was grateful for the interruption, even though the contortions through which her mind was going were a purge of her deadened emotions. After the second knock she went to the door.

"I was starting to think you were still in bed." The plumpish, brown-haired woman standing in the hall began to smile. "I didn't get you up, did I?"

"Heavens no. I've had more than my ration of coffee and cigarettes already. Come on in, Amy." She started toward the kitchen. "How about you? The water is still hot, and it'll only take a minute to fix you a cup of instant."

"No, thanks. I had an extra cup this morning, too. Hugh didn't sleep well last night, and when he doesn't, I don't." She gave a little giggle. "But I can't complain. Insomnia can lead to some very interesting indulgences."

Adrienne chuckled. "Amy Stevens, you're both innocent and earthy."

"It has advantages, being both." She sat on one of the dining-area chairs. "I came to hear how things went yesterday. Did you see the rooms, and, if you did, did you like them?''

''Yes to both questions—and I rented them.''

''Wonderful! Now you're on your way to being a real honest-to-goodness craftsperson. This apartment isn't a large enough cottage for a cottage industry; now you can expand and do all those things people who are really in business for themselves do.''

''I have been in business for myself.''

''Only halfheartedly, Adrienne. Admit it, it's been something to keep you from doing a lot of thinking, not much more. When you moved in here a year ago, you weren't much of a neighbor, you know. You were all withdrawn and pinch-faced, and full of self-pity.'' She held up a hand when she saw Adrienne about to speak. ''You had a right to be like that, there's no denying: almost broke because of misguided pride that wouldn't allow you to accept a settlement, suddenly without a job because your nerves were banging around inside you like piano wires under heavy-handed thumping. You were on the edge, you know that?''

''Yes, I know.'' She looked out the window. ''I remember. God, do I remember! But I also remember how you and Hugh helped, Amy.''

''Well, we just tried. You got hold of yourself. You started this craft thing as a therapy, and now you've turned it into a damn good business. But tell me about the rooms. What kind of place is it?''

Adrienne told her. She told her of the house, of the withered garden, of the stillness and feeling of serenity surrounding the property. She described the three people she'd met and the immediate interest they'd shown in her and how she, in turn, felt an affinity toward them. As she talked, she discovered it was good telling Amy of the house and people, because the telling turned impressions into reality. She didn't tell Amy about the south parlor window and the closed window seat, because, if she mentioned those, she feared all the good things would change into no more than a facade concealing what was an inescapable reality.

Amy got to her feet and, with a surprise move, took Adrienne tightly in her arms. "God, I'm happy for you. You deserve some good things now, so go out there and get them."

Adrienne hugged the plump woman in return, pulling her close. "Thanks, Amy. Whatever recovery I've made, I owe a big bunch of it to you."

"Let me go, Adrienne Lewis, so I can get out of here before I cry." Her arms tightened around Adrienne's shoulders. "I get maudlin very easily."

Adrienne dropped her arms and stepped back. Little pinpoints of heat were burning at the corners of her eyes. She blinked them away. "Me, too, Amy."

A few minutes after Amy left, she was preparing to shower when the telephone rang. It was vehement, demanding, its strident sound sending vibrations through the apartment that gathered momentum as they raced from room to room. Her first impulse was to do nothing, to ignore the instrument and its intrusion, but the sound became something to be escaped, like a dagger slashing inside her head. Its harshness suddenly went out of control, reaching the limits of her tolerance, and she finally hurried down the hallway to pick up the handpiece on the sixth ring.

It was Ned Anderson.

She was surprised how pleased she was to hear his voice. It was really very nice to listen to.

"Adrienne, I'm going to be in town shortly. If you're ready to start moving your material out here, I can drop by and help."

She had not anticipated anything like this, though he and Geoff had told her they would help; so, for an instant, she hesitated. Amy's visit had helped her move away from the memory of the dream, but, even so, when she spoke, she knew it sounded stilted. "That's kind of you, but I don't want you to put yourself out."

"Hey, you're not. I've got to be in town, and I'll be driving the station wagon, so maybe by using your car and the wagon one trip will do it."

"You should see this place," she laughed. "It will take a caravan of U-Haul vans."

"Okay, so it takes more than one. I'll still be happy to help."

All the phantoms had fled. "All right. I'll be ready when you get here. I'm in unit B, apartment 28. And, Ned—thanks."

"It's my pleasure, Adrienne."

She showered quickly, but stayed long enough under the sharp needles of spray to allow them to drive a warmth deep into her flesh until her body responded, quivering with little tremors as the last shades of tension disappeared.

When she opened the bedroom closet, the mirror on the back of its door swung into position reflecting her full-length image. At first she gave it no attention, but then, just because it was there, quickly ran her eyes up and down the pale curves outlined against the shadowy background. It was no more than a cursory look, a detached appraisal as she pulled a brush through her hair. She held no impossible scale of values for her figure. Only once had she suffered the inconvenience of a diet, and then only as one of the many futile endeavors to please Andrew. Most of the time she found it effortless to maintain the ripe maturity of her long-legged body within acceptable contours, ignoring or giving only passing attention to current bodybuilding fads.

What she saw in the mirror was not the straight, lank female figure Pucci and Dior originals were designed to cover. There was too much fullness in bust and hip to be squeezed into their sexless creations, too much healthy woman to be transformed into a stereotyped mannequin. She was over five and a half feet of functional female, round full breasts and deep hips hinting at abundant earthiness. Long legs, tapering to slender ankles, were strongly muscled, a leftover from ten years of dancing lessons paid for with money saved from skimpy allowances and after-school jobs when a too clumsy girl dreamed of becoming a prima ballerina. The face hinted at beauty, but did not possess the stunning symmetry cosmetic firms required for their TV commercials, though its well-defined cheekbones were evenly spaced and slanted in a smooth triangle to a rounded jaw. Under a straight nose, her lips were full but not sensuous. Her eyes, perhaps the most vivid attribute of her features, were wide set. They were the elusive blue of turquoise, their color made even more pronounced by their dark lashes and brows and the blue-black hair tumbling down each side of her face.

For thirty-one, she thought, it was a good, acceptable body. She gave a derisive laugh. Good enough to please her, perhaps; but not good enough to have satisfied Andrew.

She took a pair of faded jeans and an old yellow cotton blouse from the closet and slammed the door shut, angry at Andrew's invasion into her thoughts.

It was nine forty-five when Ned arrived. Like her, he was wearing jeans. A blue T-shirt replaced the blue sports shirt of the day before. Little daubs of paint, faded from repeated washings, sprinkled a multihued pattern across his chest.

"Hi!" His greeting bordered on shyness, accompanied with a self-conscious smile, at odds with the impression he gave of confidence. "Did I get here too soon?"

"No, come in."

"Nice," he said, his eyes roaming around the apartment. "It has a good lived-in look. That's how homes are supposed to be."

She nodded, for a moment having the strange sensation of being returned to her teens and being called on for her first date. "Most of the stuff is stacked in the bedroom in boxes. I'll help you get them down to the car, then bundle together all the things here on the table."

"Why don't I take the boxes down while you're putting together your bundles? It might save time."

She led him down the hallway to the bedroom and stood aside at the door, nodding in the direction of the cartons forming looming brown walls around the bed. "Now do you think we can do it in one trip?"

"Well . . . would you consider two?"

"Or three or four," she laughed.

The loading of the vehicles went surprisingly fast, and, with much shoving and some shifting of contents, they managed to cram all the cartons into the Toyota and station wagon.

"Damned if we didn't do it." Ned shut the wagon's tailgate with a flourish. His T-shirt was dark-stained with perspiration and his face glinted with it.

Adrienne nodded. Her blouse was stuck to her shoulders and back, her hair tumbled in a lank cascade down her neck, and she wondered why any right-minded person would take on a task like this in the high heat of a June day. "I guess it proves where there's a will, there's a way."

He grunted. "There must be another good old folksy adage I could add to that one."

"You'll do better thinking of it where it's cool. Come on up, and I'll fix us some iced tea. We can relax while the air conditioner breathes some life back into us."

Going first up the stairs, she was aware of Ned's eyes following the sway of her hips in the tight jeans. Instead of the annoyance she would have experienced just a few months past, she felt a certain satisfaction, a basic pleasure in being a woman. There was a tiny stirring in her stomach, a hint of anticipation.

Ned pulled out a chair and sat at the littered dining table

with an exaggerated sigh, stretching his legs out in front of him. While she spooned the powder into two glasses, she apologized for serving him instant tea. Ned shrugged, saying instant coffee and instant tea were the only kinds there were so far as he was concerned.

A few minutes later, placing the full glasses on the table, she sat down across from him. "Katie told me you're planning to take up painting again when you get set up in the house. Does that mean you're giving up photography altogether?"

"Oh, no. Photography is the bread and butter provider. I have accounts I brought down from Atlanta I can't afford to let go; and, to tell the truth, the role of starving artist just doesn't send aesthetic chills up and down my spine. I'm of the generation that has come to accept, practically demand, creature comforts. I suppose she also told you art was my first love, what I started out doing. It didn't pay all that well, so I drifted into photography, but now . . . well, I guess there's a siren song luring me back to it."

"Maybe it's hereditary."

He looked sidewise at her. Momentarily some of the spontaneity left his face. "She told you about Sebastian, I gather."

She saw a shadow behind his eyes. "Yes, she did."

"Well, I have to admit the desire to start painting again has grown stronger since I moved into the house, kind of as if it was a portion of the inheritance."

She took a long swallow of the iced tea, remembering the things in the garden and window seat which reached out for her. But when she held the cold glass to her right temple, the recollections went fleeing away after the other banished memories. The fragile wall between chaos and order had been strengthened.

Ned showed no reticence in talking about himself. He told her of the commercial photography studio he had owned in Atlanta, of his mother, who operated a public relations firm, and of his schooling in Atlanta and New York. He mentioned briefly two engagements which had never led to weddings because self-analysis had convinced him he was too selfish to marry.

While she listened, Adrienne watched him. She watched the play of light on his features, rippling with the working of strong facial muscles, and then, behind those features, she became aware of something she could not easily describe other than as a—a sensual sensitivity. She could see it far back in his blue eyes, unfathomable and boundless, something that reached out for new thoughts and ideas, while at the same time she sensed his main focus was inward, toward a self-imposed privacy in which unborn paintings and photographs incubated.

"Do you talk to yourself when you work?" she asked.

He looked at her, his right brow arching upward. "I guess so, yes. Why?"

"I don't know why. I don't even know why I ask. I guess you just look like a person who might do it. At least to me."

"Oh? Is there a special way for people who talk to themselves to look?"

"No, I don't think so." She looked down at her iced tea. "This isn't making sense, is it?"

"No."

She looked around the room, feeling too embarrassed to face him. She could feel him waiting for her to say something else, but there was no more to be said without making an even greater fool of herself. But there had been a reason. It was entwined with the inward searching she saw in his eyes. He would talk to himself, she was certain, when he drew forth those special ideas, questioning aloud their validity and rounding off jagged edges. If he did not speak loudly, he would at least mutter while he worked. But why had she asked the question? Something she did not know existed had stirred itself in the back of her mind . . . and she knew that whether or not he talked to himself held a relationship to something very important.

"Do you?" she asked.

"What? Oh—no. I hum."

"Okay." His right brow lowered and he smiled. "Now that we have that major problem worked out, we have one more facing us."

"What's that?" Her stomach tightened as she frantically ran down her mental list of things to do, searching for an act left undone.

"Food. It's lunchtime."

"Already?"

"Already. You eat lunch, don't you?"

"Sometimes. Most of the time. But now and then when I'm busy I don't bother—or forget it."

"Well, today we eat lunch. There's a place on the way to the house where we can stop. So go do the things a woman does before going out in public, and we'll go."

Sarah's Cafe was not new and it was not old. It existed in that limbo of establishments which have met with a modicum of success, but never become popular. The furnishings were solid, functional and clean-looking plastic and Formica. Half a dozen hanging plants and four reproduction paintings provided decorations. Two lazily turning ceiling fans indolently churned the air, stirring the warm smell of kitchen grease through the long, narrow room. Just inside the door three men were engaged in an animated conversation around a table on which the empty plates of their finished meal still sat, and far in the back a silent couple sipped tall iced drinks through long straws.

At a table halfway to the back of the room, Ned pulled out a chair for Adrienne, then sat across from her. He leaned forward, his arms folded on the table. "What do you think?"

"About this place?"

"Yes."

"It's interesting."

He laughed. "A good ambiguous answer. But correct. Geoff and I've stopped here several times on the way to Builder's Discount Supply. It's convenient and the prices are right." He glanced over her shoulder. "And also, as you'll see, friendly, too."

A young woman in a maroon uniform laid two menus on the table between them, ignoring Adrienne but smiling archly at Ned. "Hi! You haven't been in for several days."

"We've been awfully busy at the house."

"How much longer before you have the place fixed up and can start work?"

"Oh, most any day now, Sandi. It takes a while to renovate an old house, you know."

"Yeah, I guess so."

Her smile broadened at him, then she turned and strolled toward the kitchen doors at the rear of the room. Adrienne watched Ned's eyes follow what she assumed was the motion of the young woman's hips under the maroon material. Remembering her awareness of his eyes on her own hips when they went up the apartment stairs, she decided he was a rear-end man. In a moment, he turned to discover her watching him.

"She wants to model," he said.

"Oh?"

He shook his head. "She has no form."

"It looks to me as if she has quite a bit."

"No distinctive bone structure."

"Oh."

He laughed then, realizing he was explaining himself into a corner. "Okay, Adrienne Lewis, maybe I'll use her sometime."

Adrienne ordered a bacon, lettuce and tomato sandwich with nothing to drink. Any more liquid, she speculated, after the coffee and iced tea she had already consumed, would make her gurgle when she walked. Ned asked for a ham and cheese sandwich and a can of Miller.

Waiting until he finished the first half of his sandwich before speaking, he said, "Katie tells me you're divorced."

Immediately Adrienne felt the defensive contraction of her stomach muscles. For what became far too long a time, her body refused to move as she waited for Ned to make his next statement . . . waited to learn he was one of the predators who looked on divorcees as fair game and easy prey. Desperately she hoped otherwise.

Her voice was thin when she said, "Yes."

"I have a friend in Atlanta who went through it." He shook his head. "I guess no matter what the circumstances, it's a shattering experience and knocks the hell out of your emotional equilibrium for a while. Deborah was a long time recovering. I guess it's like being fired from a job after years of trusted employment; some of the layers of personal confidence are stripped away." He took a long sip from the beer can. "Well, anyway, the three of us talked a little about it last night, and we decided whatever assistance you need, even outside your business, we want to offer helping hands. You know, you made one hell of an impression on Katie, and Geoff and I've learned to respect her judgments."

Inside Adrienne's head there was a rapid swirling that moved her away from herself so she was no longer in contact with the café or with Ned but rushing through an indistinct land shimmering with melancholy beauty. It left a dampness in her eyes; she blinked away the haze to see Ned watching her with a hesitant smile. Her lips trembled.

"Thank you," she said softly, wishing he could see all the textures and colors of her emotions. "I appreciate what you've just said, Ned. But it embarrasses me. I don't want my relationship with you three to be a one-sided affair, and I don't know offhand what I can offer in return."

"I think just being the person Katie saw in you will be

enough of a return. She has Geoff and me thinking we're the luckiest people around to get you for a tenant."

"She's a wonderful person, Ned. I was very drawn to her yesterday." She looked down and picked imaginary lint from her blouse. "But don't let me become an intruder. From what I've seen, and from what Katie told me, you three have something very special between you—old-fashioned friendship. That's precious, Ned. I envy you all."

"We do, yes. It goes back a long way, ten years back, in fact, to when we met in art school. We haven't been separated since then, emotionally that is, though this is the first time we've lived in such close proximity. Katie wants you to join us. She says under your . . . well, your austerity . . . there's a companion soul." He looked directly at her then, with eyes which she saw were dancing and full of color. "And do you know, Adrienne Lewis, I think she's right."

Suddenly she felt relaxed, as if after struggling up a long hill she had reached the top and found respite.

After leaving the café, Ned followed a route which took them along the north edge of the city. At a shopping mall on the outskirts, he turned into the parking lot and drove slowly down a lane until he found two adjacent spaces near the Publix supermarket. Adrienne pulled in beside the Jeep.

He came to her window. "I hope you've nothing planned for dinner this evening, because Katie wants you to eat with us. I told her I'd bring home some steaks. Now don't say no. This will be the first time in months I've had a steak that isn't prefixed with the word 'chopped.' It's to celebrate you renting the rooms; so if you say no, there can't be a celebration and she'll fix Geoff and me macaroni and cheese with a slice of Spam. Would you believe, I'm becoming a connoisseur of macaroni and cheese—and frankly I don't want to be one."

"I couldn't let that happen to you."

"I should hope not. You stand guard while I run into the store. I'll only be a couple of minutes."

The sun slanting through the windshield burned on her lap and stomach. The boxes piled on the seat beside her cut off air circulation and she felt closed in, claustrophobic, like an occupant of an old-time prison hot box. She rubbed gathering sweat from her eyes, squinted, then looked around the lot. It could be any parking lot, in any city. With just a bit of imagination, she could pretend she was on a very special trip, from which she would come back wiser and stronger.

She leaned back against the headrest and smiled. Ned returned carrying a large package wrapped in white butcher's paper, along with two bottles of wine tucked under his arms. As if handling something very precious, he placed the package of steaks in the station wagon, then shoved the wine bottles into the floor space behind the front seat. He drove with greater care the remainder of the way, the steaks and wine apparently a priceless cargo.

Katie was digging in the herbal bed that ran the length of the carriage house front and Geoff was trimming a hibiscus bush when they pulled into the parking area. As the day before, the tranquillity of another time snuggled around Adrienne so completely that she briefly felt she was experiencing thoughts and images from those long-ago days. But this time, as she got out of the car, the feeling was so strong, so absolute, it made her shudder inwardly, as if in response to a sinister caress.

Katie came over to the cars, wiping her hands on soiled jeans, and took the steaks from Ned. "Was it your charm or the steaks that made her accept the invitation?"

"Let's just say she's going to have dinner with us."

Making no comment, Katie headed for the house with the package.

With three of them doing it, the unloading of the cartons took much less time than the loading. In less than half an hour the boxes were stacked in the smaller of the rooms. With most of the afternoon remaining, Ned decided to pick up the plywood and two-by-twos required for Adrienne's tables, and Geoff volunteered to accompany him to the building supply dealer. Adrienne mentioned adding the cost of the material to her first month's rent, but Ned rejected the offer with a wave of his hand, saying it was the landlord's obligation to provide adequate facilities for a tenant. After they drove down the driveway, she went into the kitchen, where Katie was washing vegetables for a salad and scrubbing four baking potatoes.

When the salad was tossed and in the refrigerator, Katie said, "I've got some paperwork I can't duck any longer."

"This is a good time for me to go through my order book and arrange the cartons for easy access to the material I need for due jobs."

"Okay. If you want to wash up, there're towels and washrags in the closet off the main hallway upstairs. Help yourself. I shouldn't be more than an hour or so."

"Take your time. I've been here only a trifle over an hour, and already I think I've thrown your schedules all off track."

Katie waved a hand. "No way. Don't worry. Right now we have no schedules, but when we do, nothing interferes."

"Okay. I'll see you later."

The cartons were bulky but not heavy. Using the markings she had applied with a felt-tip pen, Adrienne restacked them in the storeroom according to their content and extent of use. When they were in order, she dug into her tote bag for her order book, but two times of rummaging through it produced no book. Disgustedly she dropped the bag to the floor and stood, hands clenched on her hips, glaring at the boxes, remembering the book was in one of the drawers of the sideboard in the apartment's dining room. She puffed out her cheeks, then let the air escape with a satisfying, emphatic "Damn!"

She stood at one of the open windows in the larger room. A soft breeze drifted in to dry the perspiration dampening her. Pine and sun-warmed grass scents, blending with a medley of more vagrant smells she could not identify, floated into the room on the lazy air movement. Several moments passed before she recognized the fragrance of lilacs. It was nearly nonexistent, elusive among the stronger scents, more an imagining than an actual aroma. She was surprised, because she had seen no lilacs near the house. Then she remembered the dream, in which the scent of lilacs had added thickness to the lightning-splashed darkness. She shivered, feeling the perspiration on her skin turning cold. Abruptly she turned from the window and left the room.

In the hallway she halted, her mind divided. A very rational portion of it insisted she go upstairs, find a towel and washrag and wash the perspiration, which now felt grimy, from her. But the other portion was heeding a silent call that beckoned her to visit the old parlor. Around her the house was silent except for an occasional creak of an old timber shifting the weight it had carried for so many years, while from outside she heard birds fluttering among the pines and oaks, then, far away, in another world and time, an automobile horn blared, muted by distance. She stood very still, waiting for the backlash of the brief tension she had just experienced at the window, feeling very much alone, waiting to discover which portion of her mind would prove the strongest.

Slowly she turned toward the parlor.

The room was the same as it had been the day before. Afternoon sunlight filled it with an amber haze, striped here and there with more brilliant columns slanting from the windows. Standing in the doorway, she watched motes of dust swirling on the quiet air like gossamer bits torn from fairy gowns.

She took a hesitant step into the room, then another, feeling that peculiar silence of long-empty places curling around her, hollow like something once alive and vital, but from which life was now drained.

In the middle of the room, she stopped and looked around. She sensed again the tranquillity, but the imperfection had grown bigger. Nor was the silence as deep as she first thought. It was merely a cover, like a calming agent spread on turbulent waters, flattening the surface under which powerful currents roamed. She walked slowly to the south windows. The sandals she wore made no sounds, no echoes bounced behind her.

She could not help but wonder how, after learning of the two brutal killings which had occurred in it, the garden would appear to her today, but on the first look she saw no change, nor did she feel the strange force among the brown remains. The garden ruins lay in a deep silence under the weight of the sun. Although she knew she was seeking something which did not exist, she focused all her senses on the twisted skeletons of rotted foliage, appraising them foot by foot, wanting to become aware of a sound or sensation in the dead patch of land, no matter how artificial or imperceptible. This time she wanted nothing in her subconscious fermenting until a dream like the one of the night before reoccurred. It was, in all probability, silly, she knew; yet she told herself that what she was doing was a cure for anxiety. She wanted no accumulation of doubt.

But nothing came from the area of death. There was no repeat of the previous day's dark sensation of an entity out there waiting and reaching. Satisfied, she turned from the window.

Her pulse had accelerated while she was looking out the window, and now it was slowing toward normal as she walked to the door. Her stomach was churning, too, telling her her nervous system had taken more of an assault than she had realized.

She was within three or four steps of the hallway door when she first felt it take hold of her. By the time she was fully aware of it, it was already inside her, curling its way into her senses like a sinister odor so that she suddenly had to fight to control her breathing. She stopped, immobile, while the thing within her told her to look over her shoulder at the two front windows. Her heart began to thud again. A fist took hold of her stomach and twisted. She knew then that the thing which had been in the storage compartment beneath the window yesterday was still there. It had not become only a memory as had the disturbance in the garden. It was there and it wanted her to come to it.

Now that her senses were concentrated on the seat, whatever had crept into her mind retreated, so she stood without restraint, yet felt very sure if she tried to leave the room it would reach out for her once more.

Unable to do anything else, she took several steps toward the window. Around her the silence was so vast the room might have been moved to a place outside the world, beyond the reach of earthly sounds. Even the motes of dust, she saw, appeared to hang stationary in the yellow-amber shafts of sunlight, and she wondered if time had ceased its flow. Strangely she felt no apprehension, but a realization of vulnerability sharpened her senses. She walked slowly to the south window seat.

The window was closed, giving the sun coming through the glass a magnified warmth. Over the years that repeated warmth had cracked the white paint on the seat and rippled it, reminding her of froth solidified. Tiny yellow stains marred the sterile surface, giving it a diseased appearance like cancerous tissue.

The silence tightened. She stood looking down at the seat, squinting in the brightness of the reflected light from the white paint, forcing herself to remain calm. Twentieth-century thinking told her there was no possibility of what she was feeling, that she was behaving like a child, yet the ancient instincts submerged beneath her contemporary thought patterns knew otherwise. Adrienne was conscious of something beneath the seat lid, something down there in the dark compartment, waiting for the lid to be lifted.

She hooked her finger in the metal loop and pulled upward. The seat did not move. She gave a yank, digging the sharp metal into her flesh. Still there was no movement of the lid, though a few flakes of dried paint fell to the floor at her feet. Even as she gave it one more try, grunting from the cutting pain in her finger, she knew it would not open. Disgustedly she pushed the ring back down into its recess and stood looking at the seat, sucking her finger, tasting faintly the metal of the ring.

She moved back a step, then another, before turning to cross the room to the door. It was while she was turning, when her back was almost facing the seat, that she heard the faraway voices, muted in the heavy silence, calling her.

CHAPTER

The conversation eddied around her. She tried to find interest in it, but confusion filled her consciousness. The imagined voices of the parlor carried more reality than the ones of the three people sitting around her in the carriage house apartment.

The steaks, cooked on a grill set up in the parking area, were eaten, along with potatoes and salad, in the kitchen of the house. She supposed they had been delicious, but to her they had been disturbingly tasteless, bland fodder. She remembered the wine as no more than tart-tasting water. During the entire meal and after, she felt that something uncanny was waiting to make an appearance, that this evening was no more than a blurred interlude before whatever it was moved out of the darkness to take its place among them.

"The four of his paintings I've seen," Ned was saying, "are magnificent examples of draftsmanship. God, the restraint and control that man possessed is absolutely unbelievable."

"I would like to know why there isn't more of his work around here," Geoff said. "A prophet unrecognized in his own country, do you suppose?"

"Probably. Jesus, if only I could master his techniques, and I think I could, I'd be walking with the angels."

Adrienne realized they were speaking of Sebastian. She wondered how much of their conversation she had missed, hoping not too much, because to her, Sebastian was a strange, illusionary figure standing half concealed in the shadows of the past, from where he haunted the history of the house and the area surrounding it.

Then Ned was standing over her, pouring more cream sherry into her glass. "You've lived in this area quite a while, haven't you?"

"Eight years."

"And you haven't heard of him?"

"No." She pulled her attention together as best she could. "Orlando is like every other city with its various interests. We were in the industrial circle, and away from the office we found our outlets with people to whom art is a microchip or, at best, aerial photographs of highways. I'm afraid we were humdrum in our interests."

"We all are, when it comes right down to it. It just bugs me that a man with the talent he possessed is condemned to drift in obscurity while so-called modern artists catering to fads gain fame."

"The story of mankind," Geoff said.

"A sad commentary." Ned went back to the chair in which he had been slouching and sat down. When he spoke again, there was an intensity in his voice Adrienne had never heard, but which indicated that her first impression of his self-assurance was not entirely wrong. "I can, and I am going to, master his techniques. Someplace in this part of the country there has to be a collection of his work which I can study."

She saw a shadow of concern lay for a moment on Katie's face as the red-haired woman drew a breath to speak, but then changed her mind and looked down at the glass of wine she held in her hands. From the corner of her eye, she glanced at Geoff, but the tall, bearded man was staring straight ahead.

Without any of them being aware of it, twilight had faded into night. The intense heat of July and August was still far enough away that the darkness held a soft, velvety quality. From where she sat, Adrienne could see the distant glow of Orlando's lights spreading upward in a fan-shaped aureole on the horizon, like illumination escaping from another world, she thought. She looked away and sipped her wine.

Katie got up, poured herself another glass of wine, then went to the open window. She stood with her back to them, looking out, turning the wineglass pensively in her long fingers. "I've never seen more beautiful nights than here. There's a magic about them that keeps you from wanting to go to bed for fear of missing an enormous event." She turned to face them. "I'm going to like it here."

"I hope so, because we can't afford to move again," Geoff said.

Adrienne looked quickly at one then the other from under her lowered lashes, conscious of a sudden undercurrent moving through the room. The chances were that she was misinterpreting, but Geoff sounded as if he was bluntly telling his wife they could not leave. There had been a sharpness under the phrasing of the commonplace words. She waited, fingers tight around her wineglass, but as the minutes passed she was unable to detect any hint of dissatisfaction.

The conversation lagged after that as if the others, too, had recognized the brief exchange as a turning point in the evening. Adrienne finished her wine, then glanced at her watch. It read ten-fifteen. The lateness of the hour startled her, and saddened her, because the evening had escaped her, leaving no more than a blurred recollection of a few details. What should have been good hours with three people she admired was suddenly no more than an unrewarding loss of time. She cleared her throat, then tried to make her voice light. "Do you all know it's past my bedtime already, and I have a half an hour's drive to get home?"

Ned accompanied her to her car, telling Katie and Geoff he was going on to bed when she was gone.

"We'll get your tables put together tomorrow," he said when they reached the Toyota.

She merely nodded. She felt like a marionette with its strings at all the wrong lengths. She was tired, tired in her muscles and tired in her mind. Almost she told Ned not to bother with the tables, that she had changed her mind about renting the rooms because the house frightened her. It would be so easy, so safe, to say that, but instead, she said, "I'll help you."

"I'd like that."

"I'm asking you again, Ned, to please not throw your schedule out the window because of me."

He looked directly at her with eyes that were very frank and very open. "I think that maybe you have become my schedule, Adrienne."

"Oh?" She felt a pleasant surprise.

"It's a feeling I have. I can't describe it, and I don't know what it means, to be very truthful with you, or how to explain it. But I sense in some way it has to do with my desire to start painting again."

"In what way?"

"I don't know that, either. It's all pretty damn vague." He shook his head and looked away, toward the stars. "I have this—this premonition, if you like—that you and I will be working on a painting together at some time. A portrait, maybe. They say Sebastian did unbelievably beautiful portraits of women, though there are none around to be seen."

Around them the night stirred softly, and the remoteness which had held her prisoner all evening set her free, no longer distorting time and events. An emotion which she had not allowed to approach her for so long, a once unendurable violation of her self-protection, reached out for her. Affection. "Working on a portrait wouldn't be as prosaic as building a table together, would it?"

He smiled. "No. At least with a camera or brush, I know what I'm doing. I can't say that about a hammer and nails."

It came then, flowing out of the full-bodied night, finding its way into her as it had in the parlor that afternoon. It curled its way through her while she stood, afraid to move, afraid to speak. She had to tell him of her experience in the house; he must know of her fear. Her heart began to race, demanding more air from her lungs so she was forced to breathe in short, shallow gasps.

"Ned, may I ask a favor of you?"

"Of course."

It was as if the night, too, was waiting for her to speak. Even as she asked the question, she felt the doubt and misgivings of the past year returning. "Would you open the seat of the south front window in the parlor?"

"I'm planning to open both of them before too long."

"I know. Katie told me. But I mean very soon, Ned. Maybe instead of building the tables tomorrow we could open the seat. Do you think it would be possible?"

"Yes, I suppose so. Just the one? Just the south one?"

"Yes, just that one."

His right brow crawled upward. "But why? It's just a storage area, probably empty and smelly."

"No, I think there's something in it."

"What?"

She knew she should feel foolish, even more so than when she had asked him over coffee that morning if he talked to himself while he worked, but she did not, only perhaps a little shy. "I don't know."

"But you think there's something in it? Really? Why?"

She was becoming more and more embarrassed, having to struggle to keep her eyes on his face. "Yesterday and today . . . I could honestly feel a—well, a force of some kind reaching out from it . . . as if something—or somebody—was . . . was wanting to get out of it."

"Somebody! In the window seat? Just that one, just the south one?"

"Yes, somebody . . . and just the south one . . ."

She shook her head. She could not go on. She was making such a goddamn fool of herself. Her illusions had finally become reality.

"Damn! That's something." He looked in the direction of the house, then gave a husky chuckle. "You mean I've got a nonpaying tenant hiding in there? It must be cramped, all huddled in a window seat like that, don't you think?"

"Ned—"

"Look, Adrienne, I've got to admit this old place is somewhat creepy, especially after dark; and, with an active imagination, a person could easily scare themselves with the idea it's haunted. But I haven't seen or heard anything all the time we've been here." She had her eyes downcast, but she knew he was smiling. "Besides, it somehow just doesn't have the requisites to be a setting for a Gothic tale . . . you know, no foggy moors or thundering surf beneath tall cliffs, not even a narrow dirt road."

Listening to him, she felt, at first, ashamed, a child who had told a farfetched story to gain attention, then disappointed that Ned did not believe her, and, finally, a little angry that he did not. Though she knew silence was the best response, she said, "I—I'm not making this up, Ned."

"No, I know that."

"It's just that you wonder about my mental equilibrium."

"Oh, Christ, don't become defensive, please." His voice immediately lost its edge, became touched with whimsy. "It's not everybody, Adrienne, you've got to admit, who's told they have ghosts dwelling in the parlor of their house. It takes some getting used to."

She looked at him then. Even in the darkness, she could see, under a thin veil of humor, concern struggling with disbelief on his face, and she wondered which one would win control. When he made no move, she shook her head and turned toward her car.

"Adrienne, wait!" He took a step after her and laid a hand gently on her upper arm. "Don't be mad. I guess I've botched this whole thing, haven't I?"

"I—I'm sorry, Ned. I know what I'm trying to say sounds crazy, and the way I'm saying it doesn't make sense or make what I feel seem worthwhile, but I did, honestly, have a bad reaction in that room."

"I believe that, Adrienne. Now look, don't leave. Let's go into the kitchen and I'll fix some coffee, and while we're drinking it, you can tell me the whole story. Okay? You've got my curiosity aroused, you know." He gave a little tug on her arm. "If I do have things living in one of my window seats, I want to know about it. Come on."

Neither spoke while Ned heated water in a dome-shaped teakettle and emptied heaping spoonfuls of instant coffee into two mugs. At the kitchen table, Adrienne shifted uneasily on the wooden chair. Something deep within her was waiting to hear the muffled voices calling to her. On the table in front of her, her folded hands began to quiver, then to shake. In an instant, her entire body was trembling. Ned turned from watching the kettle.

"You're frightened," he whispered. "My God, you're really frightened!"

She could only nod.

He crossed the kitchen, pulled her up from the chair and

encircled her with his arms, drawing her close against his chest. She rested her cheek on his shoulder, for the first time in a long time aware of comfort and protection as his warmth found its way into her, deep in her where the cold twists of apprehension were coiled, then spread through her until she felt the coils melt away.

When he felt the calmness return to her, he pushed her back to arm's length. "Let's go open those seats. Now! Together."

Adrienne stiffened.

"I swear to God, you look like you're in shock." His hands tightened their grasp on her shoulders as concern overlaid his features. "Are you up to it?"

She nodded, then her voice tore free of the tightness in her throat. "Yes. I'm all right now, really." Though her face felt as inflexible and misproportioned as a Halloween mask, she managed a smile. "You've got to think I'm a nincompoop. I'm sorry."

"What I think is that you're a very scared woman."

"Not so much now. But I was—and there's no rational explanation. Not one. And that's what makes me feel like a gold-plated you-know-what."

"Okay, tell me about it."

With his strength acting as a shield between her and her fugitive self, with his warmth still flowing through her, she told him of her experience at the window, looking out upon the garden. She described the previous night's dream, trying all the while to make her words plausible, attempting to keep to a no-nonsense tone, hoping that when she finished Ned would still think of her as a right-minded person and therefore more easily forgiven for suffering odd moments of hallucination.

"God Almighty!" There was no disbelief in his voice; his arms tightened around her. "You do make it sound real."

She looked up at his face, seeing his neck and jaw muscles

rigid, straining cords holding his features together. He stared at the door to the hallway leading to the parlor.

"Let's open it," he muttered. "I've got to see for myself."

Using all the willpower she could muster, she forced herself to smile and say, "Maybe you'll be able to collect back rent if we find it occupied."

He chuckled. From the cabinet beneath the kitchen sink, he dug out a hammer and a wood chisel, saying he wished he had a crowbar.

Adrienne followed him down the hallway which passed her rooms. It was dim, lit only by the light spilling through the open kitchen door, so the long silhouettes of their shadows preceded them like guides leading them to the massive darkness of the parlor. Their footsteps on the hardwood floor echoed with a curious booming, an endlessly renewing sound that followed them through the gloom. Just inside the parlor doorway, Ned stopped so abruptly Adrienne very nearly walked into him. Even so close, she saw him only as a blocky outline of a human form, all his detail erased by the darkness of the room.

"Get the light," he said. "It's to the right of the door."

She groped along the wall, found the switch and flipped it. A thin yellow illumination tried unsuccessfully to push the darkness away, only managing to force it as far as the walls, where it piled upward upon itself from floor to ceiling, dwarfing them in a chasm between reality and fantasy.

"That's only a forty-watt bulb," he said, seeing her look around the room. "I never come in here at night."

"It should be enough." The hollow vibrations of her voice replaced their echoing footsteps.

"The south one, right?"

"Yes."

At the window, Ned laid his tools on the floor, then ran his fingers over the seat, digging his nails into the crack outlining the lid. "I think it's mostly old paint sealing it shut. It shouldn't be difficult to pry open."

Adrienne said nothing. She could still stop him, she knew, but it was beyond her right to do that now.

He knelt before the seat, took up the hammer and the wood chisel and began working at one corner. He worked slowly, carefully, like a sculptor, Adrienne thought, each short stroke of the hammer meticulously controlled. The thudding of the blows was magnified in the emptiness of the room, the noise building upon itself until the striking hammer was the focal point of all sound.

Halfway along the front of the seat he stopped. Perspiration was running in rivulets from his face, dully sheening his forearms. He ran a hand across his forehead and sat back on his heels.

"This is more than I thought." He shook his head. "I can't see why in hell anybody would paint over something so obvious as this lid."

"Maybe for this very reason. To seal it."

"You think so?" He seemed to be trying to bring unrelated subjects together, and she saw what she read as disbelief in his eyes.

"Do you still feel anything?" he finally asked.

"Not like this afternoon."

He pressed. "But something?"

"Yes."

He turned away from her to look at their transparent reflections in the window, then down at the seat again, seeking a way to say what he wanted to say, then finally saying it incredulously. "I feel it, too."

"You do?" Excitement touched her. "What kind of feeling?"

"Like yours, from what you told me . . . that there's something in there wanting out." He continued to stare at the seat, frowning, endeavoring to understand a problem that rational thinking refused to admit. "It's impossible."

She laid a hand on his shoulder. "You're not pretending, are you? You're not saying that just to make me feel less a fool?"

"No! I wish to Christ I was."

"Ned, have either Katie or Geoff felt it?"

"No." He scowled. "Well, once Katie did say she thought we were not alone in this room. But that was all, and neither Geoff nor I questioned her about it, because when she said it we were busy cleaning and waxing the floor."

Unconsciously she laid a hand on his shoulder.

He looked up at her, seemed about to say something, but instead ran a hand through his hair, then wiped the perspiration from his forehead once more before starting to tap at the lid again.

Adrienne removed her hand from his shoulder and stepped back. She watched him for another few minutes, then walked slowly to the other window and looked out on the dead garden. The darkness enfolding the area was more opaque than she'd imagined it could be, laden with the cloying scents of a fecund night. She leaned against the sill and waited, not knowing for what, but telling herself it was to reaffirm that out there, where death had been a violent visitor, nothing waited, nothing existed. The action was an idiotic show of valor, testing her freedom from fear.

Behind her Ned's hammer sent rhythmic trembles through the old wood that she could feel in her feet and in her thighs where they touched the sill. It was like the sound of digging, the steady noise of an excavation where time was being stripped away, layer by layer, from secrets long buried in silent darkness.

During the past two days she had wandered into a catacomb of fear. This was the time to find her way out before the feeding of her fear became an ongoing process. Even though Ned said he felt the thing in the window seat, she must convince him she was a captive of self-induced phantoms, nothing more, and that he was becoming a prisoner, too.

But as she was about to turn from the window to go back to him, she sensed something—as if a cosmic magnet was drawing away all the nocturnal sounds beyond the verandah—and she knew the garden was not empty. Nothing distinguishable moved through the tangled ruins of the star-dappled vegetation; yet there was a restlessness in the night, an invisible cloud drifting through the darkness.

It hovered just beyond the verandah railing, permitting her to feel its strength, feel the terror and rage and corruption swirling within it, debris in a maelstrom which had ripped from mankind all its most horrible passions. It moved back and forth outside the railing, seeking a way onto the verandah and into the house. She heard a screaming within it, mixing with the sound of her heart thundering in her chest. She fell back a step and as she did, she saw a woman's face materializing, taking shape like a photographic image in developing solution, floating toward her, drifting like a hideous will-o'-the-wisp. Its features were contorted in indescribable horror and pain. Blood streamed from its flared nostrils. The mouth stretched into a wide oval, screaming in demented terror at Adrienne through the window, appearing to both curse her and beseech her.

"No!" Her own voice was a gasp of pain torn from her throat. "Oh, my God . . . no . . ."

A blackness, more depthless and opaque than anything Adrienne had ever seen, came out of the night and swallowed the desperate face.

Adrienne turned and ran to Ned's side.

He looked up, startled. "Adrienne, for Christ's sake, what's wrong?"

"It's there—in the garden." She pointed toward the window.

"What? What you felt yesterday?" He was on his feet now.

She nodded, unable to tell him it was total horror this time, feeling the rush of something close to madness descending on her.

"Stay here!"

He hurried to the window, his hand taking a firmer grip on the handle of the hammer. He stood where she had stood, a silhouette against a rectangle of the night sky, his head slightly cocked to the right, listening, waiting. The hand holding the hammer cocked the tool like a weapon, while his body stiffened in preparation for violent movement. He stood poised, ready, but the final movement never came. Slowly he relaxed, shoulders lifting and torso swelling as he took a deep breath. After another moment, he turned from the window and came back to her.

"Did you see it?" she asked.

"No." His breathing was harsh and forced. "There was nothing to see."

"The face—it wasn't there? The face of a screaming woman?"

He shook his head.

"But surely you could feel something out there in the garden."

"Yes . . . I felt something." He stared down at the seat, then turned to gaze back at the window. "What the hell is going on?"

She was calming slightly now. Her immediate terror was gone. She drew a deep breath. "There's got to be a relationship between what's in the storage compartment and whatever's out there in the garden."

He made an abrupt negative gesture. "Goddammit, Adrienne, we're talking about ghosts, and there are no such things."

"I know."

With one quick movement, he swung away from her and bent over the seat. "To hell with being careful. I'm going to find out what's in this damn thing."

He slammed the hammer against the chisel, gouging the wood, tearing splinters from the edges of the lid and the area around it. The old paint buckled, then split into confetti as spiderweb cracks formed jagged fans in the wood beneath it. Adrienne stood silent, watching, not daring to say a word lest she cry out against the silent echo of the silent scream erupting from the face or, maybe worse, beg him to stop before the contents of the storage bin were revealed.

He hacked his way across the front of the lid, then back along each side, leaving a ragged U-shaped scar on the surface of the seat, ignoring the chipped paint and wood slivers that formed tiny windrows along each side of the grooves, giving the seat the appearance of having been capriciously destroyed.

Finally he laid the hammer aside and slowly stood up, breathing rapidly through his mouth, eyes obscured beneath his dark brows. Using the chisel like a small crowbar, wedging its tip into the groove he had gouged along the front of the lid, he pried upward. The lid trembled, then warped into a small dome over the chisel, but held, though the old wood groaned with dry squeaks of protest.

Adrienne shuddered and moved to his side. Not certain what answer she wanted to hear, she asked, "Can you do it?"

"Yes. Right now."

He jammed the chisel under the lid once more but instead of prying he leaned his entire weight on the chisel. A shrill creaking erupted from the seat. Paint chips and splinters danced on the lid, then fell to the back of the seat as the lid tore free.

He did not lift it, but stepped back and exhaled sharply, then looked at her. His voice was tight. "That's it."

Adrienne merely nodded. She did not know what she had

expected, but nothing had changed. There had been no rushing of obscene powers into the room to shake the house or fill the air with sudden, snarling evil. The darkness, still held precariously at bay by the weak bulb, was not transformed into a fetid mass hiding malevolent creatures.

But a breeze found its way through the room, carrying the faint smell of lilacs, and from somewhere in the room, there was maybe, just maybe, the sound of a childlike giggle.

Ned looked at her and licked his lips. "Well, shall we?"

Now the darkness of the room did seem to tighten around them as the circle of dingy light shrank. A tiny point of coldness touched her between her shoulders.

"Yes."

He worked his fingers into the opening at the front of the lid and lifted.

Very little light spilled into the storage area; Adrienne felt she was staring down into a well shaft, one descending to the earth's very core. But as her eyes adjusted, the shadows thinned, losing their secretiveness, and she made out oblongs of gray neatly bisecting the overall dimness of the cavity. She bent closer, and saw they were rolls of what appeared to be heavy material like tightly woven canvas.

"Jesus Christ!" Ned was at her side, one hand gripping the lip of the compartment.

"They have to be paintings." His voice was thick. "Rolled canvases."

Then she saw the frayed ends of the rolled canvases with tiny daubs of paint clinging to the loose threads. A musty smell, mingled with one she could not identify, rose from the compartment. Ned said it was linseed oil and paint pigment.

"They have to be his," he said slowly. "They have to be Sebastian's."

Adrienne did not realize she had clenched her fists, but now she felt them relaxing and opening, leaving little crescents of pain in her palms where the nails had dug in. She was experiencing the same exultant feeling when, as a child, she accepted a frightening dare and then performed the accepted challenge with no dreadful consequences. She controlled a startling desire to laugh.

Ned visibly relaxed as well. He drew a long breath while straightening up before looking at her.

"I'd feel more excited if what you saw at the window hadn't occurred, but even so"—he grinned—"I feel damn good."

"I only feel ridiculous." She looked at the canvases lying in the well of shadow. "I'm a real jackass."

He put a companionable arm around her shoulders. "No, you're not. You were dealt some heavy one-two punches and you rode them well."

His arm felt good around her, essential. "Maybe I put myself in the way of them."

"No, you didn't do that, either." His voice drifted away a tiny bit. "Remember, I felt everything you have."

"But you didn't go all to pieces."

He tightened his arm and squeezed. "It's okay."

"Oh . . ."

"Anyway, I hadn't planned to get into these seats for a long time, so the paintings wouldn't be found for months. It was rough on you, but thanks."

"I guess you're welcome. Are we going to open the other one?"

He chuckled, dropped his arm and bent to reach into the storage area. "Let's take one at a time. Personally I couldn't take a repeat of the tension we felt, and, besides, one treasure a night is enough."

Very gently, slipping his fingers carefully into the open ends of a roll, he lifted one of the canvases, stepped away from the seat and, kneeling, laid it on the floor. In the gloomy light the gray material seemed dirty and valueless.

"I'm going to need help, and we've got to be careful." He

looked up at her. "The paint is probably dried out, so it might crack when we unroll the canvas."

"What do I do?"

He pointed to the two free corners on the outside of the roll. "Hold those down while I do the unrolling."

She dropped to her knees facing him and put her fingers on the corners he indicated.

"Hold them flat on the floor."

She pressed the canvas down on the wood, spreading her fingers to obtain more coverage.

Very slowly Ned unrolled the canvas. Though his fingers were trembling, his touch was delicate, like a sensitive massaging, as he pulled the material toward him. With each new inch of the canvas exposed, his breathing quickened; perspiration dotted his forehead and clung to his chin in tiny droplets. He ignored it.

Adrienne saw a band of blue-black paint appear, watched as it grew wider while the canvas unrolled, then saw golden yellow hair inch out from under the rolling canvas. She watched it take shape to form a casual coiffure around a face of startling beauty.

Blue eyes stared up at her, and a sensuous mouth, ever so slightly curved in a hint of a smile, seemed to be ready to speak to her. Below a firm chin, a slender neck disappeared into a dove-gray neckline. Finally the head and shoulders of a young woman lay between them.

"Oh, my God." Ned's voice sounded as if it was an effort for him to speak.

"What's wrong?"

His eyes did not leave the painting. "How in hell did he do it?"

"Ned?"

"Adrienne, look at that paint. Not a crack anywhere, not a hint of fading or discoloration. It's been a hundred years, at least, since it was applied, and it looks as fresh as if it came off the palette only this morning. And the tones. My God, look at the tones! They're real. Impossibly real and lifelike. It can't be done . . . yet, look, he did it." He stared at her, skepticism fighting with near reverence on his face. "Sweet Jesus, what a genius that man must have been!"

She knew so little about art that she felt helpless before his admiration of the portrait spread between them on the floor. But she looked at it with more concentration, trying to understand.

The young woman in the painting was no more than nineteen or twenty, clean and sparkling with the wholesomeness some women show as they enter maturity. There was an innocence in the face which Adrienne could only think of as bucolic, yet which was belied by the vivacious, twinkling glimmer in the blue eyes. An overall wistfulness on the young woman's features made one think that this girl of long-past summers harbored secret desires that the artist, master that he had been, was unable to capture. And, as she studied the painting, she began to see and feel what Ned had exclaimed over. Slowly at first, then with a continued astonishment, she began to experience the eerie sensation that what they had removed from the storage compartment was not a painting, but a living, breathing woman . . . a creature clothed in warm, smooth-textured flesh.

She drew in a breath, suddenly disturbed, telling herself it was the weak light causing a hallucination, its dimness befuddling her senses.

She looked up from the painting to see Ned watching her.

"You feel it, too, don't you?" he asked. "A feeling there's life in that picture."

"Yes. What is it? The bad lighting?"

"Maybe, but mostly I think it's the way Sebastian painted it. He must have possessed a secret." His eyes returned to the portrait. "God, it's beyond belief. The rumors said the portraits were magnificent, but nothing like this."

"The other canvases in the compartment, they must be portraits, too."

"Let's see." But instead of rising from his knees, he looked around the room, scowling into the darkness. "We need something to hold this flat. I don't want it to roll up again or curl."

Adrienne said, "I don't think it will."

He glanced at her questioningly, then grunted and lifted his fingers from the corners of the canvas. Adrienne did the same. The portrait remained spread flat between them, not even the corners curling up. Ned shook his head. "I'm going to study this man, find out everything I can about him. I have to. God, there's so much here to learn."

Half an hour later, sixteen portraits lay in a semicircle on the floor, beautifully brilliant twenty-by-twenty-four-inch rectangles of color giving the impression of pulsing as the dingy light played across them.

All of them were of young women, all of them radiant like the first one, with a spectacular brilliance coming from deep inside them, as if light had somehow been captured within the pigments and was slowly being released. Each one was so three-dimensional, so disturbingly warm with life, Adrienne would not have been taken aback should the women speak to her.

Represented were women from every level of society. Aristocratic women dressed in lace and lawn and silk, with sweeping plumed hats and beaded purses. With an elegantly gloved hand, one held the leash to a Russian wolfhound. A young, plump matron grinned from her canvas, the sails of a windmill behind her. A high-wigged French courtesan from two hundred years before smiled her coquette's smile, thrusting forward a deep-cleavaged bosom. There were farm girls, wholesome and ripe with health, dressed in homespun and cotton, some wearing bonnets, some with their hair unkempt as if returning from the fields. Two domestic serving girls in gray woolens, white aprons and wide collars stared straight ahead from under their dusting caps. There were also ones who could have been nothing but whores, with their obscenely garish boas draped around them as they stood provocatively in tight satins of clashing hues, their rouged smiles knowing, their shaded eyes wise but empty.

Then there were two radically different in model selection, so blatantly sexual they were erotic, so pulsing with a life force of their own, they engulfed Adrienne with a spawning uneasiness. They were the only nudes. One was a horizontal composition, the only one in the collection, reminding Adrienne of Goya's "Naked Maja." The black-haired woman reclined on her back, surrounded by thick pillows. With her arms behind her head, she gazed boldly from the canvas with murky lights smoldering in half-closed eyes and a smile promising the unduplicated delights of the ages. The other was a frontal view of a statuesque blonde, arms held high, a pagan priestess doing homage to an unseen god. Behind her, partially lost in frail wraiths of smoke, temple columns rose. Adrienne could think of only one word to describe them. Frightening. She had the alarming suspicion that if she were to run her hand over the bodies in those two paintings, the flesh would be warm and smooth.

Fifteen of the canvases were completed, from which the young women stared with liquid eyes. Some of those eyes looked up warmly, some with more than a hint of sadness, a few exhibiting the same alarm Adrienne was experiencing. Behind each of those exquisite faces seemed a lingering awareness of torment. Adrienne had the uncanny sensation of standing, not amid a display of paintings, but within a group of living women who possessed a common but hideous secret. There was a stirring in her memory, a chilled recall of the dream in which women's voices called to her while one wailed in misery.

Ned stood with his hands clasped behind his back, examining the unfinished painting. A very thin umber wash covered the canvas, upon which the drawing, in darker umber, was completed. Even without the application of color, and with only elemental modeling, the sensuousness of the woman who had sat for the portrait reached from the canvas with erotic mystery. Dressed in what eventually would have been some sort of gown leaving her shoulders and upper breasts bare, she gazed slantwise at the viewer from long-lashed eyes already indicating the existence of an age-old craving.

Until this moment Adrienne had done no more than glance at it. Now, when she looked full at it, she saw the face suddenly in night-shadowed color, saw the even features on the canvas twisted in ghostly lines of terror and pain. The face was closer than it had been outside the window, its tortured emotions able to touch her with their terror.

"It's her," she whispered. "My God, it's the face I saw in the window."

Ned sucked in his breath. "Then . . . then it must be Sabra."

She knew she should recognize the name, that at some time it had been mentioned to her, but her memory would not pull it into focus. "Sabra?"

"Sebastian's wife, the woman who was killed with him out in the garden."

She felt a sudden frigidness racing through her body, as if the cold spot which took its place between her shoulders while Ned was opening the seat was drilling into her. At her feet, the paintings glittered like out-of-focus, peripheral images of oversize gems. She looked at Ned. He was staring toward the other window with an almost impenetrable intensity.

"Katie told me about her." She was not at all certain he heard her. "I'd forgotten."

But he nodded and said, "I refuse to believe in ghosts or phantoms."

He sounded like a man trying to convince himself that what he had believed all his life could not be jeopardized with things spawned in superstitions and ancient fantasy. Adrienne said nothing. Solid substance was fading from her rapidly, racing away to the far end of a dark tunnel. Everything around her, Ned and the shadows and the paintings, was becoming only shards of an escaping awareness.

"Adrienne! Adrienne!"

Ned's arms were around her, not in a companionable way, but solidly, girdling her in protection. She shivered and leaned against his chest, wanting to sink deeper and deeper into the peace and security he offered. Behind her eyes tears were forming, ready to spill out onto her cheeks. Her body and mind were waiting to cleanse themselves of the painful left-overs of shock and fear which had jarred them almost beyond endurance. When she began to tremble, Ned's arms tightened, drawing her closer to him, pulling her into a time and place where life was snug and understood.

"You're not going home," she heard him saying. "I'm not going to allow you to make that drive. Your nervous system's getting ready to blow itself apart, so you're going to spend the night here. I'll fix a bed for you."

She moved her head in agreement, feeling a tiny bit of his strength seeping into her, soothing her enough for her mind to regain elemental functional control.

With his arm still around her waist, he helped her up the stairs to the second floor and guided her into a bedroom. She sat on a straight-backed chair while he dragged sheets and a pillowcase from the linen closet, then made the bed. She watched him with dulled eyes, exhaustion leaving her no choice but to sit as quiet and still as possible.

He came into the room with towels and a washrag. "In case you feel up to washing, I'll leave these with you, but if I were you, I'd go right to bed. You can shower in the morning."

She pulled herself out of the abstraction far enough to

make her lips smile, her head nod. "Thanks. You're . . . you're nice, Ned."

He hung the towels and washrag on the bed's footboard. "So are you, Adrienne."

She took his advice and did not wash. In spite of feeling sticky and grimy, the bathroom was too far down the hall. As she squirmed out of her clothes, she wondered what her reaction would have been if Ned had volunteered to help her undress. She was asleep before an answer came to her.

She had no idea what the time was, if she had slept for a few minutes or several hours, or if dawn was just on the other side of the horizon, only that darkness filled the room. What she did know was that something had burrowed through the layers of exhaustion insulating her mind.

She lay on her back staring up into the darkness where the ceiling should have been. Sometime after she had fallen asleep, she had kicked the top sheet off her, and now the perspiration on her naked skin created a false coolness in the night air coming through the open window. Under her, the bed sheet and pillow were soggy with dampness.

She lay listening; waiting for noises in the darkness, for movement in the room, acutely aware of how slowly time creeps when nerves are on the verge of convulsion.

When she first heard it, it was hard to distinguish. It was no more than a thin background noise to the overwhelming silence. But she forced herself to concentrate on it, and it became not a lost remnant of sound but the rhythmic cadence of voices speaking. Women's voices. Women who were talking as women do at a party or reunion.

She forced herself to concentrate, to listen carefully, to fix them in some direction. Then she knew. The voices were coming from downstairs, from directly below the bedroom . . . from the parlor.

Stretching his legs before him on the blanket, Sebastian leaned back against the trunk of the willow tree, his sketch pad and charcoal sticks forgotten at his side. Through the willow's restless foliage the sunlight fluttered on his face as if not certain exactly where to touch. He lowered his eyelids and through his lashes watched the trees and river recede into a light-pointed mist of dusky greens and smoky blues. He enjoyed viewing the world that way, transforming it into an exquisite abstraction of line and color. Within those colors, he had always known, was a beauty beyond imagining.

"Sebastian, are you asleep?"

The woman's voice, a soft and rich contralto tone, was a poignant portion of a dream he hoped would never end.

"No." He opened his eyes to look through the drooping curtain of the willow's leaves. "I'm sitting here wishing for the ability to swim."

"I will teach you, if you come in with me."

"No, Sabra."

"Then I will be but a minute more. Just once more across the river and back. Is that all right?"

"Of course . . . but hurry. There are actions I do not need to be taught and would like to share with you."

She laughed, her very special throaty laugh, and stood facing him with the water halfway up her strong thighs, a naked, suntanned creature of the river with her browned skin golden in the afternoon light, her black hair plastered to her cheeks and shoulders. "I promise to hurry, my darling, because those things you share with me are so fascinating."

She turned and dove headfirst into the brown-green water. Halfway across the river she surfaced, stroking toward the far bank, leaving no disturbance in the water behind her.

He watched her, eyelids not lowered now, wanting to see her clearly in these pristine surroundings which murmured with summer life, imagining her, with no difficulty, as a goddess from the forest glades. In all the many, many years, there had been many women, but none like Sabra. Intuitively, from the first moment of meeting, he had known this tall, voluptuous woman offered no counterpoint in ordinary experience, and still he was unable to fit her into the perspective from which, for so long, he had viewed women.

He sighed and smiled as he watched her rise from the water at the far bank and turn slowly to her right and then to her left as she looked up and down the river, the sunlight glinting on full flanks and heavy breasts dripping with water. She belonged to another place, another time. She was an anachronism, a pagan forest nymph living within the cloistered Victorian society in which fate had placed her.

There was a sound off to his right, low like a child softly clearing its throat. He looked in its direction. Under the branches of shrub, the Siamese cat sat. Its tail was wrapped tightly around its paws, its neck stretched with its head thrust forward, ears laid back, eyes slitted into elongated slots against the brilliance of the river, watching Sabra. For a brief instant, the pose of the cat disturbed Sebastian; its thrust-forward neck and head reminded him of a serpent.

Then he chuckled and said, "You have good taste, my friend. She is magnificent, is she not?"

The cat turned its head to look at him. Something moved behind the blueness of its eyes, something he found troubling, because it did not belong in the eyes of a cat—an almost human awareness.

A week after their marriage the cat had made its first appearance at the house, accepting food, wandering through the garden for a day or two at a time, then disappearing, to return a few days later. Sabra laughingly said their house was only one stop on the Siamese's prowling of its territory, that it came to find peace and rest in the garden because, she was certain, such a raffish cat possessed a harem distributed among its other stops. It showed a fondness for her, watching her intently during its visits.

The cat blinked, gave the appearance of grinning, then turned its brown-masked face away. Leisurely it got up, stretched its body in a muscle-tautening pull and glanced over its left shoulder at Sabra swimming back across the river. Showing no hurry, it moved off into the shadows of the undergrowth.

Sebastian watched Sabra stroking through the sun-bleached water, bringing to him what he had never received from a woman, desire and beauty, offered not obliquely but with unguarded intimacies of mind and flesh.

She came out of the water superbly glorious in her sun- and water-drenched nudity. Even as he watched her push aside the willow boughs to stand before him, she seemed more a by-product of a time remembered than a vivid image of the present.

Trembling light painted arabesques on her, wavering on her flanks and across the gently doming curve of her belly. Water ran down her in tiny rivulets, following her undulating curves to form a dark stain on the earth around her feet. A smile hovered on her lips. He closed his eyes to implant her image in his memory.

"Sebastian, you were napping, weren't you?" She knelt at his side and scowled at the empty pages of the sketch pad. "You've done nothing."

"Oh, but I have, my dear." He laid a hand on her thigh and ran his palm over the smooth surface. "I've watched you, and when I do that, there is nothing else of beauty to interest me."

She looked at him from under lowered lids. "Even with only words, you thrill me."

He saw she was truly flattered and was once more amazed at the childlike shyness that shared the big, sensuous body with her enthusiastic, erotic desires. He slid his palm up the warm dampness of her thigh until his fingertips touched curls of hair. She drew a deep breath.

"Do you know what day this is?" he asked.

She smiled playfully. "Of course, my darling. It's our seventh wedding anniversary."

"And you're not bored after seven long weeks of marriage to a man old enough to be your father?"

The smile continued to hover on her lips, but now it was touched with blossoming pleasure. "I'm becoming old, too, dear. In four months, I'll be twenty-eight; so perhaps it is a mature love we possess. That is the best and strongest kind, Sebastian."

He nodded. "I think that, too . . . and I know we have the strongest kind."

For a moment, his mind slipped away from his control. All the pleasantries in it fled before a mass of darkness from which something black and shapeless peered at him. He knew it was The Master. Not since his meeting Sabra had The Master come. But he would. Someday he would make an appearance and see her—and want her.

"Sebastian? Darling?"

The darkness slithered away, taking with it the black, shapeless form. Sabra was bent slightly forward, her face over his, a look of concern on her features. He smiled with what he hoped was reassurance.

"Are you all right?" she asked.

"Certainly."

"You looked like you were gone away somewhere."

"Not from you. Never would I go away from you."

"I pray not, Sebastian." She laid a hand on his chest. "Will you share with me those things you said you would?"

Her voice was a whisper, an extension of the murmuring trees and river. She began unbuttoning his shirt . . .

"You are very dear to me, Sebastian." Her whisper came from deep in her throat, and even as close as her face was, he saw an expression of devotion on it.

The river had not washed away completely the lilac scent she wore, and its lingering fragrance was like a subtle remnant of a long-ago desire, a remembering of flower garlands and a time of frenzied creation.

Sometime later she lay beside him on the blanket, weary and spent, her muted sobs sounding like a prayer.

He put his arms around her and drew her tight. "You are my beloved."

A short distance away, in a shadowy cave beneath a flowering shrub, the Siamese sat a moment longer watching them, then slowly rose to turn and retreat deeper into the shadows.

Sabra stood on the verandah looking out over the garden. She loved what she saw: it was so much a part of Sebastian. Every day he spent a little time in it, pruning, digging, rearranging plants so colors mixed in startling juxtaposition or merged in blended hues. Within the garden's boundaries he had created a fantasy as poignant and as ardent as he placed on canvas.

Unconsciously, her mind dwelling on the seed-laden earth, she laid her hand flat on her stomach, instinct whispering that within her loins a seed had been planted that afternoon which would give birth to a life more miraculous than any in the garden.

She walked along the verandah to the steps and descended to the crushed-shell walk to meander through the shrubs and plants like an ancient stream winding its slow way through a crowding forest. Her steps were languorous as relaxation seeped through her, the aftermath of passion's omnivorous appetite under the willow tree.

At the far end of the garden she came to a wrought-iron bench set under a sapling's lower boughs. Usually the grottolike space was sun-dappled, but now a deep, gloomy shade filled it, the westward sun too weak to reach beneath the foliage as it sank into a smear of clouds above the horizon. It was the place she came to when she wanted to be alone to think. It was a make-believe secret place belonging to the little girl within her where dreams could be created. She sat down and closed her eyes.

Around her the garden quieted, the life within it seeming to hush its impulsive chatter to watch the gathering clouds forming an advancing bulwark above the western horizon. The silence pleased her, because she wanted this moment uninterrupted.

In the soft darkness behind her closed lids, her mind focused immediately on the impossible pleasure of her marriage to Sebastian. Irrelevantly she wondered what Preacher Henry, back home in the Louisiana parish, would say concerning her fleshly wants and desires, and a smile touched her lips as she thought she could hear his bellowing predictions of damnation. Poor man. How she would like to tell him that his was the soul that was lost, because he lived without sensing the beauty around him, waiting expectantly for an afterlife which might never come. He, like so many others, had never heard the notes from the magic flute, beckoning to be followed to the pleasures of this living life. She squirmed on the bench, thinking of the sensual notes with which Sebastian filled the air.

Yet she knew so little concerning the background of this man who was her husband, other than his given name was Boris, which he detested, and that he came from somewhere in central Europe. He was a strange island which held secrets hidden among craggy hills and verdant forests. Some of those secrets were dark, she felt, while others were of incredible beauty. When she discovered he did not wish to speak of his past, she did not question him; not because she was not interested, but because it made no difference to her. It was the man who shared her life yesterday and today and who would be sharing it tomorrow whom she loved, not the man of the distant past.

Yet, she was forced to admit to herself, there were some things she would like to understand better, little puzzles which, if she could put them together, would make her feel more a part of his life, more complete in her function as a wife. There were the strange moments when he exhibited an almost ancient wisdom of life, and others when an emotion that bordered on what resembled dread lingered beneath the surface of his outward personality.

However, the most disconcerting mystery was the magnificent portraits of the women he kept, stretched but unframed, leaning against the studio walls, and his absolute refusal to discuss them. She knew they were magnificent pieces of art, true masterpieces, but they belonged to one of his dark secrets.

It was during a visit to the home of Ellen Lowe, the only other young woman attending Rosemount Academy with her, that she had first seen the landscapes and mythical allegories he had painted. Their craftsmanship, executed in rich hues of dream-hazed colors, excited and touched her. So when, soon after a chance encounter when she and Ellen had met him by the river while herb hunting, he asked her to pose for a portrait, she eagerly agreed.

But when only two sittings were completed, with merely the under painting done, he refused to continue and placed it face to the wall, paying her the entire fee promised but giving no reason for ceasing work. Her first reaction was shock and disappointment; in spite of his words denying it and Ellen's encouragement, she was certain she was not suitable. But now . . . Now she smiled. What had been an ending had been a beginning. When she was convinced the work stoppage was not her fault, he began his courtship, a courtship which led to a quiet wedding in a quiet chapel two months later.

At that moment she felt eyes watching her and looked around to see who it might be. A dozen paces up the path the cat was standing beside an ixora bush staring at her. She tried to smile at it, but found she could not, that suddenly she was uncomfortable and embarrassed before its gaze. There was something almost indefinable in the cat's look. As unsettling as it was, as unbelievable, she saw lust in the blue eyes moving slowly over her. Then, as if aware of the recognition within her, the cat blinked its eyes, turned away from her and shouldered its way through the plants bordering the path to disappear behind them.

She frowned and stood up, suddenly wanting to be with Sebastian.

He was in the studio standing before the easel on which was a painting he had been working with for several months. It depicted a mythical mountainous land shrouded in a mist rising from a waterfall. In the foreground two unicorns nibbled grass at the water's edge, one with its head raised, looking toward a clump of trees on the pool's far side. Dimly seen through the foliage of the trees were the figures of a nymph and a horned satyr. It was a vision from a time known only in myths, but in spite of its ethereal beauty, Sabra did not like it. Whenever she looked at it, she experienced an odd feeling of discontent, as if she sensed a subterranean doom approaching from the far side of the mountains.

Sebastian did not hear her enter, but remained bent close to the canvas, muttering to himself while he pinpointed tiny highlights on the broad pad of a water lily. He was trying, she saw, to hurry lest he lose the north light, which was failing as the storm approached. Already the light was watery and stained with gray as the sun melted in a melancholy dullness behind the cloud bank.

She stopped halfway across the room, not wanting to disturb him, knowing instinctively that sharing her own feelings of contentment would be an awkward interruption, maybe even a nuisance, to him. She stood quietly, slowly looking around the studio, enjoying as she always did the smells of his profession, the linseed oil and canvas, the freshly mixed paint pigments and varnish.

But a restlessness settled on her, and the air suddenly had the odor of mildew and decay. Her heart accelerated. She felt a small charge in the air as if the storm on the western horizon was sending out tiny electrical bolts. She continued to stand without moving, sensing the current building in power, becoming less gentle, more aggressive. She looked at Sebastian, but he was unaware of it, still leaning into his work and muttering.

A moment later, with her eyes still fixed on Sebastian, she became aware that the main force of the disturbance was behind her. Suddenly she felt eyes staring at her, moving their gaze across the back of her head, intent, searching, seeking an opening into her mind. Holding her breath, she turned around. No one was behind her. All she saw were the portraits, which even in the dying light radiated their usual glow, leaning against the wall. She looked long at them, frowning, as she tried to associate them with the thing seeking entrance to her mind. She sucked in her lower lip and gnawed on it, telling herself that they were merely paintings, pigments piled and blended on canvas, inanimate rectangles of lifelessness. She told herself that was so, but she found she was not believing it.

Forcing herself to keep looking, she continued to study the paintings, slowly discovering things about them she never observed before. Without a doubt, the women in the portraits were returning her stare, looking at her with eyes not of paint and linseed oil, but real, moist colors. She saw human sensibility in them and a vehement turmoil of emotions directed at her with that terrible strength she had felt. She was looking into eyes brimming with jealousy and desperation . . . and consuming hate.

She was shivering, little quivering trembles that scurried like insect feet over her skin. Though her mind screamed that what she was seeing was an illusion of light and imagination, a core of terror began to build. She was trapped by the women's eyes, held helpless in the malevolent stares. Knowing she must escape before she succumbed to the spawning terror, she tried to look away, certain if she could see the reality of the studio the hallucination would disappear. But as she turned her head, her eyes met those of the reclining nude. A silent whimper fluttered on her lips. The painted irises of the dark eyes were expanded to round discs and from their deep wells a killing hate burned into her own.

"Damn! The light is gone."

Sabra whirled, the sound of Sebastian's voice driving a shock wave into her senses. The cocoon of fear wrapping around her unraveled, and she drew a deep breath, feeling foolish and embarrassed as she turned from the paintings.

"It's because of the storm that's coming," she said, thankful her voice indicated nothing of the turmoil subsiding in her.

"Uh?" Sebastian turned, his brows raised. "I did not see or hear you, my dear."

"You were busy, and I didn't want to disturb you."

"Sabra, Sabra. How many times must I tell you, you are no disturbance?"

"Many, Sebastian. I love hearing you tell me."

He laughed, glancing down at the brushes he was cleaning with a soiled rag, then out the window. Nothing remained of the laugh on his face when he asked, "You say a storm approaches?"

"From the west," she answered. "It was well up over the horizon a few minutes ago."

"Oh." He dropped the brushes into a glass jar, then his eyes moved past her to the portraits, where they lingered for a few seconds before returning to her. "It has been a while since we had one."

"Yes." What was the change she felt in him? "We do need the rain."

"It was bound to come."

Intuitively she knew he was not speaking of the coming storm. He was suddenly withdrawn, and she sensed a defensive alertness in his manner. She wanted to ask what was suddenly troubling him, but knew the answer he would give would ignore the depth of the question. Again his eyes drifted to the line of portraits while she watched a shadow darken his face. When he looked back at her, the apprehension had become dismay.

He said, "This has been a good day, my Sabra. Let us continue to make it so."

So much was wrong and something needed to be said, but he had closed the door of communication between them. It had been a good day, but now all the magic was gone.

He took her gently by an arm and guided her from the studio. When they went through the door into the foyer, he stopped to draw it shut behind them. He had never closed that door before.

"Sebastian—?"

His hand tightened on her arm. "Shhh—go upstairs."

"Sebastian, what has happened? Why are you acting so strangely?" She felt the initial weakness of fear which comes before the body reacts. "Tell me, Sebastian. What's happening?"

"Go upstairs, my Sabra, while I close the windows. Then I will come up and we will talk."

"I can help you close the windows, darling; and there's no need for me to go upstairs during the storm. It's safer down here."

"Humor me this one time, Sabra. For this one storm."

She resisted an impulse to scream at him that he was frightening her, that all the strength was draining from her body. She tried to search his eyes, but their darkness was opaque. There was nothing she could do but obey.

"All right. I'll be waiting for you."

From the bedroom window, she watched the shadow of the storm move across the land, pushed by a prowling wind that sent leaves tumbling one over another on the lawn while at the same time moaning among the eaves. Plump drops of rain splattered among the garden plants, then turned into a slanting downpour that transformed trees and shrubs into phantoms. She flinched at the first flare of lightning and the all but simultaneous thunder crash which shattered the early dusk.

When the reverberations of the thunder died, she heard the voices. With the rain rattling against the window as a background noise, she heard distinct sounds coming up the stairs from the floor below. Women's voices. She could not distinguish words. There seemed to be no words. It was a babble, garbled by the storm noise, with the voices talking all at once, but she could feel the intensity and hear the emotions in them without knowing what was being said. She distinctly heard wails of terror, louder than the raging wind, mingled with staccato whimpers. And, separate from those, she heard a sensual laugh or two.

She made herself reject what she was hearing. Someplace, she told herself, the wind had found an object which it was making into an instrument from which it drew a noise that resembled women crying and laughing. Nothing else could be possible; nothing else could be accepted within the realm of reason or common sense. There were no other women in the house but her! She started for the door to call Sebastian.

In that instant, a fire ball of lightning swept past the window, sending darting reflections of blue-green flame throughout the room, and thunder roared with the crash of a mountain falling, instantly followed by a shrieking gale that lashed around the walls. Before its force the house trembled and swayed as if trying to loosen itself from its foundations. Heavy timbers groaned. In startled fear, Sabra clutched the footboard of the bed as the floor shook beneath her, threatening to tilt in the direction of the window and pitch her out into the fury. Then abruptly the swaying of the house ceased, the hissing rain was gone, the thunder muted. Only a mild summer rain fell in the gathering twilight.

"Sebastian!" She ran to the head of the stairs. "Sebastian, where are you?"

He appeared in the foyer at the foot of the stairs carrying a lamp and what she assumed was a cup of hot tea. He came up the stairs slowly, treading lightly on the balls of his feet, twice looking over his shoulder at the closed door to the studio.

She said nothing until they were in the bedroom. She was all hollow inside; as if she was seeing Sebastian from far away, she watched him set the lamp on the dresser. He held the cup toward her. It was tea, heavy with the sweet pungency of aromatic herbs.

"I thought I heard voices," she said, ignoring the tea,

hearing her own voice reflecting the emptiness she felt inside herself. "They were women's voices, Sebastian, and they were coming from downstairs. Did you hear them?"

He took her by the arm and led her to the bed. "Sit down, Sabra, and drink this. You are nervous, and it will calm you. I promise."

She took a sip. The tea was hot. It was full of herbs she could not recognize but which were strong and pleasant. "Did you hear them?"

He fumbled with the wick of the lamp, turning it a trifle higher, then said, "The wind caused many unordinary noises, but none I mistook for the voices of women."

"I told myself it was the wind, but it couldn't have been. What I heard was too real, Sebastian." She feared what she was saying was becoming no more than a meaningless recitation. "No wind made the sounds I heard."

He watched her sip the tea. "The wind is capricious, my dear. It can do many fanciful things."

She nodded. There was no need to carry the subject further. She was only speaking of conjectures. She looked up at him standing before her. He looked so tall, a bearded colossus standing protectively between her and whatever was out there in the darkening world, whether it was real or constructed in her imagination. She took a long swallow of the tea.

"Are you relaxing?" he asked.

"Umm-umm." She was. Nicely so. The delicious euphoria of the afternoon was returning. She could see now he was not a colossus: he was much too short and much too square. No, he was Pan. She giggled. If not Pan, he was the man who played the magic flute. She took another sip from the cup. Again she giggled. Maybe when she finished the tea, they could try to plant another seed in her loins.

* * *

Concern lay a thin webbing of lines on Sebastian's face as he watched the mixture of chamomile, goldenseal and mandrake he had put into the tea take effect. He stood poised before Sabra, ready to take the cup from her and lay her on the bed when she slipped into unconsciousness. The potion, a tripling of the dosages he normally used for the drawing of blood from women, was by far the most concentrated he had ever employed. It was close to the limit the human body could withstand; so he observed closely the glazing of her eyes and the rise and fall of her breast, knowing she would suffer nauseating results when consciousness returned.

When instinct told him The Master was riding the storm, confusion mingled with his determination to hide Sabra. Though all along he had known this time would come, he had not formulated a plan for when it did, avoiding the subject as if not thinking of it would prevent it from occurring. His entire response had been generated by fear for her, along with, he was forced to admit, an underlying apprehension for himself. Without time to think carefully, his panicked mind decided to drug her into prolonged unconsciousness and keep her in the bedroom, out of sight, in the hope that she would not awaken while The Master was in the studio. Already it had been too close with her hearing the women's voices. Watching her drift away, he cursed himself for the situation his selfishness had placed her in.

Outside the soft rain continued, as it would during the entire time The Master was here, pattering like fingertips against the windowpane. He did not keep track of the hours, aware of time's passing only by the shortening lamp wick and the shriveling pool of illumination. With eyes starting to ache, he sat beside the bed watching Sabra and occasionally reached out to touch her limp hand or gently stroke her cheek.

From downstairs came the noises which over the years had lost their meaning to him, but which tonight dug like demons into his brain with all their hideous connotations. As they went on and on, he attempted to build a barrier of disinterest between them and his senses by concentrating on paintings in work or ones contemplated for future rendering. But he could not blunt the realization of the horrors being enacted in the room below.

He heard the sharp slaps of flesh on flesh and the cries that followed, guttural curses, piercing screams, hysterical pleas to be permitted to perform an act of perversion in exchange for relief from an intolerable agony. He heard the grunts of a beast accompanied by the sighs and groans of sexual pleasure and gratification. These were the sounds of a place far more terrible than hell. He looked at Sabra, knowing with a fatal certainty he would never allow her to be so condemned.

He knew dawn was not far distant when gradually a silence moved into the lower floor as, one by one, the voices quieted. But after the obscene flurry, it was no more than the lull that comes after a dreadful storm when the earth quivers in anticipation of another onslaught. In the near darkness, he sat looking at Sabra, waiting for the call he knew would come.

"Come down, Sebastian, I would talk with you."

For the first time in longer than he could remember, his first impulse was to ignore the summons. He stood up, but he made no move from the bedside as his hands balled into fists at his sides. But, while he went through the physical actions of rejecting, he knew resistance was impossible. No spirit remained with which to fight back. Long ago he had given it away.

"Sebastian, do not make me angrier than I am." The air in the bedroom heaved in convulsive waves. "Come down here!"

He nodded, feeling the familiar malice, then looked glumly at Sabra. She was lying an unfathomable distance from him, her entire form blurring, fading into a faraway limbo. Incapable of doing anything more for her, or for himself, he turned from her and walked out the door.

When he opened the door to the studio, a swirl of heat spewed past him, humid and oppressive. He hesitated on the threshold as it streamed into the foyer, carrying with it the leftover smells of the night's horrors.

Within the studio's darkness, the obscene power occupying it vibrated on the sluggish air. Like exhausted bodies unable to crawl from where overworked muscles abruptly ceased functioning, the paintings were scattered around the floor in disarray, tossed or kicked into a profane jumble by a barbaric fury. Standing among them, he could feel their hate directed at him.

"I want her, Sebastian!" The guttural voice came from within a floor-to-ceiling pillar of opaque blackness in the southwest corner of the room. "She belongs to me."

"No." Sebastian was surprised at the intensity of his answer, wondering from where his defiance came. "A portrait of her has not been done."

"Then paint one. I order it!"

"No, not of her."

"Why not, Sebastian?"

"I love her."

A mixture of growl and laugh rumbled out of the darkness, and from around the studio came the sucking hisses of indrawn breaths.

"You cannot love, Sebastian. The capability is denied you. You find solace and pleasure only in the physical dalliance with a woman's flesh."

"No longer. I love Sabra."

There was silence from the corner, heavy and menacing. Something shifted position in the pillar, a tall, bulky body turning to face him directly. He could feel the malevolent mind working, seeking channels through which to funnel punishment and retribution.

When The Master finally spoke, there was still anger, but

no rage, in his voice. "Three hundred years of life, Sebastian. That is what I have given you."

Sebastian felt his heart hammering in his rib cage. His lungs suddenly demanded more air than he could possibly give them. Very slowly, focusing his eyes on the mass of darkness, he drew a deep, long breath and said, "You gave me nothing. I traded these women, and a hundred others, in exchange for those three hundred years."

A roar tore the early morning silence. Sebastian fell back a step before the demented wrath erupting from the pillar, which trembled and appeared on the verge of disintegrating. A shadowy figure raised an arm to point at him. Red eyes gleamed like coals seen through curling smoke.

"We signed a pact. You belong to me, Boris Sebastian."

"No longer. The contract is null and void."

The Master ignored what he said. "Like these women, you are mine, Boris Sebastian—and the woman named Sabra Reye belongs to me, too."

Sebastian shook his head. "No! I renounce the pact and accept a normal life span to be with her."

"You are dooming yourself."

An unusual calmness was on him. "For the first time in six lifetimes, I know love."

"Then enjoy it while you can, Boris Sebastian; for that enjoyment is to be short-lived."

The pillar of darkness faded, siphoning into itself, becoming smaller and smaller, until early morning grayness claimed the corner. Sebastian looked around the studio, assuring himself he was alone, then slowly moved through the scattered paintings, picking them up and returning them to their places against the wall.

Finally, as with other men, death had become his companion.

CHAPTER

Little tremors scurried along her nerve network making Adrienne quivery, not permitting her to entirely trust her muscles for a task any more strenuous than standing in one place. At the moment, that was what she was doing, standing on the periphery of a remote and foreign area. Though the room was familiar and the three people in it were known and liked, she had the sensation of standing in the wings of a theater stage, unseen by either actors or audience, watching a scene unfold but unable to experience the emotions passing between the performers. Yet she felt no desperate urgency, for she was returning from the netherworld into which shock had driven her, and her thoughts would soon be collected again into a reasonable order. The jagged edges of last night's terrible memories were being smoothed away.

There had been no awakening disorientation that morning: she knew exactly where she was, but ten minutes passed while her groggy mind sorted its way through the dreadful attachments clinging to it from the previous evening. During those ten minutes she convinced herself the voices coming from the parlor were too distinct to be part of a dream. And though she told herself the face was the product of an imagination gone rampant, no matter what rationalizations she tried, those moments which had taken her to the brink of insanity could not be wishfully pushed away. Just remembering raised the hair on the back of her neck.

When she had finally gotten up, showered and come downstairs, she felt only half put together. She was without makeup and her thick hair was undone except for combing. She had descended the stairs subconsciously braced for another ordeal; so when she heard Ned, along with Geoff and Katie, in the parlor, she entered it cautiously, half expecting the ferocity of the night to be lingering like a cold malaise in the room. But it was only a sunlighted room. She had been touched with embarrassment at the genuine concern the three of them expressed, and when Ned laid both his hands on her shoulders while asking her how she felt, it stirred again those reactions such a long time dormant.

Now Ned was on his knees crawling among the paintings which were still spread flat on the floor just as they had placed them the night before. If any rawness of nerves caused by the incident at the window still chafed him, he did not show it. He was like a small boy given a new plaything and, in his excitement, was excluding all else from his thinking. He was examining the canvas weave, stroking his fingers over it, holding the back of a painting up close to his eyes while he tilted it this way and that, studying the threads as they caught crisscrossing highlights. And all the time, Adrienne noted, he was muttering to himself in a continuous monologue of questions and answers.

Geoff and Katie stood to one side. Geoff's hands were thrust into the hip pockets of his khaki slacks. His eyes were intent on Ned, carefully watching every movement of the examination.

At his side Katie stood with her feet apart and her arms folded under the thrusting ledge of her breasts. Although her attention was on Ned, she was not watching with the collected concentration of her husband. When she saw Adrienne, she shook her head, then walked over to her. "They've discovered something else to divert them."

"Oh?"

Katie looked at her husband, then at Ned. Adrienne saw indulgence in her eyes, that special understanding a woman can possess for a loved one, even though that person may at times be performing outrageously. "Sometimes I wonder how either of them get to spend time at their professions, they find so many other things to do."

"Last night Ned thought finding those paintings was important."

"He still does, more so than ever." She looked directly at Adrienne, her handsome face now clouded with concern. "I understand it was a pretty frightening time in here while the lid was being opened. You okay?"

"Yes." Adrienne fought to hold the violent memories of the previous night in their isolated places in her mind. "I guess I lost my cool."

"Not from what Ned says. I'd be halfway to Atlanta now, still running, if that happened to me." Her eyes drifted away to rest momentarily on the paintings, and her tongue flicked her lips. "It doesn't seem real, does it?"

"No. Has Ned said anything about opening the other window seat?"

"Geoff wanted to, but Ned said later."

"I wonder why he wants to wait."

"I don't know." Katie shrugged.

At that moment, Ned stood up, scowling. He was rubbing a thumb and forefinger together. Adrienne saw a powdering of color between them and knew while she had been talking with Katie that he had scratched a bit of pigment from one of the canvases.

"How does it feel?" Geoff asked.

"Like paint. I can't distinguish anything different in its consistency, except . . ." The scowl on his face became a look of puzzlement. "Except there's a warmth to it I don't understand."

"It's getting hot in the room."

"No, not that." Ned shook his head. "It's more like a heat generated by the paint itself."

Geoff frowned, then knelt beside the portrait of a brunette. Very gently he laid a palm on the radiant features. Time stretched into a long minute while he rested his hand on the brunette's cheek, keeping his eyes averted while the others watched him. Adrienne felt her breath becoming short, and she glanced at Katie to see that her lips were compressed into a thin straight line. Finally Geoff raised his eyes and swung them slowly across the three faces turned on him, then attached his gaze to Ned's, nodding slowly, his head only moving by degrees. "There's heat inside it—like body heat coming from under the skin."

"Jesus H. Christ!" Ned's voice was no more than a whisper as he continued to study the material between his fingers. For a brief instant, he looked at it as he might study a squashed insect, then returned his attention to Geoff, who was still kneeling beside the portrait. "Try the nude, the reclining one that looks like the 'Naked Maja.' It's so goddamn lifelike, if any of them are warm, it's got to be that one."

Geoff crabbed his way through the canvases until he reached it. When he turned his face up to them, it appeared he was trying to smile, but his lips remained tight and thin under his mustache as he said, "I'll bet this one will be a hot mama."

No one responded. Very suddenly the atmosphere was heavy, and while she watched Geoff place his palm on the nude's hip, Adrienne caught a movement from the corner of her eye. Katie had taken a half a step forward. With a shock, she saw the expression on the other woman's face. It was particularly strained with revulsion, as if the big redhead was reacting to an emotion directed at her alone from the painting.

"Well?" Ned walked around the paintings to stand beside Geoff.

"Warm." Geoff's voice was almost too matter-of-fact. "A little more so than the other, to tell the truth."

"What the hell is it?"

"I don't know. Let me try a couple more." Geoff placed his hand on two other portraits with the same results, then stood up shaking his head. "I'm not even sure it's real."

"Oh, it's real, all right. But what makes it real?"

Geoff merely shrugged his shoulders, his eyes jumping from portrait to portrait. "There's something we can do, though, to make sure."

"What?"

"Take some samples to a lab for analyzing."

"Where? You need a place with an interest in art as well as having a lab; someplace, too, that's versed in art history and restoration." Ned ran his eyes around the fan of paintings. "You know, maybe this warmth wasn't part of the paint when it was applied. Maybe it was a reaction that's taken place over the years. It might not even be unique to these paintings."

"I think it is. If it generated heat on its own, it would have dried and flaked, wouldn't it? I'm thinking it has some relationship to the perfect flesh tones."

"I still want people with a background in art to handle it."

"How about the university at Gainesville, then? They've a damn good art department that might be interested, and they could pull the necessary strings, too, to get samples tested in one of the school's chemistry labs."

"It might be worth a try. I'll phone them this afternoon.

Since it's summer, there might not be much going on there and they can run the test right away."

No one spoke for several minutes, all four standing, staring down at the paintings. The portraits glowed in the sunlight, brilliantly hued women of perfect symmetry smiling enigmatically.

"I'm going to fix some breakfast," Katie said suddenly.

"I'll help." Adrienne had to get away from the paintings. Very suddenly the vivid impression that these were real women lying helplessly at their feet haunted her. She hurried after Katie. Passing the door to the smaller of the two rooms she had rented, she paused and glanced at the stacked cartons of supplies, then shook her head and continued toward the kitchen.

In the kitchen Katie was breaking eggs into a mixing bowl. She glanced over her shoulder when Adrienne came through the door.

"I thought we'd have a good old-fashioned breakfast instead of a good-for-you nutritional one. I can't face fruit and fiber this morning." She broke an egg on the rim of the bowl with more force than necessary and a glob of albumen slithered down the bowl's outside. "Damn! Powerful Katrinka strikes again. I used to be hell with baby chicks at Easter, too."

Adrienne said nothing. She still considered herself too much of an outsider to inject herself into their personal moods. The well-mortised barriers against involvement were not yet completely broached, and behind them, stone-faced and tense, much of her continued to walk the path of a loner.

"I'll make the toast," she said.

"Okay—and thanks for being like you were just now."

"How's that?"

"For not asking me what's wrong. I've developed a private problem, and I don't know how it would be received if I let it out into the open. Kind of ugly, I think."

"You're welcome to bring it out, if you want to." She

dropped two slices of bread into the toaster, then pushed the plunger down. "Even just a little bit of it, if that'll help."

Katie smiled, but it lacked meaning. "I told you the other day you'd be good for me."

"You said you needed an ally of the feminine gender."

Katie stopped peeling bacon slices apart and turned her head to look straight at Adrienne. Her clean, strong features were diffused by a series of emotions, and in the depths of her youthful green eyes hints of anxiety reflected. She was a woman floundering, frustrated and maybe a little resentful.

"After what happened to you and Ned last night, and the feelings I've got after looking at those paintings—at one painting, really . . ." She shook her head. "I—I just no longer feel the way I did when we left Atlanta. But I can't describe how I feel, either."

"I know. It's a different world than it was yesterday."

"Are you frightened?" Katie asked the question in the same tone she would have used if making a shameful confession of guilt.

"Some. But not like I was yesterday—or, God knows, last night." Adrienne hoped the shrug she gave was depreciative. "Today I'm more nervous and perplexed."

"I guess that's what I am, too." Katie turned her attention back to the bacon. "Are you still going to want the rooms?"

Adrienne felt a mental door shut behind her. She had walked into a cul-de-sac and was trapped. "I—I don't know."

"I wouldn't blame you if you didn't, neither would Geoff or Ned; but I wish you'd keep them. I'd like having you around."

"I'll think about it, but . . . but, well, it's not as appealing as it was, I've got to admit."

"Dammit!" Katie slammed a fist on the drainboard. "I don't believe this happened. I will not—ever—believe in ghosts and demons or—or anything supernatural. I won't! Dammit, I won't! And I don't believe that damned naked woman lying on her back, showing everything she has, can emit emotions!''

"What do you mean?" A grotesquely heavy weight suddenly pressed against Adrienne's chest.

"That painting—the nude one Geoff touched to test its warmth. Just before he put his hand on it, I swear to God, I felt jealousy and hate coming from it."

The stability and order of the morning disappeared. Fear returned to position itself not far away, ready to rush in again with its brutality. Adrienne looked out the window. The sunlight was so brilliant, so clean, turning the greens and grays of the pepper and pine trees into multihued variations of color, and she wondered how vileness could exist in a place so warmed with that golden light.

"You felt nothing in the parlor this morning?" Katie's voice was no more than an empty echo of what it had been. "Nothing at all?"

"No, not this morning. I suppose Ned told you, though, that I felt something yesterday and the day before. That's why I asked him to open the seat."

"He didn't go into detail. Tell me about it . . . please."

Adrienne turned from the window. It was taking an inordinate amount of time to gather her thoughts. They wanted to skitter in all directions seeking places to hide, places in her mind where consciousness never reached. When at last she pulled them into an understandable pattern, she told Katie of the lure of the window seat, the impressions coming to her from the garden and the nightmare in her apartment.

The wall clock between the south windows ticked its measured cadence as Katie stared at Adrienne with a steady, serious gaze, then, without saying a word, moved to the stove to turn on the electricity under the skillet of bacon. Adrienne knew her new friend was posing unanswerable questions to herself.

Breakfast was eaten between spasmodic spurts of conversation, mostly conducted by Ned and Geoff concerning the testing of the paint. Adrienne had nothing to contribute, and Katie sat glumly silent, once reminding Geoff an order from a Memphis department store was rapidly approaching its due date.

When the second cups of coffee were being finished, Ned said, "I'll start on your tables, Adrienne, as soon as I phone the university."

"She might not be taking the rooms." Katie's voice was flat and mechanical.

Ned gave Adrienne a quick glance, then stared down at his empty coffee cup. "I guess I don't have to ask why."

There was no surprise in his voice, yet Adrienne was aware of disappointment undertoning the question. "I really haven't decided not to. I'm just hesitant, that's all. I guess it will have to be blamed on my ingrained cautiousness and an overstimulated imagination."

He shook his head. "No, it's not your imagination. We know that, so don't even think it is. What we experienced last night was real, beyond any kind of a doubt. But, dammit, I'm not sure what it was we experienced. Was it a fantasy we indulged in because of what we thought we felt coming from the window seat, was it really a supernatural visitation, or was it a natural phenomenon?" He drew a deep breath, then blew it out with a whooshing noise. "Oh, hell! I'm just throwing a bunch of words together, aren't I? I'm trying to stuff the whole occurrence into a neat, tidy package of rationalizations."

No one said anything.

Finally Ned looked directly at Adrienne. "I wish you'd rationalize, too."

The meaning behind his words was implicit and shook her. She stole a glance at Geoff and Katie. Geoff was staring with an unsuccessful attempt at nonchalance out the window, but Katie was watching her with a strained expression.

They wanted her to stay!

Although she thought of herself as an outsider, they did not. The knowledge was like a spasm within her, a jab of exquisite pain with an almost sensual urge. As she sucked in her breath, she heard the muted sound of barriers falling, and thought what a good sound it was to hear. The Hadrian's Wall she had erected to protect herself was finally crumbling.

At the instant she knew she was going to keep the rooms, she knew she was going to do many other things, too. "Okay, I'll stay."

A quarter of an hour later when Adrienne and Katie got up to wash the dishes, Ned went to phone the University of Florida and Geoff wandered out in the direction of the carriage house.

"God, I'm glad you're keeping the rooms. If you'd decided to leave, I think I might have gone away, too."

"Katie, you couldn't do that! What about Geoff? What about your work?"

"Geoff would come with me after a hell of a battle; and, let's face it, we can do the work most any place." She looked around the kitchen. "To tell you the truth, I've got an unsettling feeling about this place. It's as if—and this is silly, I know—as if the house and the whole area around it is waiting for something to occur—and not something pleasant, either. It's making me uneasy."

"What does Geoff think of your feelings?"

"I haven't told him . . . yet."

In an abrupt shift, Adrienne changed the subject by asking about the sharing of meal costs, using the just completed breakfast as an example. She wanted Katie to veer away from all talk of uneasiness concerning the house, because if they continued with such a conversation she knew their apprehensions would multiply a hundredfold.

As Katie was storing the last plate in the cupboard, Ned returned to stand with his hands in his pockets looking out the rear window. "They've got as big a collection of bureaucratic minds at Gainesville as you'll find in Washington."

"They don't want to examine the paint, I take it," Katie said.

"Oh, yes, they'll do it, but not until fall. They gave me some mumbo jumbo about reduced staff and department money tied up with other allocations for the summer. For Christ's sake, how many people does it take to look through a microscope?"

"It would be more than looking through a microscope, you know that; but academic halls are as gorged with red tape as government halls."

"Ned, maybe I can help." Adrienne suddenly remembered Sam Jethro, who was in Andrew's Sunday golfing foursome. Jethro was a partner in a local firm which specialized in cosmetic formulation. Its entire business involved formulas and chemical breakdowns. Sam, on more than one occasion while visiting the house, had bragged of their chemist, insisting he was one of the finest in the business. She said, "I know of a supposedly first-rate chemist. I can try to get in touch with him."

"Great!" He rubbed his hands together. "Okay. Now, what say we get to the tables?"

Katie made a heaven-help-you gesture as Adrienne followed him from the kitchen.

By two o'clock she was forced to admit that Katie was correct. Ned was not a carpenter. Although the tables took shape, it was by an indirect method. There was much bracing and needless extra sawing; remeasuring became standard procedure. More often than not, two nails were used where one was intended because the first either drove into the wood at an odd angle or bent under glancing hammer blows. But Ned lost neither his optimism nor his enthusiasm; so by a few minutes after three, the second and last table was shoved into position, a block of scrap wood wedged under a leg that was a quarter inch too short.

He stood in the doorway nodding his head with a smile of satisfaction riding happily on his lips, caught in a feeling of creative pleasure. Agreeing with him in an earnest voice that it really was not a bad job, Adrienne found pleasure in sharing his enjoyment. After so many months of restraint, this response to another's emotions was like an emotion in itself, fulfilling and gratifying.

"I'll help you unpack what you need from the cartons," he said finally.

She shook her head reluctantly. "Not today. I'll leave that for tomorrow."

"We've got plenty of time."

"While you have your tools out, why don't you open the other window seat?"

"Do you really want to open it?"

The atmosphere in the room suddenly became heavy. For a brief instant, there seemed to be a mini-blackout in the communication between them, like the breakup of signals on a radio or TV set when stations are changed, so she had the impression they were both rapidly shifting their thinking, that the casual moments of the table building were dissolving.

When she did not answer, he asked, "Have you felt anything coming from it like from the other one?"

"No."

"Then I'd rather wait."

Adrienne realized she agreed. She doubted anyone could take again occurrences like those of the previous night, not, at least, until nerves were calmed and sensibilities restored.

"I'd better go home," she said softly. "Honestly, I feel like the proverbial rag, bone and hank of hair."

"You certainly don't look it." His defensiveness was gone as he ran his eyes up and down her in a quick, delicate inventory of her figure. "You know, you're one of those women who always appear impeccable. You could dress yourself in burlap and rope sandals, and you'd make them look like a Como gown and Gucci shoes."

She saw he meant it as more than just a passing jest and was simultaneously embarrassed and pleased.

"Well, at least let me fix you a drink before you leave. We owe ourselves a few minutes relaxation, don't you think?" When he saw her hesitating, he said, "Please."

She wanted to sit with him, with or without a drink, because for the first time since her failure with Andrew, she desired the company of one specific man, a man with whom she could talk in more than social generalities. In particular, this man in the rumpled blue sports shirt and with the sawdust clinging to his forearms.

"I'd like that," she said.

When they left the rooms and turned down the hallway in the direction of the kitchen, Adrienne wondered if the soft, low sound she heard coming from the front of the house was the murmuring of women's voices.

CHAPTER

It was around seven o'clock when Adrienne came to the conclusion she was hungry. But before eating, she decided she would make the phone call to Sam Jethro. It was something she did not want to do, because to her Sam Jethro was repugnant. A hefty man, with the florid complexion sometimes associated with good living, he possessed a totally unmodulated voice which he used to boom insincere hail-fellow-well-met clichés to the unlucky person who came within range of it. Andrew had overlooked that. He was so certain Jethro would at some future time offer him a high-paying position in the cosmetics organization, he had given in payment a portion of his personality as an offering on Jethro's self-erected altar of ego. They deserved each other, she supposed. They possessed so much in common: greed, insincerity, hidden schemes and uninhibited strategies.

She found both his home and office numbers in the phone index book, written in Andrew's cramped scrawl. Jethro himself answered after the sixth ring.

"Adrienne honey! How are you?" The big, indomitable voice rolled along the phone line like the sound of brass gongs being struck by sledges. "I was just asking Andy about you the other day."

"I'm fine, Mr. Jethro. I—"

"Sam, darling. You were part of the gang once, so call me Sam."

Adrienne's fingers tightened around the handpiece at the sly dig. "All right—Sam."

"Now, what can I do for you? You know, I bet you have a favor to ask. About Andy. Right?"

"Yes about the favor. No about Andrew."

"Okay. It makes no difference. You just tell me what it is, Adrienne honey, and I'll see what can be done."

She spoke as fast as she could, using the impersonal business voice she had employed on the phone at Rondo Electronics, keeping him at a mental arm's length, giving him no chance to interrupt. She told him of the warmth in the paint, but not where the paint came from or of any of the happenings surrounding its discovery.

When she finished, he said, "Adrienne honey, you certainly phoned at just the appropriate time. Believe me, it's coincidental. Lucas hasn't a thing on his agenda for the next several days, and he gets grumpy as hell when he isn't playing with his test tubes. He prowls around the office like an irritated bear; so I'm going to tell you right off, he'll run the test for you. But I'm going to ask this friend of yours to pick up the tab for Lucas's time and material. That seems only fair to me."

"Of course that's fair, Sam. Mr. Anderson wouldn't have it any other way."

"Fine. Then you just bring the samples to the plant tomorrow. If anyone can find what's making that paint warm, it's our old Lucas." He hesitated, then gave a little muffled cough and, with the inflection she had been waiting for, asked, "Adrienne, how's it going with you since the breakup?"

"Very good, Sam."

"No problems you'd like to discuss with an old friend? Things must be a little tight for you since leaving Rondo, and you know, I'd be more than happy to offer some kind of assistance." It was the ageless voice of the predator. "Maybe we could have a drink sometime and talk over your future."

And to hell with your friend Andrew's feelings, she thought, but said, "I'll tell you all about what I'm doing when I see you. Now, I really must scoot, but, Sam, I honestly appreciate your help. Thanks so much. And promise me you'll give my regards to Evelyn."

The mention of his wife inserted a disquieting element to which he had no immediate response. "I'll do that, and I'll be waiting to see you, Adrienne honey."

After she hung up, she discovered her hunger mostly gone, so she bypassed the frozen chicken dinner she had planned in favor of a small salad, made from a packaged salad mix, and a glass of iced tea. She suspected it was not enough, but the preparation and the eating of a meal, even a skimpy frozen one, was just too great a chore.

When she finished with the salad and tea, she glanced through the TV listings, but found only one show of interest, and it did not come on until ten o'clock. There was a novel she had been going to off and on for the past month which interested her, but she knew she'd be unable to stay focused on printed pages.

The telephone rang, startling her. She stood looking at it, allowing it to ring several times before crossing the room to answer it.

"Adrienne, this is Gloria Wilkens of the Plum Tree." The high-pitched voice burst from the earpiece in a gushing assault, not stopping to draw a breath, persistently hurtling words along the wire. "Darling, I've been phoning and phoning and phoning and getting no answer. You just can't realize how terribly desperate I am right now. When are you going to get me the corn husk flowers I ordered? They were due yesterday, dear, and I have half a dozen customers just absolutely frantic to get their hands on them; so I must either have the flowers or a very good excuse to give these distraught people tomorrow. Do you know how desperate it makes a person, Adrienne dear, to be on the receiving end of a positive torrent of complaints and demands? It just simply frays the nerves. Now I absolutely—"

"Mrs. Wilkens? Mrs. Wilkens!"

"Yes, dear?"

"You will have the flowers tomorrow." Adrienne felt she was thrashing wildly in an act of self-preservation. "I'm sorry there's been a delay, but I'll deliver them around noon tomorrow. I moved my workshop and ran into some unexpected problems; however, I now have them all under control, so I'll be at the Plum Tree at noon. Is that satisfactory?"

"Oh, yes, and thank you, Adrienne dear. I just knew there was a very good reason. I'll see you tomorrow, then."

Adrienne sat for a moment after cradling the phone, permitting the turbulent after-sounds of the woman's voice to cease their massive swirl in her head, conceding ruefully that Gloria Wilkens's persuasive techniques were very effective. She had been outmaneuvered. The flowers, she was certain, were not due at the Plum Tree until the day after tomorrow, but in the desperate attempt to escape the inundation of words, she had used her mouth instead of her mind, speaking without thinking. Now tomorrow would be chaos as she shifted schedules and fashioned extra flowers to accommodate Gloria Wilkens.

She needed a cigarette, really needed one, and her only pack was stuffed behind the sun visor in the car.

Outside the apartment the heat was stagnant, the darkness overwhelming, dripping with humidity so thick it squeezed the illumination from the parking lot lights into tiny ovals resembling distant stars.

Adrienne hurried across the patch of lawn, noticing over her shoulder a storm approaching from the northwest sending lightning flares above the nearby buildings. She crossed the sidewalk and stepped between two parked cars to take a shortcut to her parking place. She heard a noise behind her, a scurrying sound, like tiny feet running across the asphalt. A moment later a cry full of fear, a small child's wail, came from her left. She stopped and whirled around, the first embrace of fear encircling her. There was nothing. Lightning lit the sky and she saw her reflection, transparent and ghost-like, in a car window. Her heart began to race.

"God," she whispered. "Please not again. Not here, too."

She stood waiting, one hand braced against one of the cars, knowing she was standing on the edge of frenzy. Once she thought she heard the feet running along the other side of the automobile, but could not be sure. Holding her breath, she continued to stand quietly, listening. Still there was nothing, only the nearby silence and the distant thunder. Finally, all of her muscles squeezed by the returning fear, she started for her car, not hurrying now, but walking very slowly, placing first the toes, then the heels of her feet softly on the pavement.

She was inserting the key into the Toyota's door when the thing came out of the darkness at the front end of the car. It landed with a thud on the hood, a form without shape, coming slowly toward her, rippling as it swayed from side to side.

She felt the scream forming all the way down in the bottom of her lungs, felt it rushing up to expand her throat muscles, felt her mouth opening to allow it out into the stagnant night.

Then the thing stopped its advance. A small head tilted up. Two glowing eyes stared at her.

The scream turned to a high-pitched laugh. Muscles and nerves relaxed so rapidly she leaned against the car for support.

She was exchanging stares with a cat.

They studied each other while regularly spaced sheets of lightning lit the skies with phantom flames. The cat inched closer across the hood with its face still raised up to her, its blue eyes catching faint highlights from the parking lot's illumination. It was thin, but sinewy muscles bunched and flexed under a short coat of sandy brown fur. The dark face appeared to be wearing a slightly lopsided mask, and the long tail, with an unnatural crook in it, swung slowly from side to side. Cautiously it took another step closer to her, purring softly, its inquisitiveness overcoming any apprehension.

Adrienne reached out a hand. "You scared hell out of me, do you know that?"

The cat meowed with a sound more childlike than feline and nuzzled against her fingertips as if trying to tell her any alarm caused by its stalking was inadvertent.

"You're a Siamese, aren't you?" She stroked its underchin with a forefinger. The cat sat down and its waving tail thumped rhythmically on the hood metal. "You're a stranger to these parts, I think. Just a tourist passing through, is that it?"

A raspy purr and heavy tail thump answered her.

"You're not exactly sleek, but you're cute. I wish we could spend more time together, but you've got to understand I'm a busy person, and, besides, I wouldn't be surprised if a traveling cat like you has more places to visit tonight." She withdrew her hand, opened the door and reached inside the car to take out the cigarette pack from behind the visor. As she closed the door, she said, "I'd invite you in, but there's nothing in my apartment to interest a wandering Siamese; so I guess we'll just have to remain two strangers who passed in the night."

The cat gave its peculiar meow.

She turned away to begin walking across the parking lot.

Behind her there was a sharp click of claws on pavement accompanied by a gruntlike meow. She looked over her shoulder. The cat had sprung from the hood and, ten feet or so back of her, was following, rolling slightly from side to side with a distinctive stride.

She paid it no more attention until she reached the outside entrance to the apartment building. While she was unlocking the door, it rubbed against her ankles, looking up at her to half purr, half meow in a display of shrewd feline cunning.

"No, not tonight."

She slipped sidewise through the door, closing it quickly behind her, then immediately became confronted with a twinge of shame, wondering, as she walked across the foyer, how long the cat would remain standing out there looking at the shut door. She imagined it might be considered a small act of cruelty on her part, considering the approaching storm, but she was sure the cat would demand attention which she could not give. She paused for an instant on the stairs, then shook her head and continued climbing.

Sitting at the dinner table with another glass of iced tea and a cigarette, she leafed through her order book until she found three deliveries which could be slipped a day or two, giving her enough flowers to fill the Plum Tree requirement without jeopardizing other accounts. It would mean, though, that the following day, shortened by the Plum Tree delivery, would be spent fashioning replacements. It also meant she could not accompany Ned if he took the paint samples to Lucas. Disappointment and relief fought for dominance. On the other hand, she would not be forced to face Sam Jethro. That, in itself, was a rescue from a second-rate nightmare.

While she rinsed the glass, she noticed through the kitchen window the storm was closer, transforming more than half the sky into an unpleasant black. Gusts were finding their way between the apartment complexes, catching hold of the shrubs and trees in the landscaped area to shake the smaller branches. She wondered what the cat would do should there be rain.

She showered slowly, standing still for long minutes, allowing the warm spray to pinprick her skin in a direct challenge to the tiredness seeping through her muscles. The hot stabs opened her pores and she could feel the warmth leeching into the long, taut curves of her body, replacing the tightness with luxurious laziness. When she stepped from the shower stall, all the body structural parts were functioning clinically smoothly, and her mind was completely free, all thoughts and memories segregated into nice, neat little compartments where she could comfortably control them.

She made a turban of a towel for around her wet hair, but draped nothing around her body, shivering when the mechanical coolness of the air-conditioning raised gooseflesh as she padded down the hallway to her bedroom.

Katie lay watching through the window as the storm approached. An hour before, she had come to bed. At that time her body had been a big, tightly bound-up package of exhaustion . . . not the welcome physical fatigue of work, but the dull nauseated weariness of continued tension. When she had left Ned and Geoff in the kitchen of the house nursing cans of beer, she was not sure she could force her objecting muscles to pull her thick-feeling body across the parking area and up the stairs to the apartment. She had felt like an awkwardly designed machine constructed of flexible plastic which had aged and cracked and become brittle.

But when she stretched out on the warm sheet, her mind began to freewheel, thoughts rolling forward relentlessly, racing through her consciousness, one after another.

Close to half an hour ago, Geoff had come to bed. She had not been in the mood, but when he lay down beside her she hoped he would want to make love, for, as tired as it was, her body would have responded to his demanding hands and, in turn, her rampant mind would be forced to react to the delicious urgency. But he had made no move, not even questioning her wakefulness, so she had rolled on her side, back to him, to stare out the window, her mind hopscotching from thought to thought.

Now she watched the storm. It was a great blotch of black out there in the night. She could only vaguely estimate its size from the way the edges of the clouds wavered into sharp outline from the lightning quavering within their depths. It was an easy-moving storm, not advancing across the night sky with any haste, but even so, she thought, before many minutes its preceding breezes would be stirring the sluggish air to bring a coolness through the open window into the oven heat of the room.

Behind her Geoff began to snore. It surrounded her, prodding her from all directions, suddenly becoming a malignancy from which she must escape.

She swung her legs off the bed and sat on the edge of the mattress. For a moment, the snoring hesitated, then began again with greater resonance. She pushed herself to her feet and went to the window. The storm was a looming black mountain beyond the treetops, its interior glowing from the lightning, and the thunder rumbled like avalanches falling down its sides. The temperature of the breeze dropped, drying the perspiration on her to lay a clammy veneer on her skin but sending welcome chills through her. She stood perfectly still while her body threw off its heat, then turned from the window, going to the chair on the back of which hung her blouse and jeans. She slipped into them, shoved her feet into the sandals beneath the chair, took a quick look at Geoff, who was lying on his back, and quietly went out of the apartment and down the outside stairs.

No real purpose had made her come out into the night. Escape from the room's heat and Geoff's snoring were incidentals, even the collage of thoughts racing through her mind was not primary. She did not want to think. She wanted to empty her mind. Everything that was stored in it now, she was determined to cancel out.

She walked with a measured slowness across the parking area, then down the driveway. Leaves rustled, night insects chattered and clicked. At the end of the driveway she stopped to stand looking up and down the county road, tempted to stroll along it for a mile or so, forcing her body to exert itself, so when she returned to bed it would be with a true physical weariness. But she glanced up at the cloud bank and, seeing it had moved overhead, knew there was no time.

She retraced her steps up the driveway. She walked with long, swinging strides and was nearly halfway to the house when, with heavy ploppings on the dry leaves and driveway gravel, the rain began. She could hear it hissing across the fields, gathering momentum and eliminating any hope she could reach the carriage house before the full fury of it was on her.

Disgusted with herself that she had come out with the storm so close, she started to trot toward the side door of the house. As the dark bulk of the building loomed over her, a quick jab of light sparkled in one of the floor-to-ceiling parlor windows. It was no more than an outsized spark, an instant flash of colorless light like a brief reflection bouncing from a mirror, but, slanting into the corner of her right eye, it caught her attention. She slowed her pace, turning her head to look directly at the window. It was blank, as darkly vacant as the room beyond it. Behind her the rain drew closer, drumming on the pavement of the road. Knowing she had hesitated too long, she left the driveway to cut across the lawn toward the side door, hoping the trees would offer protection when the rain overtook her.

Then she was beside the window from which the flash of light had come, with only the croton bushes between her and the dark oblong. A movement, another spark of light. She stared up at the window.

A woman stood at it looking out at her.

Katie stopped. A coldness unrelated to the storm reached out of the night to clutch her throat. She heard a guttural croak come from her wide-open mouth. The night bent in a huge distortion. She watched the woman continue to stare at her and raise a hand to spread it palm-flat on the glass as if trying to touch the wetness of the rain. Katie gasped. Even as blurred as the figure was by darkness and rain, she was able to see the expression of hate distorting the features.

A whip of wind lashed back and forth up the driveway splashing the rain against the window. Almost immediately the glass cleared, but the woman was gone, the window empty, a black one-dimensional rectangle with the rain splattering on the opaque-looking glass.

The full fury of the rain came then, drenching her, with its explosive coldness sucking the breath from her lungs, but still she stood where she had stopped, dumbly uncomprehending, staring at the vacant window. She watched the glass become smudged with rain water, saw it turn into a wavering plate through which nothing would be visible, then darkening, enfolding its secret in the silent depths behind it.

Shuddering from wind chill and trembling nerves, she eventually turned away. Immune to the pouring rain, she sloshed slowly toward the carriage house, her mind sorting and shifting, accepting and rejecting the messages that had been sent to it. She did nothing to assist it in its task, because, very suddenly, she knew whatever decision it would eventually arrive at would be unbearable.

Ned knew he was asleep. His mind was functioning with that masterful clarity accomplished only in certain dreams. The scene of which he was a part was indistinct. Red, purple and yellow flowers bloomed behind a diffusing haze, and down a winding path two figures sat on a wrought-iron bench, gesturing in choreographed slow motion. Yet in the midst of this unreality, he was completely aware of the alertness and responsiveness of his senses. He knew this dream through which he slowly glided was one of approaching transformation and climactic knowledge.

He drifted closer to the couple, and as he did the scene shifted, becoming lower keyed and bathed in a mauve-tinted half light, so he moved along the path through a dying twilight. Sensing him, the man and woman turned to look at him, slowly, like figures under water, with each movement a harmonic sequel to the one before. Under the tree boughs overhanging the bench, their faces were partially obscured in the blurring shadows, yet the woman was familiar to him from another time, another place. But it was the man who spoke.

"You have found the portraits, have you not, Ned Anderson?"

"Yes." It was his voice, but he was not speaking.

"There are secrets to them, secrets you may learn, if you are willing to leave the realm of mortal man."

It made no sense.

"We are kin, Ned Anderson, you and I—by both blood and desire. It has been difficult for me to bring you here, but you have finally come and I can feel within you the need to know about the rendering of the women's portraits . . . and perhaps the strength required to satisfy that desire."

"Who are you?" Still there was no sensation of talking while he listened to his voice.

"In due time I will tell you, perhaps the next time we meet; though by then I am sure you will have guessed my identity."

"What is it I must do to learn the secret you talk about?"

The man looked over his shoulder at the woman who had remained seated on the bench. She gave an almost imperceptible nod.

"Find a young woman, Ned Anderson; one with a comely turn of features and form who wants her portrait painted. Find her and make the arrangements for the sittings—and I will come to guide you with the work."

"You're not telling me much, you know. What do you mean by leaving the realm of mortal man?"

"Complete the first portrait and wait. If it turns out as acceptable as I think it will, then a proposition will be made to you." He hesitated, then said slowly, "In the meantime, Ned, do not open the other window seat. What is in it does not concern you now. Later its contents will be revealed to you, but for now you must ignore it."

After the man had spoken those words, the scene began to fade away, funneling into a distant twilight, gaining speed until it became ill defined and then obscured.

When he opened his eyes, Ned lay staring up at the ceiling, listening to a summer rain pattering on the windowpane, seeing behind his eyes the remnants of the dream still imprinted on his mind.

1886

Sebastian was as close to happiness as he could come. It had never been an intense emotion with him, more a feeling that for the time it was being experienced, all was well with life, that all the imminent ugliness of living was removed. This evening he was savoring the sensation without apprais-ing it, realizing once again that what joy he knew was brought to him by Sabra.

From where he stood on the verandah, the decorative paper lanterns glowing in the descending twilight gave the appear-ance of plump fireflies orbiting over the garden and lawn in endless journeys having no destinations. Under their light, the forty or so people attending the party wandered in and out of the color-stained pools of illumination, chatting, laughing, forming and re-forming groups as those within them saw friends on the lawn's far side or strolling the garden path. Watching the unending movement, hearing the spilling con-versations, Sebastian knew the party was a success.

He looked at the refreshment table set up by Jerome and

him on the lawn. The food, too, had been an immense success. Most of the platters on the table were empty, as was the punch bowl after its third filling. He smiled. Sabra had done well in finding the widow Kluver, who came twice weekly to clean and who had prepared the hors d'oeuvres and pastries this evening. His smile became a chuckle. Jerome would say Sabra had done better than well.

Not long after moving into the house, when he discovered the amount of time consumed maintaining the property, he had hired Jerome, a broad, tall man just past middle age who kept his curiosity to himself and revealed little of his own past other than being a Confederate veteran. Living in the carriage house loft, he assisted in the garden, cared for the lawn and assumed or shared the other chores of running the small estate. After the birth of Spencer, his devotion to Sabra and the baby passed an initial awkwardness to become a paternal love. Sebastian felt comfortably safe with him around.

On the days when the widow Kluver, a plump partridge of a woman in her middle forties, came in, Jerome, Sebastian noticed, discovered numerous household chores. To his pleasure a friendly, maybe even more, relationship developed between the two. He liked that: it gave him the feeling of possessing a family in every way.

Perhaps a half hour before, Jerome had hitched up the buggy to return widow Kluver home, saying, if Sebastian did not mind, he would be returning late, but would take down the lanterns and dismantle the table first thing in the morning. Sebastian suspected it would be very late before Jerome returned.

There were footsteps on the verandah. He turned to see a pleasant-looking, heavy-set woman approaching from the direction of the steps. Hastily he attempted to sort her name from the overlong list which had been stored in his memory during the evening.

The woman smiled as she reached his side, a soft smile under brown eyes twinkling rather prettily. She stopped several steps from him, her smile broadening, relating to him alone.

"I'm Lois Kingman, Mr. Sebastian." She held out a gloved hand. "We were introduced earlier, but I'm certain you've forgotten my name."

With an answering smile, he took the proffered hand gently by its fingers. "I am sorry. With faces I have no problem, but names are like wisps of fog I cannot grasp."

She laughed a trilling sound too girlish for her age and size, while indicating with a nod the people below them in the garden. "I'm the president of the Poinciana Garden Club, Mr. Sebastian. I saw you standing here alone and thought it would be the perfect time to offer a personal thank-you for the lovely afternoon you and Sabra have shown us. We're all simply enthralled with your horticulture. Your plantings are unbelievably amazing."

"Thank you, Mrs. Kingman. The garden is a hobby, a place where I find relaxation."

"Well, I must say, you're as fine an artist with the land as you are with paint and canvas."

"You are too kind." He was pleased with what the woman was saying. The sincerity of the words indicated some form of acceptance into the local society. "I must admit, I enjoy flattery."

"No! No! I mean it, Mr. Sebastian. Have you studied garden design and layout?"

"No. Whatever forms the arrangements take are purely accidental, I assure you. I merely dig and plant and prune."

"I think you're being modest; however, I shan't worry the subject. But I did want to give you our club's grateful thanks, Mr. Sebastian, for the opportunity to see this most unusual display."

"The garden party was my wife's idea, Mrs. Kingman. I confess to being a person who does not mix well with society, but Sabra has much desire to be with people and to attend functions as well as to give them."

"And you indulge her."

"I love her, Mrs. Kingman."

After the woman returned to her friends in the garden, Sebastian slowly scanned the figures below, seeking Sabra. Not only was the searching a desire to find her in order to admire her beauty, it was a necessity born of the persistent apprehension dwelling in him these past months, an act of self-assurance that the dream had not perished.

Even during times of gratification, such as this, the uneasiness was with him, utterly tireless and dedicated like a blackmailer draining from him, bit by bit, the self-confidence obtained through the years. He knew that this dread, playing with him like an insidious disease, was the result of the evil which was once the grand illusion, yet he could find within himself no repentance for the manner in which he served The Master. He harbored no wish to undo what he had done. He accepted the offer made to him those many, many years ago gladly, not permitting the suffering and terror he inflicted to tarnish the profound satisfaction received in creating magnificent art.

His life was that of half artist and half fraud and, in total honesty, he could not feel sadness or remorse, because living through the unending years was not the toil of traveling a journey with no ending. Life was too sweet, an enchantment compounded by time. But a year ago he had made the choice to change his destiny, disregarding its foreordained consequences. The decision was irrevocable, though now he was haunted by the fear that in his selfishness he might have put the sign of doom on Sabra as well as himself.

He saw her at the same time she looked up at him from her conversation with two couples examining a circularly trimmed azalea bush. She smiled and touched her fingertips to her lips, then daintily blew him a kiss. He all but tasted that kiss, warm and moist, on his lips. He smiled and, without feeling in the least foolish, did the same thing in return.

A moment later she detached herself from the couples to approach him along the winding path. There was a luxury in her movements unable to be obscured beneath the prim conventionality of her summer gown. Sebastian saw the furtive turning of male heads as she came toward him, giving him a hint of possessive jealousy which was new to him. He found it both pleasing and distasteful.

She did not come up on the verandah but stood beside a flower bed looking up at him. He could smell her lilac cologne and beneath it was the warm scent of a healthy woman.

"I'm beginning to feel alone out there, darling," she said. "Come, walk with me. Everyone so admires the garden, I want you to hear their compliments firsthand."

"Mrs. Kingman has told me."

"She's only one. There are others who have better taste than she who are stupefied by its beauty. You'd be pleased to hear what they are saying."

He leaned across the railing, placing his face only inches above hers. "I will wait, Sabra, and find my pleasure when they are gone."

She smiled up at him without pretense of not understanding or innocence. "Perhaps it's time I should tell them to leave."

"In a little while. I have patience, and anticipation adds to the enjoyment." He straightened. "Now go be the exquisite hostess for a while longer while I go up to look at Spencer. If he still sleeps, I will join you."

An expression of soft tenderness came on her features, a dramatic variation of the subtle sexual mystery which had settled on them. "I'll check on him."

"No. It is only curiosity. If he was awake, we would hear him."

"You're making me feel irresponsible."

"Nonsense." He stepped back from the railing.

"If he's awake and hungry, call me."

He nodded and smiled, then entered the foyer. The cat was sitting beside the closed studio door. It watched him pass.

He climbed the stairs slowly, his legs suddenly heavy, a vague disquiet nibbling at his consciousness. He could not help but be troubled with the thought he was possibly carrying an unspeakable horror to the seven-month-old baby in the bedroom above. In all the years, this was his first child. In the past, precautions had been taken; for there would be no explanation to give as the child and its mother grew older while the father remained as he was at the time of the birth.

The baby was asleep. He was lying on his back in the crib, his head turned on his left cheek. One pudgy hand was relaxed on his chest, the other flung up beside his face on the pillow, its thumb partially entwined in the black lock of hair which in a few months would tumble over his forehead.

Sebastian stood looking down at the little creature from his loins. The love within him for this innocent little child was a pain working through his body, a terrible ache beyond the reaches of medication. It frightened him; for it was not a love, as was the love for a woman, from which he could turn outward. This tiny beginning of life was in actuality a portion of him sleeping in the crib, and a man cannot turn his back upon himself.

He went to the window. Below him the garden and the lawn were lost in darkness except for the rainbow hues of the lanterns. He saw foreshortened figures, like three-dimensional shadows, moving toward the corner of the house in the direction of the horses and buggies waiting in the area before the carriage house. The guests were leaving and he knew he must go down to bid them good night. On the way out of the room, he stopped beside the sleeping baby.

"Forgive me," he whispered, "for what I have done."

In the foyer the murky semidarkness was different from the

few minutes previous when he passed through it on the way up to Spencer. The humid air was crisp and distorted as it would be if a lightning charge had slashed through the room leaving the atmosphere singed with electricity. He stopped with one foot on the bottom step and the other on the floor, his left hand gripping the newel-post. The room was empty. The cat had disappeared.

Silence was total. On his neck and down his forearms, hair rose in response to the seared air while the coldness of indecision threw his mind out of tempo. He felt no emotion except for a complete recoiling from what was in the air. Then his senses sluggishly began to work their way through their constraints. At first vaguely, then with a terrible certainty, he became aware of what was in the foyer with him. Anger. A physical outpouring of rage.

"Master?"

He spoke aloud. The word echoed and reechoed between the walls.

The anger sizzled, burning away the air within the foyer. He gasped, suddenly wanting to run out into the night, to escape to the outside world beyond the house where the air was fresh and breathable. But he knew it would be futile, as impossible as trying to block his brain from a jolt of agony. A vagrant kernel of his mind tried to devise a cunning scheme to counteract and escape what was awaiting him in the studio, but he did not listen. He had to do what must be done without furtiveness. Nothing could be concealed from what he faced.

Very slowly he opened, then went through the door into the studio.

Sabra felt impatience compounding within her. Why, she wondered, did these people not just get into their buggies and leave? The simple act of standing before the carriage house bidding them all good night, smiling to the women's too-often-repeated thank-yous, while the men lit the buggy lamps, was on the verge of becoming overburdening. These final moments had dragged into an intolerable lengthening of time. She wanted to remain gracious to these slow-to-leave people, to continue to smile and remain informal with the proper display of charm, but within her was the raw primal want to be with Sebastian.

"Now, remember, Sabra dear, you promised to talk with your husband about attending a club meeting. We really do want him to give us an informal lecture on botanical design in a garden." It was Lois Kingman speaking from her seat in the last buggy remaining. "I just know it would be enthralling and enlightening to listen to a man who can make such bizarre mixtures of color so appealing."

"I will, Mrs. Kingman, but don't expect too much. Sebastian isn't one to attend meetings."

"Yes, he told me that, but I'm sure you can persuade him."

"I'll try, I promise."

"Very good." She turned to her husband. "I'm ready now, Horace. Perhaps if you whip up old Dumpling we can overtake the Simpsons. Ethel and I have a few items to discuss concerning next month's meeting."

Horace Kingman made a clucking with his lips as he flicked the reins, but let the whip remain in its bracket. The waddling old mare moved down the driveway at a pace, Sabra knew, that would not change until its stall was reached.

She watched the buggy until it turned from the driveway to join the procession of lamps moving in the direction of the town, their lights winking on and off as they passed behind the bushes bordering the road. She heard a voice begin to sing. Others joined it. She could not recognize the song, but it was plaintive and filled the night with a sadness, as if the singers were lamenting the loss of transcendent beauty.

Back in the garden she stood at the foot of the verandah steps, her gaze drifting along the lines of hanging lanterns. A faint breeze found its way through the trees, rustling the summer-dried leaves with the sound of falling rain as it passed, to swing the lanterns in erratic arcs, blurring their colors. Pale ghost light from a crescent moon touched only the tip ends of tree and shrubbery branches, spreading a transparent veil over an arabesque of fathomless shadows. After the hours of gentle bustle, the garden was incredibly empty and silent.

She was climbing the steps to the verandah when she saw a lantern swinging too far in the strengthening breeze. Inside it the candle tilted and slipped from its anchor to touch the paper casing. There was a puff of flame, followed by a ball of fire streaming a ribbon of breeze-tossed smoke. The burning mass cartwheeled around the line from which it hung, then, hissing, plunged downward into the garden, etching the night with a shower of sparks that trailed it like a comet's tail.

Sabra gasped, hesitated an instant, then descended the steps and hurried along the path in the direction of the place the fire ball had plummeted. No doubt there was no danger, yet the lack of rain the past weeks left certain spots in the area that were tinder dry. If the flame fell on one of them, a fire could be started. As she hurried along the curving path, she wondered what was keeping Sebastian. More than enough time had come and gone for him to look in on Spencer and return if all was as it should be. Abruptly it became a greater concern to her than fire, and her steps faltered for a pace or two. But then ahead she saw an amber glow pulsing on the ground, the first birth pangs of a fire. She ran toward it.

The location where the lantern had fallen was farther into the garden than she had anticipated, within only yards of the grotto under the drooping boughs where the wrought-iron bench nestled. The humid air was a barrier of invisible dampness through which she struggled, cloying, filling her nose and throat with what felt to be a warm, thick liquid that cut off her air and sucked her strength. When she reached the spot where the small fingers of fire picked at a scattered pile of pine needles, perspiration was forming trickles on her cheeks and wriggling down her spine and inside her thighs. Lifting her skirt hem above her ankles, she stomped on the struggling fire, shifting the burning needles with the toe of her shoe, finally kicking dirt over them. When she was satisfied no hot needle remained to ignite the flame anew, she stepped back and fought to fill her squeezed lungs with the murky air.

The other lanterns, she saw, were doing no more than swinging in lazy circles, though the breeze still nudged them and continued to rustle the dry foliage with a curious whispering.

Then she saw something. Up along the path, between her and the house, she was certain there was movement in the darkness, something without shape but so black it gave the impression of being a depthless hole hollowed out of the night. She stared at it, unbelieving, telling herself whatever it was, was a combination of imagination and sudden apprehension. But then the blackness moved, drifting toward her, slowly rotating, a pillar of darkness within darkness. It halted a dozen feet from her, its bulk filling the path, its rotation becoming slower, tentacles, like smoke streamers, reaching out from it.

Burning through the humidity, she felt a hotness, like standing on the fringe area of a fire, and emanating from the black mass, along with the heat, came a smell, sharp, tangy, which she recognized as the stench of burning sulfur. It was then she became aware of a presence within the blackness, of something watching her, studying her with a brooding interest. A line of coldness moved up her spine. Her hands began to shake and she clasped them together in front of her. The silence of the night built upon itself to become a terrifyingly complete lack of sound filtering away even the noise of her own breathing.

"Is—is there someone there? Who—who are you—?"

A guttural rasp came from the dark pillar. It might have been a chuckle. "I am many people, or many things. I am whatever I desire to be."

Apprehension exploded into terror. The heat from the swirling darkness seared into her flesh, the sulfur fumes blurred her eyes. With a cry, Sabra whirled and began to run along the path away from the slowly revolving darkness. A chuckle followed her.

Everything looked strange. All the shrubs and plants with which she was familiar were odd in shape and position. Brutish and undefined, they bordered the path like humpbacked watchers.

It was immediately after she passed an azalea bush that she saw the woman.

She was standing in the middle of the path no more than twenty yards ahead. She stood motionless, her body taut with a challenging arrogance as she watched Sabra approach. Sabra stopped, panting, hearing her heart thunder in her chest.

Not far away one of the lanterns still burning rocked on its overhead line, its light rippling over the woman in a succession of red and yellow and orange, giving the illusion she was bathed in fire.

Her costume was a bizarre kaleidoscope of glaring colors crudely mixed. A black-trimmed scarlet dress, which left her shoulders bare and stopped at her knees, accentuated each abundant curve and soft indentation of her body. Around her shoulders a purple boa fluttered in the breeze, its feathery tentacles caressing her cheeks inquisitively. Her hose were a pale match to her dress, and through a slit in the dress's skirt a red and black garter could be seen encircling her right thigh above the knee.

"Who—who are you?" Sabra had trouble with the question. Fear vibrated along her nerves.

"Lorraine." Coming from heavy lips which barely moved, the voice was low-pitched. "My name's Lorraine, Sabra Sebastian."

Sabra shook her head. The woman had to be a hallucination, a spawn of her terror. But instinct began to send its warning tinges down her arms while at the same time it laced a network of sharp prickling across her shoulders. This woman was very real. She was three-dimensional. Shadows curved around her figure. Her perfume could be smelled, cheap and sharp and almost rancid in the heat. And . . . and there was a frightening familiarity about her, about the heavy-lidded eyes, the full-lipped mouth, the upswept brown hair. And the boa and dress. Sabra knew she had seen them before. But where? In heaven's name, where? The inability to remember pushed her further over the threshold of fear.

"I know you, don't I? We've met someplace, but I can't remember where."

The woman laughed. "Oh, we've seen each other, dearie—at least you've seen what your husband turned me into."

"I don't understand."

"Worse luck for you. I would think since you're married to the bastard, you'd know his secret." She took a slow step forward, then turned to assume a three-quarter-view pose in front of Sabra. "Look close! Look close at me, damn you, and tell me you don't know where you've seen me."

Sabra stared. If only the fear would not clog her thinking and leave her free to concentrate. The boa, that vile-looking garment, was the clue . . . a purple boa, upswept hair and sensuous mouth . . . a black background behind it all . . . the image was coming, separate fragments were forming one overall picture . . . picture . . .

"Oh, dear God! No!"

The woman threw back her head and laughed deep in her

throat. It was a blood-curdling sound in the silence of the garden, the howl of a prowling beast that had found its prey. Before its savagery the darkness gave the impression of closing in on itself so it might somehow protect the creatures that walked the night in innocence.

"So you recognize me now, eh, sweetie?" She shifted the boa on her shoulders while taking a hipshot stance. "I'm usually the fifth one from the left as we lean against the wall in that bastard's studio."

Sabra moaned. Disbelief convulsed her mind, veering it into frantic confusion. Up and down her back, and in her legs, her muscles suddenly knotted. Her mouth opened and closed painfully as she tried to speak, to form some kind of sound even if it might be a scream. She was unable to do more than gasp.

Grinning, the woman began to advance on her, her movements deliberate as if stalking a prey, her eyes dilated and glistening in the feeble lantern glow as they watched Sabra's trembling backward retreat. A potent evil reached out from her, fierce and hungering.

"You are a beauty, I do admit," the twisted lips hissed. "It's plain to see why he kept you for himself. But what's fair for one is fair for all."

Sabra's voice broke through the congestion of her throat muscles. "What—what are you talking about?"

"Freedom! The right to live the same as you with your fancy clothes and baby son. To live like the women we are—not the captive beasts your husband made us." She laughed her guttural laugh again. "But we will have our sport tonight. The Master is here and has freed us for a while, and when we are done our lives will be somewhat easier to bear, Mrs. Sebastian, knowing you and your husband are dead."

Nothing was making sense. Sabra was whirling around in the center of a time and space gone insane. Whatever this hate-filled woman was talking of would not seep into her comprehension. No matter who this woman said she was, or what she looked like, the thought of her being a painting come to life was a lunatic's illusion. But she knew she must escape.

There was a noise behind her. She spun on her heel.

From behind a clump of shrubbery, a woman leading a leashed dog stepped into the center of the path. Lunging against its leash, forepaws clawing the air, the dog thrust bared fangs at her, choked snarls erupting from its straining throat. It was the woman and the white Russian wolfhound from another of the paintings in the studio.

With a cry, Sabra plunged to her left, blindly trampling through rows of peonies and periwinkles bordering the path, thrashing her way between ixora bushes. There was resistance; something clutched the flowing skirt of her gown. She sobbed, imagining the dog's jaws clamping on it, and frantically lunged forward; her skirt tore, but the resistance disappeared, allowing her to push through another row of bushes.

She had no idea where she was going, though she knew she was headed in the direction of the grassy knoll that was the center of the garden. There were shouts from in front of her and to her left, the thudding of feet along the U-shaped path surrounding her. How many were out there? Dear God, was it all of them? All the fifteen women in the fifteen paintings? Were they all alive and hunting her to kill her for a reason she did not know? A whimper seeped through her lips. If that was so, she was defenseless with no hope of gaining the house. Even as familiar as she was with the layout of the plants and shrubs, she could not elude that many searching women: the garden was too small. By forming a circle, they could close tight upon her, squeezing her into its diminishing center. Kill her—that was what the woman named Lorraine had said they were going to do. Kill her and Sebastian. Oh, God, was that why he had not returned? Was he already dead? And Spencer? No, God! No!

Off to her left she saw an enormous black mass rising

irregularly, like a miniature hill, against the sky. She recognized it as the bougainvillea centerpiece of the garden's design. She looked across the tops of plants surrounding her to see heads and shoulders spaced along the path forming the circle to entrap her. She fell to her hands and knees and crawled toward the bougainvillea.

"Coming, coming, ready or not," a voice called.

"Get ready to die, Sebastian's bride."

Oh, God, they were making a game of hide-and-seek out of it. Only in this game, if they found her, she would not be "it" during the next game. She would be dead.

In desperation she tried to crawl under the bush, but the latticework of branches was too tightly woven. She clawed at the twisted wood, showering herself with blossoms, but only managed to tear her fingers and gouge her arms. Against the paleness of her skin, the blood formed a black cross-hatching on her forearms and an oily syrup on her fingers.

The women began a continuous calling to each other and to her, becoming more shrill and keening as they started to close the circle.

"Hurry, hurry, Leah, you're lagging."

"More to your right, Juliana. You're getting too close to me and leaving a gap between you and Antoinette."

"Are you hidden well, Sebastian's wife?"

"We're almost there."

She could hear them plainly now. They pushed through the foliage, their skirts and farthingales swishing against leaves and branches with the sound of a deadly rain drenching the newly spaded earth, their feet crunching on the dried clods of dirt just beyond the knoll. She could hear the gulping sounds of their heavy breathing as they sucked in the humid air.

She pushed herself to her feet, panting, sobbing, placing her back to the bougainvillea and raising her hands before her, fingers clawed.

One of the women shrieked in delight as she pushed through an ixora row. "There! There! See her beside the big bush?"

"Yes, yes—look. Beside the bougainvillea!"

A dizziness swept through Sabra, but she fought it away and stared at the figures thrusting their way out of the shrubbery to circle the base of the knoll. She braced herself.

The women became silent looking at her, ominously silent. Eyes glittered, facial and body muscles were tense. She could feel the bloodlust rising up the knoll from them, engulfing her, then seeping through her pores to chill her own blood. The coldness drained the strength from her, drawing away the control of her body from her.

"What is it you want?" She did not recognize the hoarse voice as her own.

"You," a tall red-haired woman in a purple gown answered.

"I've done nothing to any of you. For God's sakes, why do you want me?"

"To kill you." The redhead's voice was flat, matter-of-fact.

Two young girls giggled with what sounded like anticipation. Several others moved up the knoll a step or two.

Sabra looked from one to another of the women encircling her, seeing instead of them, the paintings against the studio wall.

"You—you can't do this," she sobbed. "You're not real . . . you're only paintings."

There were several throaty laughs, but mainly they stood staring at her.

Then, with very deliberate steps, nine or ten of the women started up the knoll. A pace or two from her they hesitated for a moment and studied her with their soulless eyes. Suddenly, their mouths stretching into screaming ovals, they sprang at her with their hands clawed into talons matching hers. The fury and weight of their attack drove her backward into the bougainvillea. She wavered, lost her balance, then, screaming in terror, fell to her knees. Twice she managed to rake her nails along soft flesh and fragile cloth bringing shouts of pain and rage. Hands grasped her arms, twisted them, then pulled them out straight from her shoulders while others dug deep into her hair yanking her forward and down as fists pummeled her neck and shoulders.

She writhed and bucked. She was being hammered into a dozen fragments of pain, yet she drew on the strength of desperation to wrench herself right and left, for an instant freeing her right arm long enough to clutch a fold of a skirt with her hand and try to pull herself erect. But the blows on the back of her neck stunned her, and, with a cry of despair and terror, she sprawled full length on her stomach, her face mashed into the dry grass by the hands pressing on her neck.

A sturdy blonde dressed in the homespun of a farm girl placed a foot on her neck and stomped viciously down. She giggled as Sabra choked on the dirt filling her gasping mouth, then glanced at the others with eyes glinting a hateful glee. "Let's make her perform before we kill her."

There were answering titters and handclaps.

"Yes," a voice in the rear cried. "Like The Master makes us perform."

"Yes, yes . . ."

"Oh, let's do it. It will be such fun!"

The hot air crackled with their excitement. Those in the front of the group swayed forward to lean over Sabra, their faces becoming rigid masks of lust.

"Make her perform like The Master makes us perform for him."

"Yes! Strip the slut's gown from her."

Eager hands clawed at the thin chiffon, ripping and shredding, until it peeled from Sabra's body in streaming tatters, then tore and yanked her undergarments until they were pulled off her. It was done swiftly and violently. Sabra lay moaning, helpless, totally alone in her terror. Even after the hands grasping her arms released her, she did not move but remained spread-eagled on her stomach, held helpless by a lethargy of pain and humiliation.

Over her she could hear them talking. They were like young girls in a school yard during a recess break, each one trying to make her ideas heard while the others chattered. Giggles and handclaps, with loud indrawn breaths, punctuated the discussion, and she knew they were deciding her manner of dying, but still she could not understand how, because none of them existed. They were paintings in Sebastian's studio.

Then abruptly the talk stopped. Completely. Not a whisper or indrawn breath or a rustle of a garment interrupted the sudden silence. The stillness became another presence in the garden, so thorough it vibrated with its own power.

"I want her!" The contralto voice curled through the silence, almost musical, but carrying beneath its rich notes the sharpness of cruelty in its inflections. "She belongs to me."

The women shuffled. One or two of them murmured blurred words that were unintelligible but which indicated objection. Then from the back of the group, a cultured voice said, "Magda, she has flaunted herself before us all. Are you going to deny us our revenge? The Master said she belonged to us, and we think that means to all of us."

"She took my man of a hundred years, Corinth. It is my right to deal with this bitch who stole him away."

Sabra heard the figures around her shifting, shuffling their feet on the trampled grass, retreating a small distance from her in response to the words of the new arrival. Painfully she moved her head enough to look in the direction of the voice. Hair was tangled over her eyes, sweat stung them, but standing at the foot of the knoll she saw a naked, dark-haired woman looking up at them. Dully she recognized the woman as the reclining nude in the painting Sebastian kept separated from the others. At the sight of the savagery on the woman's face, the terror moved inside her. Giving a helpless sob, she closed her eyes and waited.

Back and forth over her a whispered conversation intently took place, but terror and pain had driven her so far into the dark recesses of herself that the words were merely garbled scraps of sound.

Suddenly the violent hands clutched her again, digging sharp nails into her arms and entwining themselves in the heavy mat of her hair. They pulled upward. Lances of pain drove their hot needles through her shoulders and scalp. Instinctively she struggled to her feet and tried to plant them firmly on the grass.

Then suddenly she was staring, through the dirt caked on her lashes, directly into the life-size version of the face of the reclining nude. It was a wildly sensuous face of black arching brows, Slavic cheekbones and almond-shaped eyes of searing green. She heard the hissing of rage sucked into the flared nostrils, could feel the hot moist breath expelled from the curling mouth. Loathing sprang from the woman in a hot destructive power that caused Sabra to shrink back in the grasp of the hands forcing her to face it.

"Magda," one of the women said, "do what you wish with her, but do not kill her. We want our right to her also."

"Kill her?" The naked woman laughed. It chopped the night like a harsh slap. "It is not her death I want, you fools. It is her beauty."

A serving girl holding Sabra's arm tittered, then another behind her snickered. In an instant there were squeals of enthusiasm.

"Do not let her move."

More hands clutched Sabra's arms, pulling them behind her, while others dug deeper into her hair to grasp masses of it near the roots. She was pulled into an arch so the entire length of her nakedness was vulnerably thrust toward the inhuman terror of the black-haired woman.

Magda held up her hands before Sabra's eyes and turned them slowly that she might see the long, talonlike nails tipping the strong fingers.

"Behold, thieving bitch! With these I will destroy your beauty." She leaned her face into Sabra's and smiled. "Piece by piece, little morsel by little morsel. You will have much time to repent, much time to beg and scream."

"I—I've done nothing—please—you must believe me."

"You stole Sebastian from me!"

"No! We—we fell in love. I didn't know—"

"You stole him!"

With a sudden downward slash, Magda raked the daggers of her nails down the length of Sabra's belly. Then again and again, grunting and laughing with the effort, she slashed at the helpless nakedness arched before her.

Sabra howled. Her mind exploded with intolerable agony while Magda's fingernails methodically tore her body flesh, then her facial skin, away.

Sebastian opened his eyes, aware of the feeling of emptiness in the room, listening to the oppressiveness of it. Circling him were layers of darkness, honeycombed with patches of gray from the windows, through which the dismal moonlight tried to creep. All through him a dull pain throbbed along his muscles, up and down his legs and arms, across his shoulders, knotting his stomach, throbbing inside his head, refusing for a time to allow him to focus his eyes. But he could smell the dust and polish covering the floor on which he lay, its hard wood strangely comfortable against his bruised flesh.

Gradually memory filtered back. When he had entered the studio, the women were waiting, lined up in a half circle with Magda in the center. And behind them, in the southwest corner of the room, the black, smoking column of The Master almost lost in the darkness. At the sight of the undulating pillar, his apprehension had turned to a fright so strong it became a physical part of him. The Master could not be here. There had been no storm.

The voice curled at him, then, "Of course there was no storm, Sebastian. Are you fool enough to believe I cannot travel without one?"

"But—always before—"

"As a courtesy, Sebastian, to let you know I was coming." The blackness in the corner expanded. The voice rumbled. "This time you deserved no warning. This time I freed the women for their pleasure, not mine."

The column began to shrink in upon itself.

"Wait! What do you mean?"

"These women hate you, Sebastian. I do not envy you."

The mass of darkness disappeared.

Except for Magda, he had never seen the women as living creatures. All through the many years, from the time of painting each of them, they were to him only images created in oil by his brushes on oblongs of canvas, rectangles of color leaning against the wall of whatever studio he was occupying at the time. Now they faced him, each one living and breathing, warm with young, healthy life, as they had been at the time of their separate portrait sittings, each one directing at him a killing emotion. He knew his destiny had caught up with him.

When they swarmed over him, he had been powerless to protect himself from the fury of their raking nails and thrashing feet, repeatedly gouging him and kicking him, some even sinking their teeth into his more exposed parts. They were around him, over him and finally on him. Even before he sprawled on the floor he had tasted blood. At last, when the mists began to close in around him, he heard them filing from the studio, crossing through the foyer to leave the house on their way to the garden.

"Sabra!"

The name was cried in a voice which had no timbre, made no sound, yet cried with a deafening crescendo in his awakening mind.

The heavy hammering in his chest sent tremors through him, but he pushed himself to his knees, took several deep breaths, then struggled to his feet. It took all his strength to remain upright while he swayed from side to side. Nothing was broken, but he would be unable to demand too much of his body.

As cloying as the night air was, it revived him a little when he stood leaning against the verandah railing. Only two of the lanterns remained burning, one of them flickering. The scent of night-blooming jasmine was too heavy, pressing sweetly into his nostrils and nearly gagging him. Out over the garden, the blackness remained impenetrable to his squinting eyes.

When he heard the laughter and the giggles, it was impossible to immediately define their location, but holding tight to the railing, he forced his mind to concentrate on the erratic sounds. They were coming, he decided, from the center knoll over which the two lanterns still burned.

His legs were unsteady as he went down the steps to the path and began to stumble along it in the direction of whatever was happening out there in the darkness. Twice he missed bends in the path, walking into bushes along its edges, scratching his hands, tearing his coat into more ragged shreds.

"Sabra . . ."

Now there was terror in the silent voice crying in his mind.

He knew why they had not killed him in the studio. The Master knew the ultimate diabolical punishment. As he approached the knoll, he knew what he was going to see, and the terrible fear of it drove what coherent thoughts still clung to his mind away.

He left the path to push through the shrubbery, cursing the sturdy branches and lush foliage of which he had once been so proud. He could see the women moving around the knoll, dark figures in the darker night, weaving, bending, clapping their hands in the performance of what looked like the steps of a ritual dance. And now, a dozen feet away, he could hear other sounds that had not been loud enough to be recognized until this moment. Grunting sobs of unspeakable agony.

One of the women saw him, shouted, and they all whirled to face him when he thrust through the last clinging shrubbery. Their circling dance halted. High-pitched laughs and twittering giggles sank to guttural snarls; shaded eyes became devoid of merriment to stare at him with glinting hate. Their mouths hung grotesquely open as they panted with bloodlust.

Sebastian saw all there was to be seen in one sickening glance: the women standing in their circle around a naked creature on its hands and knees from which blood ran in thick, dark streams as it blindly groped its way around their feet.

"Sabra!" He screamed her name.

The naked thing raised its head to point a shredded mass of bloody flesh in his direction, then reached out a hand, crying with despair.

He lunged up the knoll with a roaring bellow, flailing his arms in berserk windmilling swings. But before he was halfway to the pitiful thing that had been Sabra, he knew he was not going to reach her. The women were rushing to meet him.

For the last time Jerome stood in the studio. He looked slowly around the emptiness, sadly shaking his head as he tried to take a personal inventory of memories which did not want to come to him. It was a terrible place, this room, he thought, filled with that special, heavy silence of death which was a totally isolated silence like no other.

His roaming eyes stopped at first one, then the other, of the window seats. Everything in the house had been auctioned off except for the items he had placed in those seats before gluing the lids shut over them. The items were personal articles belonging to Sebastian which, he felt, no one had the right to see, much less acquire. A ledger, closed with a strap and lock affixed to the cover, two ribbon-tied bundles of letters and a small notebook, through which he had leafed without understanding what appeared to be mathematical formulas jotted in it. In the other seat were the paintings, those gorgeous, lifelike portraits of young women which Master Sebastian had kept leaning against the wall and allowing few strangers to see. Jerome honored that reluctance, though he did not understand it, reasoning if Sebastian did not want the paintings seen while he lived, no one should examine them after his death. He had removed them carefully from their stretchers, rolled each one gently, and placed them in the window seat. All the things he put in the seats, he knew, would be safe from inquisitive eyes until they were meant to be found.

Now there was nothing left to do. It was time to go. The visit to the estate was the final act to be performed for the Sebastians, making certain the big house and the carriage house were sealed and locked. A distant cousin of Mrs. Sebastian, and her husband, had taken the baby Spencer back to Louisiana with them after the funeral. He understood they could have no children, though wanting one desperately, so the poor little fellow would have a fine home.

He shook his head again, as he had done so many times in the last ten days. What kind of beast was it that had orphaned the baby in such a terrible fashion? The morning following the garden party when he found the grisly remains, hunt parties were sent out, not having the least notion for what they were looking, and discovered nothing. Bears, some said. Wolves, others speculated. Nonsense, he thought. Bears and wolves had never existed in this area. They were frightened people trying to explain the unexplainable. Whatever it had been, though, it was, for certain, a strong and vicious creature.

He drew a deep breath, slowly turned away from the window seats and walked from the room, his footsteps echoing in the hollow space, the final sounds of a time passing.

CHAPTER

There were no remnants of the previous night's rain. The sky was clean, washed and wind-dried to a transparent blue with no clouds. The air was buoyant and pristine with the humidity gone until later in the afternoon.

Adrienne looked at the cat sitting beside her on the car seat. It was enjoying the ride, sitting straight with its forelegs braced against the car's motion, head held high with its nose pointed up into the draft coming through the open window on the passenger's side.

Slipping past her in the parking lot, it had jumped into the front seat. After two attempts to persuade it to leave she gave in to its tenacity and allowed it to stay.

"You like riding in cars, don't you?" she asked.

At the sound of her voice, the cat looked at her with partially squinted eyes.

"Well, say something."

The cat meowed, then turned its head back to the rushing wind.

"You're not as independent as you'd like the world to believe, are you?"

The cat ignored her.

When she had come down to the car this morning, the cat was sitting next to the driver's door, its brown-masked face lifted up at her inquisitively. Apparently it had spent the night in the vicinity of the Toyota, a small grease smudge on its back hinting maybe under it.

Taking on a pet was a duty she had refused to consider, convinced a person must be at least reasonably confident in themselves to assume that task. Then why had she so easily acquiesced to the Siamese's adoption of her?

"I'll be damned if I know," she said out loud, glancing again at the cat. "Maybe I feel a kinship to you. You're alone, wanting to be independent, but not certain of all the things it takes to be that way. But you know what? I really think it's because I feel like a stinker for leaving you out in the rain last night."

The cat looked up at her once more, then rose and crossed the narrow space between them to sit at her side, pressing against her right hip. She sighed and reached down to stroke its ears.

She parked the Toyota under the peppertree, between the station wagon and the Jeep. The cat waited, jumped out after her, then stood at her ankles looking quizzically up at her.

"Go and play—or whatever it is cats do," she said. "We're going to be here quite a while."

The cat answered her with its childlike meow but did not move; its blue eyes remained intently focused on her face.

"I can see we're heading for our first big problem, friend."

Ignoring the animal, she began to walk toward the side door of the house. Her mind moved from the cat to the Plum Tree order, and the disgust at herself welled again for permitting Gloria Wilkens to have manipulated her.

As she reached the bottom of the steps, the screen door opened and Ned came out. "What have we here?"

"You've got a tenant who's mad as hell at herself for allowing herself to be boxed into a corner last night by a frenzied customer, that's what you have."

"Oh—well, that's interesting, too; but I was referring to that creature stalking you."

She looked behind her. The cat was sitting fifteen feet or so away. It appeared to be studying them, as if considering their reactions to its presence. A wayward shaft of light struck its eyes, and, for a very brief moment, Adrienne was certain she saw in them an intelligence far too keen to belong to an ordinary cat. For a long heartbeat, she returned the cat's stare, feeling it projecting into her own brain, then turned her attention to Ned.

"He's a hitchhiker I picked up in the apartment parking lot, and I think he's about to make his welcome questionable."

Ned dismissed the cat. "Were you able to arrange for that chemist to examine the paint?"

"Yes."

"That's great! When?"

"Today, if you want. Take the samples to the Terryjean Corporation on Tomahawk Drive and ask for Sam Jethro. He's part owner of the company and promised to put their chemist, a Mr. Lucas, on it immediately. There is one stipulation, though, Ned. He wants you to pay for Lucas's time and material."

"That sounds fair. Whatever the cost, it will be worth it to find the answer." He came down the steps and grasped her shoulders with both hands; she thought for a moment that he was going to pull her into his arms and kiss her. "We can go right now. I've got the scrapings in plastic bags."

"Oh, Ned, I can't go. I'm sorry."

"Why?" He dropped his hands.

She told him of the Plum Tree order, then, trying to make light of it, of her aversion to Sam Jethro.

"One of those, huh?"

"Yes."

He hesitated, then said, "Well, I guess that means I won't be seeing much of you today, doesn't it?"

"I guess not." She wished it were different.

He nodded, and when he looked at the still watching cat she thought she saw disappointment in his face. When he swung his eyes back to her, his expression was earnest, yet his right brow had crawled up giving his features a precarious balance; however, his voice was soft and touched with nervousness when he said, "You know, Adrienne Lewis, I have this very curious feeling I could get used to seeing a whole lot of you every day."

The directness of the statement surprised and pleased her. Something trembled inside her, a subtle shifting of weight. She felt warmth seep into her and spread along all her nerves, then into her chest, where it made her heart speed up. She had to say something. When she smiled, she found it came easily. Her voice was as soft as his as she said, "I'm glad, Ned Anderson."

He laughed. It was a boyish laugh of pure joy, the sound of a moment when happiness outbalances whatever weight might lie on the spirits. Then it was gone and the seriousness returned.

"I phoned Sheila Rosenthal and Sidney Scott just a few minutes ago," he said. "Sheila's the head of the East Central Historical Society and Sidney's the lawyer who cut through the red tape getting me this place. I wanted them to know about the paintings. I think it's the fair thing to do since they both went to so much trouble on my behalf. Also," he grinned, "Sheila has access to all the available records, so we can find if the paintings are mentioned to any great extent. They'll be coming out this afternoon between three and four."

"I'd like to meet them, to hear what they have to say."

"I want you to." He glanced at his watch. "Do you think Jethro's in his office yet? It's almost nine o'clock."

"He should be. He certainly will be by the time you get there."

"Then I'm going to leave. I can't entice you?"

"Not this time. But ask me again."

"Oh, I will, believe me."

He went back up the steps and opened the screen door, holding it for her. Before she reached the steps, the cat bounded forward to scurry into the house.

"Hey, you! Come back here!" Adrienne hurried after it.

"Let it go. What damage can it do? The studio doors are closed."

"I don't know if it's house-broken."

"Well, you'll find out. But I think I've heard that cats are naturally house-broken."

Half an hour later materials were piled on both worktables in her room. After the Plum Tree order, only seventeen corn husk flowers remained, with orders for sixty more to be delivered within the next four days. That represented at least sixteen hours of steady work, but in new surroundings, she suspected, work would go slower. The strangeness of the area was certain to have a limiting effect: wire strips, soaking area and glue gun would all be in the wrong places.

She spread a layer of newspaper on the floor in front of one table to catch straw droppings, then pulled wreaths for an order of nine from the wholesaler's cartons. While the corn husks were soaking to obtain the necessary pliability, she decided to work on the wreaths.

She took a plastic dishpan to the kitchen, where she filled it halfway with water. Logically, she should do the soaking in the kitchen, but she did not want to encroach into areas she was not renting . . . and that, she admitted, was a bold-faced lie. She wanted privacy when she worked, probably because she still felt self-conscious in this new career after the regimented years of office work.

"Hi!" Katie was standing in the middle of the workroom.

"Oh!" Adrienne halted so abruptly water sloshed out of the pan. "Hi! I didn't hear you come in."

"I'm sorry. I should have called to you." The big red-haired woman licked her lips and glanced around the room. "I'm not thinking so well this morning."

"What's wrong?" Adrienne moved around her to set the dishpan on the table.

Katie was self-conscious. She looked quickly at Adrienne, then away.

"Remember," Adrienne said softly, "I'm your ally."

"May I ask a favor of you?"

"Of course."

"I'm not positive about what I'm going to tell you, but I do know what I saw last night was real and I know I'm still frightened from it." She shrugged, shook her head, then made a feeble attempt to smile. "Will you go with me into the studio to look at the paintings?"

Adrienne did not want to go into the studio, and seeing the paintings might break the fragile feeling of well-being she was experiencing, but she said, "Certainly. Just let me put these corn husks in the pan to soak."

"Don't let me interrupt, please. I'm just—"

"Hush!" She dropped the corn husks into the water. The wreaths could wait. "There . . . Okay, let's go."

She followed Katie from the room. As they turned down the hallway in the direction of the studio, a clicking noise, accompanied by a subdued murmuring whine, came from behind them.

Katie spun around, sucking in her breath.

"It's a cat," Adrienne told her. "He came uninvited with me this morning and slipped into the house while Ned and I were talking." She looked at Katie's face rebuilding itself after the shock. "I'm sorry it frightened you."

"It evens us up. One scare apiece." Katie made a negative gesture with one hand and managed a tight smile. "He's kind of cute. What's his name? He is a he, isn't he?"

"Yes, and I don't know his name, if he even has one." She quickly told the story of the cat, finished by saying, "Let me put him out, now that he's cornered and I can get my hands on him."

"No, let him stay." Katie clucked her tongue at the cat and smiled again when he meowed in answer. "You know, he kind of looks like he belongs here."

They stopped just inside the studio door. The silence and the heat of the closed room descended on them, oppressive like an accumulation of years of stillness and the absence of air, making Adrienne wonder if this was how it felt when one entered an ancient sepulcher.

The paintings still lay in a fan of glowing colors on the floor.

"God, I hate these things," Katie whispered. She was staring at the paintings with a terrible loathing. "I'd like to take a pair of scissors and cut every one of them into ribbons."

There was no sound, but something stirred, something without configuration or substance, in the sluggish air. It drifted slowly across the room from where the paintings lay. Adrienne had the sudden impression of being watched, while whatever it was waited for any other words they might speak.

At their feet the cat riveted its blue eyes on the paintings, then walked over to the canvases, a continuous deep-throated snarl coming from its drawn-back lips, a lordly sound in comparison with its usual plaintive utterances. It made a circle of all the paintings, seeming to examine each one, then walked back to Adrienne and Katie, haunches swaying. It looked up at them, then left the parlor.

Adrienne glanced at Katie. Ignoring the cat, the other

woman was standing braced and tense with her eyes aimed at the paintings. All the apprehension of the workroom was gone from the statuesque woman's face, replaced with anger.

"You're not going to frighten me again," she muttered. "You did that last night, and you're not going to do it this morning."

"Katie, who are you talking to?"

Katie did not answer. Instead, she took several slow, careful steps toward the paintings; at her sides her hands were clenching and unclenching. When she reached the paintings, she walked slowly around the edge of the fan-shaped display, looking down at it until she came to a canvas across which a bar of sunlight slanted. She stopped, feet apart, and stared intently at the portrait, her eyes moving from detail to detail, her breathing becoming increasingly sharp.

Adrienne rubbed the palms of her hands down the outsides of her jean-clad thighs, drying the sweat dampening them. She took a tentative step, then another, toward Katie, knowing it was not bravery but curiosity moving her.

"What is it?" she asked when she was at Katie's side. "What's this all about?"

With the toe of her sandal, Katie nudged the canvas which she was studying. "This . . . this one right here."

Adrienne looked down at a three-quarter portrait of a red-haired woman in a purple gown. She was standing with her right arm resting on the fanned back of a rattan chair, her left hand lightly grasping her right wrist. Her head was tilted very slightly forward, but her green eyes looked directly at the viewer with the secure stare of a complacent young matron. She was a tall, healthy woman who, one knew immediately, was inexhaustible, capable of answering physical demands with physical demands.

Adrienne concentrated on the painting, seeking whatever it was that made it different. Then she saw it. Like a transparent, shadowy veil, she had not recognized it on the other occasions when she had looked at the portraits, but now it was so obvious that she wondered what had misdirected her attention before. She ran the tip of her tongue around her mouth and looked at Katie.

"There's a resemblance, isn't there?"

Adrienne nodded. "Yes . . ."

Katie appeared to wilt. "I knew it. I wasn't sure, but still I knew it."

"I hadn't noticed it before."

"I hadn't either, not until I saw her watching me last night."

Adrienne looked sharply at her.

Katie nodded. "Last night when the storm began she was standing in that window over there watching me run up the driveway. I went out because I couldn't sleep."

Instinctively Adrienne looked back down at the portrait. Briefly she was certain she saw a difference in it. Was it a hint of a smile on the woman's lips?

"Let's get out of here," she said.

"I'm going to speak to Ned. I don't want these damn things here." Katie shoved the painting with her foot. It slid across the hardwood floor until its corner caught on the canvas next to it. "All of them. I want them all gone."

The air quivered once more as the unseen force in the room moved. Adrienne stared at the painting of the woman in the purple gown, unable to do anything more than look. Katie muttered under her breath, then spun and walked away.

Back in Adrienne's workroom, Katie stared out the window while she told Adrienne of the previous evening. There was fear and anger in her telling, and Adrienne knew there were under-the-surface contusions and abrasions within her friend. She had the feeling that Katie was performing a kind of mental surgery on herself.

When Katie finished, Adrienne said, "I have to make a

delivery. Come with me, and after I drop off the order, we'll do female things."

"Like what?"

"Like wandering through a shopping mall and invading a store or two without any intention of buying anything."

Katie turned from the window. Little pieces of a smile were trying to come together on her lips. "What about your work?"

"It can wait. What about yours?"

"Geoff's firing. There's nothing I can do."

Katie helped her take the corn husks from the water, pat them dry in a towel and put them in the kitchen refrigerator to prevent mildewing.

When Adrienne went upstairs to the bathroom, she saw the cat curled on the bed she had used two nights before. Whatever feline emotion it had experienced in the studio was apparently gone, forgotten in the comfortable satisfaction of sleeping on the soft mattress.

The car behind him blew its horn. Ned looked into the rearview mirror of the Jeep and saw an expressionless female face hiding behind outsize dark glasses and pinched between long strands of straight hair. The face pointed at him through a sun-splashed windshield. He waved as if in acknowledgment of a greeting, glanced at the traffic light to see if it was green, then casually shifted into low gear and started the Jeep across the intersection. On the far side of the intersection, a yellow Thunderbird whipped around him, cutting too close to the front of the Jeep, then immediately braked as it overtook slow-moving traffic.

"Did you a helluva lot of good, didn't it?" he muttered, then promptly pushed the irritation from his mind.

Sam Jethro. There was no need to squander precious time thinking of him. Jethro was a member of that self-important group of *Homo sapiens* whose prominence was measured by their own yardsticks. Jethro had spent thirty of their forty-five-minute conversation extolling his own achievements while beaming with an ersatz friendliness. That Adrienne wanted to miss the meeting he could now understand, and he hoped that when he went back for the test results, the man would be far, far away from the office.

Lucas, however, was the coin's other side. Ned could not help but think of the chemist as a rotund little figure who had been created by a nineteenth-century artist illustrating a child's story.

Lucas was short and firmly pudgy with a big bald head fringed by a scarf of gray hair, through which he ran blunt fingers while talking. Clear blue eyes appeared to bubble with a latent humor and a larger than usual intelligence over the tops of half-framed glasses. Standing behind Jethro during the conversation, his round face had been a shadow show of impatience, boredom and controlled disgust while the other man talked.

When he opened one of the packets containing the paint scrapings, Ned was aware of the little man's tolerant attitude. But when Lucas took the chips between his thumb and forefinger and felt the warmth within them, his eyes narrowed and his large head nodded.

"Tomorrow afternoon, Mr. Anderson," he said, "I'll have the test results tomorrow afternoon."

"So soon?"

"Yes. There is irrationality where there should be only rationality." He smiled over his glasses. "I can't permit that, Mr. Anderson."

But the meeting was no more than an incidental happening, like the impatient woman in the Thunderbird, because nothing was of the least importance this morning. Only because he was unsure of his memories had he taken the paint samples for analysis. The action was superfluous.

The man in the dream had said he would give him the secret to the paintings.

Sweet Jesus Christ!

His hands trembled on the steering wheel, and in spite of the wind tugging at him in the open vehicle he felt hot rivulets of sweat running down his sides. Around him the traffic was only another incidental blur.

He had known from the first moment he saw the paintings, for an artist to possess the knowledge exhibited in them would be to own the formula that would reestablish a long-lost order in the world of art. Minds and consciousnesses would be expanded beyond what today was considered the ultimate techniques, all made possible by the person who held the formula. The waning art of portraiture would, under that person's guidance, enter a renaissance with the palette and brush replacing the camera and film as they themselves had once been replaced. Fortune and fame would be a by-product of such creativity. It would be a time for the creation of enormities by a mind which would itself, in time, become capable of moving beyond existing restraints to create even greater enormities in the field of art.

Dream or vision, he knew it was Sebastian with whom he had talked last night, even though the man declined to identify himself. But certain phrases still rang in Ned's memory: "We are kin, Ned Anderson, you and I" . . . "leave the realm of mortal man" . . . "difficult for me to bring you here." And a portrait of a young woman must be done, a woman "with a comely turn of features and form." Then a master speaking to a neophyte: "I will come to guide you with the work," followed by the order not to open the other window seat. The words had been soft, but their meaning was strong. Certainly it had been more than a dream, more than a fanciful desire of an obsessively questing mind. It had been an apocalyptic meeting.

He turned to his right at an intersection and saw he was on

Waverly Street, a block or two from Sarah's Cafe. He was startled because while he had been thinking, there had been no conscious guiding of the Jeep in this direction. He parked the Jeep across the street from the café.

A scattering of half a dozen customers glanced at him as he entered. Did the place, he wondered, ever fill to capacity?

Sandi was at the counter filling sugar dispensers from a container made of an old coffee can. He sat on a stool opposite her.

"Your friend isn't with you today," she said.

"No, he has his kilns fired and has to stay near them."

"I mean your other friend, the woman."

He remembered Adrienne was with him the last time he had been to the café. "Oh. She's tied up with her business, too."

"It must be nice to be a photographer and artist and be able to wander around when you want to."

He shrugged. "I never thought about it."

"Can I get you anything?"

"A cup of coffee." Then he remembered he had not eaten breakfast and added, "A Danish, too, please."

Sandi poured the coffee then took a Danish roll from the pastry cabinet and held it up. "This one okay?"

"It looks good. Don't bother warming it."

She placed it on the counter beside the coffee. "Anything else?"

"Are you ready to start modeling?"

"I—" She gave a giggling laugh that was diluted with a gasp. "You mean it?"

"That's why I'm here. To ask you."

"Jeez! Well, I—sure. Anytime you say, I guess."

He wished she had hesitated, pretended to at least think about it. Her extravagant eagerness somehow possessed a touch of the vulgar.

"It will be a painting," he said. "Not photography. A portrait."

"Oh?" She wiggled and smiled. Roundness moved under the maroon waitress uniform. "That means I'll have to sit still, doesn't it?"

"You should be able to do that. We'll take a break every ten minutes."

"What kind of a portrait is it going to be?"

"A portrait," he shrugged. "A portrait portrait. The kind you hang on the wall."

"That means"—she lowered her eyes and smiled—"I won't be *au naturel*."

"No, you'll be clothed."

"Jeez, if it's going to be kind of formal, I don't have anything to wear."

"We'll think of something."

She looked over his shoulder. "Excuse me a minute. A customer wants me."

When she was gone, Ned took a sip of his coffee. He stared at the wall behind the counter without seeing it, in its place seeing the paintings fanned across the studio floor: farm girls, servants, matrons and whores. A waitress would be appropriate, but he knew she would object to posing in the uniform; and, if he did insist, for her the glamour would be taken away, the emotional high gone, and she would become merely an object without character or spontaneity. But there was another way, a modern fad in portraiture, to fit her into the theme and still keep her natural and enthused. Life-style. Portray the person and her life-style. Do it with directness, but convince the viewer reality can be a mythical state also.

"Sorry." She was standing across the counter from him again. "He's an old grump, but he's a regular and tips good."

"What kind of clothes do you usually wear away from here?"

"Oh, I guess jeans. T-shirt and jeans, or a blouse and jeans."

"Then that's what you'll wear." He suddenly saw the composition, saw it so fast because it was so elemental, so much an art school exercise, but it was one in which she could feel free and hold the pose. "Make it a man's shirt, unbuttoned a ways with the tails tied under your bust. A thin blue scarf holding your hair back. I have a stool. You'll rest one leg on it. One thumb will be hooked in the waistband of the jeans, the other hand on the stool beside you. It's simple but effective."

She nodded. "Uh-uh. I can see it."

"Good. That means you'll get into the pose better."

She nodded again, wisely. Ned felt her perception was more to do with awareness of her physical self than understanding the pose.

"When can you start?" he asked.

"I guess just about anytime you want to. I leave work at two o'clock and have Sundays and Mondays off."

Ned was going to suggest the following afternoon, but remembered Lucas's promise of having the test results ready. He wanted them before he began painting—just in case the conversation with Sebastian was, indeed, only a wayward dream.

"How about day after tomorrow?"

"Sure. That sounds great."

"Do you want me to pick you up?"

"No. I've got a car, and I know where you live. I can be there around two-fifteen, maybe just a few minutes later."

"Fine. If you don't have a man's shirt, you can wear one of mine."

"Okay—and—and thanks for asking me. I want to be a model so much, and I hope I work out for you."

There was something more than a little pathetic in what she said, he thought, at least in the way she said it. Almost humble. For the moment, she was not a sensuous animal, but a deferential young woman desperately wanting something more from life than carrying short orders from a greasy kitchen to grumbling diners.

"You will, Sandi. I know you will. We'll talk about a fee day after tomorrow."

"You're going to pay me?"

"Of course."

When he took the money from his wallet to pay for the coffee and Danish, she refused to accept it, saying, "It's on the house."

It was eleven-thirty when he pulled into the parking area. Adrienne's Toyota was not there, and he decided she was delivering the order she had told him was due today.

Funny, he thought. Really funny. And maybe a little awesome, too. In just a few days he had become aware of a presence in her he had found in other women only on isolated occasions, and the even bigger surprise was that he liked it, though it also flustered him. Behind her reclusive facade he felt there was a tender, sweet woman, just a little naive, who had spent too much time brooding over an event which threatened to make her life a cold, empty stretch of time. He wanted to erase all that torment from her memory.

CHAPTER

Sheila Rosenthal walked around the paintings half a dozen times, kneeling now and then to touch one with gentle fingertips, her wide brow frowning and her lips pursed.

"Marvelous," she muttered, making it assume the rhythm of a chant. "Marvelous, marvelous. So lifelike. So disturbingly lifelike." She rose from kneeling beside the portrait of a brown-haired girl to look at Ned. She nodded at the splintered window seat. "You found them in that compartment?"

Ned nodded, slanting a surreptitious glance at Adrienne. "Yes. I wanted the space for storing old instruction books I occasionally use for reference."

"It's quite a find, I'll have to say that." Sidney Scott, though not indicating boredom, exhibited an indifference which was a direct counterbalance to Sheila Rosenthal's enthusiasm. "You know, it's a very good chance they might be valuable in certain markets."

"They're not for sale." Ned's voice tightened.

"I should hope not." Sheila scowled at the lawyer, her

voice sharpening into a tone of challenge. "And it's more than a find, Sidney, it's a discovery."

For the better part of twenty minutes they had been in the studio, since Sheila and Sidney had arrived at three-thirty, with Ned answering and asking questions while Adrienne merely watched and listened, feeling, somehow, she was protecting Ned's back like a companion in a duel. Geoff, curiosity showing clearly on his face above his blond beard, stood just inside the door leading to the hallway, hands in his pockets, tongue occasionally running around the line of his dry lips. Katie had excused herself on the arrival of the visitors, not wanting, Adrienne knew, to look at the paintings. The big redhead's anger and fear had gradually faded away at the Altamont Mall. She had finally promised she would not confront Ned with demands that he would only ignore and at which he might possibly take offense. Now the five of them stood in a speculative group. Looking around at them, Adrienne saw their interweaving expressions of conjecture as their eyes flicked back and forth across the canvases at their feet.

As if by previous arrangement, no one mentioned the happenings in the house to the visitors, each realizing the telling would be difficult and uncomfortable. It was the same as a family keeping its more bizarre secrets to itself, Adrienne supposed.

Sheila Rosenthal had discovered the strange radiating warmth of the flesh-tone paint by herself, so Ned told them of taking samples for study. An all but invisible shadow of what might have been bewilderment crossed her face as Sheila listened. Sidney Scott had shown no emotion, his elongated features, dominated by gold-rimmed skeet glasses, remained rigid. Of the two, Adrienne liked Sheila better.

Sheila Rosenthal was one of those women who would be considered handsome rather than attractive. Dark-haired, dark-eyed, neatly tanned, she was probably, Adrienne judged, in her early forties. Though not large in stature, she nevertheless gave the impression of a domineering physical structure by the erect, positive manner in which she carried herself. Adrienne was certain Sheila was a catalyst in civic organizations. She would have paid-up memberships in the Florida Symphony, the historical society, the little theater and, of course, the Art League. She probably gave much more than she had to give, and, through her involvement, would keep a group active.

Now she raised her eyes to look at Ned. "First thing tomorrow morning, I'll go to the society's office and dig out everything, absolutely everything, on this place. Somewhere, in some sentence someplace, there must be a reference to these paintings. I know there have been rumors concerning them, but rumors abound about a place like this and a man like Sebastian. It's just inconceivable to me nothing has been put in writing about them."

"Remember, Sheila," Sidney Scott said, "no personal notes of either Sebastian or his wife were ever discovered."

"I realize that, Sidney; however, we do have a listing of the household goods which were auctioned, and there is no mention of these paintings being held back."

"Where else is there to look?"

"Oh . . . there must be someplace." She looked at, then nodded in the direction of, the unopened window seat. "Maybe even in that seat over there."

Ned glanced at her, startled; his eyes darted to Adrienne, then to Geoff. Adrienne saw that Geoff's face reflected Sheila's question.

"That could be," Ned said. His voice was unnaturally flat, forestalling discussion. "We'll have to open it before too long."

"I certainly would," Sheila said. "It might be a treasure trove like the other one. I'd have gotten into it immediately after finding the paintings in the other one."

"I'll get to it shortly. I promise."

Adrienne looked at Geoff and saw that, like herself, he was aware of, and surprised at, Ned's evasiveness.

"So we have ourselves a little mystery," Sidney said, smiling. "I suppose that's one of the fun things about inheriting an old house."

"I suppose so, yes," Sheila answered vaguely, then turned her attention back to Ned. "What are you going to do with them?"

He shook his head. "Other than studying them very carefully, I haven't thought about it."

"Well, I, for one, would like to see them exhibited in the city library and the Art League's gallery. People have the right to see truly fine art, Ned. Today we're surrounded by frauds and miserable imitations of art done by incompetents with the sense of design of toads, plus plain fakes. Let people see what type of work an honest-to-God artist was capable of doing."

"They'd have to be restretched and framed. I don't think I have the time."

"Of course you don't. It can be done at the Art League's workshop."

Ned looked at Adrienne, then Geoff, then back to Sheila. "I'll think about it."

"I think you should consider it very carefully."

"As a civic duty?" Sidney asked.

Sheila made a face, but did not answer. Then, as if remembering something, she wandered away from the others to stand beside the canvas of the reclining nude. It was the third time Sheila had singled out that particular painting for close scrutiny. Looking down at it, Sheila seemed to be fighting something inside her. Her fingers convulsed into fists at her sides, her breathing shortened, and, as Adrienne continued to watch, she saw an almost indiscernible shiver run the length of Sheila's body.

"God, there was a barbaric evil in that woman," she whispered. "I wonder who she was."

"We'll probably never know," Sidney said.

Sheila shook her head. "And I don't think I'd want to."

A few minutes later they left, Sheila promising to phone the following day if she found anything of interest in the society's files. Knowing she should resume her work, but feeling too uptight after the extended association with the paintings, Adrienne followed Ned and Geoff to the kitchen to sit at the table with them. With nothing else to drink in the refrigerator, she sipped a cold beer.

"Well," Geoff sighed, "we didn't learn anything from them."

Ned was leaning with both elbows on the table, turning the beer can around and around in his fingers while staring out the window at the parking area with squinted eyes.

"No," he said. "I made a mistake. I don't need outside help to learn what I want to know about the paintings. I'm sorry now I phoned those two, and I didn't need to take the samples to Terryjean."

"What do you mean?"

"Just what I said."

"You haven't said anything, really," Geoff muttered.

"And I'm not going to say any more." The words and the way he spoke them were an unpleasant surprise.

Suddenly the atmosphere around the table was abrasive, uneasy, ragged at the edges. The afternoon had gone out of balance. Adrienne pushed herself a little higher in her chair and took a long swallow from the can, feeling a tiny shock as the crisp beer bit her tongue and shriveled her throat.

She drew a long breath, then slowly pushed herself to her feet, trying to appear casual, attempting to fix the smile just right on her lips. "I'm going to have to start paying rent before too long, so I'd better get to work earning the money for it."

They both looked up and nodded, but neither spoke.

She began on the wreaths. They were simpler than the flowers, and with the sudden tightening of emotions in the kitchen, she did not want to return there for water to resoak the corn husks. As she had thought it would, the work went slower in the new surroundings. She felt out of place, a trespasser in someone else's workshop. What had been a private function now seemed to have gone public. She found it difficult to concentrate. Though most of the actual construction of the wreaths was routine, a small portion of her mind was required to direct the placement and gluing of the pinecones, dried flowers, ribbons and eucalyptus. It refused to do so. She was forced to fight the impulse to jam the ornaments helter-skelter around the woven straw rings.

Outside, the golden yellow afternoon light seeped away, a lavender glow edging across the sky to replace it. The shadows of the pines and oaks sprawled across the yard in long, dark bands like tentacles reaching for something at the rear of the carriage house. Up among the treetops, an evening breeze began whispering softly to itself.

When she finished the fourth wreath, she packed it in its carton. It completed an order for a gift shop on the west side of town, and she stacked the four cartons to take home with her for delivery the following morning, then went to the window to watch the day becoming lost in the lengthening shadows. The question she did not want to be forced to answer all over again surfaced from the stirring confusion to become the focal point of her skittering thoughts.

Should she stay here?

The decision had felt so final the other day, but now the doubts and hesitations were back, more so than before, more menacing and filled with disorder and spilled-over hatred from the paintings.

She found her purse, dug out her cigarettes along with a book of matches, lit one and inhaled deeply. The smoke had a toasted taste, and after savoring it briefly, she slowly blew a plume straight out the window and looked up and down the driveway. Twilight was spreading its web over the land and watching it filled her with the melancholy the ending of a day had tortured her with since childhood. A terrible sadness came to her whenever she watched the lavender darken into mauve, then to gray and finally into night's darkness.

She turned from the window and looked around the room, the desire to stay still strong. On the surface everything was so perfect. But under the tranquillity were the black shadows harboring anxieties and brooding hostility. She was close to feeling she was in a sinisterly alien world where her intellect was in danger of no longer functioning.

"A penny for them."

She looked around. Ned, holding the cat in a crooked arm, was at the door.

"They're not worth even that much, I fear."

"You're depressed, aren't you?"

"A little. How can you tell?"

"There's a veil over your face." He bent down to permit the cat to jump from his arm to the floor. "If you were a photograph, I'd say you'd been pictured through too dense a diffusion screen."

The cat clicked across the room to rub itself against her ankles. Ned leaned against the doorjamb, the distant expression of the kitchen gone from his face.

"You were thinking about leaving, weren't you?"

She bit her lip and nodded, then returned his gaze. "Only thinking of it."

"Don't," he said softly. "Please don't. I came to apologize. I was pretty abrupt and selfish there in the kitchen. No matter how I feel, or what I think, I had no right to behave like that. I've told Geoff I'm sorry, and he says he understands. I hope you will. I know there's no need to keep the paintings secret; on the other hand, I just don't want to be annoyed with outsiders until I can have a chance to study them. It's just that . . . well, I've got this feeling I can learn a great deal about them, and a hell of a lot from them, on my own. But that's not justification for the grunting Neanderthal behavior I displayed."

"I understand," she said. "And I don't really want to go."

"Then stay." He left the door to cross the room and stand in front of her. "We need you here. We appear well disciplined and adjusted, standing with our feet planted squarely on the good green earth, but we're not. We tell ourselves we're looking at life in the proper perspective, but that perspective is kind of warped. It has to be. We're artists, and artists never completely leave childhood. Our emotions race and sizzle and run rampant, zooming beyond our control . . . so we have to be stabilized, and you've become . . . well, you've become our stabilizer in the few days you've been here."

Her breath caught. She retreated from a direct response, slipping back toward the isolation in which she had existed for so long.

"No, Ned." She shook her head. "I can't accept that responsibility. Please don't ask me to do it."

"Don't think of it as a responsibility, more of a . . . well, a symbol of objectivity. The main thing is: just stay here and continue as you are. That is all I ask. You being here is the vital thing."

"How can I be an anchor when I'm as nervous as you three?"

"Because I need you here, Adrienne." He laid his hands on her shoulders as he had done that morning at the side door. "We've all been drawn into a surrealistic world, and we each must grasp what we can of substantiality. Geoff and Katie have each other. You are my hold."

"And what am *I* to hold to?"

"Me. I hope.

Adrienne knew Ned was inviting her to share their strengths, but she did not know how to respond.

His hands tightened on her shoulders. A sudden panic rose in her, then just as instantly fled. Something sensuous and willful moved through her mind. Deep inside her she began to feel the stirrings of a hunger she had not experienced for a long time. She tried to turn her mind against it, to push it back to where it had been curled dormant for so many months, because if it grew, and she acted upon it, only bitterness and frustration would await her. Still she made no move to extract herself from his hands.

With an almost hesitant movement, his hands slid across her shoulders and up her neck until they were cupping her face, following the contours of her jaw, fingertips stroking her earlobes. Inside her the hunger responded. His actions were finely wrought, graceful movements of a ritual begun back in the first light of the dawn time. So very different from the clinical movements of Andrew.

His face came closer to hers. His breath on her lips was warm and carried faintly the smell of tobacco.

"Remember what I told you this morning?"

"Yes . . ."

"Change it. I want to see you every day. I'm already used to it."

She looked into his eyes. Reborn desire soared beyond her ability to control and burst through her in torrents of heat, rippling her muscles and singeing her nerves until shudders ran down her body.

Outside, twilight tightened its web, grew darker and darker as the night descended.

Ned reached out and switched on a bedside lamp, then smiled lazily at Adrienne, studying the softness of her features on the pillow beside his in the soft illumination.

"Hi."

"Hi." She smiled in turn, not trying to find words, pleasantly content with the weariness of her body.

At the window the curtains were billowing in fat puffs of white before the night breeze that found its way into the room, making the air feel cooler than it actually was on their damp bodies. Gooseflesh rose on Adrienne's belly and thighs. A shiver ran through her.

"Cold?" Ned laid a hand on her.

"No." She turned on her side to face him. "Just contented. That was a delicious shiver."

"Oh." He spread a hand flat on her hip and kissed her on the forehead. "You're a very beautiful person, Adrienne Lewis."

"Thank you." She felt her face flush, and to hide it she nestled her head against his shoulder. She wanted this moment of happiness to be suspended in time. "You gave me that beauty."

"No, I don't think so. I think it's always been inside you. You allowed me to bring it out."

"Was . . . was . . . I . . . adequate?" Everything in her stopped as she waited for his answer.

His hand slipped up her side, warm and heavy, but tender on her flesh. It cupped the firm, thrusting mound of her breast, lingered, then slid behind her to spread between her shoulders. He pulled her slowly against him.

"You were superb."

A soft cooing came from her throat, and she pushed herself full length to him. A feeling of wholeness was coming to her. The confusion which had been her life, even the loneliness and despair, she knew now, at this wonderful moment, were no more than abstractions, only faint memories of bad times.

After a while, Ned released her and rolled onto his back once more, his hands crossed on his chest, staring up into the darkly woven shadows crisscrossing the ceiling. Adrienne felt a trickle of disappointment. Her body was awakened, wanting more of the sweet turmoil it had just experienced, but she forced herself to lie still, arms along her sides, also looking up at the shadows above them, certain he had not turned away from her but rather toward things lingering in his thinking.

"I have so much to do," he finally said.

"Well," she said, "one thing is to finish painting this room. A white ceiling is fine, but one and a half walls of blue and two and a half of old eggshell white isn't exactly the color scheme most decorators would approve."

Beside her he continued to stare up. From out on the road, a rumble of a passing truck filled the night and she listened to it fade into the distance before he answered. "I've painting to do, that's true, but these walls aren't it. They'll have to wait their turn."

The flatness in his voice momentarily disturbed her. "Oh?"

He looked at her. The remoteness which had been in them in the kitchen was in his eyes. "Remember the waitress named Sandi at Sarah's Cafe?"

"Yes . . ."

"I stopped at the café today on the way home from Terryjean to ask her to model for a portrait."

"Oh—" Was that all she could do, give monosyllable answers?

But an undertone of which she was not aware must have been in her voice, because he turned her face to his with a forefinger on her chin.

"Hey, it's strictly business."

"I know. It's not that." Now her voice was flat, too. *Should* she tell him what was jabbing her so suddenly with little pricklings of guilt and anger? If she did tell him, how was she to hide from him her feelings of confusion and fear?

"What is it, then?"

Some of the luxury of the moment before drifted away. "It's the paintings."

He looked away. "That's what I thought, but they're so damn important."

"In what way?"

"The world of art has shrunk," he said slowly. "It's given only a downgraded, passing thought, then only once in a while, by the average person. This is the accomplished age of Donkey Kong and Pac Man, of home computers and word processors. Art has become video graphics, graffiti on subway walls and pink plastic floated around islands in Biscayne Bay. Art is an ongoing process, I know; but, as Sheila Rosenthal said this afternoon, the fakers have taken control. The beauty is fleeing. Those canvases downstairs are miracles remaining from the last golden age of painting, and whoever learns their secret will become a messiah in the renaissance of truly beautiful art."

"Do you want to be that messiah?"

"Could I be blamed if I did?"

"No, I suppose not." She rolled all the way onto her side facing him and laid a hand on his chest. She did not want the hope just given her to be taken away. "Only, Ned . . . don't let it become an obsession. I haven't known you very long, but I like you the way you are."

He laughed then, the good, boyish laugh she liked so well, and pulled her over on top of him.

"From this day on, you're the only obsession, Adrienne Lewis, I'll ever have."

Their mouths came together, clinging until her lungs were drained of breath while his strong hands began doing things to her which had never been done before, things which made her healthy body strum and surge in eagerness. When finally the thundering madness exploded, she heard her voice crying in glorious agony, screaming her body pleasures.

* * *

Alexander Lucas felt pummeled, exhausted, like a man who had been through a riot. He was confused. His discipline was in danger of being lost.

He sat at his desk staring distractedly at the wall clock opposite him, watching the red second hand jump forward, hesitate, then spring forward again, driven by the pulsing quartz mechanism inside the imitation wood case. In the nighttime silence of the cramped office, the ticking of the clock reminded him of water dripping. Steady. Unceasing. In time the rhythmic, one-second spaced intervals of sound would fill the mind.

"Fool!" he muttered. "Damn fool! Be true to yourself. Admit it is not the clock which disrupts your thinking."

He looked at the notes he had carefully made in the laboratory spread across the desk top. Wrong. Every damn one of them all wrong. Calculations giving him lies for answers. A job so simple a twelfth-grade chemistry student would complete it in no more than two classroom sessions. So elemental, if one knew what he was doing—which he did—it could be performed with a home chemistry set. And he came up with gibberish. Four times. Twelve hours. Always the impossible answer.

He pushed the notes around with a blunt forefinger. No. No, he was not wrong! That he would not, absolutely could not, acknowledge. If he made such an admission, what worth, then, was his experience and confidence? If per chance the findings were incorrect, what of the feeling, the intuition of more than half a lifetime spent in the laboratory that told him the figures scrawled on the notepad pages were correct, as accurate as modern science would permit? The impossible was the possible; no matter how inconceivable. He looked at the packet of samples he had brought in from the lab, but made no move to finger it as he had the notes.

"It cannot be, but it is."

He spoke as loud as he could, wanting to hear his voice in the silent emptiness. Again he looked at the plastic packet of paint scrapings. This time with horror and fascination, because he had proven that folded in the plastic wrapper was a substance which could not chemically exist.

At the start of the testing, though the warmth emanating from the paint excited him, his approach had been routine. Under the microscope, adding the catalysts, fluoroscoping the tiny bits, he found what he knew he would find as the contents separated into individual entities: zinc oxide, titanium, cadmium, sulfoselenide, with linseed oil, and, of course, varnish. All of them what one would expect to find in an artist's oils. But then there were the other factors, the elements of the mixture which had no right to be there, which could not possiby blend with the oils, could not exist in the state in which they were mixed: sodium chloride, potassium chloride and sulfate, calcium and sodium and magnesium phosphate with traces of other organic salts.

Only the rudiments, he told himself at first. A freakish, perhaps spoiled mixture. But then the other portions showed up. Tiny traces. Mere hints. But there! There in the correct quantities. Carbohydrates, glycerides, oleic and palmitic acids. On and on, he had broken down again and again what he had, dividing compounds into compounds, until eventually all the constituents were noted and written on the pad—and always the information he could not accept formed the answers.

The paintings from which the samples had been scraped contained blood!

"So, you admit it," he told himself. "It is a fact, not a hypothesis. Now you work onward from there. Now you discover why there is warmth in the mixture, yes. You discover why dried blood is lifelike warm and remains so healthy for so long."

He picked up the packet of scrapings, stuffed the notes in

his shirt pocket, then stood up. Glancing at the clock, he saw it was ten minutes after eleven. He should phone to tell Rochelle he would be in the laboratory all night, but by now she would be in bed, having assumed he was not coming home. After thirty-one years of marriage, she was accustomed to his all-night sessions with his microscopes and chemicals. And he would not charge that nice Mr. Anderson for the time: it would be unethical, because this had become a personal quest.

He walked slowly down the hallway to the swinging doors leading to the laboratory, pushed through them into the dark cavern of the antiseptic-smelling room. His nose wrinkled. The janitors with their foul-smelling cleansers had come and gone while he was in the office. More often than not, he suspected, they poured just enough of the liquid into the corners to smell up the room, doing no actual cleaning.

Turning on a high-intensity lamp on the worktable, he hoisted himself onto a stool. Only the tips of his shoes touched the floor. With extreme deliberateness, he unfolded the plastic wrap, breathing shallowly so as not to send the chips flying. These were the last ones he possessed; the others had all been used in the earlier experiments.

When sometime later he first became aware of the noise, he gave it no thought, accepting it as part of the harmony of sounds heard as an undertone even in empty buildings. It was blurred, possessing no dominance, at once alien to the emptiness and familiar to the darkness. However, within a few moments its decibel level increased until it assumed an identity of its own to become unnormal in the fragile silence.

Lucas looked up. He could not define the sound, but he thought he felt a current of air. He mumbled wordlessly, returning his attention to the microscope. Sometimes concentration caused peripheral effects when the body and mind were tiring, he had discovered.

But the next time he heard it, he knew it was not his imagination. He looked up, slowly swinging his eyes around the laboratory, squinting into the darkness beyond the high-intensity glow. He became aware of something else. Over the antiseptic smell, there was another aroma, the faint scent of burning, though he could not decide if it was wood or wiring.

"Is there someone there?" he asked.

There was no answer, yet he immediately knew there was a presence in the room with him, somebody or something in the ring of darkness out there watching him, beyond mental and physical reach. He switched off the lamp and slid from the stool. For the first time in more years than he could remember, he felt fear. The room abruptly began spinning around him, squeezing in on him, all the laboratory furnishings streaking past him with their high-polished surfaces etching veins of silver in the hostile darkness.

"Who's there?"

To his right a mass moved along an aisle toward him. It was darkness within darkness, having no definable shape, a black hole in the blackness through which it shifted. From within it a cadenced noise rumbled.

"What is mine is mine."

"Who are you?" Lucas's heart was hammering in his chest with such force he felt his rib cage vibrating. He began to gasp. "Who—who are you? What—what do you want?"

The mass moved closer. The smell of burning came from deep inside it. Lucas could feel the heat on his face, feel it drawn into his contorted mouth and down his throat to wilt the insides of his empty lungs.

"What is mine is mine and will remain mine."

Lucas stumbled back, clutched the edge of the worktable with desperate hands, all the time trying frantically to draw cool air into the fire that was now raging in his chest. He could not do it. It was at that instant that he knew, with a horrible certainty, that his heart and lungs were going to explode inside his body, that he, Alexander Lucas, was going to die here and now. He managed a breathless sob. He did not understand. His life was being taken away from him for a reason he did not know.

CHAPTER

Time was telescoping. It had been ten days since Alexander Lucas's death at the lab, and already it was the last day of June. Fighting the repugnance which came to him at this time each month, Geoffrey drummed his fingertips on the tabletop. Feeling his shirt sweat-stuck to his shoulders, he sat hunched over the scarred and paint-spattered table shoved into a far corner of the workshop, its isolation an almost visual denial of its existence. Spread before him were the monthly receipts, the monthly bills, the inventory lists and the notes indicating required materials. They formed an irregular paper fan around a desktop calculator from which a paper tape curled with its column of gray-printed figures. From the far side of the room came the crumpling sound of paper as Katie wrapped unicorn figurines in sheets of newsprint before placing them in cardboard cartons for shipping.

Geoff tore the ribbon of paper from the calculator at the same time he pushed the machine away. The paper tore at an oblique angle, ripping away the final two sets of figures in the column. Fury raced through him, then subsided to a manageable anger which he relieved further with an under-the-breath muttering of "Shit!"

He tore free the portion of printed tape remaining in the calculator, after a short hunt found a dispenser of transparent mending tape, then carefully joined the jagged ends of the torn paper. The junction was not neat, but the column of figures assumed a legible entity which satisfied him. It was the story the figures told him that dissatisfied him.

It was a simple straightforward presentation of mathematical facts. It was not cluttered or complicated with such items as competitive marketplace standing, obsolete or outmoded product design, items too expensively manufactured to be marketable or subcontractor unreliability. What the figures were telling him, as they had for the past two months, was that sales were not strong enough to reinvest capital for necessary expansion. The business was solid, it was thriving, it could continue on indefinitely as it was now operating, but it could not grow without an infusion of outside money—and he did not know if he wanted to invest borrowed money in the operation while it was located here.

He shuffled through the papers before him until he found the letter which would be strong collateral for a loan if they decided to make an application.

Forwarded from their old Atlanta address, the letter had arrived the previous day. After dinner he and Katie had discussed it briefly, and he knew she was awaiting him to approach her for an input of her ideas. All their business decisions were jointly agreed upon in give-and-take discussions; however, as yet nothing was balanced in his mind securely enough for him to measure the extent of his feelings, so he was not prepared for a dialogue. When the time came for him to present his ideas to her, he would need to be positive, because to tell her what he intended to tell her would require resource and ingenuity.

Henerick Meir, Inc. The sepia letters on the buff-colored stationery connoted solid foundations and respect in a business sometimes thought to be shaggy with corruption. The clean, neat design gave him an amount of confidence, an added faith in the international reputation of Henerick Meir, Inc.

Months before, on the advice of a department store buyer, they had sent a query, along with a unicorn statuette, to Meir's headquarters in Brussels. In time an answer returned stating Henerick Meir was considering representing them in Western Europe. Then a prolonged silence until the receipt of this letter stating Mr. Meir himself would be conducting a buying trip to the United States. He would take pleasure in meeting with them. The letter told the quantity of pieces which would be required, the delivery times which would be expected, and ended with the suggestion they add a series of elfin characters to their line. The letter gave the date Mr. Meir anticipated arriving in Atlanta, making a special stopover between New Orleans and New York, to meet them. That date was only four days away.

He shifted his position in the straight-backed chair to look dubiously at Katie. She was concentrating with such preoccupation on the packing, he knew it was an assumed behavior and she was studiously avoiding looking at him. Unconsciously his right hand clenched into a fist on the tabletop in an unthinking try at grasping the situation. Everything recently was so goddamn wrong. In a curious way, he felt an obscene joke had been played on Katie and him, leaving him hurt and flustered and provoked, with no recourse but to turn his back on the offender. And that was the frigging problem: he was not at all sure from whom the offense came.

He watched Katie put a wrapped unicorn in the carton, then pour a layer of Styrofoam peanuts over and around it. Three more statuettes awaiting packing sat beside the carton on the long plank table. When those three were in the carton, he decided, he would talk with her. He would have to. Time was running out.

Five minutes later Katie was crisscrossing the lid of the carton with packaging tape. Geoff found himself looking objectively at her, seeing her as a woman and not the wife he had made the centerpiece of his life for six years.

In her short shorts and skimpy halter, she was stupendously female. Under the pale, rosy tan some red-haired people managed to obtain, long, strong muscles rippled with her movements in a smooth, gliding way which was more than a mere anatomical functioning. It was a movement full of resiliency and vitality, generating the almost electrical charge one was aware of emanating from her. Before she became conscious that he was watching her and turned her head to look at him, Geoff sat quietly in the chair realizing the womanhood of his big red-haired wife penetrated deeply into her. It made him feel solemn and a little frightened because she had chosen him to love.

"Are you ready to talk now?" she asked.

"Yes." He shifted in the chair to face her, placing his right arm on the top rung of the back, keeping his left hand on the table with the letter held tightly under it. "I think we should consider working with Meir and should definitely meet with him. A face-to-face conversation will tell us a good deal, don't you think?"

She nodded, as if already knowing that was the decision he had arrived at during the silent struggle with himself.

"You know," she said, "if we do supply him, it will cost us a great deal of money we don't have and will have to borrow. So we do that: what, then, of our original plans? We'd no longer be a cottage industry with the freedom it permits, but suddenly find ourselves operating a small business. Is that what we want? We've been happy doing our work our way. It's given us a lot of pleasure."

He did not know if she was speaking her thoughts or being

a devil's advocate. He said flatly, "Pleasure, yes; but no monetary security."

From the tightening of her face, he saw that the inflection of his voice might have been unpleasant to her.

Quickly he went on. "Honey, we're in limbo right now. You know that as well as I do. We've worked ourselves into an impossible corner. With any less work than we have right now, we'd be unable to make ends meet. But with more, even fifteen hundred a month gross, we could give ourselves some of life's goodies and stash a buck or two into a savings account. Yet we can't increase our production because our equipment isn't adequate. It's the Catch-22 of the nominally successful small business."

"Well, apparently you've thought it all out," she said. "So that's what we'll do, I guess."

Geoff heard the petulance in her voice, but chose to ignore it. "I honestly think it's our best move. Maybe considering the long run, it's the only one we can make."

Abruptly veering the conversation away from finances, she said, "We can't both go to Atlanta. We've a dozen orders waiting with impossibly close due dates."

"I know. I've been thinking it over. It would be best if we could both meet with him to allow him to get a perspective on our relationship and how fine-tuned our work is. He'd like to inspect the shop, too, I know, to satisfy himself we can turn out the required amounts. But that just can't be done . . ."

"So . . . ?"

"I'll drive up to meet with Meir. In all honesty, Katie, I think you'd make the better impression on the man, but I'd be so damn nervous thinking of you traveling alone, I'd not get a frigging thing accomplished here. Shit! I wish to Christ we knew his itinerary. We could contact him and maybe get him to come here."

"I'm sure he wouldn't change his plans to come so far out

of his way.'' She seemed ready to say something more, to ask a question, but remained silent.

Was she wondering why, after such long deliberations, he was making such short shrift of the subject? Usually, he knew, he went into great, all but boring, detail to explain his reasonings. Suddenly he felt trapped. She knew there was something more on his mind, and she was waiting him out.

Finally she asked the direct question, her words pointed and sure. ''You've got something else on your mind, don't you?''

He waited for a split moment for some kind of reaction in himself to the question, but none came. He was blank. He was a small boy trying to conceal from an all-knowing adult a questionable deed of which he was guilty.

''What do you mean?'' he asked, stalling while he still sought to pull his mind into equilibrium.

''Don't toy with me, Geoff. You're acting damned unnatural. I could easily get the impression this trip is some kind of covert action.'

''Holy shit!''

''Well? Am I wrong?''

He could hide it no longer, and suddenly he wanted to hide it no longer. All the hollowness was gone from him as he pushed himself to his feet, refolded the letter and stuffed it into a shirt pocket. The nervousness was draining away and aborting the misgivings which had been gnawing him.

''Let's go upstairs,'' he said, wanting to put off the confrontation for another two or three minutes. ''I can talk better up there.''

In the apartment's tiny kitchen Katie stood with her arms hanging at her sides, feeling too big physically and too small mentally. She knew what he was going to tell her was going to be very, very important, and for the first time in their marriage she wondered if it would develop into a situation with which she could not cope. Geoff took two bottles of beer from the small refrigerator, opened them and handed her one.

"Do you want a glass?"

"No." She shook her head. "Just conversation."

"Okay." He took a swallow from his bottle, then whipped the back of a hand across his lips. Without looking at her, he walked to the windows and stood with his back to her staring down into the parking area. "There is another reason, you're right. While I'm in Atlanta, I'm going to look for a place where we can move. I phoned the other day to check, and our old studio has been rented."

Katie did not answer. She felt they were standing on the threshold of a situation which could get out of control. The silence stretched into long seconds, then into an extended minute. Finally she went to an end table and took a cigarette from the pack lying on it, becoming conscious of the first stirrings of something in her, but not knowing if it was the start of excitement or resentment, yet whatever it was made her hands tremble as she set the bottle on the table and lit the cigarette.

"Everything is wrong here." Geoff was still looking out the window, speaking slowly, trying to explain an inner dismay. "It's all taken a bad turn, Katie, and I'm not sure I want to have any more to do with it."

"Leave?" She regarded his back with surprised eyes. "Is that what you're saying?"

Without turning around, he nodded. "Whatever's happening around here will never be explained to my satisfaction, Katie. I don't know what the hell it is, and I'll probably never know what it is, but I don't want you or me caught up in it, because I can't help feeling it's something dangerous, more dangerous than we can handle."

She drew in her breath with a sucking sound, wanting to laugh and weep at the same time, because listening to the words Geoff was saying was listening to a magic incantation releasing her from a horrible weight slowly suffocating her. She wanted to cry out her agreement with what he was saying, to scream her thanks to him for extending a rescuing hand to pull her from a creeping horror.

But instead of all that, she asked, "What about Ned? Can we afford to move back, considering the time and the money we've put into the move down here? Friendship and finances are big considerations, Geoff."

"Ned's changing." He finally swung away from the window to look at her. "He's becoming part of it, whatever it is; and, as for the money, if Meir accepts our line we can borrow enough to cover the move as well as add equipment."

She knew he was not yet telling her everything on his mind. Still, she decided not to question him, but wait for him to tell her in his own way and time. She drew deeply on the cigarette, then said, "It's the paintings."

He looked out the window again, but this time did not turn his back to her. "Yes. All the troubles began when they were discovered. Whether it is actually them or not, I don't know, but our lives have been changed just as if some kind of element without mercy has moved into that house to play a macabre game with us. We've all been touched by it, but Ned is the worst affected. He's become too goddamned obsessed with those paintings, to the exclusion of everything else, and that frightens me, Katie, because I'm afraid in time it will become worse with him." His eyes roamed up and down her statuesque body, then stared straight into her eyes with an expression more tender than any she had ever seen. "I can't allow anything to happen to you, Katie. I love you."

With a tiny whimper, she took a quick step forward, stood before him for an instant, then pressed herself to him. It was awkward trying to keep the beer from spilling and the cigarette away from the back of his neck, but she had to feel the warm, hard length of him. When his long arms folded around her, she knew it was as much a protective hug as it was an embrace.

"Oh, Geoff, could we do it? Could we leave here and still feel good with ourselves?"

"Do you mean, is it ethical?"

"Yes . . ."

"Maybe not all the way, but self-preservation is stronger than ethics, and I honestly think that's the choice we're making, honey. If not now, then damn soon." He ran a hand down the long curve of her back to the voluptuous swell of her buttocks, where he allowed it to remain. "Besides, I think before too long Ned might be wanting us to leave. I've a premonition his obsession with the paintings is going to take a frightening turn, and, if I'm right, I don't want to be here when it occurs."

She pushed harder against him, feeling her big curves mash themselves against the solidness of his chest and stomach.

"God, I love you, Geoffrey Clements."

"Do you want to prove it in the bedroom?"

"Yes . . ."

Sometime later they lay facing each other on the bed with their hands still tentatively exploring one another. As it had been from the very beginning of their relationship, their lovemaking had been good, completely alive and understanding, demands made and fulfilled with both strong, robust bodies performing efficiently.

The noontime sun glinted on the bedroom windows transforming them into opaque rectangles with splinters of vivid light. They listened to a car come into the parking area, its tires crunching loudly on the gravel in the midday quiet, then stop with a muted squeal of brake lining, heard a door slam, followed by footsteps going in the direction of the house.

"It must be Adrienne," Geoff said. "She probably had deliveries to make this morning."

"What about her, Geoff? She's become a true and real friend."

"I know."

They lay silent, their hands no longer caressing.

"Are you sure it's the right thing to do?"

"Yes, Katie. We've come to a decision. Now we stick to it."

"You came to the decision. You didn't talk to me about it."

"Are you against it?"

"No. I want to leave. I'm frightened." She raised herself up on an elbow to look directly at him. "Why didn't you tell me you were thinking about this?"

"Shame, I guess. Manly pride. I might have gone on for a while longer, but when Sheila Rosenthal and Sidney Scott were here you acted so goddamn strange, just like a person getting over a huge scare; so I made up my mind it had to be done. And when that chemist at Terryjean died while analyzing the paint scrapings, I knew we had to leave. This might sound like a pile of horse hockey, but to me his death was an omen."

"An omen? Darling, he died of a heart attack." She laid her head back down on the pillow. All of them had felt some shock at the man's death a week before, but now that she thought about it, although he had not ignored it, neither had Ned appeared too disturbed. Considering the intensity of his desire to learn what was in the paint, his indifference was curious. Was it, she wondered, one of the changes Geoff was referring to? "It was a natural death."

"But it was our job he was working on, honey. If Ned hadn't taken it in, Lucas wouldn't have been there alone."

"It could as easily have been someone else's job."

"Sure, but can you tell me why all of what appeared to be his notes on our job were only charred bits of burned paper?"

"No, I never thought about it."

"Well, now that you are thinking about it, don't you think that those notes were destroyed so no one could read them?"

There was no answer she could think of to reply, so she mumbled, "That's spooky thinking, Geoff."

"Of course it is. But why shouldn't it be? This whole damn setup has become spooky, Katie, and that's why I'm in favor of dealing with Meir. The trip to Atlanta to meet with him gives me the perfect reason to go there and look for a new place."

She buried her face in his shoulder. "I agree, darling, but I'm going to have to work on convincing myself we're not being unfair."

Adrienne snipped the end of a binding wire on a corn husk flower and slowly turned the pale brown creation in her fingers, examining the delicate petals. She smiled with satisfaction, then realized how very little it took to please her. With this one, she had thirty-eight pretty results of therapeutic action, elegant little examples of a human behavioral pattern under stress.

The cat was curled on the end of the table, gazing with sleep-heavy eyes out the window. She went to stand beside it and stroked its ears, thinking that someday she would give it a name. It looked up at her, murmured deep in its throat, then returned to its observation of the lawn and driveway.

From down the hallway she heard Ned's and Sandi's voices in the studio, where work on the portrait was proceeding, his voice low, a continuous rhythm, enticing transient sensuality from her, while her occasional responses were tight, scrawny monosyllables. A rapid little jolt, bordering very close to jealousy, skipped through Adrienne's mind, surprising and alarming her. It had the same effect as being struck from behind, leaving her feeling vulnerable and provoked at the same time. Ashamed of her reaction, she went out of the room, turned away from the murmuring voice and walked toward the kitchen.

Katie was at the sink washing apples. When the redhead

looked at her, Adrienne saw that her eyes carried a distant expression of satisfaction, like eyes which had just gazed into the center of a very special dream.

"Hi!" Katie held up an apple. "Want one?"

"If you've got one to spare, but they always look better to me than they taste."

"That's the uniqueness of cold-storage fruit." Katie dried two apples with a paper towel before handing one to Adrienne. "Are you busy right now?"

"No. I've got some flowers to pack for tomorrow's deliveries, but nothing pressing."

"Then let's take a walk."

Adrienne heard the strange tightness to Katie's voice. It dropped so low it was little more than a whisper. To Adrienne's ears, it was a furtive arranging for a clandestine meeting. She nodded, saying nothing but wondering why she was so unexpectedly disturbed as she followed Katie out of the kitchen, through the foyer, then across the verandah and down into the garden.

Katie led the way through the brown ghosts of plants and shrubs in no hurry to reach any particular destination. At the far end of the ravaged area, Katie stopped in front of the wrought-iron bench that was attempting to hide its rust and decay under the drooping oak branches. She stood looking at it for a moment, then said, "I don't know whether to trust it or not."

Trying to ignore her growing uneasiness, Adrienne shrugged and sat down. "I'm going to chance it."

Standing where she was, Katie turned in a full circle, her eyes slowly scanning the dead emptiness before them, holding her look for a moment on the studio windows, giving Adrienne the impression the red-haired woman was checking to ascertain if they were being watched. Apparently deciding they were unobserved, she sat down beside Adrienne heavily, stretching her long, shapely legs out before her.

al drained away from her. She did understand, b
have time to assemble herself.

Finally she said, "It doesn't surprise me. I guess it would be better if we all left this place. I've thought about it, you know that, just about every day since I rented the rooms, but—"

Katie reached over to take her hand. "It's different for you. You and Ned have the start of something good. Geoff and I, well—we're into our routine now. You know, not as many immediate memories, the vibrations are more controlled. But—well, dammit, Adrienne, be careful. There is something terrible about this place, and if I went away and something happened to you, I'd— I'd—"

"Nothing's going to happen, I promise you." She laid a hand over the one with which Katie held hers. "It's true, Ned has returned me to the wonderful feeling of being a woman, and I like that. I'd forgotten how good it felt. It's a whole new discovery, and I'm excited, but I'm too old and too cautious to completely turn my back on reality." She squeezed Katie's hand. "Now, tell me about your decision to leave."

Katie spoke with an honest directness. She told Adrienne of the Meir letter and the opportunity it offered, and she very frankly described their fears, though she made no mention of Geoff's new feelings concerning Ned. However, as she listened, Adrienne heard, in silent words beneath the spoken ones, the descriptions of the same abrasions of spirit and mind which she herself felt—and she wondered how truthful she had been when she told Katie not to worry.

A half hour later, she stood in the center of her workroom. ust when these surroundings were becoming familiar, they ere strange again. Once more in her life the good things ere threatening to slip away.

Late-afternoon shadows pooled under the table and clung to walls in grotesquely twisted lines and blotches. Leaning inst one of the tables, she watched the walls move away,

What seemed to Adrienne to be far too long a time
before Katie drew a deep breath and said slowly, "
know how to tell you what I'm going to without feeling
goddamn bitch."

Adrienne squirmed on the bench and sucked her lowe
between her teeth. A misgiving began to stir inside h
causing a film of coldness to spread across her shoulders.
general sense of numbness gripped her. She knew she should
say something, if only a word or two, to help Katie, because
the expression on her friend's face was a mask of indecision
mixed with pain, but no words came to her.

Katie fixed pain-filled eyes on her, studied her face for a long time as if attempting to memorize its features, then dropped her gaze to the apple core she held in her lap. When she finally spoke, her voice was cramped.

"Geoff and I've been talking, and we've come to a couple of decisions."

"About your business?" Adrienne asked the question cautiously, knowing she must, but not wanting to hear the answer. She was like a person drawing a deep breath before leaping into a yawning void.

"That mainly, yes." Katie looked at the house. "And those decisions led to another."

At that moment Adrienne knew with certainty what Katie
going to tell her. "You're leaving, aren't you?"

"It's not definite. We've just talked about it." Gon
the sparkle of contentment which had shone in her eyes
kitchen, their moist expression now trying to put a lie t
she was saying.

"You haven't set a time, then?" Adrienne look
from those sad eyes.

Katie was reluctant to answer. "No, but I honestl
will be soon. Maybe very soon."

Adrienne stared across the wretched ruins of th
den, knowing a shadow lay over her face as som

then rush back upon her with what was surely an intent to squash her within their blue mass. With a little murmur, she closed her eyes in a desperate try to hide in the darkness behind their lids.

When she opened them, the walls were where they should be, solid and stationary, with the shadows on them weaving graceful arabesques of looping curlicues. And Ned was standing in the doorway. Although every muscle in her face was stiff and drawn, she managed to smile at his concern. "I—I felt a little dizzy," she lied. "It must have been the heat."

He stepped into the room with his arms reaching for her. "Are you sure? You look pale."

With his hands on her waist, her body drew enough strength from them to thrust away the lingering waves of shock, permitting her to smile a true smile as she leaned into his chest. Amid all the fear, he was providing the solid anchor he had wanted her to become.

When he kissed her, she responded with instant eagerness, using her tongue as a rapier, dueling with his in the warm cavity of his mouth. At some moment during the kiss, his hands began to roam over her, stroking her shoulders, then moving slowly down her sides to spread wide on her buttocks and pull her tight to him until they strained loin to loin.

"Are you going to stay tonight?"

"I shouldn't.

"But you will."

Arm in arm, they stood looking out the window at the shadows crawling across the lawn. Unseen under the drooping boughs of a peppertree, the cat watched from out of the brown mask of his face, his blue eyes staring intently at one of the studio windows.

Just as he remembered, he was certain he was dreaming, but like then, his senses were alert, incredibly quick and strong, so he was aware of being in familiar surroundings.

Along his side, he could feel the firm, warm pressure of Adrienne's naked body pressed curve to curve against him, simmering in him a desire to take her once again on the rumpled bed. But in the room into which he drifted, she was nowhere to be seen.

Standing beside an easel, studying the painting on it, was the man who had been in the garden the previous time and, behind him, as she had been then, the beautiful, dark-haired woman was sitting—but this time on a window seat instead of the wrought-iron bench.

As it had been then, what he saw was in soft focus, details hidden behind a veil of gossamer. Yet through that haze, Ned recognized the studio. The easel was his, with the unfinished portrait of Sandi resting on it.

Turning to greet him, the man smiled. "You have done what I told you to do, Ned Anderson . . . and you have done it exceedingly well." He looked at the canvas once more. "This is a fine woman, the kind I had hoped you would find, the kind which is needed."

Ned wanted to ask what was the need, but knew he would receive no answer, so he merely said, "Thank you. I'm trying to paint her in the same theme as the others."

In the slow-motion, choreographed movements Ned remembered, the man stepped away from the easel, gazed at him with satisfaction, then went to stand beside the woman. He laid a hand on her shoulder while smiling down at her. On his face Ned saw an expression of overpowering love and devotion. "He has done all we hoped for, my dear."

The woman returned his smile with a gentle slow smile of her own. "Yes, he's very talented."

"You have guessed who we are, have you not, Ned?" the man asked.

Ned nodded. "Yes, I think I have."

"I am Sebastian, and this is my wife, Sabra."

Once more Ned nodded.

"I promised you I would assist you with this portrait, and I will, Ned; but you must open your mind without hesitation to accept those things I tell you. You must follow my instructions without prejudgment and not turn what is simple into a complex situation. By taking the paint samples to the chemist, you could have caused mischief; however, the irrational act was nullified, as you know."

Throughout the room the mists wavered, transforming the scene into a setting viewed under water. Ned looked around. Was he dreaming, or was he awake in the studio? Then, in that strange mixing of what was and what was not, he felt a warm weight press itself across his loins and knew Adrienne had thrown a leg over him.

He knew, too, that he was speaking, though he felt no vibrations in his throat or chest; the weight of Adrienne's leg was only a resilient warmth. "I'll take your instruction without question, Sebastian, if what you teach me is the secret of creating paintings such as these portraits."

"That is what I will teach you, Ned."

"Then I am your apprentice."

"In the window seat, the one you have not opened," Sebastian was saying, "there are papers and a notebook. In it is the formula for the mixing of the paints. Study it. I will come again, to explain it to you."

Adrienne moaned as she snuggled closer to Ned. Against his skin she felt warm and satiny. He ran his hand along the long, curving length of her thigh lying over his loins, feeling the strong, lithe muscles beneath the smooth-textured skin.

This leg under his hand, the even-spaced breathing fanning in warm little puffs on his right cheek, were actualities: they were Adrienne, and Adrienne was a living creature in the factual world. She was reality. To further assure himself, he moved his legs, then his arms, just enough to feel muscles responding to his commands. He satisfied himself he was out of the dream, but instead of euphoria he had the uneasy impression he was being led toward a destination where something waited that could possibly be as malicious as it was bountiful. Was Alexander Lucas's death a hint, a warning? He had just agreed to take the second step in his following of Sebastian: what would be the third? He wondered how far his consciousness would allow him to travel in quest of the secret of the portraits.

He turned his head and buried his nose in the sweet-smelling blackness of Adrienne's hair, thinking that probably he was unduly anxious.

Later, when he obtained the formula, when he was confident of his mastery of it, he would paint her portrait.

CHAPTER

It had been a long, distracted day. To begin with, he had definitely fallen in love with Adrienne; he would soon ask her to marry him; and all the while, as he turned that realization over in his mind, curiosity over the contents of the second window seat had devoured him with a passionate intensity. He had spent all of the day wishing the hands of his wristwatch would spin through the hours, only remotely aware of Geoff's long absences and Katie's withdrawal. Twice while in Adrienne's workrooms, he almost told her what he planned to do tonight, but both times a small warning voice made him halt before he spoke the words. Now he was here, ready.

A single moonbeam slanted through the glass panes to touch the window seat with an eerie blend of white and gray, forming a haze, like a fairy mist, in which the narrow seat appeared to be shrinking in upon itself, huddling back into the hollow alcove in an effort to escape the abuse soon to be laid on it from the hammer and chisel Ned carried in his hands.

Standing in the foyer door on the opposite side of the room, he studied the thin clarity of the moonlight, the opaque shadows threatening to seep into and obliterate the pale, silvery wash of light which seemed uncertain of its intrusion into the room. Finally telling himself he could wait no longer, he decided the light was sufficient to permit him to work without turning on the overhead bulb or using the flashlight jammed in his hip pocket. He wanted no light, no matter how weak, to seep through the windows. For the present, this was his secret, just as, for the time being, the dreams were his alone.

As he crossed the room through the muted darkness, his heart began pounding with a furious, heavy beat that shortened his breath, and his stomach began to flutter. Never had he experienced such excitement, but then never before had he faced an action so totally filled with improbable expectations.

When he reached it, he stood looking at the seat, staring at the yellowing paint, in which a thin black line formed the rectangle of the lid's edge. He found himself holding his breath, waiting, listening, but nothing reached out from under the lid as it had done from the other seat. He shifted from one foot to the other, an analytical corner of his mind questioning the validity of his being here in the studio alone at two o'clock in the morning.

He knelt down in front of the seat, laid the flashlight on it and began to chisel at the lid. The work went surprisingly easily. Either he handled the chisel more masterfully than the first time, or the lid was not as securely jammed, because in a little more than thirty minutes it was loosened around all four edges.

Sweating mildly, he laid the hammer and chisel on the floor, then hooked his finger in the metal lifting ring. He drew a deep breath in a final attempt to control the wild acceleration of his heart, feeling his stomach turning over and over, faster and faster, in a threat to make him violently ill.

Slowly he pulled up on the ring. With shrill screeches the lid gave, stuck, gave—and stuck.

"Dammit!"

He stood up in order to exert more leverage.

From his left came a muffled sound like that of an indrawn breath which immediately trilled into an all but inaudible giggle. He looked around, knowing he would see nothing in the darkness of the room other than those items belonging in it, yet unable to disregard what he thought he had heard.

He gave a hard upward yank, cutting his finger and bringing a high-pitched scream from the resisting wood. The lid opened three or four inches.

Once more he heard the staccato ripple of giggles beyond the fringes of the thin pool of moonlight. He spun around, gooseflesh tingling his arms and chest. Nothing. Only the darkness. But that darkness was deeper now, because the moon had lowered itself to hide behind an oak tree on the far side of the lawn. Yet, even as his eyes dilated and absorbed the darkness, he saw nothing but the paintings lying on the floor, the easel, the taboret and the assorted photo equipment. Still he felt something. A presence? A physical entity? He could not be sure if it was his imagination or if another being stood concealed in the shadows watching him from the far end of the room. Watching, and maybe . . . maybe, he felt, offering him encouragement. Hardly knowing what to think or expect, he turned back to the seat.

Giving a final, protesting cry, the lid came open with his next pull.

When he picked up the flashlight, he discovered his hands were trembling. How would he handle the disappointment if he found neither papers nor notebook in the storage compartment? He did not want to speculate. He let out a final long breath and pointed the flashlight at the black rectangular opening, reminding himself this entire episode was an answer to curiosity, no more than an act of foolishness. He closed his eyes and snapped on the flashlight.

When he looked again, he saw two bundles of ribbon-bound papers and a notebook lying in the circle of harsh light at the bottom of the compartment.

The digital clock on the bedside table read seven-thirty. Adrienne squinted at it, then closed her eyes. If she did not see the clock, she would not see anything else and maybe the morning would go away. She did not want to get up. This was Saturday, and people stayed in bed longer on Saturdays while they occupied their minds with random thoughts of weekend pleasures. Why would not her mind understand that?

Determinedly, she closed her eyes. In the light-streaked darkness behind their lids, she willed sleep to return to take her back into its escape, to no avail. Muscles tautened and twitched as they demanded exercise. Inside her head she was certain she could feel electrical charges sparkling through her brain.

"Damn," she muttered. "Damn and double damn."

She sat up, ignoring the temporary stiffness in her body that the air conditioner sometimes caused, and swung her legs over the side of the bed, feeling blindly with her feet for the slippers waiting on the braided rug. The usual shock of hair tumbled across her eyes, and, with exasperated fingers, she pushed it away as her groping feet discovered the slippers.

After she shrugged into her old blue robe, before she wrapped it around her, she stood in front of the mirror. For the first time since girlhood, when she had watched it bloom into maturity, she studied her body, examining it with an almost joyful curiosity. She looked with interest at the outward thrusts and shadowed indentations, wanting to be fully aware of this sequence of undulating curves which Ned had brought to fulfillment.

Ten minutes later, little beads of shower spray still bubbled on her shoulders when the telephone rang, its jabbing sound an invasion of the quiet little kingdom of her apartment. Wrapped in a towel, leaving a tracing of water down the hallway and across the dining area, she lifted the handpiece from its cradle.

It was Katie. Following an apology for the early hour, she asked, "Have you seen Ned?"

"Not since last night. I worked until almost midnight, and he walked me to the car when I left. But I haven't seen him since."

"He didn't say anything about going away?"

"No." Katie's voice touched an alert chord in her. "What's wrong?"

"Nothing really, I guess. But he's not here, and the Jeep's gone. It was gone when we got up at six o'clock. Geoff's leaving in a little over an hour for Atlanta and wanted to talk to him before he left."

"About your move back up there?"

There was a short pause. "No. We're not going to say anything until Geoff meets with Meir and talks with a realtor or two."

Obviously Katie did not wish to discuss their leaving on the phone. Adrienne kept her voice bland when she said, "If he comes by, I'll send him right out there."

"How about you? Are you coming out today?"

"In all truth, Katie, I haven't given it a thought. I just finished my shower when you called, so I'm still in my precoffee mental block."

"Have your coffee, then come out." Katie's voice was drifting away. "This isn't going to be one of my better days, I know."

"All right, I'll be there. If I don't make it before Geoff leaves, wish him good luck for me, and tell him to be careful."

"I will, thanks. See you soon."

After three sips of the second cup of coffee, the black liquid suddenly turned bitter. She slumped in the chair, thinking that too many things were happening she had to keep explaining to herself, a tidal wave of questions flowing over her. Her stability was close to nonexistent.

Neither the Jeep nor the station wagon was in the parking area when, shortly after eleven o'clock, she braked the Toyota to a stop beneath the peppertree. Katie was kneeling in the herb bed in front of the carriage house alternately digging and pushing away the cat, which was thrusting its nose into the soft earth turned by her trowel.

Adrienne walked slowly over to them. Already she felt tired. "Geoff's gone?"

Katie sat back on her haunches and nodded. "About an hour ago."

"And Ned hasn't returned?"

"No."

The cat wandered away from the herb bed to sit staring at her with slitted eyes and a tail curled tightly about its feet. Its neck was rigid, its ears erect. Narrow and unblinking, its almond-shaped blue eyes sought, then found, hers and locked to them. The absolute stillness of the brown body reminded her of an ancient statuette, and, for an instant, she thought of Egyptian tombs and unwrapped mummies. Unable to pull her eyes from the blue stare, she had the disturbing sensation the cat's eyes were more inscrutable than ever, and that its intent examination was going directly to the center of her mind and scanning what was privately hidden there. She was forced to swivel her entire body to look away.

"Thanks for coming."

At the sound of Katie's voice, the outside world rushed in. Whatever had been trying to intimidate her slithered back out into the ripe Florida sunshine, leaving her feeling ridiculous and ashamed.

"Remember? I'm the feminine ally."

Katie nodded. Her green eyes were openings of long tunnels leading to a place where shadows lurked.

"What's wrong, Katie?"

Leaving the trowel stuck in the earth beside a small shrub, Katie stood up, carefully brushing her dirt-speckled knees, her shadowed eyes focused on nothing in particular, and said simply, "I'm frightened. I want so much to get away from here, Adrienne."

"Oh, Katie . . ." Adrienne felt herself being drawn further and further away from any chance of holding tight to her own self-confidence. "What can I say?"

"Nothing." Katie shook her head. "There's nothing anyone can say to help. There's nothing I can even say to myself. Since I saw that red-haired woman in the painting watching me from the studio window, everything has drained out of me. I'm just an imitation of a woman without the guts to fight my way free." She looked down at her feet, then up at the twisted limbs of the peppertrees swaying under their own weight. "There's evil here, Adrienne; and I . . . I practically begged you to come and be affected by it, too."

"You did no such thing! If there's evil here, it came after I did. In fact, I'm the one who had the hallucinations and asked Ned to open the window seat and discover the paintings. No, I chose freely, Katie. Besides . . . besides . . . by coming here I met Ned, well—I don't consider that evil at all."

Katie flashed her a worried but understanding look. "Are you falling in love with him?"

"I—" She did not know what to answer, but while she stood there returning Katie's stare, her flesh began to tingle while a tightness formed in her stomach and slipped lower to her loins.

"You are! You are in love with him." Katie came forward and grasped both her hands. "Oh, Adrienne, please be careful. He's a wonderful guy, but those paintings are doing something to him."

"They've done something to all of us," she said softly. "As I said when you told me you were thinking of leaving, I'm too old and cautious to forget reality."

"I know, but—"

Adrienne squeezed Katie's hands. "I've been in love before. I'm an old hand at it."

"Nobody's ever an old hand at it."

Before she could reply, the Jeep came up the driveway to pull under the tree beside her Toyota. Dressed in a blue T-shirt, jeans and sneakers, Ned slipped from behind the wheel, then took a half dozen packages from the rear seat. His hair was tousled from the wind, and Adrienne saw a dark stubble shadow on his cheeks and jaw.

"Geoff gone?" he asked.

Katie nodded. "About an hour ago. He wanted to talk to you before he left."

"I know." He glanced at the packages in his hands. "It took longer to find what I needed than I anticipated. I'm sorry."

"What did you need so early in the morning?"

"Supplies." He started walking toward the house. "How about lunch?"

Adrienne and Katie looked at each other. Katie shrugged. "Why not?"

"I could get hungry, I guess."

While they ate the chicken salad sandwiches Katie prepared from canned chicken and drank the instant iced tea Adrienne mixed, Ned offered no explanation as to where he had been and what he had purchased, his attitude seeming to be one of vague defensiveness. Not long after they sat down at the table, he withdrew into some inner private chamber from which he remotely conducted his end of the conversation, unable, or unwilling, to fill the long depressions of silence occurring every few sentences. Before long Adrienne found herself wishing she was not at the table.

When at last they were sitting smoking, with only glasses of iced tea before them on the table, Ned looked directly at her, much of the defensiveness gone from his eyes.

"Why don't you plan to have your lunches and dinners with us?" he asked. "I know lunches are an on-again, off-again affair with you, but it doesn't make sense to work here late like you did last night and then fix dinner when you get to your apartment or stop somewhere along the way. Hell, you're one of us." He swung his eyes to Katie. "Don't you agree?"

"All the way."

Adrienne took a swallow of the tea while she willed the embarrassment away. She succeeded, smiled at him, then pursed her lips and blew a kiss at him. "I think it's a fine idea, if you let me pay my share."

He laughed. "Oh, we'll be happy to do that." He finished his tea with a long gulp, then grinding out his cigarette with more care than seemed necessary, pushed himself back from the table. The sparkle in his eyes and the quick, nervous movements of his hands were the giveaways of a person no longer able to control excitement. "There're some odds and ends I want to take care of in the studio. Mind if I excuse myself?"

They told him no.

"Tonight," he said, getting up and pushing his chair under the table, "the meal is on me. Something bordering on the lavish. Steaks, maybe, prepared and served by someone else. A real restaurant meal."

Katie watched him go through the hallway door. "I wonder what that was all about."

"Oh, Katie, don't be so sour."

Katie shrugged, saying nothing. But a few minutes later, while they were rinsing the plates and glasses, Adrienne sensed a nervousness in Katie to match her own and came to realize the big red-haired woman was suffering from a little-girl awkwardness in dealing with the situation, perplexed and very uncertain.

"When we finish here, we'd better go grocery shopping. I really eat a bunch," Adrienne said. The idea did not appeal to her, but she thought wandering through aisles jammed with shopping carts would relieve some of the fear and worry devouring Katie's mind.

"I'm glad Ned asked you to eat with us, and even more glad you agreed."

It was Adrienne's turn not to answer. The simple statement touched her. All the self-confidence which had drawn her to Katie was gone.

Hunched over and mumbling to himself, Ned was working at the taboret, with the cat, as usual, sitting near the paintings, when Adrienne entered the studio to tell him she and Katie were leaving for the supermarket. He made no effort to hide what was on the taboret top, but neither did he identify the tiny piles of powder and the crushed leaves he was mixing, weighing on an apothecary scale and then placing in small glass jars sitting in a row on the top. Though she looked at the items quizzically, Adrienne did not ask about them, hoping he would explain their meaning, wondering when he did not if the disappointment she experienced was justified. She felt she was being excluded from his confidence, and, as she left the room, she wondered if she had ever been taken into it.

Sheila Rosenthal parked beside the Jeep. After turning the ignition off, she sat a long time feeling the foliage-scented heat moving through the open windows to fill the Cougar's interior. For longer than she cared to remember, she had been drawn to this place. Every once in a while, alone, she had driven out here to walk around the weed-infested lawn and the long-decayed garden. She was enthralled with the loamy smell of the earth, the pungent rankness of the gone-wild vegetation.

She got out of the car and walked along the path circling the back of the house to the verandah, wondering as she had so many times why the wide porch was on the side of the house instead of across the front, then recalling, as she always did, it was an addition constructed to overlook the garden. Her eyes moved over the tangled area which had been the garden, along the clapboard walls of the house and around the curling fretwork clinging to the verandah. Although they were making inroads on the creeping decay, she wished Ned and his friends would progress faster with the restoration. Of course, she had to keep in mind, restoration was an expensive business, and they did own their own businesses, which, she imagined, took considerable time to operate.

She knocked rather loudly on the screened foyer door, listening as the sound ricocheted in the empty room.

"Come in. I'm in the studio."

She recognized Ned's voice. When she entered the house, she found him at the north end of the old parlor, standing at a taboret. Flooding through the tall north windows, the afternoon light created a warm haze around him, isolating him, it seemed to her, from all else in the room, even her.

She watched him place two small bottles into a drawer of the taboret, then crumple up the sheets of paper which had been covering the taboret's top. As he threw them into a wastebasket, he turned to her for the first time, and, rubbing his hands on his jean-clad thighs, he smiled, then came to greet her, stepping out of the golden haze.

"Sheila, hello. I'm glad you came by."

"I had some free time," she said, "so I thought I'd drive out to learn if you've come to a decision concerning the paintings. I suppose I could have phoned, but, well . . . I do like this old place, so I used the paintings as an excuse to come out."

"That's wonderful. You're welcome anytime, you know that. But what decision?" There was a noticeable stiffening of his body when he asked the question.

"Why, the one we discussed when Sidney and I were here; the one about framing them and putting them on exhibit."

"Oh—yes." He looked to where the paintings lay in a row on the floor along the baseboard of the west wall. "No. No, I haven't, but I really doubt if I'll want them put out like that, at least not for some time."

"I'm sorry to hear that." She was disappointed but not surprised. She had sensed when she first mentioned it, he was far less than receptive. "I'm going to keep hoping, though; and every now and then I'm going to ask again."

"You do that." The smile accompanying his words was genuine, but he appeared relieved she was not going to insist. "I know I'm being selfish, Sheila, but for now I want to keep them here to study. There's so much information they can give me. I can feel it. I know it for a certainty. And if I allowed them to hang for public viewing, they'd be seen and admired, as they should be, but by people who are unaware of their true value. It would be time lost from my study of them."

"The warmth in them, is that it? I understand the chemist analyzing the paint suffered a heart attack. Did he get his findings to you before his death?"

"No, he didn't. But you're right, it is the warmth, along with other things, I want to study."

She knew the cryptic answer was going to be all he would say, and she knew she had no right to pry further. She walked over to them and stood looking down at the paintings, wishing she had been able to find something concerning them in the few papers on file in the historical society's office.

From within the shadow in which they lay, the women in

the paintings stared up at her. Suddenly their eyes were alive in the glowing flesh tones of their faces. She could not help herself and gave an almost audible gasp, wanting to look at Ned, but finding she could not detach her eyes from the ones gazing up into them. She was unable to check the tiny shudder that ran down her spine. Along her arms and across her shoulders her skin prickled, hot and coarse like fresh abrasions, and, at that moment, she felt sure that she was not looking at paintings at all, but at a row of living women who were studying her with the same curiosity with which she was examining them.

Something akin to dread closed in on her, unexplainable and deep, filling the room around her. She became aware that Ned was watching her, an eyebrow arched, a specter of a smile on his lips, his blue eyes quizzical. At his side a Siamese cat, which had come unnoticed into the room, stared at her from eyes wide with what could be taken as nothing else but sexual desire. She felt trapped between illusion and reality. She tried closing her eyes, but the eyes in the paintings burned through her lowered lids, reaching way into her brain to see the blossoming fear there and expand it.

"Sheila . . ."

The voice came from a distant place beyond the curve of the world.

"Sheila, what's wrong?"

She opened her eyes to see Ned standing before her, a formless shape coming into sharp focus as her eyes lost their visions of the paintings. It was no great surprise that her voice sounded strained and distant when she said, "I don't really know. But for a few moments, I had the most stupid feeling the eyes in those paintings were actually alive and looking at me."

"Others have had the same sensation."

"What is it? An optical illusion of some sort, like the eyes of the Mona Lisa following the viewer around the room?"

"Perhaps. I don't know. It's one of the things I want to study."

"I can certainly understand that." She gave an inward shiver remembering the tangible fear which had claimed her only minutes before. "It would not do at all to have a viewer in a gallery experience what I've just felt."

"No."

Behind Ned, at the north end of the room near the windows, she saw an easel with a canvas resting on it. She wanted to set her mind on a radically different track, but within the room there was nothing other than the photographic equipment not associated with painting, about which she knew nothing, so she directed her attention to the easel and said, "You're working on a painting of your own, I see."

"Yes."

She waited for him to say more, and when he did not, she walked to the easel. The painting was the portrait of a young woman. Voluptuously, the subject, dressed in jeans and a man's white shirt, rested one foot on a high stool, leaning slightly forward with the heavy thrust of her bosom accentuated. Her head was tilted back with her eyes looking at the viewer from beneath partially closed lids, her expression at once vulnerable and haughty. Sheila wondered if the model was capable of registering that commingling of emotions or if Ned had supplied it with his brushes. Color had been applied to the jeans and shirt and was indicated in the blond hair, and the background appeared completed, a rich mixture of blue with reddish undertones, with the stool a burnt umber. But no flesh tones were painted in; the young woman's face, arms and midriff were still the sepia underpainting.

"It's quite good," she said, squinting her eyes to study the modeling patterns. "In fact, it's very good. You are an artist! An excellent one. Is she a local girl?"

"Yes." He hesitated as if he was going to say no more,

but then continued. "It's merely an exercise. It's been several years since I last did a portrait, and I wanted to see if I was still capable of it."

"I don't know the model, of course; however, I'd say you're accomplishing what you're trying for, Ned." Yet while she spoke, something about the uncompleted painting disturbed her. For some reason, it seemed to Sheila she was looking at a picture of a young woman without a soul. She was about to ask Ned when he was planning to add the coloring to the flesh area when he spoke.

"Sheila, maybe I'm way out of bounds with the question I'm about to ask, so if I am, I apologize right now. I've been looking at you here in the studio light. You have a wonderful bone structure. Your face is so neatly chiseled, so very delicate, yet strong with determination, so very classic in many ways. Would you allow me to paint your portrait?"

She was both surprised and flattered; and, to her consternation, temporarily at a loss for words. It made her uncomfortable. Finally she managed to force a controlled chuckle from her tightened throat. "Ned, I thank you, but—"

"Sheila, please don't take offense."

"Offense? Oh, no, Ned, not at all. I'm flattered."

"Then would you do it, Sheila?" He was a young boy with the pressures of excitement building in him. "It wouldn't take a great deal of time. Perhaps two or three hours a week for a few weeks."

Ned stood watching her, his face like that of a person who is fearful he had put together the wrong combination of words when making a very important declaration. Behind him, near the taboret, the cat appeared to be waiting for her answer, too.

She smiled. "Ned, if you really mean it, I'd be honored. I most assuredly would. There's something so old-fashionedly elegant in having your portrait painted, isn't there?"

Ned visibly relaxed. His eyes darted so quickly to the

paintings on the floor and then back to her, she was not certain if they moved or only blinked.

"Could we start next week?"

"I should think so. Let me look at my calendar when I get home, and I'll phone you Monday."

"That's fine."

He walked her to her car, explaining on the way how he visualized her dressed for the sitting and the mood he thought the portrait should convey. The little boy brimming with excitement was gone. Walking beside her was a well-trained, gifted man who worked with beauty.

As she pulled out of the driveway onto the county road, a car slowed, making ready to turn into it. She caught a glimpse of the blond young woman in the driver's seat and recognized her as the woman Ned was painting. As she accelerated, she hoped today Ned would commence to apply the flesh tones to give the young woman a soul.

From where it had taken its place beside the painting of the woman in the purple gown, the cat sat watching. Under its sand-colored fur, its muscles were wire-tense the entire length of its body, tautened to a pressure which could explode into action within a millisecond. Its head was thrust forward on a stretched neck, its ears were laid back and its eyes were merely elongated almond shapes, giving the lean body, from its shoulders to the tip of its nose, a serpentine appearance. The unblinking blue eyes followed Sandi as she sipped from a mug of hot aromatic tea, the tongue flicking in and out as if it, too, was tasting the beverage. Ned was completely ignored as he stood a trifle behind Sandi with his left hand hovering over the partially opened drawer in the taboret.

Sitting in a chair which had been brought from the kitchen, Sandi returned the cat's stare over the rim of the mug. "It sure has an interest in us, doesn't it?"

"What's that?"

"The cat."

"Oh. Well, I guess he's either an art lover or an admirer of beautiful women."

Sandi giggled.

"Is the tea relaxing you?"

"Um-hmm. It's delicious. Where did you get it?"

"I mixed it myself from an old family recipe."

"It's better than Valium. You could make a million with it."

"I might try someday."

Sandi looked over her shoulder at Ned. "I'm sorry I was so tense. I didn't feel uptight at all until you told me I was as stiff as a board. After that, I guess, I tried too hard." She took a long swallow from the mug. "But this helps. I feel all dreamy and loose already."

"Good. Finish it off, then we can get on with the work. There isn't much more I can do today on the canvas, so we won't be long."

"When are you going to color my skin?"

"I'm hoping to come up with the right mixture tomorrow, so when you come back Monday we can start on it. You can come Monday, can't you?"

"Yes."

"Great. Now go ahead and finish the tea."

Sandi tilted her head back and drank the last of the sweetly pungent liquid, then handed the empty mug to Ned, who placed it on the taboret and stood watching her expectantly.

"I think I'm ready now," she said. "But I feel so sleepy . . . Geez, I don't know if I—"

The cat leaned forward, stretching its neck to what seemed an impossible length, its eyes glinting with new interest. The pink tip of its tongue flicked out once again, giving its triangular head an even more pronounced resemblance to a serpent. When Sandi tried to push herself from the chair but settled back with a muted moan, its blue eyes twinkled with amusement and its tail began to swing back and forth, moving faster when it became apparent the woman was asleep.

It turned its attention to Ned, watching his movements as he took from the taboret drawer a hypodermic needle, a length of tubular rubber, several vials and a package of cotton swabs. With them spread before him on the taboret top, he paused for a moment studying Sandi, wiped a hand across his mouth, then took hold of her left arm. While he tightened the rubber tube around it just above the elbow, he began mumbling under his breath. The cat's head nodded as if in satisfaction. Some of the tension melted from its tight body when Ned exhibited a satisfactory skill in drawing blood into the hypodermic, finally sitting back licking a forepaw while Ned swabbed the entry mark with ointment.

Sandi awakened just as Ned placed the materials back into the drawer.

She was startled, looking around the room with widened eyes, then at Ned. "Did I fall asleep?"

"No." He shook his head. "I don't think so."

She rotated her head with a stiff-necked movement. "I sure feel like it. Are you sure?"

"I'm sure. I think you were more tense than we realized, and the tea completely relaxed you, so you just lost touch with the world for a few seconds. You feel okay, don't you?"

"Yeah, fine . . . Only . . ." She shrugged and, without looking, absently scratched her arm where the hypodermic needle had punctured her skin. "Only just kind of mixed up like you feel when you wake up real fast from a quick nap."

Ned looked at his wristwatch. "Why don't we call it quits for the day? If you can be here early Monday, say around noon, we can hit it hard, and if everything goes without a hitch, we should finish the portrait by the end of the week."

"All finished?"

"All finished, yes."

"Geez, that's great—I guess."

"You guess?"

"I like coming here. It's been real nice."

"Maybe I can use you again. Maybe in some photographs."

"That would be great! I mean it."

The cat looked at her, then turned its attention back to its forepaw.

"You're sure you have nothing planned for Monday?"

"No. Nothing."

"Okay, then I'll see you around noon."

"All right. I'll be on time, Ned, and I promise not to get uptight like I must have been today. You have a nice weekend."

"You, too, Sandi."

After the screen door slammed and Sandi's footsteps could be heard on the gravel of the parking area, the cat rose, stretched first its front quarters, then its hind ones, before pacing to a place before the easel where it raised its head to gaze at the painting.

"Well, what do you think? Do you like it, fella?"

Without looking at him, the cat meowed, then strode out of the room. Ned stood listening to the clicking of its nails fade down the hallway into the hot silence of the house.

He wanted a drink. No, he told himself, he more than wanted one: he needed one. All the harmony of the day had been destroyed when he stuck the hypodermic needle into Sandi's arm. He felt he had performed an act of defiance against nature itself, and now apprehension moved in him. He could postulate about an act of science being performed to advance the nearly lost art of portrait painting; it might make it sound neat and acceptable in this high-tech age. Public understanding might be flexible enough to accept that, but he was not sure he was. Instead, by following the instructions in Sebastian's notebook, he stood here now feeling more like Dr. Frankenstein than anyone else.

He pulled open the drawer of the taboret. At the front of it, the small jars nestled together in three neat rows, each jar containing the ingredients of the tea he had brewed Sandi, and the powders to be mixed with the paints, the herbs obtained from the old man living out in the countryside, just this side of nowhere. Goldenseal. Henbane. Foxglove. May-flower. Mandrake. A remark overheard in the drugstore where he had purchased the hypodermic and cotton swabs had directed him to the old man, who gathered and compounded the herbs and who, it seemed, had been waiting for him in his wretched shack in the cypress hammock. Coincidence? Or manipulation? He had run it through his mind so many times that the only answer he was certain of was doubt, and the repeated asking of himself the uncomfortable question: was he a fool involved in a mess over which there was no control? He slammed the drawer shut.

He looked at the uncompleted painting of Sandi. Other than a passing physical weakness and a small confusion, she had not shown ill effects; however, if he was to be truthful with himself, he was using her as an experimental animal. He could think of no other description, and the deception could become heavy on his conscience, yet looking at the uncompleted rendering, the late afternoon sun tinting it with a thin golden patina, he knew he was going to complete it, that he must complete it. Not to finish it would mean only frustration and emptiness, and the terrible sad wondering of what might have been.

CHAPTER

''Something's bugging Katie.'' Ceramic clinked hard on ceramic. Coffee spilled over the lip of the cup into the saucer, but Ned paid no attention, continuing to study the candle flickering in the glazed bowl between them on the table. After a moment, he lifted his attention to Adrienne.

''Oh?'' Adrienne picked up a spoon and dropped her eyes from his gaze.

''Haven't you noticed the way she's behaving?''

Adrienne kept her eyes away from his, aware of the brooding thoughts beginning to pry into her mind. She kept them away by concentrating on the long-handled iced tea spoon that she turned over and over in her fingers, watching the diffused restaurant lighting wink at her in tiny stars from its polished surface. She felt a pulsing in her temple and wondered if her face appeared as pinched as it felt, if in some offhand manner Ned was throwing down a gauntlet, challenging her to lay her thoughts on the table for examination.

''Did you hear me?'' If a frown could be in a voice, she thought, one was in his.

"Yes. And I agree." She lifted her eyes from the spoon to look straight at him, not wanting the conversation to become a clinical tabulation of Katie's actions. She would lie without compunction if he insisted on continuing the discussion in this direction. Any dissecting of her friend's doubts and fears would be betrayal. She said carefully, "I think she's uptight about Geoff's trip."

"I suppose you're right." What hint of chill had been in his voice melted. "You know, if Geoff comes back with a working agreement with Meir, they'd be forced to make drastic operational changes; and, for all her self-assurance, I've the feeling Katie might not be too certain of that. She likes their present life-style." He picked up the linen napkin lying beside his coffee cup, neatly folded it into a triangle and laid it back on the table before looking around the restaurant's smoke-hazed dining room. "I'm sure that's part of it, but I've got this feeling there's something else, too. There's a remoteness about her lately. She's just not the woman I've known for ten years. Instead of behaving like a person who's on the verge of having things break for her, she's reacting to everything like someone defeated by life."

"We all have moods."

"Well, she's in a dark one . . . and I think it's directed at me."

"Oh, Ned."

"That's right, Ad. I think she's discreetly avoiding me, but at the same time, I swear, she seems to be watching me with more than average interest and concern. It's kind of like she's made it her responsibility to always be aware of my whereabouts. I could get a case of nerves, for Christ's sake."

"I think your imagination has slipped into high gear." The first lie—would there be more?

"Maybe so, but I know I'm not spinning my wheels. What about tonight, for example? Why didn't she come with us? I invited her. I wanted her to come, I really did, because I know she's having a hell of a day with Geoff gone. What's she going to accomplish sitting there alone in her apartment? To tell you the truth, I'm beginning to feel shitty about this whole thing—but the problem is, Ad, I'm not sure I should feel that way."

"Katie's an incurable romantic. She undoubtedly thought we should be alone on our first real date." Only a partial lie, but still number two.

"Our first date!" He looked startled, a man just informed he had entered a critical survival experience. "My God, you're right. This is the first time we've actually been out together."

"How do you like it?" There was a touch of mischief in her tone.

"The best date I've ever had." He looked at her for a long time, and as he did she saw his eyes widen, then narrow, as they would when viewing a very valuable, very cherished object. Something in his voice was slightly out of balance, on the soft side, when he spoke. "The very best."

His reaction was not what she had expected. Her cute little question had trapped her. She was aware of the shifting and tugging inside her again of desire. It occurred so frequently, she no longer felt embarrassed. She was aware of the inner warmth rise to glow on her cheeks as the juices in her healthy body stirred in response to the unique man across the table. Self-containment was gone.

When she heard Ned speaking to her, she looked at him, but he was blurry because of the misty dampness in her eyes. The golden light from the candle in its bowl was a vagrant illumination on his face, giving his features a mystic form.

"Adrienne," he said very slowly, his voice still unbalanced and soft. "I'm going to tell you something, but I've got to be honest and inform you that what has happened, I didn't mean to happen. Too many things needed to be done, I thought, before I was ready to allow it to occur, but within the last two weeks everything has slipped away from my control.'' He reached across the table to take one of her hands, then very simply said, ''I've fallen in love with you, Adrienne Lewis.''

''And I with you, Ned Anderson.''

How easy it was to say. The words must have been incubating in her for a long, long time.

Each had the wisdom to say no more.

Eventually Ned gave her hand an extra squeeze. ''Should we go?''

She nodded.

They were using Adrienne's car. Ned, who was driving, fumbled for the headlight switch, turning on the windshield wipers before finding the correct one. Adrienne laughed at his mumbling comments but nodded toward the southwest. ''It's probably good you found the wipers, because you might need them. Look down there.''

He leaned over the steering wheel to look in the direction she indicated. ''Holy Christ, yes. That's a storm and a half.''

Against the blackness of the night sky, a thunderhead towered upward, clouds piled upon clouds, their billowing mounds laced with the flares of rampant flame as lightning bolted through the caverns inside them. Over the earth's noises, rumbling closer and closer, thunder rolled.

At the exit from the restaurant's parking lot, Ned stopped the car and grinned at her, but his voice was filled with a very special caring in which there was no capacity for lurid meaning when he asked, ''Your place or mine?''

In the stifling heat of the car, she could feel the warmth of him. She wanted to slide across the seat to his side and throw her arms around him, but instead, with an audacity she did not know she possessed, she returned his grin. ''Mine's closer . . . and it has air-conditioning.''

Twenty minutes later, when they were walking from the car to the outside door to Adrienne's apartment unit, the first splattering of rain came. It fell in big, plump drops which hit the asphalt of the parking lot and the cement of the walks with solid ploppings, and by the time they reached the building's door, the wind began, chilled, pushing before it the smell of dust-dry earth and wilted vegetation.

Ned looked up at the fat storm fingers reaching across the sky from the thunderhead. "It's going to be a bad one."

Adrienne put an arm around his waist. "We won't notice."

When it spread over the city, the storm stalled. It hung like a finely architectured vault in the sky, bombarding the air with lightning jabs and monstrous thunder jolts. At first the rain came in wind-whipped tatters, but shortly, wave after wave of it lashed across the city, cascading down closed windows and backing up inadequate sewer systems.

Adrienne and Ned lay side by side on her bed. Purring in its room somewhere in the building, the central air-conditioning held the muggy heat of the storm outside the room while spreading a layer of chill over their naked flesh. The muted illumination of a bedside lamp floated a misty pool of amber around them. So far they had only lain quietly listening to the storm, neither wanting to hurry the affirmation of the flesh, already knowing the needs and the willingness of the other.

Eventually, with what seemed a shy, almost exploratory, movement, Ned laid a hand on the flat sweep of Adrienne's belly, then gently began slipping it in delicately patterned circles over the taut flesh around the small mysterious cup of her navel. She shivered, then moaned and felt the desire within her exploding into want.

Neither of them knew or cared how much time had passed before they lay in silence as deep as a vacuum. The storm had moved on as fast as it had arrived. Around them the amber mist of the lamp was a soft membrane between them and the sudden pains and irrationalities of the outside world.

Adrienne sighed. She looked down the length of her body, at the round, thrusting breasts and the sleekly domed belly. Once more she was aware of it as a joyous possession capable of bestowing as well as receiving unbounded pleasure, not merely a tightly structured framework of bone, muscles and flesh. What she had just experienced was very valuable and miraculous, and she wanted it to happen again and again. She wanted this newly discovered, strong body to delight this man by her side in as many ways as it would function for his pleasure.

"Are you awake?" Ned's voice was drowsy.

"Um-hmmm."

"Come live at the house." He rolled onto his side and propped his head up on a hand to look down at her to study her response to the abrupt statement. "It makes all kind of sense, you know. Convenient for your work. No apartment rent and utility expenses. All kinds of sense, really."

"Including?" she smiled.

"Oh—" He cupped his free hand over the mound of her right breast. "Togetherness."

It was a replay of the day she had gone to the house to look at the rooms. Once more there was no clinical analyzing of pros and cons. Complicating factors were ignored. Only briefly did her mind try again to send warning impulses, but as before, very weak ones, already knowing that the unpleasant memories of the house would be rejected.

"When?"

"As soon as you can."

For the first time in her adult life, she was coy. "I will, if you make love to me again."

He laughed a big, booming laugh, wrapped his arms around her, then rolled onto his back, pulling her on top of him. "Then you'd better start packing, Adrienne Lewis."

The rain splashed with steady force against the windows, transforming the smooth pane into a rippled mirror. Katie stood staring at the distorted creature peering in at her from out of the storm-torn darkness. Its face was wavering, melting into thick globs which snaked in rivulets along the jawline, then down a neck becoming shorter and shorter, while from either side of the dissolving features, strands of red hair squirmed across the decomposing flesh like plump earthworms gorging on the liquefied features. She clenched her teeth, shook her head and watched the head out there in the darkness mimic the movement.

"Jesus!"

She turned her back to the window, wondering how much of the grotesqueness she had been looking at was in the rain-distorted reflection and how much was in her mind. Drawing deep breaths, she fought a rapid beating of her heart and a trembling in her hands. She saw a spread book lying facedown in the wicker chair, but could work up no interest in it, so she ignored it and went to the kitchen and took a Diet Pepsi from the refrigerator. Going back to the living room, she stood in the middle of it looking at the window from this safer distance, knowing that there was a darkness in her mind which was an extension of the darkness outside. Never in her life could she remember having felt so all alone.

He had only been gone thirteen hours, but already her mind and body were missing Geoff. She took a swallow from the Pepsi bottle, wiped a drop from her chin with a forefinger and thought with luck, and some manipulation of circumstances, they would be away from this damn place by the end of the summer. From then on it would be no more than a bothersome memory of a badly discordant time.

With all the windows closed, heat was building up in the apartment. Already the Pepsi was warming, with droplets of condensation running down the bottle, and under her blouse and shorts she could feel sweat dampening her skin. Not only was she lonely, she decided she was uncomfortable and bored. Tonight all the laws of nature had become vindictive mandates proclaimed against her personally. It had been a ruefully adolescent act, she knew, to refuse Ned's invitation to dinner; still, Adrienne deserved this time to learn more about the man with whom she was certainly falling in love. God, it seemed a stupid, ponderous joke, this whole episode of paintings and Ned and Adrienne.

She carried the half-finished Pepsi into the kitchen, tried to find a stopper to seal in the carbonation, and when she could not, poured the drink down the drain, rinsed out the bottle and set it on the narrow drainboard. The wind momentarily howled in a whipping gust that rattled several loose windows, then somewhere found what must have been a loose plank to bang with the erratic beat of a demented drummer. Lightning crashed, its brilliant flare turning the area into the center of a booming explosion that shook the carriage house to the foundations of its solid construction, causing the tired wood to groan in protest against the assault. The air filled with the scent of hot, rampaging electricity, touched with the smell of what Katie took for the scent of burning sulfur. Almost immediately, the wind and rain scrubbed the smell away.

She went back to the window. A wave of rain washed across it, opaqueing it for an instant, then receded. The night suddenly calmed. Only a drizzle misted the darkness, as if the storm had blown itself to extinction with its final onslaught. She raised the window, drawing a deep breath as cool air flooded into the apartment. With the tension releasing its grasp, a synthesized peace settled on her, no more than the spreading of a thin balm over the jumbled nerve tangles still coiling in her, but enough so she savored the freshness of the rain-washed night with an all but sensuous pleasure. Enough, too, to realize that what was occurring in her mind was a malignancy which warped thinking in such a way that evil and foreboding became its prime topics. Giving a small shiver, she left the window to pick up the book, thinking she would turn on the radio to an easy-listening station.

The cry was that of a small child.

Startled, she returned to the window and looked down into

the parking area. In the darkness there were no details, only a cavernous spread of black within black. She heard only rain dripping from foliage, a car swishing on the wet asphalt of the county road. She shrugged and turned away.

It came again. Louder, as it would if the child had moved closer, pleading with her to come to it.

She leaned against the screen. "Who's down there?"

The cry was more a wail this time, reaching up at her from the parking area.

"Answer me, dammit!"

There was no answer, but she thought she heard movement, or rather sensed something going from one place to another in the black emptiness beneath the window. A cold thing took position between her shoulders and began to uncoil and spread down her spine.

"Meow—"

"You! You!" She screamed in rage and disbelief. "You crummy cat, I'll wallop you a good one."

She saw it now, in the middle of the parking area, looking up at her with eyes impossibly glinting in the night. Neither moved, their interlocking stares holding them bound to each other, until, slowly, like water leeching through a porous container, Katie felt her anger, then her will, draining away, siphoning along the path of sight toward the cat's eyes.

Then, either tired of the game it was playing with her or recalling something awaiting it in another part of the night, the cat stood up, stretched and walked in the direction of the house.

An oppressive stillness settled on the apartment and surrounding area. A tiredness laid claim to Katie, not a welcome, wholesome tiredness, rather one which made her stomach queasy and her head fill with fuzz. She was disgusted with herself, because the pea-brained nonsense with the cat had restoked the fear she had managed to smother, scaring the hell out of her. Neither the book nor the radio interested her. She snapped off the apartment lights and went to bed.

She did not know what awakened her. She was sprawled nude across the wide bed, looking straight at the gray rectangle of the open window, which was no more than a pale blotch in the surrounding darkness, until her eyes focused and her mind awakened enough to receive the image.

Needing a drink to moisten her mouth, she swung her legs across the bed, stubbing her toe on the footboard, then sat staring at the window, watching only wisps of clouds drifting across a moonlighted sky. Nothing remained of the storm.

At first she was not certain what was holding her attention, but, whatever it was, it was something not belonging in the view from the window and elusive enough she could not define it. She hunched forward and began a section-by-section scanning of the view. When she was a third of the way across the scene, she saw it. A transparent fan of thinly hued red light spilled from the parlor windows into the driveway, washing the undersides of the overhanging tree limbs a pale, watery pink.

She pushed herself off the bed and went to the window. At first there was nothing more than the eerie light to be seen, but then the moon-shadowed darkness relinquished its hold enough for her eyes to discern movement in the red, dark forms crossing and recrossing, growing and then receding. Shaking her head, she left the window, went to the chair on which her blouse and shorts hung, put them on before slipping into her sandals, then walked swiftly to the outside door.

She damned herself as she walked slowly across the parking area, emphatically telling herself that she had allowed herself to be ensnared in the trap of her own fears. From the first time she had seen the paintings of the women, there had been a slow transformation in her character. Even while she tried to stop its disintegration, little bits and pieces of her were chipped away each day, leaving only a fear-corrupted person.

The night breathed an unusual chill on her, withdrawing whatever hospitality its clean freshness originally offered after the stuffiness of the apartment. Haunted by the remembered woman in the purple gown watching from the studio window, the driveway became a path enticing her to stroll to a dark land where nightmares dwelt. She hesitated, looking slowly around.

Ahead of her, the pale, red glow lost its fan shape. It became no more than a blurred, undefined stain in the night. For another moment, she remained still, waiting for what she was not sure, but uneasily aware of danger. Finally she moved on toward the looming bulk of the house, carefully placing one sandaled foot before the other on the noisy gravel. Playing a game of hide-and-seek, the moon hid itself behind the trees in the front lawn, so now, except for the red glow, the darkness was complete, unending and muffling.

When she was a dozen paces from the parlor window, she heard the voices and the music. The voices were a jumble, all speaking at once in no unified cadence, while the music came as a faraway echo of ghostly pain. She stopped, holding her breath, listening intently to sounds she knew it was impossible for her to be hearing because they did not exist, and as she listened to them she became aware of vague movement, then saw shapes going back and forth across the driveway as well as slipping among the trees lining the driveway's far side. Then slowly she saw them for what they were. Shadows. Shadows cast by bodies moving in front of a light source.

There were people in the studio!

Her first impulse was to run back to the carriage house to phone the sheriff. If Ned and Adrienne had returned bringing friends, there would be cars in the parking area, but not even Adrienne's Toyota was there. Yet she hesitated, continuing to listen to the voices and music coming from what should be an empty room. And while she stood there, something hideous began reaching for her from the half-opened studio window, something drifting on the frail strands of music which, with a terrible strength, enticed her toward the window. She took a forward step, then another. Now she could define the voices better: they were women's voices. Women moaning, whimpering or singing. A voice or two speaking sharply. Inside her veins, she felt her blood turn raw and cold as she took the final step to the window.

She pressed herself against the side of the house, pressing her shoulder on the hard wood to help her keep her balance, then cautiously looked through the window.

She stared into the center of a savage dream.

The diluted red glow spreading across the driveway was thick inside the room, like a blood-tinted liquid, filling it from wall to wall, wavering with distorted ripples in a slow-motion replica of firelight. The music was soft, sensuous, a vagrant blend of sweetness, passion and despair coaxed from what sounded like the strings of a lute. Whether from the redness or a source she could not see, a stream of warmth came through the window drying the moisture in her eyes and tingling the skin on her forehead. An odor accompanied the warmth, causing her nose to wrinkle and her throat contract. Sharp, pungent. It was the smell of dark things burning.

Throughout the red gloom moving figures appeared to weave like underwater growths caught in passing currents as the magenta ripples laced like tentacles around them. All of the ghostly figures were women. Most of them were nude, but a few had remnants of clothing clinging to them. Looking more beastlike than human in the eerie movement of that red haze, some of the women were kneeling with their faces pressed tight against the hardwood floor, moaning deep in their throats. Others, sweat gleaming like a delicate coating of crushed jewels on their hides, their pliant muscles and tendons bulging under taut flesh, twisted and writhed in a languid parody of a dance in time to the spiraling murmurs of the lute.

Wandering through the fluttering tentacles, a tall, stately woman, at whose side a dog paced, wove her way among the women, swinging a censer, leaving behind her a fragrant trail of cloying scent, strong and sensuous. At the side of the room opposite the front windows, two women, a black-haired one and a blonde, stood against the wall, watching. Now and then one of them would leave her place to walk around the room, stopping to watch a dancer or study a kneeling woman, then, uttering a snarling sound of anger, slap the hapless one who had been the subject of her scrutiny, laughing at the cry or whimper of pain her blow brought forth. Under the sharp, unknown smell and the heady aroma of the incense, Katie picked out the scents of terror.

At first, struggling with her senses, Katie could not define the behavior she was witnessing, but shortly what each of the women in the studio was doing became apparent. Each of them was performing an act of ritualistic supplication.

The music struck a wild, discordant note. In the southwest corner of the room something stirred. The redness undulated in waves from the motion in the corner. The kneeling women clawed their fingers into the floor. The dancers stopped in midmotion, straining to hold firm the poses in which they found themselves. Both the black-haired woman and the blonde pulled themselves to rigid attention facing the corner. The dog whimpered, then lay down at the feet of the tall woman, who held the censer high.

A more definite shifting swirled in the red haze. A shape, tall and manlike, but bulky and without definition, stood in the corner looking at the women, studying them one by one, giving the impression of formulating a dark decision. As it stood there, its presence filling the room, it grew larger and became blacker and was touched with malevolence. The strange, acrid scent grew more pungent and drifted throughout the room. All the women were breathing hard, trembling in spite of obvious attempts to hold muscles still, each one consumed with her own brand of terror.

"Lorraine, come to me!"

Heard like a sound coming through a tunnel, the voice in the eddying mists was guttural, rasping like burned tree limbs rubbing together in a hot wind.

A bleat of fear came from one of the kneeling women, a voluptuously sturdy, brown-haired woman in her late twenties. She looked up, her eyes showing white all around the irises, the birth of absolute terror shining in them. A tiny smear of blood appeared on her chin from the underlip she bit through. She looked pleadingly at the other women around her, but they ignored her as they would an unwanted creature which had managed to find its way into their midst. She was alone in her terror. She knew it, knew there was no help to be offered her. With a final look around the room, she made a meaningless little noise, then lowered her head and began to crawl toward the southwest corner of the room and the dark, waiting figure. It stood quietly, watching the workings of shoulder and hip muscles in the strong body as it approached.

When the woman was before it, the black shape reached down with what might have been a hand to clutch her by her hair. A vicious yank brought her to her knees, then another pulled her toward the bulk of the hidden thing. The haze swirled around them, reddened and thickened to an opaque whirling of tentacles which closed tightly upon themselves.

A long, slow moment passed. The women remained as they were in their labors to hold overstrained muscles in rigid stillness. Finally from the corner came the sound of a meaty slap and a squeal of pain, followed by a gruff laugh.

Immediately the women became animated in a quick succession of body movements accompanied with a warbling of giggles and chattering. It was the giddy release of compressed emotions tautened by terror.

"Dear God, no!" Katie heard the whimpering, not at first recognizing it as her own.

She stepped back from the window, her legs working stiffly as though unused to movement. Inside her mind, there were no thoughts, only a great warping as it fought to understand the insanity to which it had been exposed, but it could not cope, and around its edges it began to crumble.

She had just seen the unbelievable.

She had seen the women within the studio over and over again, and she had hated them each and every time she saw them. She frantically fought to reject the information her crumbling mind was screaming at her, because if she accepted it, she would be forever lost in the netherworld of insanity. The women she had just watched performing their rite of fear were the women in the paintings.

"No!"

She stumbled back to the window. Despite the horror raging in her, a splinter of reason told her she must look into the window once more.

"Oh, no . . . no . . ."

The red-haired woman who had watched her that rainy night when her womanhood had been drained away was once again staring at her through the open window.

Naked this time, the purple gown discarded somewhere in the depths of the red haze behind her, the woman stood framed in the casement. Elegant in a tall, rounded sweep of taut curves, she gazed out into the night, remote from all that was occurring behind her.

Before Katie could escape into a shadow, the woman saw her. Her handsome face twisted into a mask of raw hate, and through that mask her green eyes snapped with such potent rage there were darts of blue-green flame Katie could all but feel singeing her own face.

The darkness that had descended on it momentarily lifted from Katie's mind, allowing her to ask, "Who—what—are you?"

The woman laughed.

"Answer me! Please . . ."

Ignoring her, the woman looked back into the studio, calling out, "Come and see who is here."

Twittering laughs, accompanied by the padding of bare feet, came from behind the veil of the red haze. Forms rushed through it, and suddenly the window framed a dozen peering women.

"It's the red-haired one who looks like you, Corrine."

"She's the one who hates us so."

"No more than I hate her."

Katie tried to cry out, but too much of her strength had been drained away. The flow of time ceased; only the naked figures, the contorted faces and the eyes watching her with burning malice existed. All else was lost in a contorted darkness rushing around her. Her legs started to give way. She stumbled back a step, then another until the gravel of the driveway rolled under her sandals.

A screech from the window burrowed into her escaping consciousness. It was a fathomless scream, a fury tearing the night assunder.

"Kill her! Kill her! Kill her before she kills us!"

"Yes! Yes! She says she wants to cut us to ribbons with a pair of shears."

Katie heard answering cries within the studio, then running feet. She heard herself screaming in reaction, felt her heart trying to rip itself loose in her chest. The night became charged with hatred and approaching violence. With another scream breaking through the constricted muscles of her throat, she stared back at the women to see two leaning from the window, arms and legs braced on the sill, preparing to crawl out.

From off to her left came a sharp banging, immediately followed by wood creaking. For an instant, a silence, as terrible as the screaming voices, descended on the night, creating an insulation behind which Katie sensed things stealthily moving in a circle around her. Realization jammed its way into the clogged cells of her brain. Some of the women had crept out the side door and were now standing out there, between her and the safety of the carriage house.

Instinct took command of her action. She shot a fleeting glance at the window, saw that one woman had crawled through it and was advancing toward her with upraised, taloned hands. She spun and ran along the driveway in the direction of the carriage house. A scream of rage rose in the darkness, repeated itself, then was accompanied by another. Answering cries echoed back and forth beneath the pepper and oak trees. With pale skin sheening in the night light, tangled hair drifting in clouds around burning eyes, long-fingered hands formed into taloned claws, she saw them coming for her from under the peppertree and from behind the parked Jeep. Her heart pumped huge amounts of adrenaline through her veins. Her long legs stretched their strides, and across her shoulders muscles bunched to brace themselves for the coming impact of butting into the solidly fleshed bodies.

Approaching from each side, two of them rushed her simultaneously. They collided with her in the middle of the parking area, knocking her off balance and breaking her stride. Four hands clutched at her hair, grasping for handfuls of it with which to pull her to her knees. Screaming, eyes wide but unseeing, she kicked and twisted and wrenched, driving a fist into a leering face, an elbow into an arched stomach. The powerful muscles in her legs expanded with explosive force, lunging her forward with a burst that broke her free of the clutching hands, then carried her nearly to the bottom of the outside stairs leading up to the apartment.

Curses snarling from her twisted lips, a brown-haired woman, doubled forward from the waist, charged with her head aimed directly at Katie's stomach. Katie sidestepped, whirled, threw her hips out to take the blow from a shoulder on her flank, then, completing the move, spun and raked her nails along the woman's back. Howling in pain and frustration, the woman fell to her knees on the gravel, and with a final leap, Katie sprang away from her to reach the bottom step of the stairs.

Behind her, in a shoulder-to-shoulder semicircle, the women crept closer. Crouched low, darts of hellfire erupting from their eyes above hands clawed before swinging breasts, and thighs bulging with tensioned muscles, they resembled a pack of predatory animals surrounding a hunt victim.

Katie backed up one step, feeling for the tread with a quivering foot, never removing her eyes from the women gathered below. Another step, then another. She was more than halfway up the staircase now, with the women bunched at the bottom making no attempt to follow. Three or four more steps, instinct told her, then she could chance turning her back on them to make the final dash for the landing and the door. Shadows loomed around her. Her legs shook.

She knew she was near the three-quarter distance up the stairs and stopped to ensure herself of her footing, not removing her eyes from the women below, then drew a deep breath and whirled around, springing upward in a leap to clear two steps. In the middle of the leap, a scream of shock and terror tore from her throat.

On the landing outside the apartment, two women stood. The black-haired one and the blonde from the two nude paintings, the two who had behaved as enforcers in the studio, grinned wickedly down at her. From her low angle, they both looked far too tall against the night sky, giantesses partially silhouetted before the distant stars.

At that terrible instant, Katie's mind shrank in upon itself, turning off its circuits, as if ceasing to function would save it from destruction. It became a dead mass within her skull. She stood helpless as the two women began to descend the stairs. Her eyes followed the movements, trying to alert the turned-off brain behind them with their images of approaching death. They did not succeed.

Her lips moved in words that whispered into the night. "God, please help me."

The black-haired woman was on the step beside her, laughing, then raised a hand to place it flat on Katie's chest. Katie stared down at the spread fingers between her breasts, then at the woman's face. She felt a great depression, but no longer any fear. While their stares locked to one another, both women knew that death was only a moment away.

Then the woman gave a sharp push. Katie stumbled backward, lost her balance and felt her feet slip off the tread of the step. Her right arm swung up instinctively, and her hand caught briefly in the other woman's hair, clutched a strand, held tight to it, then tore it loose as her body weight pulled her backward. As she fell away, a fingernail scraped across the woman's left cheek, opening the skin from below the eye to the corner of the mouth.

Silently the women at the bottom of the stairs watched her tumble into a backward somersault, twist halfway down to bounce twice on her left side, then flip into a final forward somersault ending on the hard-packed earth at the bottom of the steps. On the way down her big body made heavy thudding noises against the wooden stairs . . . and mixed with those sounds were the snapping noises, like twigs cracking, coming from inside it as its sturdy framework broke.

She lay on her back beside the herb bed. One arm was bent beneath her with its hand clenched into a fist around a strand of black hair. Blood crawled in wriggling worms from her nostrils and the corners of her mouth, drawing scriggly lines of stickiness across her cheeks. Under her head, the ground was warm and damp, and she knew it was from the blood seeping out of the break in the back of her skull. She did not know how long she had lain at the foot of the stairs, but all the pain had finally gone from her; only the drawing of a breath was difficult, near to impossible, yet by panting she could suck in gulps of air to partially fill her hungry lungs.

After the chattering women had stopped looking down at her to walk away into the night, the pain, for a long while, tore at her in great, gnawing bits. Now, though, she felt only jumbled up and squashed inside. She could not move, and she knew some of the things jumbled in her were broken bones in her legs and pelvis.

No one would believe her when she told them what had occurred. They would be sure an accidental fall had turned her into a demented paranoid. But Geoff would believe her. When he returned, he would help her convince people of the terrible truth about those paintings.

"Oh, God, I want him here now . . ."

She heard paws on the gravel pacing slowly from the direction of the house, and she suddenly felt grateful to the cat for coming to her. Until she heard the paw sounds, she did not know how alone she really felt, thinking that at least the cat would give her company until Adrienne and Ned came home.

The cat stood beside her looking down at her face with its wide blue eyes following the blood curling from her nose and mouth, its tongue flicking in and out as if tasting the salty liquid. All of a sudden, she was apprehensive before its unblinking stare. Abruptly she wanted the cat to go away.

The cat purred far down in its throat and moved away, slowly strolling down the length of her left side, brushing along her thigh, then came back up her right side, brushing along her right leg. Back beside her head, its eyes once more locked with hers to force their blue gaze into the center of her pupils, then bore through them into the most private parts of her being. Helplessly looking back at it, she knew it was evaluating what it saw in there.

With no tensing of muscles, no shift in eye contact, the cat sprang onto her chest. Its claws dug into her as it turned twice in a circle, then sat between her breasts, its eyes refocusing on hers.

She tried to scream at it to move, to yell that she could not breathe with it sitting on her. Its weight was upsetting the delicate balance of her broken rib cage, forcing it down so hard on her lungs that her torn muscles could not lift it. New pains washed over her. She felt the little strength remaining in her flooding away. For the first time, the fear of death came to her. Her tortured lungs, mostly empty now, begged frantically for air as down in her throat she felt a cough moving upward, tickling the membranes. It erupted from her mouth with a hacking noise and a foam of blood. Her lungs deflated.

The cat stretched out its neck so its face hung only inches from Katie's as it watched the death throes deforming her features. It shifted its position in excitement when her eyes bulged upward out of their sockets and her mouth gaped wide in an impossible try at gulping air. In a frantic last bid to throw the weight off its chest and save itself, her strong body arched. The cat hissed, dug its claws into the dying flesh and continued to watch.

A wan first dawn's sky silhouetted individual tree branches when the cat finally jumped from the dead body. Stretching its front, then its hindquarters, leisurely, it sniffed twice at the cold flesh, then paced in the direction of the house. It did not stop to look back.

Adrienne laid her inventory list aside and sat quietly on the verandah steps staring out across the brown ghost of the garden, listening to the chatter coming from the hidden world of insects. Through the open foyer door behind her, the voices of Ned and Sheila Rosenthal were a quiet murmur in the stifling heat, a part of the tidy sound of life going on. She looked at the slanting light from the afternoon sun touching the barren stalks and flimsy weeds with patient fingers of gold, trying to tease from them the beauty they had once displayed. It could not. The plants and shrubs were dead, dead, dead . . . just as Katie was dead, dead, dead.

A week and a half had only splintered the pain so the horror of it no longer challenged the sanity, but the emotional fragments were still scattered in the limbo of dormant sorrow. Eventually the pieces would reassemble and time would blunt the despair. But was the length of time required? And throughout all that time, the world would move on in indifference.

She stuffed the inventory list into a crack between the tread board and a riser on the steps, stood up slowly, then walked just as slowly through the weeds, all but obliterating the garden path. There was no way for her to extract herself from the whirlpool drawing her toward a darkness where nightmares were spawned.

She came to the bench without realizing she had walked the entire length of the garden, and wanted to immediately turn away from it to retrace her steps to the verandah, but, instead, she stood looking at its rust-stained, crumbling curlicues of iron. For a few short moments, it had been her and Katie's secret hideaway where the big red-haired woman spoke the cold truth of her fears, truths which had found a nesting place in her own mind. She took a step toward the house, but stopped; running away would acknowledge her cowardice. She sat down.

During the final days of her life, Katie had been a frightened quarry stalked by personal predators. Something unique inside her had decayed, so the woman who had died twelve nights ago, Adrienne knew, was not the exuberant woman who had greeted her in the parking area a month before. The paintings had destroyed the first woman before the fall killed the second one.

She shifted her position on the bench. Unloosened by the moment, the terrible memory curled in her head as it had been doing for the past week.

When she and Ned found Katie's body, its right hand was clenched tightly around a lock of black hair. Making no comment, Ned had pried the hair loose from the stiffly closed fingers and stuffed it into his shirt pocket. Later, when the sheriff's deputies came to investigate, then to give their verdict of accidental death, and when the reporter from the Orlando *Sentinel* came for details, he made no mention of the lock of hair. Why? she wondered then, and still did. And why had she said nothing? She shook her head, drawing in a deep breath of the heavy air that smelled of foliage rot. Do not seek esoteric answers, she told herself; leave the scattered remnants of your thinking as they are.

The time she knew Katie had been all too short, with the pleasant memories now defaced by the brutal argument between Ned and Geoff, whose grief-burdened accusations of Ned's obsession with the paintings became howls of loathing. She never saw Katie again after the horrible moments at the bottom of the stairs. Geoff sent the body to Atlanta, loaded his equipment in a U-Haul truck and stormed away from their lives. Decency demanded she attend the funeral in Atlanta, emotional judgment said no. Neither she nor Ned had gone.

A mockingbird in a nearby oak tree began a repetitious call of meaningless gossip. The sound returned the estranged world to her, made her aware of the soreness in the back of her thighs from the rust-serrated edge of the bench's seat, the petty pain telling her she must do something, any little physical action that would pull her mind back from the rim of depression it was skirting. If only hurt thoughts and memories could have bandage and splints applied like hurt arms and legs. She stood up. Startled, the mockingbird gave a compulsive cry and flew away.

She felt eyes watching her. She looked around and saw no one. She knew she was alone in the hot desolation, but the feeling persisted, would not be explained away, and as it continued she became aware, those unseen eyes were staring at her with barely suppressed carnal want. She drew in her breath sharply, startled at that impression. She looked slowly around again, and still saw nothing other than the long-dead vegetation. What kind of power, she wondered, was in a stare that she was able to identify the expression in the eyes from which it came? She ran her tongue around her lips, feeling the dread move in around her at the thought of an unknown thing in the garden with her, studying her. Across the dead patch of land, the afternoon shadows shifted like dark ribbons riding a thin current of warm air.

Something rustled in the dry stalks off to her right, something, she saw, that was golden brown prowling through the tangled thicket in an unhurried retreat. The cat. As she watched it, it turned its head to look at her over its left shoulder. She could see its eyes in what could only be described as a grinning face: pale, intense blue, gleaming with a sexual desire, in the shards of light among the rotted stalks of foliage. She gasped. A coldness slithered inside her rib cage, and, for a frightful moment, she felt it was not a cat but a demonic presence in the feline body, a creature existing on evil.

Sheila and Ned were standing at the verandah railing when she reached the steps. They ceased their conversation so abruptly when she came within hearing distance she had the impression they were discussing her, but, as if sensing her awkwardness, Ned said, "Sheila's telling me she's going to find funds in the historical society's treasury to restore the garden."

"Oh, that would be marvelous." The pleasure she felt was out of proportion to the information. She climbed the steps to stand beside them at the railing, implausibly content to be with people as she scanned the garden in search of the cat. "It must have been very elegant in its day."

Sheila nodded. "It was one of the most beautiful gardens in the central portion of the state, Mrs. Lewis. And without question, it was unique in its design and layout."

"What a shame Sebastian's and his wife's horrible deaths occurred in it." Adrienne swung her eyes across the dead brown area, pockmarked with weed stubbles, and remembered the subdued apprehension she had experienced the first time she looked at it, and then the torn face floating through the night as if trying to escape the death the garden contained. And now . . . now the thing that looked like a cat prowling out there.

"Yes." Sheila's voice trailed away into the heat. "It gives the place an eerie feeling, doesn't it?" She looked at Ned with a shallow smile. "Somewhat like the paintings."

Sheila was dressed in tennis togs. A powder-blue knit top stretched tightly across surprisingly full breasts, and a pleated short skirt gave strong-muscled legs a sturdy look. Her dark brown hair was held back from her forehead by a blue, white and yellow paisley headband. She was a compact woman when seen in this style of dress, Adrienne noticed, with a well-rounded, ripe figure, though the healthy sexuality was somehow out of character with her charmingly confused participation in social promotions.

Apparently she became aware of Adrienne's oblique appraisal of her, because she smiled self-consciously, then gave a comfortable laugh. "This is not really the outfit one might select in which to have their portrait painted, is it? Ned at first suggested a formal gown, but I persuaded him to let me wear this. I don't play very well, but I'm a tennis buff, and I feel comfortable in it. Besides, I do have a formal photographic portrait with my husband in which I'm wearing a gown." She stopped, as if aware she was on the verge of rambling, looked down at herself, then sighed. "Well, maybe it's a little out of line. I look at what Ned has done so far, and I feel more risqué than athletic."

"Sheila, there's no need for that." Ned appeared embarrassed.

"If you can do with me what you've done with that young woman Sandi, I'll be delighted. Her portrait is exquisite, absolutely beautiful. So lifelike . . . so nearly human. It's every bit as fine as the ones done by Sebastian, Ned. I mean that." She turned to Adrienne. "Don't you agree, Mrs. Lewis? Whatever he discovered in his studies of them, he's certainly applying it."

Ned's smile became rather fixed. His eyes narrowed slightly, then he gave a deprecatory shrug of his shoulders. "I think I'm learning."

Sheila then gave her full attention to Adrienne. "I hope we weren't out of line, Mrs. Lewis, but Ned wanted me to see your work, so he took me into your workshop. You know, you're very much an artist, too. You must be very nimble with your hands."

"Just patient and determined."

"No, it's more than that. In your field, you're as much an artist as Ned is in his."

"Thank you."

"No, no. That's a statement of fact, not a mere compliment. In fact, I've a corner in our family room where a bouquet of your flowers would fit nicely. Would you sell me a half a dozen?"

Sheila was so obviously sincere, Adrienne felt no discomfort by the request. The woman was, it had to be admitted, a social animal who was artfully employing her charm to burrow through another's self-defense, without even a hint of patronage or bribery. Adrienne quoted her a price 25 percent below her usual three flowers for $12.50. Sheila said she would pick them up at her next sitting, then insisted she must absolutely leave, telling them there was a City Council meeting that evening at which she was scheduled to present a petition to eliminate entrance fees charged by a city-owned park. Behind her back, Ned grinned and shook his head, then told her he would walk her to her car.

As they disappeared around the corner of the house, Adrienne looked again at the garden, studying the shadows around the ghostly plants for a hint of the cat. When she saw nothing, she shook her head and entered the foyer.

Just inside the door a floorboard creaked when she stepped on it. Startled, she sucked in her breath, then stood with quickly stiffened muscles listening to the echo. For a long time, she stood in the middle of the emptiness listening, even when the vibrations had lost themselves in the silence of the house, waiting for the sound to repeat in some phantom form.

Though she had seldom entered the old parlor in recent days, in spite of the fact that getting to her workrooms from the foyer was quicker through it than by way of the kitchen, she entered the silent room now, and was immediately tempted to go back to the foyer and use the kitchen route. Traces of whispers came from her shoes on the hardwood flooring. A frail scent of dust hung in the tepid air, with motes of it floating in the window light. Throughout the house, and in the parlor in particular, the silence was intense, as heavy as the walls and ceiling enclosing it, and she thought she could sense a vague brutality about it. She kept her eyes averted from the row of paintings lying along the baseboard of the west wall, but even with that precaution, by the time she reached the doorway to the hall, tiny beads of perspiration dotted her forehead.

She made herself stop on the threshold to the hallway to look at the north end of the room. Beside the two tall windows, Ned had created an area in which he did his painting, divided from the remainder of the room by the taboret, an old chair and a pile of empty canvas stretchers. Whether or not he intended it that way, the area possessed a comfortable, productive appearance like the photograph of a studio reproduced in *American Artist* magazine.

North light streamed through the windows to slant across the two canvases resting on two heavy studio easels, brushing the already warm-hued paint lightly with an ocher-tinted glaze. With the first interest in Ned's work she had felt since Katie's death, Adrienne walked slowly to them, stopping several feet in front of the canvases.

Looking like a beautiful miniature woman, Sandi smiled at her from the oblong canvas. Her blue eyes, under their half-lowered lids, stared directly at Adrienne, their corners ever so slightly crinkled from the smiling expression. On first glance, the vibrant blue tones in those eyes highlighted a happiness touched with mischief, the eyes of a young woman living a joyous new experience. But then Adrienne noticed a curious alien reflection in them. In the corners and along the lower lashes, there was a glinting of moisture which had no relationship to the unself-conscious smile. What looked to be tears hung poised on Sandi's long lashes, ready to spill down her cheeks. Adrienne saw an all but unnoticeable curve in the set of the smiling lips, a vague curling which made them seem on the verge of trembling with a sob.

Adrienne looked away, realigned her thoughts, then returned her gaze to the blonde's face. A sadness, not depicted by the paints, was trying to come forth on Sandi's face.

"Dear God," she whispered. "It's almost like the others."

There was a difference, though. It was like the same color seen in two variant lights: the color remains the same, but the chromatic prism is different. She frowned, slowly moving her eyes over the painting. During her fourth scan of Sandi's face she realized what was missing. The inner glow. The skin tone was astoundingly rich and natural, but the mystic inner pulsing coming from within the paint on Sebastian's canvases was missing on Ned's. Some of the tautness departed from her nerves.

More from curiosity than a desire to compare, she walked to where Sebastian's paintings lay. From their line at her feet, the women stared up at her. Like dull jewels in the deepening shadow, their eyes caught wayward bits of light which they directed at her in what seemed to be a mingling of hate and envy that caused her to think of prisoners watching her as she walked along a corridor outside their row of cells. But she ignored the eyes and paid no attention to what vibrations she might imagine coming from the paintings, concentrating on the flesh tones only. As she knew it would be, as it had always been, it was in all of them, that deep inner warmth beating like a pulse beneath the skin.

Ned had not discovered Sebastian's secret.

She saw the two nudes on the unopened window seat. In the sun's full light the soft pulsing glow from their skin was magnificently hued, giving connotations of extraordinary pleasure and mystery. Her eyes lingered only a few seconds on them, then moved away. Too long would bring the inner fears to tighten her chest as she became aware of the evil, imagined or not, fanning out from them. But as she took the first step back toward the easels, she noticed in the strong cross-lighting bits of paint and wood scattered on the seat, casting tiny arabesques of shadow on the smooth surface. Looking closer, she saw the rims of both the lid and seat were gouged. Though not as mutilated as the one she had helped Ned open, this lid, too, had obviously been pried free by a chisel and hammer.

Ignoring the paintings, she hooked a forefinger in the metal loop embedded in the lid and pulled upward. Offering no resistance, the lid lifted. Beneath it the dark well of the storage compartment was empty; only the musty, cryptlike smell of a long-closed area came from the opening around the canted lid. She stood staring dumbly down into it, not knowing how to react, her mind, for an instant, as vacant as the storage space. Then suddenly the two women in the paintings were exacting control, looking directly at her with sullen eyes while both their mouths twitched in depraved smiles. Adrienne slammed the lid shut and turned her back to them.

Only one person could have pried open the seat: Ned. In his quest for Sebastian's secret nothing was to be overlooked or go untried. A sadness brushed her with a cold hand as she partially admitted that his desire was in danger of becoming a peculiar form of gluttony, just as Geoff and Katie predicted during the last days of their faltering relationship with him. She shook her head. What, if anything, had he found in the window's storage compartment? As she walked slowly toward the taboret, she remembered the dried leaves and small bottles she had seen when she came into the studio that afternoon before Katie's death. That was her answer. Whatever he was working with had come, in some form, from the window seat, something he had discovered during secret prowlings.

Suddenly everything stopped inside her mind and she felt her eyes narrow. There was a small squirming in her memory. Something was trying to nudge itself into her consciousness, and she stood very still allowing the circuits in her mind to seek out the disturbance, isolate it, then feed it into her memory banks and display it on the screen of her awareness. It came slowly at first, a bit of this, a portion of that, but then it was there, and, although she did not understand it, she turned to walk back to the two nude paintings on the window seat. She stood examining them.

She did not have to search long. On the face of the reclining woman, running from below her left eye to the corner of her mouth, was a scratch, not a scrape in the paint surface, but a thin line like dried blood on a gouged cheek. Gingerly she reached down to run a finger lightly across it. The paint was smooth and undisturbed. The scratch was in the flesh, as if it had been painted as a feature of the face. And just above the figure's left ear the black waves of hair were disarranged, mussed, like they would be if fluffed by a careless hand. Or clutched by a grasping one?

Clutched? Grasped by a hand? The frantic hand of a violently dying woman reaching out in desperation could become entangled in the thick black hair of her assailant. At the same time, a fingernail of that desperate hand could slice across a cheek. It could do that.

No!

The thought was ludicrous. Absurd. But the muscles in her face tightened. At her sides her hands clenched into fists so tight her nails stabbed her palms. No, in no way, she repeated to herself. Dear God, in no way could that strand of black hair clutched in Katie's dead fist be associated with what she was seeing in the painting.

No! She screamed silently. Not even though Katie had thought she saw one of the women from the paintings standing in a window. No! It was grotesquely impossible.

She hurriedly returned to the taboret. At first she hesitated, guilty about going through another's private belongings, but still a little giddy about her victory over fear, she pulled the top right-hand drawer open. Neatly placed in it were the six unmarked bottles the size of spice bottles. Four contained what appeared to be crushed leaves, the other two held white powders. She lifted one of the bottles of crushed leaves from the drawer and was about to pull its glass stopper when she heard the side door open and close, followed by Ned's footsteps in the hall. She replaced the bottle, shut the drawer and took a position facing the paintings of Sandi and Sheila.

Ned had obviously gone to the mailbox at the end of the driveway, because he came into the studio carrying a handful of mail. All but one envelope he dropped on the taboret, and that one, using a paint knife, he opened, ran his eyes down the letter he pulled from it, then smiled.

"The T. J. Wyles Company wants some shots of a wholesome young woman sitting on a boat dock at sunset. I wonder why they want me to do it. It would be cheaper for them to go to a stock agency; but, you can bet, I'm not going to mention it to them." He moved to stand by Adrienne's side to look at Sandi's portrait. "I can use her. I promised her I'd give her a chance in front of the camera. What do you think?"

"I think she deserves it."

"This is the first time you've seen the paintings, isn't it, since—"

"Yes."

"What do you think of them? I've got to admit to a certain pride, but I think Sheila's praises were—well, kind of flamboyant. Maybe on their own merits they're good, but they aren't what I was after, either. They just aren't comparable to Sebastian's." He replaced the letter in its envelope, then studied the portraits again. "I haven't figured out his secret."

"No. Almost, but not quite." She continued to look at the portrait of Sandi. "It's the inner glow that's missing, that . . . well, that life pulse, I guess you can call it. You don't have it in them yet."

She wanted to ask him about the jars in the taboret drawer, the scratch on the face of the reclining nude and the empty window seat compartment. And, most of all, she wanted to ask him about the hair clutched in Katie's hand. But she said nothing.

He put his arm around her waist. "Are you going to stay tonight?"

She shook her head.

"Why not?"

"I wouldn't be good company. I feel all tied up inside, and I think it would be best if I spent the night alone so I can get rid of the knots."

His fingers pressed softly into her waist. "What's wrong?"

"Nothing in particular, everything in general. It's just one of those times a person has to have no companionship but their own." She leaned her head on his shoulder. "I wouldn't be any good in any way you wanted me tonight."

"I take exception to that, because you've become nothing but good for me in all ways . . . but I guess I understand." His hand dropped to her hip and patted it. "I'll try to share you with yourself, now and then."

It was a long evening. The sun hung too low above the western horizon, shadows lay across the lawn and garden in stripes that were too long, and hidden in the vegetation insects chirruped their twilight songs for too long a time.

Until the light failed, Ned touched up details of Sheila's portrait, then cooked two hot dogs, which he ate smeared with horseradish mustard, folded in slices of bread, accompanied by a glass of milk. Saying she was not hungry because of the heat, Adrienne had left shortly after their brief conversation in the studio. How sad, and yet how remarkable, he thought, that a person can become so interwoven with another he feels a portion of himself missing when that other is not present. He was becoming that way with Adrienne. Tomorrow he would talk to her again about moving into the house. Katie's death was long enough past that affairs could be pulled into a certain neatness.

For the time between the final sunglow and the rising of a quarter moon, he sat on the verandah steps lighting one cigarette from the butt of another, watching the smoke spread a wispy veil in the languid darkness. The cool solitude was like a poultice on the abrasions of the preceding days, allowing him to understand Adrienne's needing quiet moments alone.

He knew these hushed moments were the time he should be working on the portrait of Adrienne he was painting secretly. From the beginning, from the instant he and Geoff walked into the kitchen that first day to see her at the table with Katie, he was taken by the clean angles and curves of her features. He began to work on the portrait simultaneously with Sandi's, spending an hour or so on it after the young woman was gone, finding his memory of Adrienne's features gave him the same detail as would having her sit for him. His secrecy had grown excessive, he knew, but he wanted the painting to be a complete surprise when he presented it to her: something like a very young boy, he supposed, giving his secret love a talisman after a long interval of poetic planning and self-examination.

He sighed and blew another plume of smoke into the darkness. There would be no work done under the diffused lamp tonight. He was just unable to function.

God, he missed Geoff and Katie. Two thirds of his being had gone away with them. The ending of friendships destined to endure a lifetime had been such a bloodletting, so literally and so figuratively. The healing would be slow, and the scars would remain forever.

Was he obsessed with the paintings as Geoff, on that ugly day a week ago, screamed he was? He did not want to answer that. Perhaps there was a bit of madness in his impatience to simulate Sebastian's techniques; but he was certain he had it controlled. Someday, when he had redone the tradition of portraiture, people would understand his struggle; maybe even Geoff would realize the justification for his intensity.

He flipped his last cigarette out into the night and watched the comet tail of sparks shower behind it, then stared up at the cold-eyed stars looking down at him. If it was not for the one thought which kept surfacing over and over, he would be free of concern. But that thought held an emotional horror he was helpless to explain.

When Adrienne and he had found Katie's body, a strand of black hair was clasped in its right fist. Knowing it was important, he had pried the tuft free from the tightly curled fingers and put it in his shirt pocket to give to the authorities when they arrived to investigate the accident. But the violence of the night distracted him. Phone calls to the sheriff and Geoff turned into agonies of cold bureaucratic nonchalance and uncontrollable agony. Events had jumbled together in confusion, so it was not until Katie's body was taken away that he remembered the hair in his pocket.

Now it was in a plastic film container buried beneath a pile of handkerchiefs in a drawer of the dresser in his bedroom, its presence haunting him.

The morning following the accident he had gone to the

studio. He found the paintings of the women scattered across the floor as if they had been held high by a giant hand, then tossed throughout the room. Stunned, his eyes swept from painting to painting, looking for damage. He recalled how his skin tingled, how in the dense air of the closed room were the dying scents of heady perfumes. He had stood for a long, long time staring, then replaced the paintings along the baseboard of the front wall, suddenly not wanting to search for explanations, knowing with a chill that he did not want a reason to present itself.

At first he nearly overlooked the scratch on the reclining nude's face, but then, immediately after discovering it, he saw the out-of-place hair on the side of her head, tangled and twisted like hair which had been pulled. He had wanted to vomit.

Since then, reason and common sense had been in constant struggle with doubt and fear. He knew he should confide in Adrienne, but he cringed from the encounter, fearing to add to her burden.

A little after ten o'clock, the night lost its soothing effect and he went to bed. But sleep stayed beyond his reach. His mind whiplashed, hunting justification for his continuing to follow Sebastian's directions. Too much—nearly everything, in fact—was unreal and implausible, yet a mere hint of approaching success made all the actions excusable. Drugging Sandi with the chamomile and mandrake tea was a strange but essential procedure. The taking of her blood was flirting with ghoulishness, but mixing it with the paints, and its impossible chemical assimilation into the pigments, was a stimulant to the imagination. All those tasks he had conscientiously performed, all the notes in Sebastian's book he had followed as he would the instructions on conducting a sacred ritual—but still his painting was lacking.

Sebastian and Sabra were standing side by side before the two easels in the studio concentrating on the portraits of

Sandi and Sheila. Both of them were more clearly defined than on previous occasions, this time almost real. The mists which had eddied around them before were now no more than dust motes, a thin diffusion screen between them and him. When before he had glided through the scene, tonight he heard his sneakers slapping the flooring and his senses were tuned to the scent of lilac and an eerie stillness which held within it even deeper realms of consciousness.

Sebastian turned, smiling, nodding his head. "You have done exceedingly well, Ned. My faith was not misplaced. You are a master artist who will carry on where I stopped."

When he answered, there was a hollow timbre to his voice, but Ned could feel, this time, his throat muscles working. "I followed your notes, word by word, sequence by sequence."

"Yes, it is apparent."

"But I've fallen short someplace, and I don't know where."

"In what way?"

"The radiance, Sebastian. The flesh of your women feels warm like living tissue." He pointed at Sandi's picture. "That one doesn't. I did everything you said, and I came up with excellent tones, but the paint's cold and the pulsing realism just isn't there. What did I do wrong?"

"Nothing, Ned. You've done nothing wrong. The warmth will be in it soon."

"I don't understand."

"Soon you will."

Vagueness, Ned thought. He never gives me a concrete statement. Frustration began wedging into his thinking.

"Be patient, Ned," Sebastian was saying. "In a few days, perhaps by the weekend, the blonde's skin will be as warm as that of the women in my portraits, to both the sight and the touch. It is a gradual process."

He knew Sebastian would tell him no more, and he had not the slightest idea what to do next or say. Through the shimmering haze, he looked around the studio, at Sebastian's paintings, at his own canvases on the easels and then at Sabra.

This was the first time he had seen her standing, and he was surprised how tall she was. Under a white gown, a voluptuousness boldly pushed at the thin material which was vainly attempting to minimize an abundance of breast and hip. Her raven hair tumbled in a thick mane down each side of a sensuously chiseled face, from which, under dark high-arched brows, blue eyes watched him in a vaguely disturbing way. Floating around her was the fragrance of lilacs. He was awed by how closely, except for perhaps an inch in height, she resembled Adrienne.

Sabra's eyes widened and darted from his face to stare with ill-concealed alarm over his left shoulder. Her breath made a cold hissing sound as she drew it sharply through her teeth. With his own breath all of a sudden clogging his throat, he turned to look behind him, already sensing the presence of someone else in the studio with them. The air became curdled and granulated like sawdust, filling his nose and mouth, resisting his movements.

He first saw nothing in the depths of the surrounding darkness, but then in the southwest corner of the room he became aware of a shape blacker than the darkness in which it lurked. It hovered silently. While his eyes struggled to bring it into some kind of recognizable form, it faded backward into a mass of deeper gloom. He knew that whatever it was, it was watching them, examining them, waiting, like a nightmare creature, in its den of darkness.

Sebastian and Sabra clasped hands, moving closer to each other.

"What is it?" Ned asked.

"One who you will come to know," Sebastian muttered.

"Who?" he insisted.

"The Master," Sebastian said.

Every fiber in his body was suddenly tense. Some dim part

of him insisted this was nothing but a dream event, no more than a fragmentary part of a nightmare which was forming, but a disturbed voice whispered he was beyond dreaming, beyond illusion, that he stood within a niche of time which had no place in the past, present or future.

"He will be your patron, Ned," Sebastian whispered. "Like the Medicis and Borgias of medieval times, he will buy your work and pay you very handsomely if it strikes his fancy."

Ned looked hard at the corner. He could feel frightful power lurking there in the darkness.

By his side, Sebastian cleared his throat. It was a careful, discreet sound. The heat became more stifling. It channeled through Ned's nose and mouth to his lungs and dried them out.

Sebastian spoke. Ned looked at him, then realized he was speaking to what was in the corner. "You have seen the painting of the young woman? The blonde?"

There was a small shifting in the darkness. A ripple of heat moved from the corner across the room. With it came the aroma of faraway worlds burning, caustic and acidlike, which caused the temperature in the studio to rise and made the darkness quiver in heat waves.

"Yes. It is acceptable."

The voice was rumbling, but it was clear and, Ned thought, eager-sounding.

"The blonde will be yours in a few days," Sebastian said.

"I know." There was a low laugh. "Three to be exact. She will come to me on Sunday—the day which you all hold sacred. I find that amusing."

"Yes," Sebastian murmured. "After she is yours, you will speak with Ned, will you not?"

"Yes."

"Then you and I can have our talk?"

There was no answer for an extended moment during

which Ned felt a stirring in the corner that might have been the presence reactivating itself. Finally the voice said, "Perhaps. But I still do not feel kindly toward you; know that well, Sebastian. Being forced to wait one hundred years for a new lady cannot easily be forgiven."

"I know." Sebastian sounded meek.

The mass in the corner shifted. The rumbling voice reached out from it. "Perhaps when I have the woman, I will think on it, Sebastian."

"If not for me, then Sabra, please . . ."

"I will think on it, I say!" The darkness within the darkness became darker still, very nearly assuming a definable shape, the voice touched with anger. "Leave well enough alone, Sebastian. Now go—all of you! I must deal with Magda. She was careless with the red-haired woman."

Ned looked around. The pale light sprinkling silver dust on the chair and chest of drawers was not the frail diffusion in which Sebastian and Sabra existed. He blinked his eyes, then looked around once more, now recognizing the place for what it was, moonlight coming through his bedroom window to blanch the walls and touch the furniture with ivory highlights.

Sweat was covering him, hot and sticky, oozing from his pores in heavy drops and running across his belly, then down his sides to soak the already damp sheet beneath him. He rolled over to sit on the edge of the bed, then pushed himself to his feet and slowly walked to the window. His legs quivered the same way they would if he had been running for miles, his heart pumping in a hammering attempt to escape his rib cage. He wanted a cigarette, but was afraid if he lit one the first inhale would blow his racing heart apart. Never in his life had he known such fear, and he could not reason his way through the maze of dismay his mind had created. What he had witnessed was beyond reason, what he had heard beyond belief.

He thought of the strand of black hair in the plastic box in the dresser drawer and the disarranged hair and scratch on the face of the reclining nude—and the thing in the studio saying Magda was "careless with the red-haired woman." His ravaged senses desperately tried to repudiate what he knew was more than coincidence. They nearly succeeded, but then behind him, coming up from the floor below, he heard a woman's choked sob of pain.

CHAPTER

Adrienne awoke slowly, hearing a murmur, almost inaudible, coming from beyond the little puffy clouds hovering on the fringes of her consciousness. She recognized it as the unending whisper of the air conditioner. She opened her eyes into narrow slits and peeped through the blur of her lashes to see half-lighted bulks of familiar bedroom objects, then squeezed her lids shut again in the hope of drifting back to sleep.

She rolled to her right side and languidly reached out with an inquisitive hand feeling for the warm firmness of Ned's shoulder. Her fingers brushed only rumpled sheet. Shocked, she opened her eyes wide. She was alone in the bed. For a moment or two, she felt like a disappointed child whose expectations had been shattered. Then a slow warmth spread through her under the covering sheet and in response to it she smiled, rolled lazily onto her back while taking a long, deep breath and arched herself in a great feline movement pulling sleep-loose muscles taut, continuing to smile up at the sun-reflecting ceiling.

While she sat on the edge of the mattress a few minutes later, she felt no aloneness.

The shower spray stung her still sleep-tender flesh like needles, digging and scratching her breasts and stomach, then her back and buttocks, until her muscles spasmed and her breath came in quick little puffing gulps that set her heart beating at the same pace it would had she jogged a mile. Out of the shower, she toweled herself vigorously, deliberately using the rough terry cloth in an overzealous therapeutic rubbing, keeping the blood running fast to loosen her muscles. When she was finished, she slipped into her old blue robe and padded barefooted to the kitchen, for the first time in longer than she could remember happy in both mind and body.

Before she finished the second cup of coffee, she had gone full circle in her thinking and was still as determined in her decision as when she had made it before turning out the lights the previous night. While she sipped the coffee, she thoroughly searched her mind to satisfy herself there was no speculation remaining in her thinking. Compulsiveness she ruled out. No irrational force was driving her. No desire to apologize to a society which really did not care. No spawning of moralistic guilt.

She was going to move in with Ned.

She dressed hurriedly, surprising herself now and then when she heard a tuneless humming coming from her partially opened lips. Her fingers on the buttons of her blouse and the zipper of her slacks were quivery with excitement.

On the drive across town she tried to visualize Ned's reaction when she told him he would henceforth be sharing his house with her. It would be a very special moment. He would take her in his arms, as around them a benevolent world backed away to a respectful distance. She was no longer a part of the dull and ordinary society she saw through the windows of the Toyota; she was escaping the nowhere life of the people scurrying along the sidewalks. She pitied them, and wished they could share with her the magic of this morning.

Behind the house, the parking area was empty. Disappointment abruptly turned down the edges of her excitement as she pulled under the peppertree and switched off the ignition. With the car stopped, the morning heat rolled through the windows to saturate the interior with steaming humidity, transforming the Toyota into an upholstered sauna so her nose and mouth quickly clogged and her blouse stuck to her like a far too heavy skin.

She sat stiffly behind the steering wheel watching the dappled shadows weave their designs on the car's hood, listening to the metallic crackings it made as it tried to cool in the ardent heat, all the time struggling to keep the escaping excitement from melting entirely away, feeling doubts begin to gnaw around the crimped edges of the good feeling.

As if preparing to dive into a tepid pool, she drew a deep breath, then opened the door and got out to stand in the shade of the peppertree, hoping for some little movement of air, feeling the fabric of her blouse becoming sweat-glued to her shoulders. She walked slowly toward the door, now and then kicking at the gravel crunching beneath her sandals.

Inside the house, the stillness was timeless and deep, never having been disturbed by the sounds of human activity. It was, she felt, bigger than the house, an unearthly calm stretching beyond the limits of the walls and passing the boundaries of the property to form a huge invisible canopy under which imagination and premonition took root to solidify into terror.

In her workroom, she managed to regroup her thinking. As was always so, she told herself, sweet fantasy was subjugated to stern reality. Sadly slipping the now dulled excitement to a rear corner of her mind, she directed her attention to the piles of work stacked on her two tables. But while her fingers nimbly performed their tasks, her mind drifted, refusing to concentrate on the well-remembered movements of twisting wire and gluing pinecones.

The sound of the Jeep passing outside the windows brought stability with it. She looked up in time to see Ned driving slowly toward the parking area.

She heard his shoes crunching on the gravel, then climbing the steps to the side door. His footsteps came slowly down the hallway, the rubber soles of his sneakers making soft slithering noises on the hardwood. Adrienne stiffened. His shambling approach gave her the terrible sense of waiting for an unknown intruder to appear, so much so, the gooseflesh rose and tickled her entire body like electric shocks darting through her skin.

At the door, Ned looked in, hesitated, then stopped.

"Hi," she said. She tried to make her voice bouncy, but knew it sounded forced and unreal.

"Sandi's in the hospital." He looked past her to the windows, but with a vacancy that indicated he was not seeing anything outside them.

"Oh? What's wrong?"

"Hepatitis. They say she might not live through the weekend."

"Oh, my God, Ned!" A coldness settled in the special area of her stomach where fear is born. "When did she come down with it?"

"According to the people at the café, about three days ago. I stopped in to speak with her about the Wyles assignment, and they told me she collapsed at work last Tuesday."

"Hepatitis doesn't strike that fast. There must be something else along with it."

He looked directly at her now. "There is. They said the doctors are baffled."

"We should visit her."

He shook his head. "We can't, she's in isolation. They're

afraid of it being more contagious than normal because of whatever else is accompanying the hepatitis."

The news Ned brought was something repulsive that sprawled between them, polluting the air with a decaying stench. Ned dropped his eyes, at the same time giving his head a shake, then turned to continue down the hall to his studio.

Long seconds dragged by. She stood staring dumbly at the material arranged on the table across the room, feeling beads of perspiration molding on her forehead and arms to join the wetness already sheening her skin. She returned to her work, mentally setting herself a goal of six wreaths completed before leaving the room, assuring herself a concentrated effort would hold away any new uncertainties that might try to slink into her thinking.

From down the hallway, she heard Ned moving in the studio. Despite her resolve not to leave the room, she wanted to go to him, to stand at his side, but a latent discretion convinced her to stay away. Events were in one of those moments of precarious balance when gratefulness and animosity were equally placed on the scale. He was being exaggeratedly affected by Sandi's illness; so it was a time for him to be alone.

When she finished the last wreath, Adrienne went to the kitchen to find him tossing a salad. He said, "I thought we could have the fried chicken that's been in the freezer for a couple of weeks and some rice to go with this."

She saw the oven light glowing and knew he had already put the chicken in. "I'll help."

Neither spoke while she boiled the rice in its plastic bag and brewed tea.

During the meal, Ned made no endeavor to start a conversation. He gave the impression of a man looking inward, studying himself, perhaps discovering things about himself he had not known before.

When the dishes were washed and replaced in the cupboard, he said, "I'm sorry."

"You should be." Her voice was snippy. After the magic morning hours of high-key exhilaration, the day had become one of discontent. When she spoke again, she made no try at smoothing the abrasiveness from her voice. "I'd like to help you if I could, because I know something's bothering you; but there's no way I can even pretend to be of assistance if you don't confide in me."

"I know." He concentrated on scratching the back of his left hand. "I'm letting Sandi's illness get to me, I guess."

"Is there a reason you should?"

"No." He looked out the window.

"Then I think you're overreacting."

"I do on many occasions. Sometimes I think what adult actions I do exhibit are all pretenses, that the years matured my body but bypassed my mind, leaving it floundering around in its midteen era."

"I don't believe that, and neither do you. That's just a combination of words you're putting together to hide behind so you won't have to tell me why Sandi's hepatitis upsets you so much."

"You're persistent, aren't you?"

"When I think I have the right to be, and I think I do here." Her voice faded away on the last words, turning the statement into a question.

"You have every right." He closed the space between them with two steps and laid his hands on her shoulders. "You know, don't you, you're one of only two people I love in this world. That earns you some kind of priority, I should think."

"Then you're going to tell me what's troubling you?"

"Let's wait until Monday."

"After the weekend?"

"Yes."

"After the time Sandi will either be dead or stabilized."

"Jesus Christ, Adrienne!" His hands tightened their grasp. "What the hell are you implying?"

"That I'm afraid, Ned. I'm terribly afraid." She reached up to grasp his wrists, then gently stroked his forearms. "I'm afraid you're into something that's better left alone. I don't know what it is; you won't tell me, but I know it has to do with the bottles of crushed leaves and white powder you have in the taboret."

"Oh, Adrienne. Adrienne baby." His arms slipped around her and drew her tight to his chest. "What can I tell you?"

"The truth."

"I will, I promise. But give me time, please." His hands moved soothingly up and down her back, efficient, strong and persuasive. "Until Monday."

"All right."

He hooked the forefinger of his right hand under her chin and lifted it, then placed his lips on hers. It was more of a kiss given between friends than lovers, but after it, he asked, "Are you going to stay tonight?"

She nodded, not wanting to, but her physical want was overpowering her intellect. There was not even automatic resistance as she leaned back in his arms and lowered her eyes. "Yes—and longer if you want me to."

He placed his hands on her shoulders again, but this time pushed her out from him so he could look into her eyes. "Longer? You mean move in?"

"Yes . . ."

"God, that's tremendous! Oh, Jesus, how I love you, Adrienne." He pulled her to him once more, harder this time, squeezing her in a hug that was tight with both tenderness and protection. "When?"

"Tomorrow?"

"Can you do it then? That quick?"

"If you help me."

"I'm willing to start now."

She snuggled against his chest, fitting her curves to his, feeling her softness flatten on his solidness. "I think there are better ways we can spend the evening."

The following morning was clear and pristine bright, still fragile with rosy tints and wisps of coolness. Clean night scents lingered, haunting and voluptuous, when they pulled the Toyota and Jeep into the apartment's parking space. Four car-laden trips later, the bed in the southwest corner bedroom of the house was hidden beneath stacks of clothing, jewelry boxes, books, and mysterious cartons which had been pulled from the back corners of closets.

Dropping an armful of towels on top of what was already on the bed, Adrienne picked up a pamphlet which had fallen from a pile of publications. She slumped into the room's only chair, gave an exaggerated groan as she stretched her legs out before her, then began fanning herself. She pushed a curl of hair back from her forehead and softened the groan to a sigh.

"You know, I'm never going to be able to use that bed. Look at it! I'll never get it unloaded."

"You'll never have to use it," Ned said, laughing.

She made a face at him, sticking out her tongue. Once more, as the previous morning, she was all happiness and anticipation. All the needs and necessities of living were with her in this hot, airless room.

"What else is there?" Ned was leaning against the door-jamb looking at the bed.

"Not much. The TV set, and some dishes and silver-ware." Although the bed was overflowing, and surrounded with scattered items on the floor, she thought what was there was very little to show for thirty-one years of living. "I'll get them later. I want you to meet Amy, too. She's been more than a friend to me during the last months, and I can't move out without telling her."

"Amy?"

"Amy Stevens. A good, solid housewife type who kept me from going round the bend."

"I'd like to meet her." He looked around the room. "I guess there's nothing more I can do here, so I'm going to phone the hospital. I imagine they'll give me information on Sandi, don't you?"

"They should, but I wouldn't say for sure. Hospitals have taken lessons from the government, I think, in bureaucratic runarounds."

"What are you going to do?"

"Hang up these clothes, I guess. I should have done that instead of just throwing them on the bed. Then I'm going to work awhile. I've orders due the first of the week."

"You always have orders due. Maybe you should get yourself some help."

"No, just learn to budget my time better."

"That might be a little difficult from now on."

"Oh?"

"I don't know how much self-control I'll have with you around."

She held up the pamphlet in an imitation of a vaudevillian version of a southern belle coyly hiding behind her fan, rapidly blinking her eyes as she looked at him from their corners. "Mr. Anderson, I do declare, I believe you are oversexed."

"Frankly, Miss Adrienne, you have every right to assume that."

It was a struggle to arrange the room within the hour she allowed herself, hanging her clothes in the closet, filling the drawers of the old cherry-veneered dresser with lingerie, handkerchiefs, towels and assorted odds and ends which she should have disposed of in the apartment's trash bin. The unopened cartons she shoved in the back of the room's closet, with two left over which she slid under the bed. An hour and ten minutes after starting, she stood in the doorway looking into the room which was to become an intimate portion of her life. It was void of personality. As she went to the stairs, she wondered how much of her character she would impose on the room.

Ned was sitting at the kitchen table sipping from a can of Lite beer while looking out the window at shadows tangling into opaque designs on the gravel of the parking area.

"Were you able to get any information?" she asked.

He nodded. "It's not good. She's slipped further away than yesterday. They said they won't give any more reports over the phone."

"Does she have a family?"

"I don't know."

"It sounds serious, doesn't it?"

"It is serious." He looked at the can in his hands, then moved its damp bottom in a tight pattern of interlocking circles on the plastic tablecloth. His eyes drifted through the window once more. "I have the feeling she's going to die."

There was nothing Adrienne could think of to say. Something was disintegrating but she was unable to define it. She took a Pepsi from the refrigerator, then a glass from the cupboard, and carried them both to the table.

Minutes passed with neither of them speaking. She sipped from her glass, feeling the strong carbonation bite the back of her tongue. Obliquely she watched Ned. His eyes never wavered from the shadow designs in the parking area, but she knew he was not seeing them. When she finished her drink, she got to her feet to stand looking down at him, seeing the brooding in his eyes.

"I'll be glad when Monday arrives," she said.

He looked up. "I'm sorry." He reached out to take her left hand and squeeze it. "I guess that's become my most used expression yesterday and today, hasn't it?"

"Just about." Her voice was more sour than she intended.

"Provoked at me?"

"A little. Actually, more worried, I think."

"Don't be."

She pulled her hand from his, then took the glass to the sink, aware that if she stayed any longer her thinking would become a morass of confusion.

When she was going through the hallway door, he called after her, "I thought I'd get us some carry-out hamburgers for dinner. Does that sound okay?"

She nodded and continued down the hall. She had the unsettled sensation she was walking down an unending corridor in a labyrinth.

She worked without interruption until seven o'clock. Just after six-fifteen, she watched Ned pass the window in the Jeep: a trifle before seven he returned with a red-and-white-striped box, surrounded with several sacks, on the seat beside him.

She entered the kitchen determined to make their first meal under the new arrangement as perfect as it could be, even if it consisted only of fast-food hamburgers and fries. She hoped Ned was in a like mood, that he would inhibit the inner turmoil torturing him. So far, her own disappointment of the day had been held in check only by a constant application of willpower, and she did not want to be forced to retreat into some darker side of emotions.

If not exhilarated, the meal was tension-free. Though conversation was minimal, it was simple and personal with no either-or alternatives. Adrienne's wariness gradually slipped away as she realized Ned, too, was attempting to avoid areas where dispute might lie. When only two or three bites of the hamburger remained, she discovered she was enjoying its bland, sauce-smothered taste, which meant, she supposed, the world was slipping back into balance.

A vagrant afterglow of twilight still lingered when they finished rinsing the dishes and glasses they had used. In its distilled haze, the greens and browns and yellows of the foliage were drained into a monochrome gray in which shadowed nooks appeared as entrances to secret places.

"It's cooler outside," Ned said. "Do you want to try it?"

She nodded, thinking that maybe this evening would be an ally and not an adversary.

It was the hour when nature rests. The gilding vibrancy of the day was gone, ended in the blaze of sunset; the languid shadows of the night were still hollow pools beneath the croton, jasmine and bougainvillea bushes. The early evening breeze had not as yet approached from beyond the horizon, so around them the oak and pepper leaves still hung in limp exhaustion from the sun's flogging. Out across the fields somewhere, a crow sent its nerve-nibbling caw through the dusk, the raucous sound a challenge to the coming night. They walked to the end of the driveway, where they stood looking up and down the empty road.

Ned groped for, and found, her hand. "We should have gone out tonight. It's a time for celebrating."

"There're other ways to celebrate." She tightened her hand in his. "It's who you're with, not where you are, that makes the night enjoyable."

"I knew there was a reason I loved you."

"Because I say the right things?"

"Well, there are others, but it will do until later tonight."

It was a strange night, she thought. They seemed not to be a part of anything, standing here beside a lonely road in lowering darkness in a world which it was difficult to believe existed. Time and place were without dimension. Grays and blacks intermingled endlessly, eventually fading into a phantom light.

"Come on," he said abruptly, pulling her hand and starting up the driveway. "There's something I want to show you."

"What?"

"A surprise. I was going to save it until I was certain I was satisfied with it, but tonight's the night to show you."

He hurried her along the driveway, then through the side door. At her rooms, he stopped, saying, "Wait here. I'll call you when I'm ready."

She had never liked surprises. A surprise required a response, and the one receiving it must make a rapid judgment as to what kind was expected by the one who presented it. It was an unfair act. She stood at the table at which she had been working earlier in the evening and picked at bits of straw, putting them in the wastebasket beneath the table, then walked to the window but could see only her own reflection, which showed her in the first stages of disarray and the hen scratchings of fatigue at the corners of her eyes.

The waiting began to set up a strumming along her nerves. She was about to leave the room to walk down the hallway when Ned appeared at the door.

"Okay, ready," he said. Excitement was mirrored in his eyes, but behind it, like the shading of a color, Adrienne was certain she detected a flicker of nervousness. "This is something new I've never tried before, but I think I've managed to accomplish a little bit of what I was after."

"Oh?" She was still feeling displaced and was unable to dig deep enough into herself to bring forth enough pleasure to match his fragile show of it.

The studio was a vast cavern of shadows, most of them an unfathomable black, giving the impression of continuing on and on into the night; but, here and there, oblongs of gray only a shade lighter than the surrounding darkness reluctantly stretched from the windows across the floor. Though the windows were half raised, there was no movement of air. Their footsteps echoed hollowly, with the sound building upon itself until it formed an arch in the darkness over their heads, and Adrienne felt she was picking her way through a place where grisly obstacles waited to entangle her. She wanted to turn and leave the room and slowed her walking at Ned's side, falling behind him a pace or two, until he reached for her, and took her right arm to guide her between the taboret and chair, leading her to a place where they stood side by side before the two easels. In the faint light seeping through the north windows, she saw Sheila Rosenthal's portrait had been replaced by another, though it was impossible to pick out details with which to identify it. Ned moved away from her side and fumbled with something in the darkness, then slowly his silhouette turned to her.

"Okay, this is it."

A soft white light from a scrimmed photoflood washed the painting on the easel before her. Adrienne sucked in her breath, felt herself retreating until her hips came in contact with the taboret. She was looking at a perfect image of herself smiling at her through the brilliant, diffused light.

Dressed in a pale blue blouse and dove-gray slacks, she stood with her arms crossed below the thrust of her breasts, one hip resting casually against what appeared to be one of her worktables. Around her, only hinted at in the dark background tones, were subtle arrangements of corn husk flowers and wreaths. Everything was clean, sparkling color—everything but her arms and face. No flesh tones had been applied, leaving her features and crossed arms blended shades of ocher undertoned with sepia. But already the emotional impact of a fine piece of art reached out from the canvas to command attention.

"It's beautiful." She did not really know what else to say. The surprise was pleasant, but her startled mind tried to grasp an illusive phantom gliding through its back chambers, leaving behind it an embryo sensation of uneasiness. That it should have invaded her emotions, no matter how briefly, made her feel shoddy and ashamed.

Ned was smiling at her from the other side of the light. "It's from memory, and the first time I've worked on a portrait without sittings. But, maybe because it's you, it went easy . . . no trouble, just as if you were standing right beside me."

"When have you worked on it?"

"Whenever I had the chance; an hour now, a half hour then."

"I didn't know. I never suspected."

"I didn't want you to. It was to be a surprise."

"It is." She moved a step closer to the painting, squinting her eyes to study the delicate shading in the clothing and background. "It's better than the other two, isn't it? Or am I being egotistical?"

"No, it's better." He came through the light to stand at her side, and his left hand wandered around her waist and slid up to the outside bulge of her breast. "Those two were exercises. This is not."

She leaned against him, seeking his shoulder with her head. He was perspiring and the smell of it, tangy and keen, stirred ancient responses in her. She turned a bit, sliding her breast into the cup of his palm.

"What is it?"

"What I feel about this one. It's you, and I love you; so it was more than just combining an abstraction of techniques. I could sense subtleties I didn't with Sandi and Sheila and I applied them." He gave a low, self-conscious laugh. "Maybe the easiest way to explain it all is to say: this is a labor of love, if you'll excuse the triteness."

"Hmmm, I think I can excuse you. What are you going to do with it?"

"Give it to you, but hope you'll allow me to hang it in the foyer when we redecorate."

She snuggled tighter against him. "I'd be proud to have you do that. When are you going to finish it?"

"As soon as I get Sheila's out of the way." His voice became lower, like a sound following a series of thoughts that were drifting away. "I didn't want to do the flesh tones until I came as close as I could to Sebastian's secret. Now I almost have it."

"It's sweet of you."

He turned her to face him. "I'm not good at saying the things I feel, especially when I feel so deep and personal . . . but just know that I love you, Adrienne, love you with all the emotion the word 'love' can mean."

She raised her lips to his. "I'm the same way, darling, but know that I do love you, and, maybe, someday I'll be able to tell you in the ways I want to tell you."

"You already have told me in many, many ways."

She put her arms around his neck and pulled herself tight against him. "What we have here is more than any word, darling. It's too big and wonderful and personal to describe."

He placed his mouth on hers. As his tongue sought its warm secrets, the brazen passion she had never known but with him unleashed itself within her. She felt the first shivers of it racing back and forth through the network of her nerves, realizing that very soon all thoughts and worries would be scourged from her mind, freeing it to drive her healthy muscles in response to the frantic urges her body soon would generate.

The noise was both soft and sharp, a padding sound accompanied by a clicking, circling through the darkness beyond the edges of the floodlight, the slow cadenced paces of something prowling in the opaque shadows.

More than the sound, it was the awareness of another presence in the room with them which caused them to break their embrace, stepping back from each other to look out into the uncertainties of the darkness.

"Jesus . . ." Ned blew out a long puff of air. "It's the damn cat."

Adrienne saw it then on the fringes where the light and darkness struggled with each other. Sitting back in the shadows, only its blue eyes and brown mask were visible. Glinting with sharp slivers of reflected light, those eyes were fixed on her with an unblinking stare.

A trickle of apprehension ran through her, and she reached out to clutch Ned's hand. The cat, she saw, was not looking at her with mere feline curiosity, but with the concentration of a guard intently watching the movements of a captive.

CHAPTER

The morning was sultry, unnatural in its stillness. The sun had melted darkness's mists and replaced the delicate night fragrances with the tangy smells of withered leaves and warm earth. In another hour or so, it would blanch the cobalt sky to a hueless dome arching over a steaming, ocher-tinted land.

At the bedroom window, the curtains hung without moving, appearing already exhausted in anticipation of the heat which would soon be forcing its way between them into the room. Adrienne lay on her left side looking at the window, hoping, for the sake of comfort, she would see a tremble in one of the limp curtains, but knowing she would not. She felt safe and secure beside Ned, and anything remaining not exactly as it was might shift the precarious balance of her senses. She wanted them to stay in the neutral, motionless mode in which they drifted.

"You awake?" Ned's voice behind her still carried the soft blurr of sleep.

"Hmmm. Hmmm."

"Did you sleep well?"

"After you allowed me to."

"After I—?"

She laughed at his sputtering and rolled over to face him. He spread a hand on her hip, permitted it to rest on the rounded warmth for a long moment, then slipped it slowly up the curve of her back. With its movement, she felt her mind and body respond.

"You're so soft and warm in the mornings," he whispered. "All covered with silk and velvet."

Security became want. She arched herself, legs and hips quivering, as she thrust her belly at him, her mind heeding only the convulsive language of eager flesh. Sometime later she lay beside him, her cheek pressed to his shoulder, tears squeezing from under her closed eyelids, waiting for time to return to the world and realign itself.

He ran his fingertips down the curve of her side. "You are Juno," he murmured, "come to give your luxury to a mortal man."

"That man deserves it," she whispered, "because if I am Juno, you transformed a very dreary mortal woman into a goddess."

He chuckled, slapping her across a flank. "This mortal man is hungry and wonders if the goddess will help him prepare breakfast."

She rolled away from him, rubbing her hip. "My divinity didn't last long, did it?"

"Like fame, divinity, for some, is fleeting. However, it's an ongoing process." He leaned over and kissed her on the tip of her nose. "You can try to attain it again later on today, you know."

"My God, you are oversexed!"

"Don't you like it?"

She gave an exaggerated sigh. "I'm afraid I'll have to admit I do."

Adrienne scrambled the last four eggs in the refrigerator, found in the cupboard a small can of Spam, which she sliced and warmed, then toasted two slices of whole wheat bread. Ned made instant coffee, which he poured into a carafe to steep.

"Our cupboard's something like Mother Hubbard's," Adrienne said.

"We'll go shopping this afternoon. The crowds aren't so bad on Sundays."

Later, after the breakfast cigarettes were smoked, Adrienne said, "I want to see my portrait in the daylight."

"Even without the skin tones?"

"Yes. I can visualize what they'll be like." She reached across the table and took his hand. "I'm so amazed that you've been able to do what you've done with it from memory."

He squeezed her hand. "Like I said, it's a labor of love."

She smiled, and felt terribly sorry she had not met this man six years ago.

The late morning sun was kind to the paintings. Seen from the hallway door, they were vivid areas of color in the hushed light of the room, commanding attention with the strength of their design and colors that were washed with the gracious north light.

Eager as she was to see the painting, when she and Ned entered the old parlor, Adrienne felt her automatic resistance to the room. It had set its barb of fear within her that first day, embedding its hook more deeply on successive occasions, making her ever more vulnerable and wary. Now, somewhere in her, the apparatus for defense set itself in motion, more so than usual, until she became uneasy, then apprehensive, falling a pace behind Ned as she had the night before, unexpectedly not wanting to see the painting now.

Simultaneously they both saw it. Instantly everything around her turned thin and vague, with the world retreating headlong from the easels. At her side, Ned gasped with a tight hissing she could interpret as either shock or excitement. She reached for his hand, could not find it, then clenched her own hands into fists at her sides.

Sandi's portrait was shimmering with the elusive inner glow of life.

"It's happened," Ned whispered. "Sweet Jesus Christ, it's there like he said it would be."

"What? Like who said, Ned?" She could not see him. Her eyes were suddenly aching, as if an intense light was boring through their irises to short-circuit a portion of her brain. "Like who said, Ned?"

"Later. I'll tell you tomorrow when I tell you all the things I promised to tell you."

He emerged from the light that was blinding her. She watched him walk toward the portrait with a hand outstretched. Her heart started hammering, and the apprehension that had met her at the doorway formed into the first sensations of fear. Ned laid his palm flat on Sandi's face, then trailed his fingers carefully down her forearms.

"Is it warm?" She was not sure she wanted to know.

He dropped his hand but did not look at her as he nodded, all attention remaining on the painting. Cautiously she took a step, then another, until she stood at his side. The sunlight coming through the windows changed to a vicious stream of heat and unmerciful brilliance. Slanting across the portrait of Sandi, its harsh cross-lighting added a three-dimensional depth to her features while its heat spread a flush over the honey-hued skin.

Then she saw what was holding Ned's attention, and the blossoming fear was touched with revulsion, leaving her not knowing whether to scream or weep.

Through the smiling expression of Ned's creation, Sandi stared out at them from eyes flickering with the fires of a horror so abysmal it was touched with madness. Looking at those eyes, Adrienne knew she was seeing the accumulation of all the terror all the minds since the start of time had experienced. She made no attempt to hold in check the whimper which escaped her lips.

"What have you done?" she whispered.

He looked at her. His eyes were hooded, hiding the true thoughts in his mind behind their lowered lids. "What I set out to do—duplicate Sebastian's paintings."

"No! No, it's more than that. My God, it's more than that."

"What do you mean?"

"Ned, don't play like this with me! Look at Sandi's eyes and tell me there isn't stark terror in them. Look, dammit!"

He shook his head, not looking at the painting. For a long moment, he stared past her, then he muttered, "She can't have any expression but what I painted, you know that. How could she? That's not a living person, honey; that's a painting, pigments applied to canvas representing Sandi. The paint is warm on her face and arms, that's true, but it's still paint—and paint, for Christ's sake, has no emotions."

Adrienne stood staring at him. Jagged shards of brilliant light scraped at her eyes while the knot of fear in her stomach expanded. Ned was lying to her. The realization hurt. He was smiling and looking at her with the expression of infinite pleasure and longing she had come to know and weaken before; muted desire mingled with affection. She shook her head and backed away before he could reach out to touch her.

"Adrienne—"

"Whatever you've done, you've made Sandi's portrait as evil as the ones by Sebastian. Is it the evil you wanted to duplicate, Ned?"

"Adrienne, listen to me!"

Knowing she should give him a chance to explain, but not wanting him to see the loss of confidence she knew must be showing in her eyes, she whirled and ran from the studio.

In her workroom, she sat on a stool with her arms on the table, her face buried in them, very much alone. She could not clear her mind: doubts and fears were crammed in; alarm and dismay filled the corners. A little pain found a place to settle between her shoulders, then climbed its way up her neck to burrow through the base of her skull.

Sounding far away and muffled, the telephone in the foyer rang. She counted six or seven rings before Ned answered. His voice was an inaudible murmur coming through labyrinthian corridors, a whispering taking place somewhere beyond the edges of consciousness.

She felt rather than heard him standing at the door.

"Sandi's dead." The word dead . . . dead . . . dead came like a chant from out of a great black void.

"Did you hear me?"

"Yes."

Adrienne swallowed hard, feeling the pain expanding in concentric waves, then raised her head slowly and looked at him over her shoulder. "That's why the portrait is glowing."

"What? What the hell are you saying?" He sounded out of breath and his cheeks reddened. "What in hell are you implying, Adrienne?"

She swung around on the stool to face him, gripping its edges until her knuckles whitened.

"Did you use any of the crushed leaves or powders in those bottles?" She leaned forward. "Tell me the truth, Ned. Please."

"They have nothing to do with it."

"Tell me!"

"All right, dammit! I brewed a tea from the leaves to relax her when she got uptight. Sitting still made her nervous—so within a half hour she'd be twitchy and couldn't hold the pose."

She wanted to ask what the leaves were, but knew she

would receive no answer. Instead, she asked, "What else? What else did you do with her?"

"Nothing else. For Christ's sake, what are you trying to do? These questions sound like a cross-examination. Are you sitting there saying I had something to do with Sandi's death?"

Her hands tightened even more on the stool. She should stop talking; desperation was unraveling her thinking. But she could not cease merely because Ned was showing signs of anger.

"I'm not accusing you of anything, other than being overzealous." Her voice did not sound bitter, only factual. She tried to keep it that way. He had given her his love, a marvelous dream in which her tattered life had been mended; so she could not, would not, say things which would lead her to eventually despise herself. "You're totally unaware of what has happened to you. You don't know how you've changed even in the short time I've known you. There's something terrible about those paintings, Ned, and there is this horrible thing with Sandi—if only you'd permit yourself to recognize it. If you'd do that, you'd know, like Katie and Geoff and I, they're not only unnatural, they're unholy."

"You've read too many Gothic tales." Growing anger twisted around the words.

She pushed herself erect on the stool. Something cold and glutinous replaced the blood in her veins.

"You know," she screamed. "You know, and you're not admitting it, damn you! Don't tell me you haven't seen the scratch on the cheek of the reclining nude or the way her hair is mussed up. And don't tell me that the hair clutched in Katie's hand was just an unexplainable occurrence. It was pulled from the woman in that damned portrait!"

"Adrienne, get hold of yourself. You're going round the bend. You don't know what you're saying."

"I do know, dammit! I know—and so do you."

"Then say it. Tell me what we both are supposed to know. Come on—tell me."

"Do you really want me to? Do you really want me to tell you?"

"Yes."

"Those paintings are alive!"

"Oh, holy sweet Jesus!"

"Do you deny it?"

"Of course I deny it. How can I do anything else but? What in hell has happened to you, Adrienne, that you can even think like that?"

"I can remember the feel of those paintings' eyes on me when I've been in the studio. I can remember the screaming, bloodied face coming at me the night we opened the window seat, and I can remember, just now, the horrible look of terror in the eyes of Sandi's portrait. And, God help us, I can remember Katie seeing one of the women standing at the studio window watching her. That's how I can have thoughts like that, Ned. That's why I'm frightened of the paintings and the house—and, now, a little bit of you."

"Adrienne, listen to me. Tomorrow I'll—"

"No! Tomorrow's too far away. I gave my love and trust to you. You still have my love, but my trust . . ."

"Oh, shit!" He flung his hands out in an empty gesture. "You're hysterical. I won't even try to cope with you. Maybe later we can pull things into some kind of proper perspective."

He turned abruptly and walked down the hall toward the studio.

"You haven't heard me," she screamed after him. "You haven't been listening to a thing I've been saying."

He made no response.

The scene had been unexpectedly ugly. Like a wayward child, she had been unable to suppress her emotions, so they exploded in a tirade which menaced their future, tangling their relationship. Both of them had done their utmost to destroy each other's hold on happiness, hammering into each other's minds, with a terrible ferocity, words which could do nothing but become bad memories.

The house closed in on her. Somewhere outside, a bird chirped but was choked off abruptly, as if silence had seeped from the house to smother it in crushing folds. With a little moan, Adrienne pushed herself from the stool and left the house.

In the grotto of shadows beneath the trees, a remnant of coolness entwined itself on the bench's curlicues of iron grapes and vines. Trembling in the sluggish air, dried leaves far up in the treetops whispered secrets to one another while the twisted tangles of the shrubs rattled their husks in monotone.

Much of the fury was gone from her as she sat down. She had to think, to make some sort of plan. Think. Think. Her mind wandered away. She pulled it back. Think, plan. She sat stiffly. At last a pattern took form. She sat for a little while longer looking over the sun-leeched garden ruins, aware of, perhaps because of her decision, a peacefulness she had never experienced before spreading throughout the area. She rose from the bench and walked leisurely toward the house.

When she entered the foyer, she knew the house was empty. Standing with her hand on the doorknob, she swallowed hard, suddenly aware that she felt weak and shaky, because though she had decided what must be done, her plans had not called for the action to be performed immediately. Now she was presented the opportunity to do it quickly, and nervousness flooded her.

Once again she felt the relentless pressure of the silence, like a solid weight, which had become a perpetual inhabitant of the house, knowing that if she stood here too long, the silence alone would defeat her. She went rapidly to the kitchen.

She knew exactly which knife she wanted. Breathing faster, running her tongue around lips continually going dry, she removed it from the drawer beside the sink, tested the sharpness of its nine-inch blade with a thumb and nodded her approval, though she was not certain what amount of keenness was required to slice through canvas.

Passing her workroom, she stopped to look at the array of supplies lying on the tables. Such a small amount of work had been accomplished since she moved here so bursting with plans; now tomorrow, instead of listening to Ned's explanations, she would be packing all those items, along with her personal belongings in the bedroom, to return to the apartment. She gave a dry chuckle. What was she thinking of? Tomorrow she might well be in jail.

She stood slumped in the doorway to the studio, leaning against the jamb, the butcher knife hanging straight down from the limp grasp of her numbed fingers, feeling that an obscene joke was being played on her. Tears were near the surface, and she felt her strength of will ebbing.

All the paintings were gone, the fifteen of Sebastian's and the three of Ned's, including the one of her.

Her stomach cramped, her throat filled. For a hideous instant, she thought she was going to vomit.

''Dammit, no,'' she muttered. ''No, you're not going to be sick.''

She heaved herself away from the door, managing to swallow the bile rising in her throat, and walked slowly to the taboret. She pulled the top right-hand drawer open. All the bottles were gone. Very gradually, as she stood there with her head lowered, she felt everything slipping away until inside her, like in the drawer, there was nothing.

She lay the knife on the taboret before going to one of the north windows. Outside along the driveway the foliage was wilted, curling in on itself, bowing its shoulders under the crushing weight of the July sun. Seen through the top branches of the trees, the sky was a blanched blue-white, with one bedraggled, skinny cloud hanging above the northern horizon.

The pain which had settled in her head before the argument returned, and with it a sudden exhaustion transforming her legs into trembling, frail columns of flaccid muscles. At that moment, she knew she could no longer cope with the relentless distortions of reality.

When she left the window, the throbbing in her head blossomed beyond a distracting irritation, swelling to an intensity she thought surely must be opening a crack in the back of her skull. As she walked with overly careful steps toward the foyer door, the pain cascaded down her body like a waterfall of expanding agony, each movement sending a new jab of torment through her, filling her stomach with a bitter nausea.

She was very nearly upon it before she saw the cat sitting in the doorway watching her approach. Its head was raised so the brown mask of its face pointed directly at her, and through that mask, its slitted eyes glinted with a pale, cold-blue hardness, veiled with a terrible blankness. She caught her breath. Confronting her was not a pet cat, but an evil intelligence directing a campaign of terror, pain and death at all who dwelt in the house . . . a warning coming to her from a place deeper than conscious thought.

"Get out of my way!" she screamed. "Move!"

The blue eye slits widened, mocking her. She felt a frenzy building in her. "Move, damn you!"

Not taking its eyes from her face, the cat leisurely stood up, its tail stiffening behind it, and stretched. Slowly, insolently, it backed into the foyer.

Adrienne had the eerie sensation time was collapsing around her, that she was standing where two worlds overlapped, one dark and brooding where mankind was subservient to creatures prowling on four legs, and the other where that same mankind erroneously thought it was master of the universe.

Very slowly she sidestepped through the doorway, then across the foyer to the stairs. From just inside the verandah door, the cat followed her with what were now round eyes, their blue tinted a pale lavender. From the way their gaze crawled up and down her, she was suddenly certain the animal's interest had shifted to the physical movements of her body rather than the workings of her mind. After ascending the first two steps backward, she turned her back to those eyes and ran up the remaining steps. At the top, she looked back down. The cat was staring up at her. On its face was the same lurid grin she had seen in the garden.

She found a bottle of aspirin in the bathroom's medicine cabinet, took two, then went to her room.

She wanted to pack quickly and leave the house before Ned returned. But the pain had reduced her muscles to foam rubber; her mind had the sensation of being glazed over with a coating substance that dried into a hard shell and smothered her thinking, emotions and senses, blocking any thoughts before they could be brought to fruition.

The bed looked inviting, extremely soft and comfortable. She stood looking at it dumbly, feeling its uncanny lure drawing her toward an escape into blissful sleep. Instinct told her to resist. This particular pain must be endured if she was to retain any amount of sanity and pride. But mental and physical weaknesses were too overpowering. With a choked moan, she fell across the bed, stretching full length on it, knowing the brutal fatigue consuming her was beyond all reason in relation to the physical and mental actions which gave birth to it. A dulled knowledge whispered to her that somehow, in some way, she was being manipulated.

She heard a low, continuous sound, hushed like a soft and gentle lament. She listened intently, thinking how sad it sounded, then discovered it was coming from her, that she was sobbing. Her body began to quiver, then to jerk. In a little while she heard her sobbing fade away until all around her there was depthless silence in a ghostly world of whites and grays.

Through the mists she saw figures moving, leisurely, smoothly, coming toward her, then retreating. Two women and a man, and behind them, like shadowy silhouettes, female figures weaving through a peculiar dance. One of the foreground women advanced. Tendrils of mist clung to her and streamed behind her in entwining ribbons, making it appear she strode through the edge of a cloud. When the woman might still have been a dozen paces away, the mist swirled in retreat, leaving her vividly defined and looking straight at Adrienne from blue eyes harsh with terror. It was Sandi. Adrienne watched Sandi's lips moving, but the sound they were creating took far too long to form into words and drift across the space separating them.

"Go away, Adrienne Lewis. Go away . . . go away . . ." An eruption billowed in the mists behind her. "Save yourself . . . go away . . . away . . ."

Then another woman was standing in a clear pocket from which the mists had retreated, smiling at her. At her feet a great white Russian wolfhound lay watching Adrienne. The woman she recognized as the one in Sebastian's painting. She felt no shock, not even mild surprise. She desperately wanted to say something, but when she tried to speak she discovered she possessed no vocal cords.

"Adrienne." The woman smiled, extending a hand. "There is nothing to fear. You are welcome here."

Still she could not speak, even though she tried with a frantic force of will. While she fought to find her voice, she saw that the twisting, weaving figures in the background were the other women in Sebastian's paintings, all of them with their eyes watching her intently while their lips curved in unreadable smiles.

"You will never grow old, Adrienne," the woman was saying. "The years will pass while you remain forever as you are at this moment. Forever young, Adrienne. Forever and ever and ever . . ."

The woman came closer. The dog padded at her side. "Permit Ned to complete the portraits of you and the woman named Sheila Rosenthal. Allow him to do that, Adrienne, and you and he will live with your love until there is no more time."

"No! No!"

In one frantic movement, she rolled over and sat up on the edge of the mattress, hearing the after-sounds of her scream in the stifling confines of the bedroom. Hair was woven in tight skeins across her forehead and down her cheeks, held there by the sweat covering her face with sticky dampness.

She gulped the stagnant air in an endeavor to slow the rampant beating of her heart, clutching the mattress with desperate fingers to keep herself from pitching forward. From the store of horror that was her memory, leering skeletons, pretending to be women, beckoned to her from the far side of a swirling fog to join them in a danse macabre.

A gasping moan escaped her lips as cramped muscles protested when she heaved herself to her feet and stood swaying in the heat. Her suitcase was in the back of the closet. She would fill it with just enough items to get through a day or two at the apartment, worrying at some distant time about coming back to obtain the rest. With the overly cautious movements of a person learning to walk again following a prolonged illness, she made her way to the closet and dragged the suitcase from behind a pile of cartons. The physical action was enough to shove the dream memory out of the way.

She laid the suitcase on the bed. While she fought to open it with suddenly thickened fingers, the sunlight began to fade, retreating across the room and withdrawing out the window. Crisp furniture shadows melted, then disappeared. The corners of the room filled with gloomy puddles of dingy gray. Looking up from the suitcase and out the window, she saw a fragile skim of clouds drifting over the western horizon. With a mental shrug, she dismissed it, knowing it was no more than an interaction of heat and humidity that produced convective thunderstorms. She would be gone before it advanced as far as the house. She began to pack, hurrying, knowing she would be trapped if she was not away before Ned returned.

She laid the last blouse she planned to take on top of a pair of folded slacks, looked at the dresses still hanging in the closet, decided against them and closed the suitcase, telling herself that at that unknown future time, she would ask Amy to return with her to gather what was left. Something warm and salty-wet clung to the corners of her eyes as the hurt which had been muted the last few minutes returned.

She looked around the room, feeling depressed, knowing that once more she had become the victim of fraudulent emotions that were empty of permanence. She was alone as she had never been alone before.

She swung the suitcase off the bed and faced the door. The cat was sitting in the middle of the threshold.

"Get out of here!" Fear shrilled in her voice. "Get out of my way!"

The cat stared at her through the veils which had dropped over its pale blue eyes, showing no indication of moving as it sat there mocking her.

"Damn you!" She hefted the suitcase in her hand, testing its weight and balance, knowing she would not hesitate to swing it at the leering animal. "I'm coming through. This is your last chance to move. Do you hear me?"

Suddenly she was aware of the dark intelligence behind the

blue eyes, but she took a tentative step forward, her hand tightening on the suitcase handle, unable to think of a reason, but knowing that her apprehension of the small creature was justified.

If there had been amusement there, it instantly vanished from the cat's face. Pointed straight up at her, the brown mask suddenly distorted into furious rage, the lips curling away from needle-pointed fangs, tiny nostrils flaring. Very deliberately, it rose to its full height with its paws spread and claws extended. She watched its back arch and muscles in its legs draw tight in tension. A continuous, almost serpentine, hiss came from deep in its throat.

She stood rigidly still. The cat took a step toward her, then another. She could hear its claws on the floor sounding viciously sharp, and unconsciously retreated before it, her eyes held captive by its blue stare. In her hand the suitcase became overly heavy, unbalancing her and sending a quiver up her arm.

"Stop," she hissed. "One more step and you get this suitcase over your head."

It happened so fast even her reflexes were caught unawares. She did manage to scream, hysterical and twisted, as the cat sprang at her throat. Flailing wildly, she dropped the suitcase as she stumbled backward, then frantically clutched the fur on the cat's back in a desperate attempt to pull the animal away from where it hung on her chest with its claws ripping her blouse.

It snarled, freed a paw and slashed at her face. She jerked her head back, the movement forcing her to take a backward step to retain her balance. Her knees struck the side of the bed. Unable to counteract her backward momentum, unbalanced by the weight of the clinging cat, she sprawled heavily across the bed. The cat rode her down. Its claws dug into her flesh through the tattered blouse, spitting and hissing with its fangs exposed and its eyes glinting wildly with naked fury.

Whimpering, as much from frustration as fear battering down her resistance, she lay staring up at the cat perched on her chest.

The cat's weight seemed out of all proportion to its size, like a great stone pressing on her chest. She gulped for air while her fingers clawed handfuls of the sheet at her sides. The room darkened, the shadows merging into each other, as the cloud on the western horizon thickened its folds over the sun and drifted nearer. From far away, a muffled rumbling rolled across the sky. Adrienne turned her head to look at the window. The cat hissed, raised a forepaw with its claws extended and rested it on her cheek. She felt her skin pierced and quickly turned her head back.

She did not know how much time passed, but the darkness from the storm crept closer and closer. Her body ached and her mind drifted in fuzzy detachment. She had not moved from the position in which she had fallen across the bed, the cat allowing her only the slow, labored cadence of her breathing. The terror which had driven her toward a black abyss after the initial attack receded, but she still lay dangerously close to the edge, a cinder of burned-out reason somewhere deep within her repeating over and over that what was occurring could not be possible.

On her chest, its claws partially retracted, the cat sat watching with the discs of its unblinking eyes roaming up and down her body seeking a muscle twitch or a quiver of tiring flesh. Pain burned through her as she lay staring at a spot on the wall above the dresser where the paint was flaking to form an abstract design, the shape of which began more and more to resemble a gargoyle's head pointed in her direction. She had the feeling she was experiencing some kind of rape.

A cramp formed in her lower back. She tried to ignore it, but the muscles sheathing her shoulders picked up the pain and drew it upward until it ran hot little wires into her neck and down her arms. She was going to have to move.

She kept her eyes locked on the round blue ones above her head as she cautiously dug her fingers into the mattress for leverage, then very gradually arched up, ever so slightly rolling to her left.

A sound of untamed fury erupted from the cat's mouth, a snarling, hissing explosion that held no relationship to its normal cries. Heat came from its mouth as if its breath was rushing through internal fires before fanning from between its pulled-back lips. It sprang to its feet, balancing easily on her stomach, its eyes narrowed and gleaming with a demented flame, then lunged for her face with its right forepaw sweeping out in a slashing cut that sank its claws into her hair. It curled its paw and tore at the hair caught in its claws. She screamed, then shot her right hand up to try to grab it behind its shoulders. With a yowl, it slashed at her hand. She dropped it to her side. The cat spun from right to left on her stomach, slashing its claws at her face, throat and arms, its hind claws shredding her blouse and slacks. Something far more than feline fury guided the attack, something that gave the small animal an appalling strength. Yet, not once did its lethal claws graze her flesh. Suddenly she realized what was happening was a warning, that the cat was demonstrating what horror it could perform, that her throat and face could be torn into ribbons like her blouse.

With a defeated moan, she lay still. Instantly the cat resumed its quiet sitting on her chest.

She looked up into the brown mask. The cat tensed, its eyes darting over her, monitoring her, ready for any other movement she might try, then finally, apparently satisfied she was not going to make another attempt at escape, it relaxed and shifted its eyes to hers.

She was unable to pull her eyes away from the blue stare. The cat sat relaxed and quiet as if inviting her to peer through the blue mirrors of its eyes. It stretched its head downward, its triangular skull becoming the familiar serpent shape with the nostrils quivering and the tip of a pink tongue flicking out as if testing the air for vibrations. In its eyes were the dual expressions she recognized from times before—greed and sensual desire.

"Who are you?" she whispered.

The cat appeared to grin in answer, and she felt herself being pulled more and more into the power of that pair of blue watching eyes as one second after another slipped by. Mute and powerless, she lay waiting.

From not too far distant, thunder rolled. The cat pulled back its head and looked in the direction of the window, breaking the contact between them, tiny tremors running the length of its body as sleek muscles knotted and bunched for movement. Adrienne held her breath. Another drumming peal of thunder vibrated across the land. As if responding to some dark signal hidden in the booming sound, the cat retracted its claws, then leisurely stood up to stare down at her for what seemed time unending, finally jumping to the mattress, followed by another spring over the footboard. Without looking at the bed, its rear haunches rolling, it paced slowly to the door, but at the threshold it stopped and turned the brown mask of its face to her. On it was an expression of satisfied smugness. Then it turned and strolled away.

She felt empty and soiled. She had allowed herself to be stripped of resourcefulness and imagination, and once again she could not help but feel she had been raped. With misted eyes, she watched the cat move down the hallway, sensing that something obscene went out the doorway with it, leaving the room immediately clean and quiet like the washed emptiness of the air following a thunderstorm.

Adrienne lay with an arm thrown over her eyes, trying to regain a small portion of psychological balance. She did not know if she could. Her nerves were stretched beyond their limits.

A crash of thunder tore the silence. The walls of the old

house groaned and trembled in the concussion, continuing to quake as the sound waves rumbled around them in ominous stampedes. Under her, the bed trembled. Its shivering loosened her cramped muscles with a hint of new danger.

She stood up, ignoring the slackness of her legs and the cold churning of her stomach, sucking in deep lungfuls of static-charged air while she stood at the foot of the bed waiting for a mild dizziness to subside, then made her way to the closet for one of the blouses and skirts she had not packed.

As her movements became more confident, she hurried through the preparations for leaving. When she was dressed, leaving the torn blouse and slacks in a heap on the floor, she straightened some of the tangles in her hair with a quick combing, then went to the window to see the approaching storm. It loomed high above the trees, as dark as night, a pile of clouds across the western world. Through the open window, she could hear the first heavy, exploratory drops of rain rattling on the dry foliage, and, just beyond the road, the hissing advance of a solid downfall. She left the window, picked up the suitcase and ran down the stairs. Only when she was on the verandah did she think of leaving a note to Ned, then dismissed the inclination immediately. Later, maybe, she would worry about salvaging what might remain between them.

She was halfway between the house and the Toyota when she saw the black, shapeless form in the darkness beneath the peppertree. A thick blackness like a column of heavy smoke hovered beneath the boughs; from within it came the sensation of something waiting, watching.

Just beyond the garden, lightning sizzled, sending a pummeling shock wave across the lawn. Her startled eyes focused on the landing outside the carriage house apartment.

The women from the paintings!

"No!" she screamed. "Oh, my God—no!"

Lightning crisscrossed over her head. The ground heaved, and around the edges of the parking area the oaks and pepper-trees trembled as a cannonade of thunder roared across the earth.

Adrienne screamed again. Inside her head, a roaring grew louder and louder. Rain came in one great cascading sheet, drenching her and driving through her skin to chill her blood and suck the air from her lungs. She began to run, hoping it was toward the car, her terror-frozen mind telling her she was fleeing from all the horror and calamity mankind knew. Through the mat of hair spread across her eyes and the blurring curtain of rain, she saw other women coming from the carriage house apartment to follow the first two down the steps. They were moving faster now, unheeding of the rain. She ran faster. Another dozen steps would have her to the car. The suitcase was a great weight pulling at her right shoulder and thumping against her right knee. Lightning caroomed between her and the carriage house, lashing at her eyes like a thousand candles. The world sizzled and hissed. Burning ozone stuffed her nostrils. She screamed, stumbled to all fours, but continued crawling toward the dark form that intuition said must be the Toyota.

"This is how Katie died," a silent voice whimpered from the center of her terror. "Just like this . . . alone . . . killed by women who do not exist . . ."

"Hurry! Hurry!"

The voice carried on the wind like a cry from somewhere beyond the edge of existence.

She heard feet scraping and stumbling across the gravel to encircle her. Frantically she dug her fingers into the wet gravel, thrusting forward with the toes of her sandals at the same time, pushing and pulling herself toward the looming grayness of the car in a terror-surging crawl.

"Stop her!"

"Hurry, Corinth! Go around this thing. Hurry!"

Then Adrienne was at the car's side. It rose up into the rain above her, shining and cold-looking, curving into the blackness of the watery curtain like a glistening wall. She struggled to her feet, her grimy hands slipping on the wet smoothness of the door until her fingers wound around the handle.

"Don't let it be locked," she prayed. "Dear God, don't let it be locked."

Her fingers slipped from the wet chrome, then clutched again, digging themselves beneath the oblong of metal and jerking upward. The door swung at her, almost knocking her over. Breath emptied from her in a long whimper as she half sprang, half slithered, into the front seat, curling her legs in after her, her right hand grasping the inside armrest to pull the door shut after her.

A hand reached out of the rain, fingers clawing for her wrist. With a cry, Adrienne looked up to see a hate-filled face thrusting toward her through the door opening. A snarl twisted the lips like murderous hunger.

Adrienne slammed the door against the arm and head. The woman yowled in pain as she slipped and fell against the side of the car. Again Adrienne slammed the door, then again, barely hearing the woman's cries of agony above her own screams of rage. Then the arm was withdrawn and she slammed the door shut with such force the car rocked. She drove a fist down on the lock, leaned across the seat and did the same to the lock on the driver's side.

Rain drummed against the metal and glass as if it had taken sides with the frenzied women circling the car and, like them, was trying to find a way inside. Adrienne sat up, drawing a deep breath and pushing the soggy mass of her hair from her eyes. Her head was full of awful noises: the out-of-control thumping of her heart, the great sobbing gulps of her breathing, the hammering of the pelletlike rain striking the car's exterior and, through them all, the fierce shrieks of the women.

Only after a moment or two did she become aware of the faces, their muscles writhing with viciousness, pressed against the two front windows, and the fists striking the rain-rippled glass. Inside her, the terror re-formed, its intensity burning through her like hot wires thrusting along her nerve networks. She could almost feel her brain shrivel inside her skull.

Her head turning from side to side as she looked at the hideous faces pressed against the glass, Adrienne cringed in the middle of the seat. Beginning with the hour sprawled beneath the cat, terror and disbelief and wave after wave of horror had torn away the foundations on which she had been lifted above the primitive beast. Now she was the basic animal struggling for survival.

Then she saw the keys in the ignition. The sight sent an electric jolt through her. With a cry, she slid beneath the steering wheel. On the other side of the window, a brown-haired woman screeched curses and drove her fists in smashing blows against the glass. It creaked, and Adrienne thought she heard a cracking noise come from down in the door panel.

"Start," she said. "Please, please start."

She was surprised how deliberate her movements were in turning the key and pressing the accelerator. The engine started, coughed, then died.

"Don't panic," she told herself. "Try again. It always stalls the first time. Now easy . . . easy . . ."

Carefully she repeated the key turning and the pressure on the pedal.

The engine turned over immediately, hiccuped, then idled smoothly. Sensing what was happening, the women threw themselves at the car, their screams demonic as they kicked and beat their hands and feet along the sides and back and across the hood.

Adrienne shifted into reverse. The Toyota moved back. Rain-drenched, the women clung to it, trying to hold it stationary by digging their heels into the loose gravel, desperation suddenly as much a portion of their attempt to stop her as hate. They slipped and stumbled along with the car as Adrienne backed across the parking area.

When there was room to swing toward the driveway, Adrienne stopped, shifted into drive and jammed her foot down on the accelerator. The car sprang forward, the sound of the rear tires spraying gravel as welcome to her as the engine's instant roar.

As the car swayed down the driveway, she did not look in the rearview mirror.

CHAPTER 14

From behind the wheel of the Jeep, Ned saw the scrub palmettos, the patches of Queen Anne's lace and the scattered clumps of top-heavy ordinary weeds blurring past his peripheral vision.

Staring straight down the road in front of the Jeep, he wondered if a murderer felt as he did during the first hours after committing the crime. Unbelieving. Full of resentment, with fear spawning cold in the stomach. Everything he had done today, he had done badly, because of the inability to coordinate his cartwheeling thoughts. The boggling disbelief which struck him when he and Adrienne stood before the paintings after breakfast had shattered everything into grotesque shambles, and, since then, there were moments when he wondered if his mind might be on the verge of becoming shredded by revelations of things far beyond any awareness human emotions could sustain.

His defense against Adrienne's accusations had turned belligerent. He had gone so far as to lie when she'd asked if he had done more than give Sandi tea. Why had he refused to admit to withdrawing blood to mix with the paint? He shook his head. What had prevented him from telling her? The one person who deserved the truth, she was also the only one with whom he could confide and from whom he could expect assistance—and now he had destroyed that relationship. Smashed it all to hell and back. He beat a tightly clenched fist on the steering wheel.

Certainly he saw the glow emanating from the flesh tones of Sandi's face and forearms. God, you would have to be blind not to be aware of it. He would never be able to erase from his memory that unspeakable terror underlying the smiling expression he had so carefully given her. Dear God, he had even felt her begging him for help! Could almost hear her cries.

But still, his goddamn mind was torn into warring halves, one portion of it revolting at the horrible implications, the other part awestruck at the meaning behind the horror. It was only natural, he tried to tell himself, that after those moments before the easel, and those black ones following the phone call from the café owner, he needed to put distance between himself and the rest of the world. Then came Adrienne's hysterics, another attack upon the shambles of his senses. Everything was so hellishly wrong.

Three miles back, at the closed and boarded-up Texaco station, he had turned from Highway 50 to this secondary road, returning to the place where the brutality had begun. The macadam ceased abruptly. The Jeep bounced and swayed from side to side as its wheels sought purchase in the rutted dirt and sand of what was no more than a trail curving across the veldt of scrubland in the direction of the distant cypress hammock.

He fought the steering wheel as he let up on the accelerator. Dust swirled around the windshield, blinding him, then finding its way into his nostrils so he was forced to gulp air through his mouth, drying the membranes of his throat, making him cough. He cursed, wiped a hand across his face and slowed the Jeep. Over the horizon, off to his left, he saw a bulge of clouds creeping up from behind the greenish-brown curve of the earth like mountains heaving their snowy shoulders out of the flatness of the land. He knew they would build fast, that within them the afternoon showers rode and that he would get wet before the day was finished. He did not care. What happened to him physically was only a remote concern.

He knew when he had stood, with the bile crawling up his throat, before Sandi's painting this morning, he was responsible for the events which had taken place. He was the catalyst. Through him all the horror was funneling.

When he had heard Adrienne go to the garden, he had quickly gathered the paintings together, Sebastian's and his own three, and taken them to the empty carriage house apartment, because this morning in the studio was the first time he had been able to associate the canvases with the evil dwelling in the house. He knew moving them was not enough, that nothing would change, that there was only one act which would end the horror—the destruction of the paintings—and that he could not do. He would never be able to perform an act his aesthetic and professional training considered a sacrilege. At least not yet. Not until he gathered more facts.

That was why he was on his way now to learn the true contents of the bottles in the camera bag on the passenger seat of the Jeep, the bottles he had removed from the taboret after putting the paintings in the carriage house. It was out here where he had received the leaves and powders. It would be out here where he would discover if they had turned him into a murderer.

In Sebastian's notebook chamomile and mandrake and laudanum were named, along with goldenseal, henbane, mayflower and something referred to as "the hastening potion." After inquiries at three pharmacies, that morning Geoff had left for Atlanta, he was told by a middle-aged stranger who overheard his request at on of the drugstores that out past Oveida, at the end of a secondary asphalt and dirt road off Highway 50, lived an old man who grew, compounded and sold herbs. The informant drew a crude but accurate map. Vividly remembering the first trip now, it seemed the old man living in the cabin had expected him, for the items he wanted were laid out on the only table in the cabin when he arrived. Would the old, hollow-cheeked fellow in his dirty shirt, patched bib overalls and orange-visored cap be willing to answer the questions which should have been asked the first time?

The dirt portion of the road melted into, then eventually disappeared into, a tabletop flat field. Ned drove carefully, fearing rodent holes and weed-hidden patches of soft sand. Behind the cypress hammock, the clouds were higher, becoming touched with gray the farther up into the sky they climbed. Slowing to little more than stalling speed, Ned ran his eyes, inch by inch, along the base of the hammock seeking the dark arch of the circular indentation in which the old man's shack nestled. On the second scan he found it.

He saw no one at the squat, weather-tarnished building, though its one door hung open. A dented pitcher and washbasin rested on the bowed wooden steps that gave the impression they were crawling laboriously up to the door, and not too far away a broom lay in the dust, discarded and forlorn-looking. As on the first trip, he had the odd feeling that the shack, crouched in its deep shade, was a setting stolen from the pages of one of Grimm's fairy tales. When he was still perhaps thirty feet from the shack, he caught the pungent odor floating through the sun-heated air. It was a smell he recognized, but he could not put a name to it, though it tantalized his senses.

It was when he braked to a stop in front of the dilapidated building and switched off the ignition that he suddenly knew what the scent was. Sulfur. Burning sulfur. It was coming from behind the shack, heavy, not smudged anymore by distance and air current, strong enough to make him blink his eyes. The old man must be brewing some kind of concoction, he thought, in the few feet of backyard separating the shack from the trees. He walked around the building, trying to think of an appropriate opening statement with which to greet the old fellow. There were so many things he could have, should have, done. He could have, after obtaining the herbs, inquired into their potency. An hour's trip to the library would have been enough. But oh, no! He was keyed up and more than a little unthinking, plus suffering from a touch of smugness. Yes, sir, he was going to be the messiah of portraiture. Bring enlightenment to the masses. Give them culture. Shit! What it looked like he was, was a murderer. But dammit, in a few minutes he was going to have answers, even if he had to wring them from the scrawny old geezer's turkey neck.

The narrow plot of yard was empty. Knee-high, strong-stemmed weeds standing straight and undisturbed indicated no one had trampled through them for some time, but the sulfur smell floated on the still air like a kind of invisible shadow. A chill raced along his back and neck.

He went back to the front of the cabin to stand at the bottom of the three steps leading up to the porchless door. Through it, and the windows, he sensed the deserted emptiness of the cabin.

He mounted the steps to where he could stand looking through the door into the dust-covered emptiness of the one room. Shafts of sunlight slanting through the windows burned squares of intense light on the rotted floor planking creating blotches in which nothing could be seen, like segments of an overexposed negative. Inside, the smell of mildew blended with the musty scent of rotting wood combined with the sulfur odor. As his eyes adjusted to the gloom, he began to realize he was looking into a building which had not been occupied for many months. Dust spread across the floor, piles of sandy grit formed tiny windrows in front of cracks between the wall planking. But that was impossible! No more than three weeks ago he had talked with the old man who lived here, had walked around the wooden chairs and table and unmade cot which furnished the room. He shook his head. Uncomfortable, he looked once more around the empty room, trying for one last time to make things add up, then turned away. He walked to the Jeep, where he stood staring back at the desolate shack, still smelling the sharpness of the sulfur in the air—still not knowing if he was a murderer.

There no longer was a reason for him to remain here, because the answers he needed were to questions which could not be asked; yet he had the uncanny sensation that something was about to happen. His throat tightened. Suddenly, he was aware of how alone and small he was. He began to feel he was the last undiscovered player in a game of hide-and-seek, with the seeker closing in on him, coming nearer and nearer, stalking quietly, bringing evil and terror toward him.

Even though he was expecting something, when the voice called to him Ned drew in a rapid, shallow breath and his heart raced.

"Mr. Anderson, may I have a moment of your time?"

He looked around. There was no one, but the voice could not have come from more than twenty feet away.

There was a chuckle. "You will not see me, Mr. Anderson; so do not divide your attention looking for me."

"Who are you?" His breathing still came in short gasps. He told himself not to panic, and, without turning his head, he moved his eyes in a semicircle across the cabin and the trees on each side of it. "Where are you?"

Again the chuckle. This time it was more guttural and tinted with derisiveness. "It makes no difference, Mr. Anderson. I could be in your mind, in the cabin or among the trees in the cypress hammock. It only matters that I am here to talk with you."

"Then who are you?"

"You would not know me if I told you, Ned." There was a heavy sigh. "I was eons old before mankind crawled from the seas. In the visitations I permitted Sebastian to make to you, he gave you a name by which he knows me; so we shall use it—though it is no more than his coined name for me."

A dark, intangible shadow settled on Ned, confusion accompanied by apprehension. Was this another dream? Somehow he seemed to have moved from sunlight to shade. If he reached out, would he feel the sun-hot metal of the Jeep? He tried it. The hood burned his palm.

The guttural laugh burst from a place among the trees. "This is no dream, Ned Anderson. As people say today, this is for real. We are in the middle of a desolate field preparing, I hope, to have a discussion which will ultimately be beneficial to us both."

Ned forced himself to draw another deep, long breath. He said, "If what's happening is real, then you're real; but you only identify yourself with ambiguities. How can we hold a discussion if I must talk to nothing more than a disembodied voice?"

From wherever it came, the voice dropped half an octave and was bruised with anger. "I have told you what identity I have given myself for the purpose of this meeting. Think of me as that."

Nervousness slowed Ned's mind seeking through its memory banks, and for several long moments he could not think of a thing.

"Do you remember what Sebastian called me?"

From a hidden niche in the subterranean depths of his memory, he heard Sebastian speaking of "The Master" who would someday become his "patron." He spoke the words out loud.

Now the voice was smooth with the rasping tones and harsh anger missing, the patient voice of a person offering a relationship upon which could be built a profitable association.

"Ned, I have seen the portrait you completed of the young woman named Sandi. It is very, very good. I am impressed and would like you to continue doing that type of work, doing all the same things you did with hers."

Ned looked toward the portion of the hammock from which the voice seemed to originate. Was there a hint of dark movement among the intertwining lower branches? He could not be certain. "How did you see it? It's never been out of the house."

"It does not really matter, Ned, but I do have ways. What we are here to discuss is my proposition: provide me with portraits as fine as the one of the woman named Sandi, and you will find me a very generous patron."

"I can't do that."

"Why?"

"I can't paint like that again."

"You did it once, why not again?"

"Because Sandi died, and she died, I'm sure, because of things I did to her while working on the portrait."

"No, Ned. She lives on and will continue to do so for years yet to come."

"What do you mean?"

"In the painting, Ned. Her life and beauty are captured within the painting and will remain forever there."

He heard another voice then, one crying hysterically in his memory. It was Adrienne screaming, "The paintings are alive."

He felt the sweat burning on his forehead. The heat was wrapped around him in layer upon layer like a mummy's binding, making it difficult to breathe. He squinted his eyes to try to see into the darkness of the hammock but was unable to distinguish the form he thought he had glimpsed a few moments before. A tiny tremble rippled through his muscles, but he told himself to hold together, that given just a little more time his thought processes would function normally and he would not be so much on the defensive with the disembodied voice calling itself "The Master."

"What's the proposition you're offering?" His voice was hollow in his ears.

When the voice answered, it was varnished and slick, but with an eerie quality which removed it even further from reality. "Three portraits of three women a year, Ned—all executed in the same manner as the one of Sandi. That is all I ask. You have done one, and you have two others near completion; so, you see, you will not be overburdened to meet the first year's requirements."

Ned ran the palms of his hands down his thighs, drying the sweat from them.

"That is not asking too much, is it?" the voice asked.

"What do you give in return?"

"I will put you apart from other men. I will place you beyond the realm of nature."

Ned shook his head. There was madness in the air, insanity in the dark cavern of the trees. He stood very still and tense, his arms hanging at his sides, realizing he was being broken into little bits and pieces which were being scattered too far for him to gather and reassemble. He asked, "What do you mean?"

"Life, Ned Anderson."

"Life?" He was missing something, something he must understand if he was to remain a whole person. "I have life."

"Temporarily."

"What do you mean?"

"Life is transitory, Ned. In a few years it will pass you by."

"What are you saying?"

"That in exchange for the three portraits a year, your life will no longer be a temporary state."

He stood staring straight ahead, not seeing.

"Do you understand what I'm saying, Ned Anderson?"

He nodded.

"Is that not a satisfactory bargain? Has a patron ever offered more to an artist than unending life?"

He shook his head. In a very short while, he would be able to speak, he knew, but right now it was a far too complex technique for him to master. His mind was twisting in almost painful convolutions in its attempt to reject the statement coming from the trees. It could not. What had been said was not the ramblings of an egomaniac. The voice had made the statement with the assurance of the ability to perform. It had been a basic statement of fact.

"Do you agree?" There was a touch of impatience in the voice.

Whatever hid among the trees possessed unlimited powers. It had to be a thing outside of nature—like the paintings: something beyond the boundaries of human knowledge.

"Did you have this agreement with Sebastian?" he asked.

"Yes, for many years. Many, many years, Ned."

"But he died."

"He did not honor our pact." This time Ned was certain there was a dark movement among the trees. A form advanced close to the edge of the hammock. "I do not hesitate to give, and I do not hesitate to take away. I am fair with those who are fair with me, but my vengeance is brutal to those who become disloyal. Now, Ned, what say you? Do you agree to strike a bargain with me?"

He felt a little stronger now.

"What," he asked, "did Sebastian do that you broke the pact with him?"

"He broke the pact!" The gutturalness returned to the

voice. "He became greedy, wanting something which should have been mine."

"And you killed because of that? You killed Sebastian and his wife because you think he cheated you?"

"Only their physical bodies. Sebastian and she who was to be mine wander alone in a time and land unremembered. It seems a more fitting punishment than absolute death." What might have been a chuckle came from the cypress hammock. "The terror of waiting for my final vengeance is their constant companion, and they have died ten times a thousand deaths, Ned Anderson, while awaiting the final one, should I decide to grant them that escape."

Ned said nothing.

"Well, what have you decided?"

"Nothing yet. I want to know more."

"What more is there that you need to know? You give me three women a year, and I give you unending life. Is that not simple enough to understand, Ned Anderson?"

"You just said three women. I thought it was three paintings a year you wanted."

"They are one and the same."

"A woman and a painting are one and the same? I—" He stopped, physically wincing, as an appalling thought gouged him. He stood staring at the trees, feeling the heat radiating from the metal of the Jeep as only a nebulous abstraction, and when he spoke, his voice had a curious throaty tone. "They're the same, aren't they? The paintings and the women *are* the same! That's why the woman's blood must be mixed with the paints to be used in the flesh tones." He hesitated, suddenly aware of the terrible power lurking among the cypress trees, and he knew, as he looked in the direction of the place he thought The Master stood, his face showed a reflection of the fearful disbelief laying hold of him. "Adrienne was right. The paintings are alive."

He leaned against the Jeep, ignoring the branding-iron heat

of the metal burning through his jeans. For what seemed to him a long time, his mind replayed memories like old motion pictures he could recall scene by scene: the brutal argument with Geoff, Katie's death and the black hair clutched in her hand, the bloody face at the studio window, Adrienne's ongoing uneasiness and eventual terror. Maybe those were the reasons why, at this moment, he felt no surprise or skepticism. His immunity was built up.

The voice began to speak again with disagreeable arrogance. "I will be overly generous with you, Ned Anderson. You have studied Sebastian's paintings. Certainly you have found a favorite among them; one woman whom you perceive as more beautiful than the others, and with whom you believe you could find satisfaction. Is that correct?"

The trees whispered in a young breeze and the clouds rose higher, forming pictures in the sky, as he felt within him stirrings of dark revulsion at what he knew The Master was going to say. But he also could not keep the memory of a tall blond woman wearing a tiara and dressed in a sweeping blue gown from forming.

"Ah, you have good taste, Ned, in beauty and in breeding. Sebastian was more basic and chose Magda, an earthy type of creature."

Ned was not surprised that The Master had read his mind, and he felt if he could see the other's eyes they would be appraising him.

"Her name is Lila, Ned. Two hundred years ago she was the adored bride of a central European duke. She is one of my favorites, I admit, but I give her to you as a slave for your desires and pleasures. She will be your very own demimondaine, Ned. Helpless, powerless and obedient to you."

Under the sweat, he could feel the gooseflesh on his arms and a chilled line running down the center of his back. A dry, metallic taste formed in his mouth, which he assumed was associated with the sudden acceleration of his heart. He pushed himself away from the Jeep.

"You want me to give you Adrienne Lewis and Sheila Rosenthal?"

"Yes, in return for eternal life and Lila's charms."

Once more there was the sense that in some way he held a bargaining agent to be used against the power hidden in the trees. If only there was time, maybe he could winnow it out of the chaff cluttering his thinking.

He asked, "What do you do with the women?"

"It does not concern you."

It was the wrong approach. He stood staring at the ground, trying to appear speculative, hoping he was making The Master assume he was deliberating on the proposal. Finally, shaking his head, he said, "I'm going to have to think on it. I can't give you an answer right now."

"I do not have time!" It was a hoarse bellow, a rasping sound of anger and frustration combined.

Quickly Ned looked up. In the dense shadows beneath the trees, there was rapid movement, a solid mass thrashing among the cypress branches. For one very brief instant, he was certain he saw two malevolent eyes directing their stare at him, and the smell of burning sulfur thickened, assaulting his nostrils. He clenched his teeth to hold in check the grunt of relief rising in his throat. He had found The Master's weak spot! Time.

"I will not wait." The voice was heavy.

"Then you'll have to find someone else to paint your portraits." He started to get into the Jeep.

"Wait! Do not be hasty, Ned. There is room to negotiate." It was another voice entirely, the rage-torn shout gone, giving way to an unctuous rippling of sibilant tones which cajoled with an almost wheedling whine. "At times I lose my patience, but I try to understand and be fair. Surely you know how pressures from outside sources can cause short-temperedness. I require two women to fulfill an . . . obligation; however, I can wait a fortnight. Surely that will give you time to complete the two portraits."

"Then what?"

"Then our pact is completed, Ned. The day you deliver the portraits will be the first day of your everlasting life."

Ned nodded, but said nothing.

Behind the cypress hammock a whirlpool of fire flared, seethed for a short moment silhouetting the trees in a black tangled pattern in front of the boiling reds and oranges, then vanished with a roar of exploding air. A gust of wind swept across the veldt, howled among the trees, then rushed at Ned to strike him on the chest, causing him to fall back a step. On it the smell of scorched air replaced the sulfur odor. Invisible air waves flung clods of dirt and twigs at the Jeep in a rattling stream as heavy slabs of oversize raindrops thumped into the dry earth and clattered on the Jeep's hood and fenders.

Riding the air currents, the voice rose above the splattering of the rain. "A fortnight, Ned Anderson. You have a fortnight to give me the two women. If you do not, I shall be forced to deal with you as I did with Sebastian. Remember that, Ned. As I did with Sebastian. My secret must remain a secret."

Ned crawled into the Jeep, his muscle action mechanical. His senses were deadened.

He sat without noticing the rain as it molded his shirt to him and chilled his face and forearms, staring at the hammock, seeing its dark mass huddled, brooding, as if the trees were stopped in shame at what had hidden itself among them moments before.

"No, goddammit! No!" He shouted it aloud, his face turned up to the rain, his hands clenched on the steering wheel. "There is no such creature."

The world was a cold, gray torrent of solid falling water through which he fought the Jeep across the field, twice nearly bogging down in sand transformed to quagmire, never sure if he was edging forward in the direction of the road or traveling in a repeating circle. Deep inside the grayness, distant flashes and boomings gave him the uncomfortable feeling of driving through a no-man's-land between dueling artillery emplacements. The cold accompanying the rain chilled him beneath his soggy clothes, at the same time trying to suck the air from his lungs so he felt he was breathing in a vacuum.

The storm front rolled eastward, rumbling with still unleashed anger toward the distant horizon while behind it the rain slackened, then settled into a moderate summer shower that left a vague disquiet sprawling across the land, an unnatural silence and the sharp smell of wet vegetation.

He discovered he was probably a quarter of a mile from where the road dissolved into the field. He guided the Jeep to the two ruts of mud curving toward the macadam he could see darkly glinting between its low walls of dripping weeds. When he arrived at the pavement, with all four wheels of the Jeep solidly on it, he stopped, leaned back and closed his eyes. He needed a cigarette, but the package in his shirt pocket was a flattened mass of brown-stained paper and torn cellophane. He crumpled it into a ball, which he threw into a clump of weeds.

When he laid his hands on the rim of the steering wheel, he saw they were trembling and tried to think it was because of the physical strain of driving through the storm, but knew it was because of the revulsion and fear slithering through him. What had occurred between him and the thing in the cypress trees could not be molded in any form but the one of reality. It had happened. He had experienced it. It had been ultimate and grotesque realism.

He stopped at a 7-Eleven to buy a package of Benson & Hedges. The clerk was reticent about accepting the two soggy dollar bills he gave her.

It was after he left the store that the shock wore off. When the sharp, dry smoke of a cigarette curled in his lungs, the air was filled with the rank smell of weeds and he could feel the fast, heavy beating of his heart and hear the thick noise of his rushing blood. Though the main thrust of the storm was gone, the overhead clouds were growing darker again, setting up a boiling motion which made the heavens appear uneasy.

The lead gray of late afternoon was deepening into dingy twilight when he turned the Jeep into the driveway. At first he was aware only that Adrienne's car was gone; but then he saw a suitcase, its tan leather glinting and polished-looking with raindrops still clinging to it, lying beneath the tip of a water-bowed branch of a peppertree. There was a terrible loneliness in the way it lay on the wet gravel, a kind of representation of everything which had ever been abandoned and forgotten.

He slammed the Jeep to a stop, jumping out without switching off the ignition, and ran to the suitcase, knowing it was Adrienne's, feeling the earlier coldness intensifying within him.

Around the suitcase the gravel was scraped and scrambled into erratic ridges and ragged craters; not far from it, the stones were scattered by what could only have been wheels spinning under rapid acceleration.

There had been a struggle, he knew immediately. Then a frantic escape by automobile, and with Adrienne's Toyota missing, that was more than an assumption.

Adrienne was gone. Her departure did not come as a surprise, but the scattered stones in the parking area told a tale of violence which he found all too terrifyingly easy to read. Almost to her car, suitcase in hand, Adrienne had been attacked. While she fought, she had dropped the suitcase. But who was her assailant?

He picked up the suitcase, irrationally grateful at how light it was, and ran to the house. For the first time, he realized how little he knew of Adrienne's associations and circle of friends.

He knew no place other than her apartment to try to locate her.

He put the suitcase in Adrienne's workroom. The room was filled with the silent echoes of laughter and hammer blows along with the urgent words of the conversations which had begun the things which were eventually to become more immediate than life. The material spread on the two tables looked neglected and forgotten, abandoned because fate held no regard for human dreams. Using his right foot, he pushed the suitcase under one of the tables, took a final look around before going out into the hallway and closing the door behind him.

With all the doors leading to it closed, the hallway was dark, so he stood for an extended moment with his hand remaining on the doorknob while his eyes adjusted. The first several times he heard the noise he paid it no attention. It was part of the low monotone of background sound the mind learns to accept. But then the sound separated itself from conformity.

He looked up and down the hallway, trying to focus on the sound. Finally he isolated it as originating behind the closed studio door. He waited for it to identify itself, but it continued with the same repetitious murmur as when it first crept into his consciousness, not varying in intensity, a low, soft humming like a woman crooning to herself while brushing her hair or applying makeup. Scowling, he walked slowly down the hallway toward the door, wondering why he was being so stealthy.

He stopped at the door, still unable to explain his hesitation. He bit down hard on his lower lip as he reached for the doorknob. At the same instant he turned it, a draft of wind hit the house, whipping rain solidly against it. Startled, he swung the door open faster than he intended.

The newborn night filled the studio. Floating in the dimness, the windows were pale gray oblongs rattling in the hollow silence as the rain splashed against their glass. Ned stepped over the threshold. One of the windows was open, because he could smell the rain-soaked grass outside, tangy and astringent in the stale air of the room. Then the noise ceased and the silence moved in, but he was immediately aware of something alien sharing the darkness with him, something in which, he knew, life pulsed. He licked his dry lips and squinted into the gloom, then reached to his right for the light switch.

"If that is the magic thing which makes light, do not bother with it, Ned Anderson; for we do not need light."

The woman's voice came from the north end of the room, low, little more than a throaty whisper, flavored with a ripeness of tone and an abundance of intimate warmth.

"What?" He felt more foolish than shocked, standing there with an upraised hand and a slack-jawed mouth. "Who in hell's here?"

"My name is Lila." The voice traced sweeping curves and lovely lines through the darkness. "I belong to you, Ned Anderson. The Master has made you a present of me."

He could not help himself: he leaned against the doorjamb as a sudden numbness ran through his body. Deep inside his nostrils there seemed to be the smell of burning sulfur, and from somewhere far away he heard the voice from thc cypress hammock chuckling.

"Come, Ned, come. Find pleasure with me." The soft tones carried images of moon-gilded nights and meadows drowsy in the sun. "I belong to you. I am yours to use."

He turned on the light.

She was standing beside the easel which had held Sandi's portrait. Tall, blond and sleek in the blue gown, she stood with her tiaraed head bowed, staring at the toe of a golden slipper peeping from beneath the gown's hem. Her arms hung limply at her sides in a carefully practiced pose of sexual subjection, allowing all the curves and indentations of her proffered body to be examined.

He wanted to scream. It was impossible for this woman to be standing before him. She did not exist. Desperately he wanted somebody human at his side whom he could touch and who would tell him he was not alone with this thing.

She raised her head and smiled. "If you will not come to me, Ned, then I will come to you. I must pleasure you, Ned. The Master and the others insist I show you unlimited joy."

He watched the taut swaying of her hips, the trembling of her breasts under the bodice of the blue gown, as she came slowly to him with her gloved left hand outstretched. She emerged with a slow stateliness from out of the mists of unreality, and when she stood before him and her gloved hand closed around his right wrist, he knew Lila was a living woman with warm blood flowing through a strong and vibrant body.

She squeezed his wrist, then gave it a little tug. "Come, let us go to your bedchamber, Ned."

He tried to pull away.

She hesitated, blue eyes searching his face, then, with a gliding step, pressed her entire length to him, grinding her loins to his, mashing the heavy weight of her breasts on the firmness of his chest. She laid a cheek to his, her lips toying with the lobe of his ear, and whispered, "Do you not feel the primal urge, Ned?"

He felt his arms rising, though he was sending them no commands, felt his left hand spread between her shoulders, then stroke the long, sweeping curve of her back while his right one, having been released by her, rested on the thrusting shelf of her buttocks. Way down in Lila's throat, a purr rippled. She slipped an arm around his waist and began to lead him toward the foyer door.

* * *

He looked around. The room was familiar, but there was a strangeness to it as if it were a reproduction of one he knew but with a detail or two missing. He heard the rain still falling out in the darkness, more of a caressing whisper on the windows than the rattle with which it had clawed at the studio windows.

"Relax, Ned. Why are you so tense?"

He looked up, startled, and squinted his eyes to peer into the darkness beyond the edge of the illumination from the bedside lamp. Just outside the light, a tall blond woman was standing with her head cocked a little bit to her right, staring at him with a quizzical smile. But for the dully sparkling tiara topping the blond hair, she was nude. Only half visible in the shadows, she did not seem quite real to him; yet he knew she was as much substance as he in this scene that was occurring between the realms of life and death.

He shook his head. "I don't believe you're here. You can't be."

She laughed very gently. Against the background sound of the rain, its muted notes filled the room like a vagrant whisper of desire. She took an indolent step toward him, then another and another, emerging into the thin distilled light. Taut golden-tinted flesh rippled as beneath it long muscles flexed. She stopped a step or two in front of him, looking down into his face from what seemed to him to be a place far too high, then reached out and ran cool fingers down his left cheek.

"But I am here, my darling. You must believe it." She smiled slyly. "I will have to work very hard to please you, so you will be sure I am here. We are going to spend a long time together, you and I, Ned."

She moved another step closer, so he could feel the humid warmth coming from her, along with an elusive scent, very faint and not belonging as a part of her: a scent reminding him of . . . of paint and linseed oil and raw canvas.

Gracefully she lowered herself to her knees before him. Her overly full breasts swayed from side to side with the movement, then thrust audaciously at him. He looked at them, still not understanding how spheres which were only an illusion created with dark and light shades of paint could tremble as they did.

"Is there anything you wish me to do to please you?" She leaned forward, her lips glistening from the wetness of the tip of her tongue. "I will do anything you wish."

He shook his head.

"Is there anything you want to do to me? You can do anything to me you want to do. I belong to you."

Again he shook his head. Fragments of memories were gathering, fitting themselves together, beginning to form a recollection of things past. Anger, then fear. An empty cabin, a voice speaking to him from nowhere, driving through a storm, Adrienne gone. His awareness expanded; the memories fell into place faster. He looked down at the woman kneeling before him, looked into her blue eyes and saw behind the wanton lust humiliation and fear, and, over the pattering rain, he heard the faraway voice in the cypress hammock telling him he would be given Lila as a personal slave to be used as he desired.

"Please," she whispered. "You must find enjoyment with me."

He leaned forward and cupped her upturned face in his hands, knowing the answer he would receive, but asking anyway. "Who are you? Just who in hell are you?"

"Lila. My name is Lila."

"You know that's not what I mean." His hands tightened along her jaw. "I want to know who you are. You, the woman. The person. Not just a goddamn name. Tell me about yourself: where you come from, what in hell is your relationship to the portrait Sebastian painted of you. And one other thing: tell me who The Master is. Those are the things I want to know. Do you understand me?''

Her eyes widened and returned his look from the shadows of her long golden lashes. In them, there was an unnatural brightness, tiny highlights sparkling in their corners and along their lower lashes, and, very suddenly, she was not a big, golden-hued animal watching him and stalking him, but a young woman in whom he sensed, along with the fear and humiliation, charm and sensitivity.

''Are you going to tell me?'' he asked softly.

She continued staring up at him, and he saw a resigned sadness join the emotions already in her eyes at the same time her lips tightened, then slackened, as she slowly circled their fullness with the tip of her tongue. She closed her eyes, holding them closed for a long, long time, then opened them and nodded her head.

''I will tell you,'' she whispered, ''but only because you are a very special person. The Master says you are going to help us.''

His head filled with noises like wind hurrying through hollow reeds. He knew it was the sound of his racing blood being pushed by the heavy pumping of his heart.

''How am I to help you?''

''Why, by giving The Master new slaves for his pleasure.''

He dropped his hands from her face to rest them limply on his thighs. ''He hasn't told me much.''

''He has promised us that with each new woman you give him, he will free one of us.''

''Free you?''

He began to decipher the urgency in the voice coming from the trees. The Master had made a promise to these women, which, if he could not fulfill, would, even with his power, become an explosive affair. There were pent-up passions in the women, smoldering against The Master. A broken promise could be the poking of the embers of those promises.

"Tell me what you mean, Lila." He reached out to gently lift her face with forefinger under her chin. "Tell me everything. Everything."

He watched the expression in her eyes retreat from dawning excitement to opaque fear. "Please . . . he would punish me terribly, and I have been hurt so often. He is cruel to us, even when we do nothing, because it pleases him to hear us scream and watch us suffer."

"Lila, you said you'd tell me."

"I spoke too hastily." Tears spilled from her staring eyes to wiggle in fat rivulets down her cheeks. Whimpering, she reached up to clutch his wrists with both hands, holding tight, digging her nails into his flesh. "I beg you, give him the portraits and the women's souls. Let new ones suffer as we have for so many years. Please, kind Ned, allow us who have been his slaves to become free women so we may live the lives we have been denied."

"Their souls? He has your souls?"

"Yes. That is why we are his slaves."

"How? How in—the blood! That's it! The blood in the paint. He uses it somehow." He clenched his hands as his thoughts raced away from the kneeling woman. He had never really believed in souls, thinking of them as no more than carryovers from religion's early doctrines when the poor looked with hope for relief from a lifetime of frustrations. Again he cupped her upturned face with his hands.

"Tell me, Lila, what is your master's name?"

Definite terror took its place behind Lila's eyes.

His hand tightened on her jaw. "Tell me. Tell me his name."

"He has no name."

His hands tightened more. She whimpered, and he knew he was hurting her. "He must. Tell me! If you do not, I'll not help you and the others regain your souls. Tell me, Lila. Tell me, is he who some people call Satan?"

"No!"

"Who, then? Tell me, Lila!"

"The Master. That is all. He has no other name . . ."

Sweat broke out on his forehead, ran down his brows, then down his cheeks so it appeared he, too, was crying. He did not bother to wipe it away. He closed his eyes. "Sandi, Sandi. Poor, hopeful Sandi. In your innocence you trusted me . . . and, dear God, what have I done to you?"

He opened his eyes to see that Lila was no longer between his knees. He stood up, then walked slowly to the rear window, where he stood looking at his reflection in the rain-spattered glass, then through it in the direction of the carriage house.

The carriage house! The paintings of Adrienne and Sheila!

He whirled from the window. Even though they were not completed, he must get those two canvases out of the carriage house, away from the others. Nausea twisted his stomach. Bile rose up his throat to fill the back of his mouth. He gagged it down.

"What are you doing?" Lila was looking at him from beside the south window, where she was standing watching a new storm rumbling in the southwest. When she saw him running for the door, she screamed, "Where are you going?"

He did not know why he answered, but he said, "The carriage house."

"You cannot! He is coming to pleasure himself with the new woman you gave him today."

He was out of the bedroom, down the stairs and opening the verandah door when he heard her screeching. "Come back! Do not go! He promised to free us, do you not understand? He promised to free us. One of us for each one you give him."

The gravel in the parking area crunched under his shoes with a sharp rattling, louder than he had ever heard it before. It rolled under him so that he had the irrational fear of turning his ankle. Though the rain was still falling moderately, it struck his face as if driven by a storm wind, forcing him to half close his eyes and hold his breath. Over and over, he reminded himself not to panic, that the violence of the emotions sweeping him must be contained until he removed the two paintings.

The wooden steps leading up to the apartment were slippery with water dripping from tread to tread, forming tiny puddles in the depressions of the worn planking. It squashed under his soles in the same way, he imagined, that blood would sound if puddled beneath his feet. The thought made him grip the railing so tightly his palm chafed. When he was three quarters of the way up, a flurry of wind buffeted the building, making it creak and the steps tremble. He stopped briefly, clutched the railing with both hands, then gulped in a shallow breath, as, for an instant, he thought he was tottering on the edge of an abyss which yawned down into the darkness that went on and on without end to eventually become the place where terror and evil dwelled.

He was mildly surprised and grateful at the ease with which the apartment door opened, though his fingers felt rubbery and swollen as he inserted the slippery key into the lock. As he stepped into the apartment, another gust of wind slashed at the building, once more causing it to groan on its foundations and shiver as if it was experiencing some of the fear he brought into it with him. He slammed the door shut and leaned with his back to it, unmoving.

"Just get the portraits," he told himself. "Don't try to figure anything out. Just get the paintings and get the hell out of this place."

He tried the light switch with no results, then shoved himself slowly away from the door, starting to move in the direction of the far wall beside which he had placed the paintings, feeling his way with outstretched hands while he took halting steps in case he bumped into one of Katie's hanging plants. Only a glimmer of gray came through the windows, a half light more disturbing than total darkness because of its cold, eerie hue.

Lightning raced across the sky sending its blue-green flare through the windows. Ned looked around the room, hoping what he had seen in the flash was no more than an illusion, but as his eyes accustomed to the near darkness, he saw what he had glimpsed in the lightning flare. The paintings were not arranged on the floor in six piles of three each. They were placed around the room, rectangled color receding into the enveloping blackness.

For the length of two deeply indrawn breaths, he stood without moving. He pulled his butane lighter from his pocket, flicking it twice before the flame shot up with a tiny hiss.

The portraits were arranged around the room: three below the windows with four fanning out from them. The others were scattered about the floor. In the first few moments of light, he received the impression all the women were looking at him, regarding him through heavy-lidded eyes as their lips curved ever so slightly in wet smiles. Ned felt a chill run along his spine. He would have sworn he had entered a room where women had arranged themselves to meet a guest.

The lighter flame retreated into its nozzle. As the darkness folded in once more, he saw Sandi's portrait. Before her face disappeared within the blackness, he caught a glimpse of unimaginable terror spread across her features, bulging her eyes into round blue spheres which caught the flame from the lighter and shattered it against the opaqueness of their blind agony, twisting her mouth into a silent scream of mindless horror.

The lighter was hot in his hand. He thought he heard a rustling like a dress's material, followed by a hushed giggle.

Then the lighter was cool, and he lit it again. Sandi's face was the way he had painted it, smiling, dreamy-eyed, with a vaguely matured innocence softening her features. The fear building in his stomach began to churn: time was running out. Even if The Master was not coming, his own senses could not much longer survive in this place peopled with these women who drifted between life and death.

A long roll of thunder strode over the roof of the carriage house. It set vibrations quivering throughout the building, shivering the floor. Giving one final, desperate look around the room for the unfinished portraits of Adrienne and Sheila, he saw the door to the bedroom, took a step toward it, hesitated, then, out of desperation, hurried across the room to look into the empty blackness beyond it. Almost invisible in the ghost light from the windows and the spluttering flame of his lighter, he saw the two canvases leaning against the far wall. Rain splashed with a sudden increase in force.

He crossed the empty room, gathered up the two canvases and put them under his arm. He did not examine them. He ran back across the bedroom, then through the living room. At the door, he stopped for a brief instant, wondering if he should take Sandi's portrait with him, if he should gather them all up to carry away from whatever was approaching within the storm. But he knew it was too late; too late for Sandi, and long, long too late for the other women.

He left the apartment and raced down the slippery stairs.

CHAPTER

It was no ordinary storm. It stretched far beyond both rain-obliterated horizons, its boiling clouds churning across the heavens. Beneath it, the land, in spite of the rain, had assumed a charred appearance, vegetation turning purple-black, buildings becoming smudged, their windows, with no light to reflect, empty and haunted. Night crept beneath the clouds, a hot, humid darkness that lay too heavy on the earth as if the storm desired to smother every living thing beneath its bulk.

For the first few minutes after leaving the driveway, Adrienne guided the Toyota blindly through the rain-gray world, her concentration directed on the desperate struggle to hold away the terror riding at her side. She was not aware of where she was headed; she did not care. She was alive. Over and over, her bludgeoned senses repeated the phrase: I am alive, I am alive.

She had no idea where she was or how long it had taken her to get to wherever that might be when she saw two glowing arches high in the black sky approaching her on the right side of the car. At first glance, she did not know what they were, afraid they might be the initial visions of a new nightmare, then they were looming over the car, wonderfully brilliant and gay, and she sobbed with relief as she recognized them as a McDonald's sign. Suddenly, she knew, she was no longer a fugitive in a disintegrating world. Almost laughing, she turned into the parking lot behind the arches.

Four cars, looking like fat bugs with their gleaming backs turned to the rain, were parked near the restaurant's entrance. Condensation from the building's overworked air conditioner covered the inside of the plate glass windows. After she pulled into a space beside one of the parked cars, she sat for a long time staring at the entrance, feeling a little more of her bewilderment slipping away, a little more of reality coming back.

It was then she remembered her purse was still on the chest of drawers in the bedroom of the house, and the lights of the entrance faded away, disappearing into that place where all the good things in her life had gone. She continued to stare through the rain-blurred windshield at the lighted interior of the building, desperately wanting to become a part of a group of people, no matter if they were strangers, to drink hot coffee, even if it was served in a plastic cup.

To do those things would be a declaration of her existence, but the fluorescent salvation was to be denied her. She had no money. With her hands curled tightly on the steering wheel, her eyes focused on the steamed windows of the McDonald's, she made no attempt to hold back the sob of frustration welling in her as an overwhelming sense of despair gripped her. Soon, an uncontrolled voice in her cried out, soon the women from the paintings would be marching across the parking lot, their rage-filled eyes glaring at her, taloned hands raised to shred her flesh to ribbons. Already, in the shadows where the parking lot lights were swallowed by the night, she was certain she could feel something standing, observing her, waiting for her to leave the protection of the lights. The sob became a muted scream.

A gust of wind shook the car, lashed it with a cascade of rain. She looked behind her, through the rear window, at the shadows fringing the rain-washed lights, searching the shadow caves, but seeing nothing move, nothing that appeared darker than the wall of night, but the fear remained, intensifying into a high pitch. Whimpering, she began to fumble with the ignition key to start the car. While she struggled with the lock, her eyes flicked around her, and, from the corner of her eye, she saw the center console. Money! There were coins in a compartment in the console that she kept for tolls and parking meters. Frantically she opened the console and stared at five quarters lying in the shallow coin tray. Clutching them in her right hand like an excited child, she flung open the car door and ran through the rain to the welcoming glitter of the entrance.

In the chrome and glass fantasy that reflected the too-bright fluorescent lighting, there was a shadowed corner into which she could withdraw. She picked a table, then sat at it facing the room, needing to watch the coming and going of life, giving no heed to the people at the other tables who stared at her: some kindly, some worried, some with distaste. Dear God, never, never had she been so aware of living, or had life seemed so incredibly precious.

The coffee was hot, if bland, nipping her tongue and scoring a hot line down her throat to her stomach. She moved her eyes back and forth across the sparkle and glitter, wanting to transform it into a snug and warm place where her senses would relax.

In the chilled air, the coffee cooled too fast. Holding the cup in front of her lips, slowly turning it in her fingers, its warmth was a measured medicine rebuilding her awareness with each sip. She sat staring straight ahead trying to harness the renewed strength the coffee had given her, and feared that maybe from this day on, she would only peer at the world, never becoming a part of it again.

The coffee was not even half gone when little dark images began to circle outside her thinking, phantoms floating through that special darkness that exists only in fear. If she listened close, she knew, she would hear them gibbering in a language only understood by the mindless ones.

She screamed and dropped her half-full cup.

"Ma'am? Miss?" A young man stood looking down at her. Behind dark-rimmed glasses, his brown eyes were wide with concern. "Is something wrong?"

"Yes. Oh . . . no . . . No, I'm sorry."

"Ma'am, you don't look at all well. Are you sure you're all right?"

She nodded, fighting frantically to hold in check the return of the fear she thought she had left outside. She looked down at her hands lying on the table, and for the first time noticed the dirt caked under the broken nails, the scratches along their backs and the dried blood crowning several knuckles, and knew then the ugly sight she must be to the people at the surrounding tables. Embarrassment wedged its way into her along with the returned terror.

She looked up, shook her head and tried to smile, thinking how ghastly that smile must appear on her dirty face, framed as it must be with tangled hair. "I'm much better than when I came in, thank you."

"Let me get you another cup of coffee to replace this one." He nodded at the cup lying on the table with the brown puddle surrounding it. "It's the least we can do."

"Thank you."

He took the cup to the counter. When he returned, he carried a towel with which he carefully mopped away the coffee spill.

"If you'd like," he said, "you may use the ladies' room to clean up in. One of the girls will help you."

"After the coffee?" she asked.

"Sure," he said, and smiled. It was a good smile, mature yet touched with a lingering, childlike innocence.

The second cup of coffee warmed her even more than the first: she did not know she had felt so chilled. After three deep swallows of it, she found she could return the tentative smile directed at her by one of the girls behind the counter, but it was only on her lips. Inside her, all reason to smile was gone.

Her anger with Ned had faded, not strong enough to compete with the terror, but now annoyance directed at herself slipped inside the fear, an annoyance and a shame at her reactions when Ned informed her of Sandi's death. Ned deserved better than she had given him, because under the anger with which he had answered her fury, he, too, must have been battling fear.

Suddenly she saw him arriving at the house, driving into the parking area to be surrounded with the women-creatures, coming at him from their place in hell, their fingers, those terrible fingers, clawed in preparation to rip and tear and gouge.

She had a quarter left. She got up, steadied herself by leaning against the table for a moment, then walked across the room, cringingly aware of the eyes following her, to the public telephone clinging in its plastic shell on the wall. When she dropped it in the slot, the quarter rattled downward, then fell into the coin box with a loud plunking. Her hand trembled as she dialed.

There was no answer. She allowed the phone to ring fifteen times, fighting away visions of the women swarming over Ned before he could get out of the Jeep. With a silent whimper, she hung up. Now the laughing demons were in her mind to stay, their chortling becoming mocking taunt. She ran from the restaurant, forgetting the returned quarter.

The choked moans she heard in the car were her own, and she did nothing to check them. The building and parking lot lights reflected in a rain-hazed, soft-focused blur, while the rain fell with a steady drumming on the car's roof and hood. Through the misted windshield and steamed windows of the building, she saw faces pressed to the plate glass watching her, their pale ovals resembling the wax features of puppets melting in the smearing rain.

At first, she again drove aimlessly. She thought of trying to find her way back to the house, but panic and revulsion welled up within her with such a thrust her hands tightened on the steering wheel, and she screamed at the night.

She wandered off the arterial street on which the McDonald's was located to a narrower one with less lighting and fewer cars. After a few blocks, she pulled to the curb and lowered the window, welcoming the spray of rain in her face, running her tongue around her lips to lick from them the cool dampness. Squinting, she looked up and down the street trying to locate herself. Nothing was recognizable. Leaving the window down, she drove slowly on, entertaining a vision of the wet pavement glinting in the Toyota's headlights as curving on and on into a darkness no light could penetrate.

Then, spraying across the night, there were streaks of color so vivid she at first thought they were bursting flares from a minor explosion. She blinked and sucked in her breath, seeing there was no movement among the flaming tendrils and abstract shapes. She slowed the car, willing herself to concentrate, then felt the smile curve her lips and heard the giggle break from them when she discovered she was at the intersection of Orange and Seminole Drive with its flashing neon lights. She turned the car south on Orange in the direction of the apartment complex.

She parked the car in her assigned space, then walked

slowly to the building. She did not feel the rain. Half a lifetime ago she had moved from here to the house.

Without closing the door, she switched on the living room's overhead light, then hurried to the telephone, thanking the lack of time which had prevented her from having the utilities and phone turned off.

This time she listened to the phone ring twenty times before hanging up. The possible meaning of Ned not answering replayed itself in her thinking, creating distorted images of the rain-soaked parking area with the women screaming their bloodlusting fury while they clawed him into ribbons of torn flesh. Uttering a deep-throated moan, she covered her eyes with her hands in a desperately hopeless try at blocking out what she was seeing, knowing that under the accumulative weight of all her terrors she would soon be pushed below the surface of dark quicksands of insanity.

She sank onto the sofa, wanting to close her eyes but unable to lower her lids, though she sensed her mind withdrawing, slowing its processes, here and there flicking off circuits as the need for their functions diminished, until inside her a great nothingness began to form.

"Hey, what are you doing here?" A pause, then a gasp. "What in hell has happened to you?"

Adrienne looked at the open door. Amy was standing on the threshold, her eyes wide under a furrowed brow.

"I've come back home, for a little while."

"My God, I guess you have, and you haven't come back the best for wear, either." Amy stepped into the room. "Adrienne, what in God's name happened? You look . . . well, I don't know what, but something awful, anyway."

Adrienne stared at her friend. Almost immediately she felt tears welling in her eyes. She sat still with her hands folded in her lap as the warm tears spilled over her lower lashes to trace scalding little tracks down her cheeks.

"Adrienne!" Amy covered the space between them in

long, heavy strides, almost falling onto the sofa beside Adrienne, instantly enfolding her in a too-tight hug. "Go ahead and cry, and when it's over, tell me what's going on."

She sobbed hard, in a grief-filled panic that she could not control. Amy said nothing, but sat holding Adrienne's bowed head to her breast while stroking the soggy mass of her hair, scowling across the room at the rain-spattered windows.

Slowly the great hacking sobs subsided. Hiccups that jerked her body and made her gasp for breath took their place. Reluctantly she raised her head and looked around the room, exhausted, for the moment only vaguely remembering her return to the apartment as she listened to the rain still rapping at the window, then to Amy's short, rasping breathing, finally making herself struggle to sit erect.

Leaning against the sofa's back, she glanced sidelong at Amy, immediately feeling an instant fear, because she knew the aura of horror surrounding her would claim anyone with whom she came in contact. She ran both hands through the tight tangle of her hair, then made a useless attempt at straightening her blouse, trying to think what she would tell Amy that would not give the impression her mind was torn loose from its foundations of sanity.

"You okay now?" Amy's broad face registered concern.

"Yes, I guess so." Her mind was still working its way through a labyrinth. "Thanks for being here."

"That was a combination of luck and friendship. I was going down the hall to visit Jewell and Steve Lester and saw your door open. When I looked in, you were huddled on the sofa like a little girl who has lost her last friend in the world."

"I guess I was feeling that way."

"You want to tell me about it?"

"Yes, but you wouldn't believe me."

"Try me."

Adrienne shook her head. ''Not yet. I—I've got to make sure I believe it myself.''

''You're being very mysterious, do you know that?''

Adrienne nodded.

''Has it got something to do with Ned?''

''Something, but not everything.''

Amy scowled while she roamed her eyes around the room, then brought them back to Adrienne. ''Well, you know when you're ready to talk, I've got two well-tuned ears.''

''I know, and I appreciate it.''

''I take it you're going to spend the night here. Do you have everything you need?''

Adrienne nodded. ''I think so.''

Amy got to her feet to stand looking down at her, studying her inch by inch, her brown eyes reflecting the misgivings she was feeling.

''I don't like leaving you, but . . . well, you don't really seem to want my help.'' Amy ran her tongue around her lips. ''Adrienne, are you certain that you're all right? You look and act like—like a rape victim, to be frank. That's not what happened, is it?''

''No.'' She shook her head, suddenly wanting Amy to go, afraid complications would arise if she stayed, though she had no idea what they might be . . . just complications. ''No, I wasn't raped, honestly. I'll be all okay in the morning and will be knocking on your door for a cup of coffee.''

''And you'll tell me what occurred?''

''I'll try. I promise.''

Amy nodded, looked up at her from a lowered face, then gave an almost imperceptible shrug before walking slowly to the door, where she stopped. ''Why do I have the feeling you don't trust me?''

''I don't know. You shouldn't. If there's anybody I could talk to, it would be you—you know that. You'll be the first person I do tell, believe me, please.''

"All right. I guess I'll have to."

Adrienne watched her friend go out the door, then head toward her apartment, fighting down the apprehension that she was watching Amy walking out of her life. When she heard Amy's door close, she closed her own, turning the night lock, then sliding the bolt.

On the way to the bathroom, she turned the air-conditioning thermostat down, then stood listening to the first puffs of cold air coming through the vents, the whirring of the mechanism like a welcome voice filtering into her consciousness.

In the bathroom she leaned against the washbasin returning the stare of the disheveled creature gazing at her from the mirror. Skeins of hair were like twisted black veins crisscrossing her forehead and cheeks, and smeared under her left cheek, a smudge of dirt formed an irregular crescent. The round, blue eyes pointed in her direction showed no more life than plastic disks, empty, dispirited, with what vitality and intelligence had once been behind them missing. Shuddering, she faced away from the mirror. What she had seen in the glass was a picture of a woman in the process of disintegration.

Though there was no soap, she performed the ritual of shower taking, bending and twisting in the jets of hot water while she rubbed her body vigorously with her bare hands, obsessed with the idea of washing away all the dirt particles from the parking area. If she could, she would have opened a hole in her skull to pour water in to cleanse her mind as she was her flesh.

She dried herself with one of the two old towels left behind in the linen closet, then wrapped herself in a frayed sheet in which she had intended to bundle small odds and ends for the final move to the house.

It was nine-fifty when she wandered back into the living room. Listening to the rain still driving against the windows, she felt the closing in of impatience, and became fully aware of the foolishness of sending Amy away. If ever she needed a hand to hold, it was tonight. But when she had reached the apartment, her brain had shut itself off, leaving her like a machine operated too long and hard that had automatically cut off its power supply before disintegrating.

She went to the telephone to stand staring down at it, wanting once more to phone the house, but fearful of what her reaction would be if Ned did not answer. She walked away from it.

She looked at the door, then at the windows, then around the living room. Her mind stored away nothing of what she saw, shedding the images as quickly as her eyes sent their messages. She could not concentrate, she knew she would not be able to settle down tonight. A short time later, a perverse urging demanded that she go to the windows to look out, but she had the irrational premonition she would see rain-soaked women standing on the lawn watching the apartment. She shivered, feeling hopeless and lost.

Why didn't Amy come back and demand to help?

When she looked at her watch, it read only ten-ten. Hours had ground past, yet the watch's hands stubbornly indicated only twenty minutes since she had come from the shower. The shower had not helped. Dirt she would never see still clung to her. Like a sickness dehydrating her life's juices, the accumulation of fear began a slow, relentless spread through her until, certain that her sanity was finally on the verge of being siphoned away, she gave a cry and fell full length on the sofa, then slowly drew her legs up, unconsciously shrinking herself into a protective ball beneath the sheet.

She did not know how long she lay huddled, knees pressing into her breasts, before she heard the heavy hammering on the door. It pounded on her senses, and she covered her head, burying it deep in the dampish, cold folds of the sheet as she sought a hidden place where her nerves would cease their screaming, where the pain in her head would go away before exploding her skull. The hammering followed her, depriving her of sanctuary.

"Adrienne!"

She continued to lie very still with her eyes closed.

"Adrienne! Are you there?"

The pain in her head expanded until her temples throbbed and her skull felt on the verge of shattering. Whimpering, she lowered the sheet from her face and peeped over it toward the door, the pain in her head flooding all the way through her to squeeze droplets of perspiration out of her skin.

The door swayed on its hinges under the blows.

"Adrienne, this is Ned. If you're in there, for God's sake open the door! I have to talk with you."

There was something familiar in the voice. Moaning low in her throat, she pulled the sheet around her shoulders, then carefully rose to her feet, never removing her eyes from the door, tentatively spreading her feet to balance herself.

"Adrienne, do you hear me? Adrienne!"

Each step was a precarious undertaking, one foot shuffled before the other, as she tottered to the door.

"Ned?"

"Yes! My God, yes! Open the door, please."

Undoing the lock was the most difficult action she could remember with the cold metal and little sliding things resisting the clumsy workings of her unfeeling fingers, while on the door's other side, Ned continuously twisted the knob and pulled on it, causing the door to quiver and her to forget where she was in the unlocking sequence. She heard herself whimpering, was ready to cry out in defeat, when the lock came undone and Ned stood before her.

He pushed past her, slamming the door behind him. "Thank God, you're safe."

She nodded.

Ned went to the table in the dining alcove where he laid down the two objects he carried under his arm, then turned to stare at her. Beneath the rain dampness sheening his face, he wore the expression of a person who was stunned, betrayed.

"You were right," he said. His voice was only a dull tonal vibration coming from a great distance. "You were right about the paintings."

She could think of nothing to say except, "I know."

He stood looking at her, saying nothing as time stretched between them. Watching him, she knew that what had happened to her this evening had also happened to him.

"I did wrong," she said. "I should never have left the house."

"No." He looked directly at her. "You did right."

"I was mad and hysterical, and thinking mostly of myself. I—I was being selfish."

"Maybe. But for whatever reason, you did right in leaving."

"I phoned twice . . . I was so worried." She shifted her position, resting her weight on her left leg. "I'm glad you're here."

"I am, too."

"Where did you go? When I came back from the garden, you and the paintings were gone."

"To find answers. I saw what happened to Sandi's portrait, and I thought I knew where to find an explanation."

"Did you?"

"Yes." He stared blankly over her shoulder.

Adrienne opened her mouth, then closed it. Under the sheet, her flesh crawled. Again Ned looked around the room, his head cocked slightly to the left, then shrugged, finally shaking his head as if in dismissal of some thought. He turned away and walked to the windows, where he stood with his back to her, looking out into the night. After a short while, in a voice that was clenched and hoarse, he said, "I'm a murderer, Adrienne. I killed Sandi just as surely as if I drove a knife through her heart . . . and by doing that, I condemned her to eternal pain and terror."

"What are you saying?" A horrible coldness formed in her chest.

"I don't know for sure." He shook his head, watching his distorted image on the glass pane imitate the motion. "But now I believe in things that are unbelievable. Stories and legends that to me were only old wives' tales this morning, I discovered are irrefutable truths, because I learned today there's terror and evil beyond anything we can imagine roaming among us." He paused, drew a breath. "I killed Sandi, and I've been asked—no, more than that—I've been ordered to kill you and Sheila Rosenthal."

"Ned!" The coldness in her chest exploded around her heart.

"It's true, Adrienne." He turned to face her, his face twisted with a terrible pain. "It's true."

"What happened?" She took a step toward him. "Where did you go? Tell me what you found out."

He nodded at the objects on the dining table. "Those are your death warrants."

She looked at them. Now she recognized them as the stretched, unfinished portraits of her and Sheila, their colors bravely trying to appear bright in the alcove's gaunt light.

She pulled the sheet still tighter around her. "Tell me."

He nodded. "But first, tell me what happened in the parking area. Were you attacked?"

"Y—yes." She tried to keep the memory pictures from forming.

"By whom?"

"The—the women in the paintings." She heard herself speaking the implausible words, and as she did, the terror was reborn. "They were alive, Ned! They were alive, just like I said they were, and they—and they tried to stop me from leaving."

"I know," he said. "I know."

"But why? How can they be alive? Why did they try to stop me?"

He moved swiftly to her with his arms outstretched. "Oh, Adrienne baby. Adrienne."

His arms were heavy and solid and comfortable around her shoulders, giving her the sanctuary she needed, so, with a grateful whimper, she leaned against his chest.

"God, I was frightened when I saw the way the gravel was torn up . . . and your suitcase lying there on the ground." He stroked her tangled hair. "That was when I knew for sure that you are the most important person I've ever known."

She pressed tighter to him. "I'm—I'm so ashamed of myself for running away, because I know you needed my help, too."

"Should we forgive each other?"

"Hmmm-hmmm."

His arms wrapped even farther around her to hold her tighter. Tears sprang to her eyes, but this time they were good ones, while her body trembled with the release of tension.

"Tell me," she whispered against his shoulder, "where you went and what you found."

"All right." He pushed her back to arm's length, then looked directly into her eyes. "Let's sit down, because it's long, and it's frightening, and it's—and it's so goddamn unbelievable."

"I wonder if anything is believable anymore."

"Probably not."

Ned had trouble finding a starting point. He juxtaposed events, then backtracked to incorporate them in sequence. Sweat broke out on his face again and again as he described specific occurrences, while all the time his hands kneaded themselves in a continuous washing motion. As he spoke of his conversation at the cypress hammock with the disembodied voice of The Master, Adrienne felt her mind twisting.

"Who is he?" Her voice was weak, because she discovered her lungs could not force enough air past her vocal cords to vibrate them above a whisper.

"I don't know. Maybe it's only a force that has acquired the ability to assume shape and identity when it desires and has learned the secret of mind control . . . and knows how to capture a person's soul. I don't know."

Dully she asked, "Why didn't you tell me about the dreams?"

"You were selfish about running away from me, you say. Well, I was just as selfish about the dreams. I wanted to be the only person with the secret of the paintings."

"I—I guess I understand." She laid a hand on his leg. She needed physical contact. "Go on."

He spoke of Lila very slowly, seemingly wanting to dismiss the episode as an impossibility but knowing it had happened and no amount of rejection would make it otherwise. Adrienne was aware of the sorrow and compassion in his voice when he spoke of the woman's pleading, then the terror running through his sentences when he told her of the imprisoned souls. His voice melted to no more than a whisper when he explained the trade The Master was demanding and the women he expected to receive.

When he finally concluded by telling of his taking the unfinished portraits from the carriage house, she heard herself whimpering, "No, no, no."

"I'm not going to enter into that pact with him."

"What are you going to do?"

"I don't know. I swear to God, I don't know, but it's not going to be what that damn thing wants."

"Not even if it means you can live forever?"

"Knock that shit off, Adrienne!" He lunged to his feet to stand towering over her. "What kind of a goddamn sick question is that, anyhow? Man, would I have a big fun time living forever when every few nights I'd be listening to you scream in pain or beg for mercy. Year after year after year. No way, love. No way!"

"Ned, please—I'm sorry." She shook her head. "I know you wouldn't do that. It's just that I'm so . . . so mixed up, all turned upside down." She reached up a hand, hoping he would take it. "I've lost all control . . . and . . . and I'm so terribly frightened."

He took her proffered hand, then dropped to a knee in front of her. "I know, sweetheart, I know. We're both so damned uptight, we're ready to blow ourselves to smithereens. We're not going to get anything accomplished right now, except maybe another argument; so why don't we use our brains constructively and call off everything until morning. What do you say?"

"I'd like that."

Under the sheet, he and Adrienne huddled together but made no conscious attempt to touch, their nearness sufficient to hold at bay the primitive fear.

After getting out of his soggy clothes and drying himself with one of the two towels, he had crawled beneath the frayed sheet knowing there would be no sleep for him this night; his mind was too filled with the poison of apprehension. But exhaustion gradually spilled over him so that he drifted away from Adrienne's side, away from the darkness and the sound of falling rain, through shifting colors of pale pastel and finally into the swirling mist he so well remembered.

They were standing holding hands. Behind them, a huge bush, nodding with red blossoms, gently shifted its foliage in a passing breeze. He thought it was the bougainvillea he had been told was once the center of the garden at the house. Though their faces appeared to be misted in sadness, each was smiling at him as he approached.

"Welcome, Ned." Sebastian took a small step toward

him, but retained his hold on Sabra's hand. "We are happy to see you."

"And I you, Sebastian. I've questions to ask you. Damned important questions."

"I know, Ned. That is why we are here." He drew Sabra forward so she stood by his side. "We have things to tell you—important things, and when we have told you, perhaps your questions will be answered."

Sebastian made a slow, sweeping motion with his free hand. "Come, let us walk through the garden. There is a sensuousness about it, Ned, which dulls the reticence in one and permits open discussion."

The path was wider than he knew it, wide enough for the three of them to stroll abreast along its sand and shell surface. On each side of it, plants and flowers he did not recognize drew shimmering borders of yellow and red and blue, interspaced with tones of pink and russet. Heavy and warm, the air was redolent with sharp scents, laden with muted aromas as if a huge sachet had spilled its contents somewhere behind the taller shrubs. Dragonflies darted in and out of sunlight shafts or hovered momentarily in front of their faces, studying them with some kind of special insect curiosity.

They were nearly to the bench when Sebastian asked, "You have met The Master, have you not, Ned?"

"I talked with him. I didn't meet him. He stayed hidden in a cypress hammock."

"Yes," Sebastian sighed. "That is how it would be. He never shows himself. For the two hundred years I served him, I saw him only three times, and he assumed a different form each of those times. Only the cat—the cat was always the same, a Siamese. I am sure the cat was him."

A momentary remembrance of the cat which had befriended Adrienne passed through his mind, but he pushed it aside. "Answer me one question, Sebastian, before you tell me what you intend to tell me. What, or who, is The Master?"

Sebastian shook his head slowly. "Something terribly evil, Ned, that is filled with rage and fury. I cannot give you a formal name: he has refused to tell me one, if, in truth, he possesses one. But this I know, from conversations with Magda and occasional references he has made, he is a thing which has existed before the dawn of time, a thing created in the turbulent atmosphere of a world that was no more than burning sulfur mountains and steaming seas, and which somehow escaped extinction. He is one of the things which exist beyond the borders of Nature that give birth to dark legends of abomination and appalling evil. I know he is consumed with fury that puny creatures such as we humans now control the planet which once was his, and so he uses his powers to toy with us and torment us, though it is more than a game with him: it is a campaign of revenge. When he is not with the women, he is out roaming the world, I know, creating disputes among men, causing unnatural catastrophes."

"As usual, you're leaving a lot unsaid, Sebastian. No matter what he is, he does things that are impossible. He grants unending life, he holds women prisoners in paintings, he controls minds. Only a deity, or maybe Satan, could do that."

"Today, Ned. But how much power and knowledge was lost during the millenniums between The Master's time and the beginnings of mankind? How much since? Some of that knowledge has been rediscovered, but how much of it remains lost?"

"The paintings . . ." Ned heard his voice trailing away to a hoarse whisper. "Why the paintings?"

"He is a vandal, a destroyer. He exists to corrupt and abolish, driven by his jealousy of mankind. Nothing in our species is as beautiful as a beautiful woman, Ned; so, by ravaging splendid women, he is aware of his power and gains additional satisfaction."

"You knew that, and still you painted portraits for— *it?*"

"I did not know for years what the nature of his—*its* pleasure was with them."

"And when you learned?"

"I—I continued to paint."

"Mr. Anderson, please. I beg you to listen to what we have to say." Sabra's eyes were haunted, and in the corners of them tears reflected the brilliant sunshine. "What Sebastian did was wrong, yes, but the women are not dead, so he is not a murderer, as you are not with the young woman Sandi. Sebastian is more a—a—"

"Pimp?"

"Yes, Ned." Sebastian's eyes drifted away. "I was a—a procurer, if you will. But I was born in a time, and a place, that regarded women as no more than chattel, so I felt no repugnance in trading them to The Master for what he gave in return. I admit I was too long in learning otherwise."

Ned felt a great disappointment lay hold of him. The mystique was gone from this man to whom he had been willing to do homage; the idol's feet were clay.

They reached the bench. Around them, Ned was aware of the mists swirling, but they were thin and weightless, like floating gossamer which spread a rose tint across the path and bench. Sebastian smiled at Sabra. "Sit down, my dear."

Sebastian drew a deep breath, then combed his beard with his fingertips. He looked at Sabra, who nodded.

"Ned," he said slowly, "we are related, you and I. Very distantly, it is true, but we share the blood of common forefathers. That is how The Master, as thin as the bloodline is between us, could manipulate events so easily, permitting you to become owner of the house."

"All those manipulations took place just to bring me here so the slavery of other women can begin? Is that it?"

"Yes, Ned, that was the original plan. He demanded you be brought here not only because of your talent but because it was assumed, with that tincture of my blood flowing in your veins, you would be eager, as I was, to live until time's ending."

Ned turned away to look out over the blaze of color surrounding them in the garden. "I felt honored carrying your blood in my veins, Sebastian, and I was excited to be the recipient of your knowledge, but now, frankly, I dislike you and I'm going to try to forget everything I've learned of your art."

Sabra gasped.

Sebastian said, "I do not blame you, but please hear what we have to say. I will not attempt to change your mind about me, but I hope to change it about our purpose—about Sabra's and my purpose."

"Please, Mr. Anderson . . ." Sabra's voice was as haunted as her eyes had been.

"All right." He did not turn back to face them. "I'm listening."

"The Master desires that you supply new women to his harem as replacements for the present members of it. He is one who likes change, and there has been no change among the women for a hundred years, so he has become greedy for new faces, new bodies—and new spirits to be broken. Remember, as I said, Ned, it is from the devastation of beautiful women that he gains perverted satisfaction in his power, and the women of today are as beautiful as any who have ever existed. They possess spirits unequaled in history, along with a sense of determination and the knowledge of accomplishment women have never experienced before. They are the perfect subjects for his ego."

"Whatever he is, he must be mad."

"And consumed with raging frustration, Ned. One must keep in mind he comes from a time when the earth was no more than a cruel place of erupting volcanoes, smoldering plains and bleak seas. He is forced to admit that his kind could not survive while creatures physically smaller, perhaps, and with less power of the mind have conquered the earth."

"If he, or it, is what you say."

"Yes . . ."

"I won't do it. I will not doom women to that."

"No, Ned, we are not asking you to."

Throughout the garden the mists swirled like the solid portions of a vibration, quavering the unseen world in which this place without definition existed.

"So what is it you want of me? What can I do?"

"You can give us small amounts of freedom, allow us to, in a small way, live again."

"Live again? You're dead, Sebastian. You and Sabra have been dead a hundred years. How can you live again?"

"We are only half dead, Ned."

"I don't understand."

"We are in a limbo, Ned, a place of continuing horror The Master has created. Where he keeps us is a twilight place half hidden in darkness. It is a place existing deep inside the most terrible of nightmares." His voice became taut, and what might have been a shiver trembled across his shoulders. "Always there are the sounds of things prowling out there in that darkness lying on the land, unseen creatures seeking something—and always the thought that what they seek is Sabra and me. Always the terror, forever the fear one of those hunting things will eventually find us. During the time I was indoctrinating you on the secrets of the paintings, he allowed us to come to this borderline place of mist to meet with you. It was a ruse, Ned. This re-creation of the garden was to lull you into a receptive mood by indicating only friendship and tranquillity. We are here now because he thinks that is our purpose, talking to you about the paintings; but we must return to the unending terror within a short while. Sabra can no longer accept it. She is prepared to give herself to The Master and become one of the women in his harem in exchange for my release. She says it is because of her that I am suffering.'' Torment showed on his face above the black beard. ''I shall not allow that to happen, Ned Anderson!''

Ned looked at Sabra. She sat perfectly still with her hands in her lap, her expression numb, anesthetized.

''You would do that?'' he asked. ''Knowing what it means?''

''Yes. I love him.''

Sebastian moved to stand behind the bench and laid his hands on his wife's shoulders. ''When first we learned of you, Ned Anderson, I tried to reach an accommodation with The Master, our release in exchange for my instructing you in the secrets of the painting, because since the painting would be resumed, he would have a source for new harem members. But that is no longer our desire.''

''What is it?''

''To thwart The Master.''

Ned stood looking at them. Some of the indignation toward Sebastian was leaving him, being replaced, if not by compassion, then at least a minimum of understanding. Even if what he was being told was no more than 80 percent truth, he could recognize the trap Sebastian had fallen into, because without Sebastian's revelations, he, too, might have been ensnared—had been, in fact, with the portrait of Sandi.

''Can that be done?'' he asked. ''Can you oppose the unknown? A thing with the unnatural powers it possesses can be damned hard to defeat.''

''I do not know, and I must admit the chances are unlikely, but we must try. Sabra and I can no longer accept the horror of providing women to his harem. I know what an appalling violation of life it is, and I can never forgive myself for the misery of those poor creatures in the paintings.''

''You were killed—or placed in that limbo you mentioned—because you went against his will. If I helped you and we failed, what would happen to me . . . and to Adrienne, because she is to me what Sabra is to you.''

"We were placed where we are because we had no help, no guidance."

"You've helped me before, Sebastian. In our other meetings you showed me the secret of your paintings, and after listening to you and following your instructions, I've come to the place I am: in spite of what Sabra says, the murderer of Sandi."

"I am sorry, Ned. I truly regret what has occurred. It is her death which has finally made us realize this cannot continue, that The Master must be deprived of more subjects for his harem."

"How can you help?" he finally asked.

"By asking you to do two paintings to give to The Master," Sebastian answered. "You have a fortnight before you must give him the portraits of Adrienne and Sheila Rosenthal, is that not so?"

"Yes . . ."

"You can paint two others in place of them, can you not?"

"I suppose so, yes. But of whom?"

"Of Sabra and me."

"To give to him? That I don't understand."

"The Master made a mistake, Ned. He put our spirits in limbo moments before we died, to keep them there until time came for him to claim them. But our souls still belong to us. And I am sure he will be unable to claim them. To take our souls, to claim them as his own permanent possessions as with the women in the paintings, he must capture them at the instant of physical death. He did not do that. He was not in the garden when we died; he had driven the women back to the parlor and was with them there; so, you see, I do not believe he can remove us from where we are. He can toy with us, as he does, but he missed his chance to capture our souls and is forced to leave us in the place we are."

"Even if we continue to suffer in that terrible place," Sabra said, "we will have each other."

"And I know," Sebastian said, "that because they are our spirits and not our souls he controls, there will be times, now and then, when we can slip his guardianship and enjoy brief visits into the real world."

"And you," Ned said to Sabra, "would not give yourself to The Master."

She lowered her eyes. "No."

"Okay, but how do I give him portraits of you two instead of Adrienne and Sheila? He'll see that right away."

"Listen carefully, Ned. Paint the portraits of Sabra and myself. You have the one I began of her, and you can remember my features well enough to create a fair duplication of them. When they are finished, you will place them wherever the agreed place for delivery is, at the time arranged to present them—he will contact you before too long, I am sure, asking for progress and establishing a place for delivery. Have them draped and well covered, Ned. The Master likes ceremony and will want to make a ritual of the unveiling of them."

"And when he finds what they are, that they're not what he expects, what then, Sebastian? What will he do?"

"I do not think there is much he will be able to do. He is powerful, Ned, that is undeniable; however, you have made no pact with him, and the portraits of Adrienne and Sheila are incomplete. There is nothing for him to grasp to obtain control of you. With Sabra's portrait and mine, unlike those of the women in my paintings, there will be no handhold for him because he has, with his mistake, lost our souls. Do you understand what I am saying?"

"Not completely, no; but I'm willing to try anything. If this scheme should work, Adrienne and Sheila are safe, and I'm not obligated to him because I've entered into no agreement—is that it?"

"Yes."

Ribbons of yellow and green and red fluttered through the

mists looking like streamers flying in an unfelt breeze. Ned watched them for a long moment wondering what, if anything, their haunting movement meant. Never before in his dream times had he felt anything physical, but now he was aware of perspiration dotting his forehead while around him he felt the garden pressing closer and closer like a jungle growth of primeval plants and ferns creeping across the land.

"Well, Ned?" Sebastian's voice was removed, coming from a greater distance than previously, though he stood only a few paces away. "Are you willing to try?"

He knew it was ending and looked around at the mists, then back to the two people before him. They had receded some as if melting into the grayness shrouding the tree behind them, moving away from this meeting, which might be his final contact with Sebastian.

"Will I see you again?" he asked. "Will I talk with you again?"

"I cannot say. But perhaps if our scheme is successful, yes. You will paint the portraits, will you not, Ned? You will try to defeat The Master with them?"

"Yes . . . I'll try. I promise you . . .

. . . I promise you, I'll try."

At his side, Adrienne, who must have fallen into a fitful slumber, murmured while she twisted tighter in the sheet, pulling it from him so a chilled draft of air from the air-conditioner vent turned the perspiration on him to gooseflesh. Only vaguely did he hear the rain washing the windows with a soothing, steady sound, just loud enough that he knew the storm was over, leaving only a mild summer shower as its legacy.

He grinned up at the dark ceiling. In spite of the cold air, he suddenly felt warm and cozy.

CHAPTER

Sunlight ricocheted from the windows of the neighboring apartment unit creating splashes of vibrant brilliance. Storm-washed, the air was pristine, like a warm crystal sparkling between the two buildings, yet there was a heavy stillness out there in the morning sun, an oppressive silence. A waiting.

Dressed in her dried but wrinkled blouse and skirt, Adrienne stood looking out the living room windows. She could feel the outside heat pressing against the glass pane, trying to push into the room's coolness to squeeze around her and suck from her what little energy she had managed to regain during her fitful sleep. The draining tiredness lingered in her still, leaving her old and brittle-feeling. Exhaustion spread a web through her body. Her mind was aware of it, but refused to uncurl itself to combat the weariness, fearful of absorbing more pain and abrasion.

"Is 'good morning' an appropriate greeting?" Ned was standing in the middle of the room, his hair tousled, a black shadow forming a crescent along his jawline.

She looked over her shoulder and nodded, made herself smile, then said, "Yes, when you think what the alternatives might be."

"Do you have an unreal feeling? As if all this is happening, but on some other plane of existence?" He came to stand beside her at the window. "Nothing seems to have perspective, does it?"

"No."

He squirmed a little nervously, then said in a low voice, "I had another dream . . . or visitation . . . or whatever last night."

She waited for him to say more. When he did not, she asked, "From Sebastian?"

"Yes. Him and Sabra." He continued staring out the window, speaking slowly, his voice sounding cracked and strained. "They told me of a way to end this . . . to possibly save ourselves."

Adrienne was unable to ignite the first spark of excitement. The emotional exhaustion was too much: it shuttered out all but her fears.

"Did you hear me?" He looked directly at her now, his eyes seeking a response on her features. "In the dream Sebastian told me how to possibly defeat The Master."

"I heard you. I was thinking how appropriate the name we've given it is: The Master. We are being absolutely controlled by it, aren't we?"

"Yes." He remained silent awhile, then laid a hand on her shoulder. "Adrienne honey, we have to try to do something, you know that, and maybe what he told me is the way. God knows, *I* can't think of anything. Can you?"

"No." She turned to face him. "It's so unthinkable, that's all. Here we are caught in a situation gruesome beyond imagination from which the only hope of salvation comes from the dreamlike figure of a man dead for a hundred years. I want to, I have to, believe; but, dear God, I can't understand."

"Don't try, darling. Just react, deal with it. It's all we can do." Ned pulled her to him.

She laid her cheek against his chest. "What does he say we should do?"

Very slowly, his hand moving up and down her back in feather-light strokes, he told her the plan Sebastian had presented. While he talked, he referred to Sebastian and Sabra in the same manner he might if they were living acquaintances. Listening to him repeat the dialogue, she could feel Sebastian's presence in the room. It was eerie. She was certain he was standing very near, watching, listening, and she pushed away from Ned and looked over her shoulder, but the living room was empty. All at once, she felt like she wanted to shiver, but only her throat tightened and she swallowed hard.

The knock on the door caused them both to jump.

When Adrienne opened it, Amy was standing in the hallway holding a coffeepot in one hand and balancing three cups in the other.

"I wasn't sure you'd come for coffee," she said, "so I decided to bring it to you. From the way you looked last night, though, I've a feeling it's going to take more than coffee to get you going." She looked over Adrienne's shoulder toward Ned. "I heard you banging on the door last night, so I brought you a cup, too."

Amy set the three cups on the dining table, filled them with coffee, then carried the pot to the kitchen, placing it on the stove and turning the burner to warm. The hot, brown aroma of the coffee was strong and pungent in the sterile atmosphere of the apartment.

"God, that's good!" Ned had just sipped from his cup.

The hot liquid exploded in Adrienne's mouth and throat, shocking her nerves and senses into function, clearing away the nonthoughts in her mind.

"Thanks, Amy," she said. "You always know what's needed."

"It doesn't take much common sense to see when a person needs some kind of pick-me-up; although I'm thinking a good boot in the tail would be the best help in your case." She sipped at her coffee through pursed lips, finally, without looking at either of them, asking, "Are you going to tell me what this is all about?"

For longer than she intended, Adrienne watched the steam ribbons rise from her cup, then gave what she hoped was a dismissing shrug. "It's not really all that interesting. I had some problems—car problems—a flat tire south of town, out in the country, you know. Trying to change it in the rain just got to be too much for me. I became frustrated and mad . . . and, I guess, just upset in general. Anyway, I stopped here instead of driving all the way back to the house. I'd had enough of automobiles and rain for one Sunday afternoon."

Disbelief showed in Amy's eyes. Around them her face pinched with the start of indignation.

"We were shooting some photographs on location," Ned quickly added. "Black-and-whites of a stream and a country dirt road. I'm going to sepia-tone the prints, and Adrienne plans to add them to her product line."

Amy sighed and shook her head. "You two certainly aren't any good at lying: your story's as full of holes as the proverbial sieve. Do you know that?"

"We . . . we just can't tell you," Adrienne said. With a tiny sob, she reached out to lay a hand on her friend's forearm. "Oh, God, Amy, it isn't that I don't want to tell you, it's that I'm afraid to tell you. It could mean danger for you. Please, please, believe me."

"What are you mixed up in?" Slowly the hint of indignation was fading from her broad features. Concern began to replace it. She looked from one to the other. "It's nothing illegal, is it?"

"Of course not! You know me better than that."

"That was a dumb question. I'm sorry." Amy laid a hand over the one Adrienne was resting on her forearm. "I guess what is happening is that I'm starting to get worried, and maybe a little frightened. This is all so unnatural. I've seen you down, Adrienne, down so low after your divorce you could walk under a snake's belly, but this is different—you're not despondent, you're frightened. I really want to help you, because you're a friend. Don't you know that?"

"Yes, I know, and you are a friend, the best kind of friend. And that's why, right now, I can't tell you what's occurring." She squeezed the firm flesh under her fingers. "Oh, Amy, believe me . . . trust me."

Amy glanced at Ned, saw the intent frown furrowing his brow while he looked at her, then nodded. Sighing, she pushed her chair back, then stood up to lean her knuckles on the tabletop.

"I don't feel not wanted," she said, "but I do get the impression I'm intruding. Why don't I go, then when whatever it is that's upsetting you both is straightened out—well, maybe we can talk. Okay?"

Adrienne went with her to the door. "Amy, please, please, don't take this personally. I do promise to tell you all about it when I know for sure myself."

Amy nodded. "You know this whole thing is weird, don't you?"

"It's more than that." She felt terribly guilty and looked away from the other woman. "It's frightening, that much I'll say. When I can tell you, I'm not at all sure you'll believe me."

"I just wish you'd try."

"Later."

"All right. If that's the way you want it, that's the way it will have to be, I suppose."

After she closed the door, Adrienne leaned her back against

it. "We handled that very badly. Amy's my best friend, and I just treated her like an unwanted stranger."

Still sitting at the table, Ned only nodded.

She refilled both their cups before she took Amy's to the sink, where she stood for too long a time running hot water into it, watching the tiny cloud of steam rising. The episode with Amy made it apparent that henceforth no action, no matter how trivial or benign, would be without pressures.

Ned was playing with his coffee, moving the cup in tight little circles so the liquid swished around inside it creating a spinning whirlpool. Without looking at her, he asked, "Are you going to continue living at the house?"

She swung her eyes around the apartment, seeing the familiar furnishings, the spots of color accentuating areas where shadows might grow, the sunlight slanting through the windows to touch well-known objects. This was home, where there was no darkness and no chill, where danger did not lurk among dead flower stalks and under peppertrees. She looked slowly at him and shook her head.

"I don't blame you. I don't want to either."

She sat down again at the table. "Move in here. We'd be crowded, but we'd be away from . . . from the women. You could do the paintings of Sebastian and Sabra here, couldn't you?"

"Yes, I don't see why not."

"Then do it." She reached out to stroke his forearm. "Please. You shouldn't be out there alone. I don't want you out there by yourself."

He ran a hand along the stubble on his cheek, then wearily through his hair. "It would be the logical thing to do, wouldn't it?"

"Yes. Not only logical, but safe."

"Okay." He drew a deep breath, allowing it to escape his lips with a swooshing exhale. "We'll have to go out and get our clothes, and I want to bring my photographic equipment in here, too, along with the art supplies."

"It may take several trips. I want to bring my supplies back, too."

"The great experiment that didn't work."

"It will. Only in another way, maybe a better way."

"Do I detect shades of Pollyanna?"

"No, you hear hope."

Funny, she thought as she drove up the driveway, how nothing about the house's appearance had changed since the first time she saw it, that day in another life an eternity away. Though the ladders were gone, the new and the old paint still clashed on the outside wall, the entire house still looked spread with middle age, the shadows of the oaks continued to play among the fretwork. Death, the destruction of friendship, and the horror and terror piling one upon the other until minds had been overcome with that special monstrous exhaustion which bordered on insanity; all of them had visited the house, but the house sat as it had for a hundred and fifty years, dominating, with its fretwork and verandah, the pines and oaks which surrounded it, slipping with pride into Gothic old age. She wondered, as she parked the Toyota beneath the peppertree, how long the house could continue to conceal from the world the fact that hate and terror were now its occupants.

Ned parked the Jeep beside her, then sat for a long moment looking without expression around the area like a suffering man whose pain was giving way to numbness. Finally he swung out from behind the wheel. "You gather together the stuff you want while I get mine. Let me know if you need help."

Up in the bedroom she had never used, Adrienne once more piled the bed with clothing and personal items, emptying the closet and dresser drawers which she had so neatly filled two days earlier. When her two suitcases were packed, she stood looking around the room, touched with a deep sadness for all the things which might have been.

Only a little over two hours after they arrived, they were ready to leave, both the Toyota and the Jeep so heavily laden each of them squatted low on their springs.

"I think we can do it in one more trip," Ned said. "How much more do you have?"

She tried to run through a mental inventory of the materials left in the workrooms, and found she was unable. "I don't know. I'll have to go see."

"Okay. While you're doing that, I'm going to bring the paintings back to the house."

"Why?" Sharp fragments of disbelief sliced at her mind. "Leave them where they are."

"They'd be safer in the house."

"My God, who in hell cares about their safety? We'd be better off if someone stole them, or if they just disappeared."

He shifted gravel around with the toe of his sneaker. "I suppose you're right. That would solve our problems, but I can't help thinking of them as examples of magnificent art, Adrienne."

"Think of them as what they are! What they really are! Crazed women who have attacked me and who probably killed Katie. My God, leave them alone, Ned. Stay away from them. Let them rot and fall to pieces up there in the carriage house."

He moved his head in what she took as a nod of agreement, giving the impression of a person whose mind was playing hide-and-seek with a problem it did not want to face.

"What would happen," she asked, "if we went up to the apartment and destroyed the paintings right now, cut them to ribbons like Katie wanted to do, like I thought once about doing?"

"No!" He looked up to the carriage house apartment's windows, then back to her. "It's too late, Adrienne. The whole affair has moved too far to back away from; we're caught too tight in its web. I'm scared as hell, but I want to try to defeat that thing. I don't want there ever to be another Sandi. We need those women until after our attempt."

She nodded. She supposed he was right. "Let's go, right now." She wanted to get away. Already she felt all the hideous things which had become a part of their lives starting to gather in the shadows beneath the peppertrees. "I'll go through what we have when we get to the apartment, then come back tomorrow to pick up the odds and ends."

He looked around, turning full circle, his eyes moving slowly from the house to the garden to the trees to the carriage house like a person memorizing each tiny detail of the area, storing it away in his mind so at some future time he could pull it forth and make believe he was standing where he was at this moment. Then he looked at Adrienne, and she saw he was attempting to smile, but there was only sadness on his face when he said, "It could have been such a good inheritance."

She wanted to cry out her understanding and draw him close to her, but instead she took him by the hand. "It still can be, darling."

He squeezed her hand. "Actually, it really was, because I met you. Without the house, I would never have known you existed."

The following week moved along a course of events which never gained definition, like the murky actions of a dream, when the mind puts great distance between itself and events which tend to be strange and unfamiliar. They told Amy and her husband the house had developed plumbing problems, that until repairs were completed they would be staying at the apartment.

After carefully restretching the canvas, Ned completed the portrait of Sabra in three days, working from morning to evening beside the small north window in the dining alcove. He spent a day with a sketch pad, drawing from his memory, making studies of Sebastian. Adrienne put together some of the smaller orders in her book, but found she was unable to stabilize her mind enough to concentrate on new designs. And all the time fear and worry coexisted with them in the small rooms.

The second Tuesday after returning to the apartment, Ned was well along with Sebastian's portrait, Adrienne had completed and delivered fourteen orders, facing the irritation of gift shop owners because of late response. Instead of working until twilight's gloom dulled the colors, Ned cleaned his brushes in midafternoon, took two beers from the refrigerator and sat down at the dining table at which Adrienne was working.

"Here," he said, pushing a beer toward her. "I know it's not your favorite beverage, but it's all we've got, and I think we owe ourselves a longer-than-usual break."

She took the beer.

He ran a forefinger up, then down, the moist side of the bottle, studying the smeared streak it left behind on the condensation. "Do you think we'd know how to have a rational evening? You know, one during which we might be able to behave like other people for just a few hours—a good meal, a try at conversation not about paintings and deadlines and angry gift store managers . . . and then maybe . . ."

Suddenly the beer bottle became very cold in her hands, at the same time she felt a tingle squirm up, then down her body. She looked across the table at him. How sensitive his face was under the black shock of hair. How had she become less aware of that during this past week? And why, during that time, had the warm contentment she felt with him been lacking? Now it came hurrying back to her, making the beer bottle even colder.

"I think we would be able to do that," she said. "Especially the . . . maybe."

He laughed, the first laugh she had heard from him in over a week. It sounded so very, very good.

"I'll make a deal with you," she said.

"What's that?"

"I've got to make a delivery." She indicated five wreaths lying on the table. "I'll pick up some steaks if you'll broil them."

"That is a deal I can't turn down." He took a swallow from the bottle, looked at it, then shook his head. "How about some wine, too?"

"I think that can be arranged."

A half hour later, carrying the boxed wreaths in front of her, she was in the parking lot approaching her car. Walking through the warm, copper-toned sunlight, she was suddenly certain the nightmare was about to magically turn into an endless summertime. She began to hum an improvised, off-tune melody.

The cat was sitting on the hood of the Toyota.

The brown mask of its face was pointed up at her, the blue eyes, partially squinted, were watching her approach with brazen interest, glinting as if reflecting an inner private joke.

The new, wonderful mood crumbled. Cold fear grasped her as she stumbled and felt a flurry inside her chest. "What are you doing here?"

The cat appeared to grin, then made its peculiar, babylike meowing. It did not move.

Adrienne stood staring at it, determined to hold her eyes in contact with its squinting blue ones for as long as they continued to watch and examine her. Once its tongue came out to run slowly around its lips as it would if licking them after a satisfying meal, and the action revolted Adrienne because she knew the cat was undressing her with those damned eyes, seeing all the curves and indentations of her flesh beneath the blouse and slacks she wore. Her revulsion became shock, then anger.

"What is it you want?" She did not feel in the least foolish talking to the animal.

The Siamese seemed to smirk as it raised and lowered its head, which took on that peculiar serpentine appearance, its neck stretching with the movement, its eyes drifting insinuatingly from her face to her ankles and back up, lingering momentarily on the flare of her hips.

"Damn you!" she screamed. "Goddamn you!"

The cat rose to its feet, arched its back in a slow, languorous stretch, then walked slowly to the front of the hood, where it stood looking at her over its left shoulder. She knew it was mocking her, as it had in the garden at the house, and something substantial and important in her well-being drained away. Still clutching the boxes to her breast, she leaned against the car.

With a meow, the cat jumped from the hood and padded across the parking lot, casually strutting between the parked cars, leaving her slouched against the Toyota's sun-warmed metal, trembling and feeling unclean.

When she got into the car and rolled the windows down, she sat staring sightlessly through the windshield, listening to the unnatural stillness of the apartment complex. Within it, she thought she sensed a menace she could not define. She had almost forgotten about the cat. Its return to her life was the return of all the horrors of the house, and all the stability of emotion she had obtained during the past week was unraveled.

For the first few minutes after Adrienne left, Ned felt at odds with himself. He wandered idly around the apartment, examining, but not actually studying, Adrienne's work spread on the table, looking in the kitchen cupboards to stare at the barely adequate supply of dishes and cooking utensils brought with them from the house, then walking along the hall to the spare bedroom to stand in the doorway gazing at the neatly piled cartons and not so neatly arranged photographic equipment. Once he passed a mirror, stopping to inspect his reflection. He was not satisfied with what he saw: eyes shadowed and deeply sunk, hollows under his cheekbones which tended to slim his face into a cadaverous triangle, a day's stubble of beard giving his features an overall unclean appearance. He walked on, knowing what he wanted to do: he wanted to leave all this, everything, house, equipment, apartment, and, taking Adrienne, run away to a place where such things as fear, worry and irritation were unknown.

Back in the dining area, he saw Adrienne's wastebaskets were full. It gave him an oddly satisfied feeling, because taking them down to empty into the dumpster would give him something to do, a physical action to eliminate the distortion warping his thoughts. He emptied the contents of the wastebaskets into two brown shopping bags, taking more care than was required in the transfer, forcing himself to think about the elemental movements.

Amy was standing at the dumpster looking at a hedge of ixora marking the property line between the apartments and an area of undeveloped lots. Hearing him, she turned, then pointed in the direction of the hedge.

"There's a cat in those bushes," she said. "I've been trying to lure it out for the past five minutes. From the glimpse I got of it, it looked like a beauty; a big, healthy Siamese."

"Oh?" He stopped and looked where she indicated. At first he saw only tight-woven shadows among the starlike red ixora blossoms, but then he distinguished two glowing blue points which might have been cat eyes. "I think I see it."

"It must be lost. I thought it might have an indentification collar."

"It's probably spooked now and won't come out."

"That could be. It appeared such a beauty, I'd like to help

it get back to its home. I'm sure its owners are worried." She gazed again at the hedge, then shrugged. "I can't spend any more time with it. I've a roast in the oven that needs checking. If you and Adrienne aren't doing anything this evening, why don't you come by and watch TV?"

"We might just do that."

"Plan on it. You two have become recluses. That's not healthy, you know."

"It won't be for much longer. Everything should be fixed at the house next week, so we can move back in, then you and Hugh are invited for a barbecue to inaugurate our return to the social whirl."

Amy smiled. "That sounds good, and I accept for both of us."

Ned watched her walk away. Though she could not be more than thirty-five or thirty-six, with her somewhat plump but well-curved figure, Amy gave the impression of matronly competence. She was, he decided, a very comfortable person to know.

The chuckle came from somewhere behind the dumpster. "You might think about painting her portrait for me, Ned Anderson."

Confusion burst in his head. He looked with startled eyes at the black-painted dumpster.

As it had at the cypress hammock, the chuckle became derisive. "Oh, come, Ned. You should not be so disbelieving when your patron visits you. You will be useless to me and yourself if you allow your nerves to explode each time we have a discussion."

He forced himself to calm down and think reasonably, almost marveling at the feat when he found himself able to do it.

"Why are you here?" he asked.

"To remind you that your fortnight ends in five days."

"I know."

"And . . ."

"I'll have the paintings completed and ready to deliver."

"Excellent, Ned. Excellent."

Ned's eyes darted around the area adjacent to the dumpster, then along the rows of the apartment's rear windows to see if anyone was observing him. No one was in sight.

The voice laughed. It was lilting, fluting, full of the sound of excited expectation. "We are very much alone, Ned. Even should a person wander by, they would hear nothing. Only those I am speaking with will I allow to hear me." The laugh lowered itself an octave. "Privacy is an obsession with me."

Ned did not answer.

Though more guttural, when it spoke again the voice still held more than a few remnants of excitement, giving Ned the impression that chortling laughter was being suppressed.

"The fortnight ends on Sunday. That is the perfect day for me to receive the women—the most perfect of days. It is the one your kind holds as somewhat sacred, which makes it all the more pleasurable to me."

He saw movement in the ixora, a shadow, then a brown mask of a face pointed at him from which two blue eyes glowed as they watched him, twinkling with a fiery enthusiasm. It was the cat Amy had seen. It was . . . the cat! Adrienne's cat. It was the cat at the house! He sucked in his breath, unable to move, frozen, as a realization he did not want to acknowledge slammed into his senses.

"You!"

The two eyes continued to stare at him unblinking, reaching into his own to burrow into his mind, little blue circles from which he suddenly knew there was no escape. For an instant, he felt things stirring in his head, and had the insane, terrible thought that maggots were gnawing at his brain. Desperation gave him strength. Using all of his will, he turned away and closed his eyes.

He knew now what, or who, the cat was!

"Do you have something to hide, Ned Anderson?"

He shook his head.

"That pleases me." The voice paused for emphasis. "Now, hear me. On Sunday evening, two hours after nightfall, bring the two paintings and place them with the others. That is all you are required to do. When you have done that, leave. Do not loiter. Walk away. Walk away to a life without end. Do you understand?"

Ned looked at the spot where the eyes had glowed, saw nothing, then nodded his head. "Yes, I understand."

"Then we are finished for now. I await Sunday with great anticipation."

He heard nothing in the ixora bushes. From Orange Avenue, the muttering traffic noises held to the same cadence and volume; from an open window in one of the apartments, a cheap radio erupted tinny rock music into the humid air; but he sensed a change, a weightlessness in the atmosphere as might occur if it had been compressed by a great force and was now expanding to its natural state. He was not surprised, as he walked from the dumpster, that his body shook and sweat dampened his clothing.

When Ned told her of the cat and the subsequent talk with The Master, the menace reached into the apartment. Adrienne felt that whatever she might do was essentially useless because there was no assurance of time existing after the coming Sunday.

Ned completed the portrait of Sebastian, muttering it was not an exacting likeness but would do for the occasion.

On the insistence of Amy and Hugh, Friday night they went to a neighborhood restaurant, then to a dark, too-noisy lounge where amateur musicians simulated blue-grass music. Adrienne could not bring herself to thank God this was a Friday, and Ned, she knew, was withdrawn into a private place from where he was counting the passing hours until nightfall Sunday. Watching the crowd around them, feeling none of the prevailing end-of-the-week exultation, she had a frightening appreciation of how inadequate and diminished she had truly become.

To Adrienne, Saturday passed slowly, but, at the same time, with the swiftness which accompanies the destruction of the natural state of affairs. There was no frame of reference for the day; nothing could be judged dangerous since there was nothing in her past with which to compare it, no past consequences to remember. Yet she knew there was danger because she lost her sense of self-importance, feeling her individualism forfeited to the terrible magnitude of events.

She put together three orders while Ned made work for himself by cleaning his cameras. As the day crept onward, the apartment became small and shadowy, the rooms seeming to partially fill with menace, the air-conditioner laboring to hold away a heat which had no relation to the outside temperature. As she taped the carton containing her last order, Adrienne wondered how, if they survived The Master's wrath, this affair would affect their future.

Twilight became dusk, which turned to darkness. The evening stretched before them like a tunnel leading to a place far removed from the scenes and passions they knew, and, looking out the window, Adrienne wondered what damnation waited at the far end of that tunnel with the morning's sunrise.

Ned came to stand at her side. Peripherally aware of his movements, she continued staring out into the darkness. Though she did not want to admit it, not even to herself, she was scanning the small lawn and manicured hedges for a shadowy form with two glowing eyes.

He put an arm around her waist. "It's going to be a long night."

"Long . . . and unreal." She laid a cheek against his chest. "But it is real, isn't it? It's actually happening. We're not just working ourselves up with a lot of imaginings, are we?''

"No, we're not imagining this. As much as we want to disbelieve, honey, this is happening."

She closed her eyes with the vain hope of shutting out the world around her, but memory pictures flashed behind her lids: Katie lying dead at the bottom of the carriage house steps, howling women attacking her from out of the rain, a dead Sandi and dancing women visiting her in a dream. She pressed her cheek harder to Ned's chest. Finally the pictures faded, but their intrusion had set her heart hammering and now her breath came in short, ragged gulps.

Ned's arm tightened around her, then pulled gently. "Come on, let's find something to occupy our minds."

She let him lead her down the hallway to the bedroom. She walked with a kind of mechanical acceptance as her mind swung between freeing itself of the after-images of the memory pictures and the anticipation of the ritual of the yearning flesh awaiting her.

CHAPTER

"I wondered when you were going to wake up." Ned grinned at her from the threshold of the bedroom.

Adrienne lay looking at him waiting for her senses to draw together. Finally, she moved a little, aware of her nakedness and the too-cold air filling the room and raising gooseflesh on her. As she continued to look at him through the wisps of hair spread over her eyes, she slowly realized that the man standing in the doorway was different from the one she could recall from recent days: he was smiling.

"Why?" she asked.

"Why what?"

"Why are you smiling?"

"Am I?"

"Yes."

"Maybe it's a kind of defense. Smile and the world smiles with you. That kind of jazz."

"Oh. I suppose I'd better get up and shower."

"I've got the water heating for instant coffee."

"Okay. Give me ten minutes."

"Adrienne—"

"Yes?"

"I love you."

The day passed slowly, the hours jumbling one into the next with no measurable intervals. More than once, they found themselves performing tasks which brought them close to each other, frequently touching in an anxious giving and taking of physical assurance, making pointless conversation in order to hear the other's voice.

In the middle of the afternoon, Ned wrapped the portraits of Sebastian and Sabra in a bedspread and leaned them against the wall beside the apartment's entrance. He made no comment, but Adrienne could not help but feel it was a defensive action.

Sitting at the dining table, her arms crossed on it while she looked at the folded bedspread, she asked, "Why do you suppose Sebastian hasn't appeared to you?"

"I don't know. Maybe it's something to do with getting through to me from wherever it is they exist. I thought he might come, at least I hoped he would, because I wanted him to see what I've done. If he gave his approval, it would sure as hell give me more confidence than I'm feeling now." He stopped and looked at her, then shook his head. "Jesus, I'm talking about him as if he was a living person."

"You've been doing that lately."

"Oh?" He frowned. "I wonder what that means."

"Probably nothing. It might be just a side effect of your involvement. You know, nerves and tension—something like that."

"Yeah, I guess."

"It's not that important, anyway, is it?"

"No, I guess not." He smiled. "The fact is, right now I think we're both talking just to hear ourselves talk. Nervous chatter, you know."

The hint of humor in his voice made everything seem nearer to being all right, allowing her to push her preoccupation with the coming evening's events a little distance away.

Then suddenly it was twilight. The sun was below the horizon with the orange hue in the western sky darkening, then melting and finally fading into a mauve which already blended into deep purple up near the arch of the sky.

Ned turned from the window through which he had watched the evening approach. "I don't suppose it would do a bit of good, would it, if I asked you to stay here?"

"No."

He nodded, expecting that answer and not prepared to argue with it. "Then it's time to get ready."

It was five minutes until nine when he put the paintings in the Toyota's back seat, then slid in under the steering wheel. Adrienne leaned from her place on the passenger's side to give him a quick kiss on his right cheek.

"For luck," she said.

He swiveled in the seat to look at her. He saw in her face what he had seen in his own that day in front of the mirror: strain lines reaching downward from the corners of her mouth, her eyes so tired they reflected abstractions, with faint purple smudges forming crescents beneath them.

He reached a hand behind her head and pulled her face to his. The kiss he gave her was long, a kiss of encouragement and controlled passion, and Adrienne felt herself responding in spite of her weariness, aware of the fatigue, worry and apprehension siphoning from her as if, through the kiss, Ned was taking much of it unto himself.

When he drew his head back, she felt momentarily incoherent, a portion of her wanting the kiss to continue while another part knew there was no time. She managed a smile, saying softly, "I love you, Ned Anderson."

He gave her a quick kiss on the cheek, then started the car.

He drove slowly. He seemed to be forcing himself through

a mental hesitation, fighting a reluctance to continue toward the house, but unwilling to go back. Traffic was light, most people having finished their weekends. Adrienne sat quietly. The wind coming through the open windows was warm with a touch of stickiness, and, as they drew nearer the house, her nerves became alert, senses sharpening to spark at the suspicion of danger.

When he turned into the driveway, Ned almost stopped the car, then fed it enough gas to crawl past the house into the parking area. Away from the city lights, the darkness was heavy, concealing within its depths the oaks and pines and peppertrees, allowing the house to be seen only as a great bulk devoid of detail looming in a brooding mass over them.

Adrienne felt her heart hammering in her chest cavity, not rapidly but with a solid thudding which sent tiny trembles down her arms into her fingers. The silence between them froze. She felt very human and very vulnerable.

The air outside the car began to assume a fraudulent coolness as a night breeze stirred itself among the unseen trees. Adrienne shivered. All too clearly in her memory she saw the women coming out of the darkness, felt the terror they brought with them rebuilding within her, detail after detail horribly taking shape.

"You okay?" Ned asked, carefully examining her face as best he could in the dark.

"Yes. Just a bad moment or two. How much longer before we can take the paintings up to the apartment?"

"Most anytime now."

In spite of herself, she shivered again. Something other than the night breeze coming through the window was caressing her cheek. As she looked at Ned's profile, then squinted to see the carriage house in the darkness behind him, she felt the slipping away of her will.

"Let's do it," she said. The trembling in her fingers was

becoming worse, and she suddenly felt an enclosure being erected to prevent her leaving here. "Let's do it now, darling."

Ned pulled the paintings from the rear seat, careful that the bedspread did not slip from them. Holding them under his arm, he looked at the carriage house, then around through the darkness as he would if expecting to see something among the trees, now that his night vision was more acute.

The crunching of the gravel under their feet seemed to Adrienne to build upon itself, becoming louder and louder as they approached the bottom of the outside stairs, each individual step they took a call to whatever might be waiting for them; then, when they reached the stairs and began to climb them, an overwhelming doubt clutched her.

On the upper landing outside the apartment door, Ned dug in his pants pocket, fumbled momentarily, then brought out his keys. She watched him balancing the paintings under one arm while using the other hand to unlock the door, wondering why he did not give her the key to do the unlocking. When the lock clicked, he stood aside, then opened the door and fumbled along the wall to find the light switch.

As soon as they stepped across the threshold into the apartment, she felt them, like electrical currents, snapping in the darkness, weaving around her a web of passions in which she knew she could become entangled: the hate and greed and fury erupting from the women.

The paintings were arranged around the living room in the way, she assumed, women attending a meeting would arrange themselves, some on the chairs, several on the sofa, with the others scattered around the floor in what could be considered conversational groupings. She stood just inside the door looking from one to another of them, trying to think of something to say to Ned but unable to override her balking mind. Each one of the women, she felt, was staring directly at her.

Finally she asked, "Did you arrange the paintings like this when you brought them here?"

"No." What confidence he had been displaying, she sensed, had dangerously lessened. He held the two paintings in front of him. "I'm going to put these on the sofa. That will be the best place for them to be seen when he unveils them."

She nodded. The women were now, she was sure, watching Ned as he walked slowly to the sofa, the atmosphere in the room suddenly lighter, expectation and excitement replacing the hate and fury.

He removed the three paintings from the sofa, placed them in the center of the floor, then leaned the two wrapped canvases against the sofa's back. They dominated the room.

"That's about right, don't you think?" he asked.

"Yes." She felt inarticulate.

Uncertainly Ned approached the painting in one of the chairs. In front of it, he stood gazing intently down at it, withdrawing, as she watched, into a place where his thoughts were private and distinctly his own. She saw his hands clench, then unclench, at his sides, a muscle cord into a ropelike ridge in his neck, then watched while he drew a deep breath as he shook his head. She moved a half step to her left into a position from where she could see the portrait.

It was of a statuesque, golden-haired blonde who, while giving a regal effect, was basically a sturdy, full-bodied woman dressed in a curve-accentuating blue gown. An awesome woman, Adrienne thought, who had been designed by nature for a primary function and who certainly must have performed it with incredible charm. But then she saw the woman's eyes. Their blue depths were glistening unnaturally in a way no artist could ever paint them. She knew what it was. Both she and Ned had seen it in Sandi's eyes. Tears. Then behind the tears, she saw a dark fluttering which reminded her of cringing shadows, something which could be nothing but the reflection of sickening despair. She closed her own eyes and moved away.

"It's Lila, the woman The Master sent to me," Ned said at her side.

"She looks so . . . so full of fear."

He took her by the arm. "I think they're all terror-stricken underneath their hate. Their madness is a mixture of envy and despair, I'm sure."

She nodded, having the terrible impression that this was no longer an apartment, but rather a crypt or tomb, and she and Ned were ghouls participating in an unspeakable act of cruelty.

"Where's Sandi?" she asked.

"I don't know." His hand tightened on her arm and gave it a tug. "Let's go. There's nothing more we can do here, and time's running out."

"How long do you think it will be before he arrives?"

"Not too long. He was so damned excited about this occurring on a Sunday, I'm sure he'll want to entertain himself and gloat as much as he can before the day ends."

"And when he finds out he's been tricked, what then?"

"Sweetheart, I don't know. You know that. We've talked about it."

Just before Ned flipped off the light, Adrienne looked for the last time at the paintings, seeing here and there, she was certain, eyes that were too wet and lips parted in either partial smiles or grimaces of fear. She could feel hysteria and fury beginning to pulse in the hot air of the room, intensifying, frighteningly so, until she no longer saw oblongs of paint-covered canvases but living women gripped in savage passions returning her stare from the depths of soulless horror.

"Come on, let's get out of here." Ned was once more tugging at her arm.

She stepped to the landing outside the door at the same instant he flipped off the light. As the room returned to darkness, she heard a woman's voice, high-pitched and trembling, crying out words she could not understand.

"Ned?"

"Just keep going, sweetheart. We've got to get away from here." He guided her to the first step. "Come on."

Once again the gravel crunched in tiny rattlings under their feet. Somewhere in the distance a dog barked, protecting its territory against things it imagined it saw or smelled in creeping shadows. Adrienne shivered. She felt out of balance, as if she and Ned were scurrying along a path leading to some strange new menace while dark things prowled in the night just beyond their hearing.

When they reached the car, Ned glanced at the house, then around the area and finally at his watch as if measuring time against distance. "I'm going to get a few things out of the house."

"Ned! You said we don't have much time."

"I know. I just want to pick up the linseed oil and varnish. I've used up the little bit I took to the apartment, and I might be wanting to do more work."

Adrienne stared at him incredulously. "Why not tomorrow? You don't need them tonight. You can't possibly be using them for a day or two—maybe never if we don't get away from here."

An extended minute passed while Ned neither moved nor spoke. He stood rigidly beside the car. Finally he looked at her with eyes which seemed to hover on her before sliding away in the direction of the carriage house.

"All right. I'm going to get Sebastian's notebook. I didn't take it to the apartment. I don't know how much danger is connected with possessing it, but if there is any, I didn't want to expose us to it at your apartment." He looked straight at her. "I want to destroy it—now. I don't want it ever to be passed on as it was to me. I want it all to end tonight."

"You can do that tomorrow."

"There might not be a tomorrow for us, darling."

She felt the color leaving her face while at her sides her hands doubled into useless fists.

"I won't be long. Just a couple of minutes. I know right where it is."

Still she made no comment while imagination grew upon itself to combine with fear. She continued to stare into the darkness folding more and more tightly around them, more than certain now that something must be watching them from the shadows.

He handed her the car keys. "Here. While I'm in there, move the car down to the side door."

She took the keys, surprised at how cold they were in her palm after being held tightly in Ned's hand.

Without another word, Ned hurried toward the house.

At first the sound came from a long, long way away, faint, ethereal, without any meaning. But as she became attuned to it and listened more closely, it drifted gracefully nearer, undulating through the night, at moments sweetly sensuous, at others blatantly strident, a melody blending all the notes of all the music since before time began.

Adrienne felt it seeping into her, entering through her skin, to find the places inside her where her blood ran, then turning it into streams of fire rushing through her veins. She shivered as it leeched along the channels of her senses to numb her mind of everything but a sudden, desperate desire which bordered on ecstasy.

She was growing warm as the rivulets of steaming blood in her veins ignited tiny fires throughout her body. Her loins began to pulse, her breasts swell. Gasping, she looked around—and saw it!

Light filled the windows of the carriage house apartment. It was a diffused, wavering light such as might come from the reflections of glowing embers or a multitude of candles. It rippled across the glass in blending shades of pink and green and orange, sending sparkling shards of color fanning through the darkness to sprinkle the gravel of the parking area with shimmering patches. It was from somewhere in the direction of that kaleidoscope that the exquisite melody came.

She realized she was walking across the parking area only when she moved through one of the places where window light splashed on the gravel, and, for those brief seconds while she was in the illumination, the night became a burst of radiant pigmentation in which she could not remember where she was or what was occurring . . . and did not care.

At the bottom of the steps leading up to the apartment, she hesitated, listening. Coming from above her, like an intricate interweaving pattern of the music, yet alien to it, were voices. Some were singing, others crying, and the songs and cries were accompanied by other voices laughing and giggling.

Wanting to run up the steps, she forced herself instead to take them one at a time. Now the music roamed unhindered through her, beating with a great pulsing surge.

She turned the knob. The door swung in without resistance. The wonderful sound floated out and encircled her, burrowing deeply into her to find the secret place where the primal urges coiled. Gasping, she did not move, wanting never to lose this experience of pure sensation in which all memory of life was removed. She followed the sound across the threshold.

Colors which appeared to come from a melted rainbow filled the room. Deep within them mauve and black shadows played a game of hide-and-seek, while from out of their swirling movements fanned heavy fragrances she thought she recognized as musk and sandalwood. A few feet inside the room, she was aware of the scent of candle wax, too, along with cloying frangipani. All around the room what appeared to be hundreds of candles burned with straight, unwavering flames like tiny slots of fairy fire in the multicolored haze.

Behind her the door closed.

At first, she was only partially cognizant of figures other than herself moving through the pinks and greens and oranges, then recognized the specters as women roaming sensuously through the vagrant light, women whom she had the remote feeling she had seen and met before.

She felt she should say something, to make herself known to these women drifting like ghosts through the fuming light, but her mind was slipping further and further from her control until she was left with no thoughts, only implausible sensations.

Very slowly she began to perceive a steady throbbing beneath the lightness of the spiraling music-sound. It found the rhythm of her heart, matched itself to it, then surged through her like the rememberings of a bodily passion she had never known. She stood breathing deeply of the fragrant air as her mind pulled in, removing her even more from the outside world, enclosing her for what might be forever in this witching illumination.

The women were dancing, their naked bodies contorting to the trailing beat of the undertoning throb. Sweat had transformed their rippling flesh into reflective curves on which the colors sheened as if the pliant hides had been bathed with oil. She watched heavy breasts sway and soft bellies heave above sturdy hips, which were rotating and thrusting fecund loins forward in erotic invitation; but slowly, as her concentration became more fixed, she saw that on all their strained faces rode an unconcealed terror, that their half-closed eyes shadowed the harshness of despair. She could hear them grunting and sobbing as they struggled to fill their laboring lungs with the room's rancid air. Bending, arching, strong muscles flexing under tautened flesh, they were responding to the throbbing with a brutal grace; yet, as she stared at them, she did not see the sensuous movements of healthy women, but the bestial struggling of naked animals.

Dismayed, she looked away. She felt herself swaying with the relentless beat. The air in the room grew hot, stifling, becoming clogged with the smells of incense and the sweating bodies of the dancers. Dizziness made her wipe a hand across her forehead as a weakness, along with a creeping clamminess, seeped through her.

Something passed before her, dark, almost opaque, making her think of a wisp of sooty smoke. For the length of an indrawn breath, whatever it was hesitated in front of her and examined her, studying her as someone might an object for purchase. Coming from it was a stench that she was certain was burning sulfur.

A guttural sound, resembling a voice, spoke in her ear. "You have come early, Adrienne Lewis."

Before she could react, the darkness drifted away. She watched it approach two of the women standing in the center of the room whispering to one another, then saw it expand into an all but definite shape as portions of it encircled their bodies. With fluting squeals and little-girl giggles, the women permitted it to pull them to the floor.

She felt the sweat run down her face and arms as, through the fog of wavering light and cloying scents, she watched the women writhing on the floor and the dark, boiling thing between them stroking and caressing their proffered flesh. She was, she realized, watching a harsh lovemaking, with the dark thing taking brutally what the women were forced to offer. In a little while, one of them whimpered, then cried out in pain as what might have been a hand or paw clutched a plump breast and clawed into its malleable firmness. In answer, a laugh rolled through the room, hoarse and guttural like the baying of a night beast. The two women moaned uncontrollably but made no attempt to squirm away, remaining sprawled on each side of the thing within the smoky cocoon, waiting docilely for whatever it desired to do next.

Adrienne tried to scream, but the hot air gagged her, allowing only a whimper to slip through her stiffened lips.

"We, ourselves, are gentle to each other," a voice beside her said.

She whirled, startled. A tall woman with flowing chestnut-colored hair stood near her, studying her with luminous eyes of equal chestnut hue.

The woman shrugged wide, strong shoulders, looked perplexed for a moment, then used the tip of her tongue in a slow wetting of her lips. "You will be my very special friend."

"What do you mean?"

The woman nodded to her right, indicating something in the haze she wanted Adrienne to see. Adrienne looked in the direction the woman had nodded.

"You see," the woman whispered, "we are kind to one another in our love."

Clinging together with long legs and eager arms entwining, two women smoothly rolled and twisted deep in one of the chairs. Faces hidden, pressed together as lips ground against lips, their gentle hands fluttered along spread thighs and over thrusting breasts. A low sound, a cooing, came from them, breathless and eager, as they gave flesh to flesh.

Adrienne felt an odd dissolving of substance within her, but at the same time a strange sensation of witnessing a dark kind of beauty left over from the dawn time. Within the growing heat of the room, the fragrances of the incense mixtures blended into a heady combination of springtime blossoms which drew her further and further away from her senses, so she stood without moving, staring through the saffron haze at what she plainly saw as the exquisite beauty of the act the women in the chair were performing.

"My name is Esther," the woman whispered. "What is yours?"

"Adrienne." How difficult it was for her to speak. "Ah." Esther reached out to run cool fingers down Adrienne's cheek.

Around them the mists eddied as women who were not occupied drifted through the room stirring little currents in the oppressive air. Hesitantly, several of them approached to stand a respectful distance from Adrienne and Esther, their eyes curious as if in Adrienne they were beholding a creature somewhat different from themselves.

"She will be mine," Esther said, looking hard at them. "Is that understood?"

A redhead laughed. "Until someone else takes a fancy to her."

But the others nodded and turned away.

Esther chuckled deep in her throat as she cupped Adrienne's face in both her hands and drew it toward her own. Adrienne rocked forward on the balls of her feet. She knew what the other woman was going to do, and she wanted her to do it, so when their lips met, she pressed hers hard against Esther's, darting her tongue into the moist warmth of the eager mouth seeking its sweetness. Esther made a crooning sound as she ran her hands down Adrienne's neck, then across her shoulders and finally down her sides to rest on her hips. Their touch was hot as their movements became more sure of themselves. They slipped around Adrienne's hips to spread on her buttocks, where they began a greedy stroking. Adrienne moaned. She shifted her hips beneath the demanding hands and through her clothing became aware of the heat of Esther's naked body pressing against her own from breasts to loins. She felt a sensitiveness of the tissues in her body she had never before known, and with a low, continuous purring, which she only vaguely recognized as her own, she ground her breasts and loins tight to Esther's, opening her mouth as she did to welcome another of the woman's kisses.

"Adrienne!"

It came from a great distance, a shout by a voice calling from another world.

She heard it as no more than an isolated sigh in her mind, yet she felt a stirring of suspense and confusion in her consciousness. She pulled her mouth from Esther's.

"Adrienne, where are you?"

She pushed herself away from the woman. Uncertainty touched her. She looked at Esther, who was smiling at her with what she could only think of as hunger, and suddenly she felt repugnance. She stepped back, looking around the room, feeling Esther's hands tightening on her buttocks in a slight restraining effort.

The candles began to flicker, their flames weaving back and forth like tiny serpents searching for things in the shadows to attack, until she sensed a darkness she had not seen before closing more and more tightly upon the saffron-misted area. Still in their circle around the walls, the women were continuing their dance, but with their primitive writhings slower as their exhausted muscles and overstrained flesh refused to respond to new demands.

"Adrienne! Where are you? Answer me."

The voice was nearer, but still far, far away. Her body tensed and for a split moment became that of another. She pulled herself completely free of Esther's hands.

Esther's smile remained. "You will belong to me, Adrienne, for a long, long time. There are many who are to be set free before my time comes."

There was something she should remember, which, if only she could bring it to mind, would combat the horror she felt at the woman's words. But whatever it was, it was too elusive for her to find in her memory; so she stood mutely, unable to return Esther's stare, feeling more naked and vulnerable than the women surrounding her.

"Perhaps I will not be as gentle with you as I thought." Esther was still smiling, but a huskiness in her voice was counter to the smile. Then, with her eyes narrowing and a little shrug, she turned away.

"Adrienne! Adrienne! For Christ's sake, answer me!"

Others heard the calling. There was a murmuring among the women.

Adrienne shook her head dully. She was desperately tired.

In a very obscure cell in her mind, a mote of knowledge whispered that she should do more than stand helplessly where she was, that she was as much a prisoner of herself as of the environment surrounding her.

From somewhere a tinkling bell began to send sharp, crystal-pure notes through the haze. Another joined it, then another, until the stifling air quivered with what might have been the music of an ethereal carillon.

The women began to whisper among themselves, their exhaustion apparently forgotten as they drew together in what could only be expectation. A few of them hastily combed fingers through their tangled hair. Within a moment, they had all settled themselves, their whisperings and gigglings stilled, so that other than the tinkling of the distant bells, there was absolute silence within the room.

Adrienne saw the dark column drift toward the sofa, where its darkness began to fade, separating into wisps of sooty gray. The women began to tremble.

Slowly, as if reluctant to enter even the subdued illumination of the apartment, another form took shape within the remnants of the spiraling column. At first, it was transparent, then portion by portion, like a statue without detail being hewn by unseen hands, it blocked itself into arms and legs and torso, and a figure partially emerged. Feet apart, arms folded across a massive chest, it stood beside the sofa.

Scattered moans came from the women as the wisps of darkness became no more than streamers circling the figure. Adrienne felt her insides were about to give way while the heat moved upward, becoming filled with the smell of burning sulfur. Terror held her rigid. All the strength in all her muscles was sucked away into the heat.

The figure, if that was what it was, appeared neither human nor beast, but behind the twisting black wisps, it was tall, yet stocky, combining both man and animal, with neither predominant. It was a pulling together of shadows into a solid form, an ancient structure which had survived the changes of uncounted millenniums that mankind, and the creatures which had survived along with it, could not even guess at. Adrienne thought she saw a massive male torso, but instead of sleek thighs, strong-looking columns of fur descended into what might have been a feline's hind legs. Large bracelets studded with what looked like semiprecious stones that encircled its wrists and golden armlets gleaming on bulging biceps were its only adornment, its only clothing. It was a thing which dwelt in myths and legends. And it was a thing without a face.

In their weaving, the streamers crossed and crisscrossed its face, never permitting even a brief glimpse of its features, but through the dark ribbons, Adrienne received the impression of animal handsomeness, of harsh lines blending to create a near human face bordering on strong ruggedness. Once, as a streamer drifted away from in front of it, she saw a blue eye focused on her with a piercing stare, and as she returned its look she felt a sudden numbness, a slipping away into a sensation of being drawn slowly in its direction.

"Eugena. Marcella." The voice came through the ribbons of darkness in surprisingly modulated tones. "Tomorrow your servitude is completed, as I promised you. You will live, then die, as free women, and He whom you call God may have your souls."

An excited murmuring came from the women.

"You have been a long time with me." The figure reached out a hand to the bedspread-wrapped canvases on the sofa. "But with these two to replace you, I emancipate you."

As his hand closed on the bedspread to pull it from the paintings, Adrienne heard footsteps on the landing outside the door, then a rattling of the knob.

"Now! See those who are to take your places."

With a magician's flourish and a swirling of the dark

ribbons around it, the figure yanked the bedspread from the canvases.

Sebastian and Sabra smiled at the women from their places on the sofa.

Silence. A frozen silence, huge and distorted, in which not even the tinkling of the bells was heard. It filled the room. It pushed at the walls in an effort to spill out into the night and when it could not, piled upon itself, layer upon layer, until it became a burden too heavy for those within the room to bear.

A woman screamed.

Then another.

"You have cheated us!"

"You have broken your promise again!"

Time stretched into an intolerably long moment while the figure, ignoring the women, stood staring at the paintings, then threw back its head and roared with a terrible animal rage into the shifting haze. Howling with a demented fury beyond comprehension, it snatched up the stretched canvases, stared at them an instant longer, then flung them with a crazed violence across the room. They smashed into a wall to fall with a deadened thump to the floor. The putrid stench of burning sulfur choked the room, and, as if a gale wind swept through the saffron light, the candles whipped and guttered.

"He lies to us!" a woman screamed. "He will never let us go."

"We are forever doomed." The voice of another broke with hysteria. "We will always be his slaves. We will belong to him forever."

"Silence!" The black streamers whipped around the figure in increasing spirals. "Quiet!"

But a chant of rage and horror came from a dozen throats. "No, no, no!"

"I warn you, you caterwauling sluts—be still!"

"Mother of God, help us . . . please . . ."

"Put no faith in her," a voice cried. "If we are to be helped, it must be by our own actions."

The cold tone of command in the husky voice quieted the women for an instant, then a calmer voice spoke. "What Magda speaks is true. Heed her."

"Heed her, you pampered bitches," the figure shouted, "and you will dance for one hundred years."

The absolute fury in the voice made a few whimper and some step back. A snarl came from the figure's hidden mouth, then what might have passed for a laugh. "Down! Down into the beast position, you worthless cows. Down!"

Here and there, women dropped to their knees, then bent forward pressing their faces hard against the floor. Others stood trembling, some holding hands, looking nervously around the room.

"No!" Magda stepped forward. "No! Tonight we free ourselves. We can. You see before you proof he is not invincible. He has been tricked. He can be defeated—and we can do it! He is nothing but a dumb brute!"

"Yes! Yes! He is no Master!"

She took a step toward the figure, then another. Taking courage from her, other women moved forward, at their sides their fingers curling, long nails becoming talons.

The figure watched them for a moment or two, then raised an arm, pointing a forefinger in their direction, streaks of blue fire burning where its eyes must be.

Magda laughed, the demented laugh of a person who had experienced close dealings with terror too many times to be affected with its advance upon her. With a yowling scream, she lunged forward, then leaped full upon the figure with the entire length of her body, driving into him with all the force her strong muscles could project. He stumbled backward, tottering, nearly falling to one knee. Earsplitting, guttural screams of inhuman fury echoed and reechoed through the hazy light as the women fought one another to swarm over him.

"Adrienne! Adrienne! Are you in there?" The door rattled on its frame behind her. "What in hell is going on? If you're there, answer me!"

She knew the voice now, but could not give a name to the person calling to her. Yet she did cry out as she thought of trying to open the door to allow whoever it was to enter.

In the center of the room a pile of writhing bodies squirmed like things unearthed beneath an upturned rock while wet flesh gleamed red and orange as, circling it, crouching women paced, eyes glaring with lunatic rage and mouths twisted into distorted ovals spewing words of ugly vengeance. Beneath those squirming bodies, she knew, was The Master, yet instinct would not permit her to believe he would remain there long.

There was a heavy thudding against the door.

From within the pile of naked bodies, a woman screamed. A leg jerked outward in a spasmodic kick of pain. Adrienne watched its pointed foot strike a candelabra standing near a chair. The top-heavy fixture swayed in a teetering arc with the candles dragging their flames in tiny comet trails through the swirling mists, then it toppled, plunging the dozen little fires into the chair.

The intermittent thudding at the door became repeated blows slamming into the paneling until it creaked on the verge of splintering.

"Adrienne! For God's sake, answer me, if you're in there."

She did not know what to do. The dizziness was on her again. The hot scents of the incense and struggling bodies were choking her. Sweat bathed her, running into her eyes, her nose. Her hands began to tremble and her legs shook while her heartbeat filled her throat. She stared dumbly at the twisting bodies, then at the door, trying to find a way out of the terrible cul-de-sac in which her mind was trapped.

"She is to blame, too!" A tall brown-haired woman who was standing on the edge of the pile of writhing flesh pointed at her. "She tricked us, too!"

Adrienne heard another blow on the door. Quietly sobbing, she forced her quivering legs to take a step in the direction of the sound, partially aware it somehow had to do with escape from the horror which was trapping her.

They rushed her. Screaming curses, they clutched her hair, pulled her arms, tore at her face with their slashing nails. With a wild cry, she flailed out with her arms, made one of her legs swing in a kick which drove her foot deep into soft flesh, and all the time a noise somewhere between a whimper and a moan made a continuous sound in her throat as she turned her own fingers into hooked claws which she raked along wet skin. But there were too many; they piled on her as they had on The Master, using their weight to drive her to her knees as their lashing fingernails shredded her blouse and skirt to expose her skin in which they gouged bloody channels. Hands clutched her hair, dug in deeply, then pushed her face down toward the floor.

Frantically she lunged forward, driving her shoulders into several pairs of legs before her. She saw one pair stumble backward, then swing out to the side as the woman to whom they belonged lost her balance. Through the screams of the women on top of her and her own sobbing, she heard the falling body crash into something which, in turn, fell with a splintering, metallic crash. She heard a cry of fear, immediately followed by another. The blows on her hunched back ceased momentarily, the hands in her hair relaxed their twisting. Nerves and senses instantly alerted themselves to the hesitation, then reacted spontaneously as she lurched to the left, using her hip and shoulder as a battering ram against the women kneeling around her, thrusting forward as she had before, but this time drawing herself up into a tight fetal position. She rolled free of the women.

Terror drove her body. She pushed herself to her feet. She gasped. New fear shoved the old aside.

Along the entire south wall of the room, already claiming the sofa, flames crackled in widening sheets. With bright red tentacles reaching out, spreading like greedy fingers up the dry paper of the wall, the fire was racing toward the front wall. From the burning chair into which the candelabra had plunged, runnels of flame scurried across the floor and were teasing a corner of the old rug into a smoldering combination of smoke and fire.

Some of the women were doing no more than looking with blank eyes at the fire's advance, all their functional responses apparently deadened, though several others were moving cautiously toward the two centers of flame, an auburn-haired woman holding a gown in her hands with the obvious thought of smothering the rampant fire. But six of them remained crouched in a circle around Adrienne, their mouths stretched wide in silent screams behind the long strands of hair fallen over their faces. A violent shiver shook her as she made herself return their mad stares, all at once knowing with a terrible certainty that these were crazed animals whose minds had been driven out of focus by the consuming hate and terror building in them for so many years.

She took a tentative step backward, then another, with the women following her. She could see muscles bunching in their bent legs as they prepared to spring, hear the hissing of their breath through teeth now bared like fangs.

There was a scuffle, a flurry of movement, as Magda elbowed her way through the circle. "Damn you! Damn you to the hell we have suffered! He has escaped, but you will not."

Without a pause, she sprang. Adrienne stumbled backward as she slapped away with stiffened fingers a hand which darted at her eyes. Missing her face, Magda clutched at Adrienne's breasts. She pulled and twisted, sending streams of pain lancing across Adrienne's chest and down her belly. Adrienne heard herself screaming with a blinding rage and drove her knee hard into the woman's abdomen while lashing with her nails across the contorted face before her. Cut deeply and surprised, Magda howled as she released her hold and fell back, blood flowing from a lacerated cheek.

The other women shuffled closer, but made no attempt to join the attack. Back of them, even through the saffron mist, Adrienne could see the fire had climbed all the way up the north wall and was reaching with the tips of its outrunners for the front window curtains. On the other side of the room, the flames were devouring an end table, exploring portions of them, like scurrying snakes streaming from their nest, starting to crawl up the east wall. More of the women were fighting the fire now, using pillows and discarded gowns in an attempt to smother it.

Then Magda was on her again, snarling, clawing and kicking. In spite of Adrienne's catching her wrists, she managed to dig both hands into Adrienne's hair, and with a strength far beyond her stature she yanked Adrienne's head forward, slamming her face down to meet an upcoming knee. Adrienne squealed as pain split her head like a hatchet sunk into her skull. Blood squirted from her nostrils. She could hear Magda laughing and the other women giggling.

Shrieking as incoherently as the women surrounding her, Adrienne butted her head and shoulders into Magda's belly, driving herself forward with all the power in her leg muscles. Off balance from the kick, Magda could not react. She teetered for an instant, air rushing from her mouth, her hands spasmodically digging more viciously into Adrienne's hair; then, with a startled cry, she fell to her back, dragging Adrienne down on top of her sprawled body. Momentarily Adrienne lay with her face buried in the mound of Magda's left breast, but animal instinct combined with the terror and pain that were mounting to a climax within her, and with a snarl, she bit the firm flesh and mindlessly gnawed her teeth into the warm tissue. Magda screamed a howl of dreadful anguish. Adrienne did not hear it, her mind no longer within its human dimensions, an unused intelligence from the cave time wresting control, communicating nothing but the knowledge that she must preserve herself. Snarling, she chewed at the flesh, spitting out mouthfuls of blood and ignoring the hands tearing at what remained of her clothing and lacerating her bare back and sides in deep furrows. Suddenly the hands picked her up from Magda's writhing form, held her helpless, then threw her halfway across the room.

She lay still where she fell, not too far from the burning sofa, panting and spitting out blood and flesh. She saw women kneeling beside a screeching Magda, along with others milling aimlessly like fright-befuddled cattle, through the mist which had become too full of red and too shifting with movement. And too hot. She watched the flames cascading down the walls from the arc of fire spanning the ceiling. The realization that the fire was beyond control came slowly. She stayed as she was on the floor with only her eyes shifting from time to time as she watched the women and the approaching holocaust with detachment.

When she finally remembered the battering at the door, the distorted darkness disappeared from her mind, torn away with an almost audible ripping sound as something clean and shimmering replaced it.

She sat up, grimacing at the salty sweet taste in her mouth and the warm sticky substance around her lips. She wiped a hand across her chin, then looked dumbly at the blood smearing her fingers, and all at once she felt tired, more tired than she could ever remember, with pain lying like a web across her face and laddered down her back in burning strips.

Ignoring that pain, she pushed herself up from the floor to stand with her feet widespread to maintain her balance, looking around the room. Two walls and the ceiling were lost behind solid masses of flame. Smoke was blackening the saffron haze, turning it into an opaque thickness through which she barely distinguished the women, who were now showing signs of fright. None of them were any longer trying to fight the fire; instead they huddled together like beasts trapped in a burning barn, watching with fear-blanked eyes the encircling fire creeping toward them. Seeing their muted terror unleashed an onslaught of panic in her. She was trapped with them in a burning coffin!

"Ned!"

She did not know she had screamed his name out loud; it had just entered her mind and she responded, but the women stared at her.

Where was Ned? Surely it had been he at the door trying to get into the room before the fire started. She knew that now, now that it was too late. Was he still out there on the landing, or had he gone away when she had not answered?

Rekindled terror tightened its grip on her. From the corners of her eyes, she saw red tongues of flame at her shoulders. She screamed. Behind her something crashed. Sparks swirled around her in a shower of searing dots which burned pinpoints of pain on her shoulders and along her back where they touched her skin. She sprang forward, directly at the befuddled women blocking her way to the door.

She was still on her feet, in the middle of the women, exchanging raking scratches and slaps, trading kicks with them, her screams as loud and demented as theirs, when she saw Ned standing in the frame of the opened door.

"Oh, my God, Adrienne!"

"Ned! Ned, save me . . ."

"Adrienne! Hold on, honey, hold on. I'm coming . . ."

She had read of actions occurring too fast in times of stress to be individually recorded by the mind. During those times, no conscious directions are given to the body; it reacts under the guidance of an ancient instinct stored in remote cells of that portion of the brain which today is never used. Ned leaping through the door, then using his fists and feet to drive the women away from her, was such a time. It was all a blur punctuated with merciless, ugly screams in her ears and jumbled areas of woman-flesh distorted before her eyes.

Then they were near the door with Ned between her and the women, still lashing his fists at them, matching their screams of fury with grunting curses of his own, shoving Adrienne in the direction of the landing at the top of the stairs with his back and shoulders. Throughout the room, the flames were roaring in the draft from the open door, arching in a great vault from wall to wall and dropping from the ceiling in fiery stalactites. Smoke billowed, whirlpooling around them like an oily fog that plunged down their throats to clog their lungs at the same time it was filling their eyes.

He gave her a final shove, just opening his mouth to shout at her when a scream of unimaginable terror rose above all the others. It was a bloodcurdling wail beyond the range of panic. Adrienne felt a chill race through her, then cold prickles on her neck and back. She saw Ned's hands drop to his sides while he stared past the women into the inferno the room had become. Like creatures instantly frozen in time, the women halted their attack, remaining into the positions they were in except for looking back over their shoulders.

Once more the scream soared, even more torn with terror than before, fluting into a shriek in which horror and desperation sounded the descent of a mind into dark madness.

"Our portraits! They are burning! *We are burning!*"

All the voices were completely stilled. Only the roar of the greedy flames crackled and hissed as they devoured the room, sending forth smoke that whorled in thick clouds through the open door.

A piercing wail rose from within the black clouds, immediately accompanied by another that brimmed with a panic so utterly shrill it soared out of human hearing.

"No! Noooo . . ."

Wildly wheeling, the women who had been attacking Adrienne and Ned struggled among themselves to plunge toward the flames.

"Get downstairs," Ned gasped. "Hurry."

She hesitated, her eyes on the ghastly scene in the room.

"Get going, dammit! I want to close the door and lock all that evil in there. Now, get going! I'll be right behind you."

She was halfway to the bottom when an explosion thundered into the night, rocking the old structure and shaking the stairs beneath her. Glass from the apartment's front windows shattered with a booming crash, then shattered again as it smashed into the parking area. Inside the apartment, the fire renewed its rumble. Dizzy, she grasped the railing with both hands and stood swaying with her eyes closed tightly, trying to swallow the metallic taste flowing into her mouth.

Coming down from the landing, Ned slammed onto the wooden planking, then he caught her waist with an encircling arm. "Come on, honey, come on! The door's closed and locked."

He partly dragged, partly carried, her the remaining distance to the ground, then pulled her to the car under the peppertree. She stumbled along at his side, panting with deep wheezing sobs as heat from the fire added its weight to the humidity of the night, forming a mixture so thick she found it next to impossible to suck it into her lungs. Not until they were leaning against the Toyota's metal coolness did she realize she was naked.

"The whole building's going," Ned said. He spoke more to himself than to her. "There's no saving it now."

"No."

The loss of the carriage house seemed overwhelmingly inconsequential to her. Watching the fire spiral its blood-red flames high into the darkness in what looked to be an attempt to singe the night sky, she felt a drowsy indifference creeping over her. The accumulated terrors were a portion of a huge design she could no longer really remember.

"No," she said. "There's no way of saving it . . . any of it."

From under a hyacinth bush beside the driveway, the Siamese cat watched the spraying fountains of sparks as the carriage house fell, timber by timber, in upon itself. In its blue eyes, squinted against the glare of the flames, red reflections danced like tiny demons cavorting in an orgiastic ceremony, while from low in its throat came a sound somewhere between a purr and a growl.

When the final wall collapsed, the cat stood up. It swung its eyes from the stunted flames struggling to remain alive within the ruins to the man and woman leaning against the automobile. It studied them, its narrowed eyes becoming opaque as if behind them its brain was forming, then discarding, then re-forming ideas. Finally it arched itself, then turned slowly and walked down the driveway. Just past the dark bulk of the house, it stopped to gaze back at them over its shoulder, its eyes now dull red, its small, curving fangs bared. The sound coming from its throat was no longer a purr.

SEPTEMBER

1986

There is no wealth of sight or feeling to the Florida season change; so, though the air was fragile, there was no crispness to hint of approaching autumn. True, the mornings had become gossamer, shimmering with the jewels of dew idly scattered during the night on crotons and hibiscus and glimmering on manicured lawns and weed-choked fields alike, but by midday the humidity would return and the smell of warm earth and overripe vegetation would replace the delicate night fragrances.

Sheila Rosenthal sauntered through the old garden, stopping now and then to pull a weed which had encroached too close to the path, studying the empty areas from which she and other members of the historical society had cleared long-dead brittle stalks. Looking at the emptiness, she tried to envision what replacements to set out the following spring which would as closely as possible duplicate the extravagant beauty of the original garden. Other than repeated mentionings of the bougainvillea, which had been the centerpiece, the records told little else concerning the types and arrangements of flowers and plants with which Sebastian had created his pattern of rainbow hues. Like everything else about the man, there was a shadow of depressing mystery over this dismal place where he and his wife had so violently died. Sheila imagined that time had slammed a door on events and memories, shutting the long-dead couple in a dark, unknown cell in history.

She followed the sensuous curve of the path until she came to a spot from where she could see the black pile of rubble which had once been the carriage house. It appeared to be sucking into its depths all the early afternoon sunlight as if it was trying to recapture a tiny leftover of the heat that had reduced it to that ugly, charred mound of twisted timbers, some of which, she thought, pointed at the sky like handless, pleading arms.

Or . . .

Or were the ruins trying to warm the still-unfound bones missing from the sixteen partial skeletons discovered within them?

Sheila shuddered, swung her eyes away, then took a shortcut to her car through the dry remains of the garden and the nodding weeds starting to encircle the parking area. Inside the car, she knew, she would feel protected, her heart would slow and the coldness in the pit of her stomach would disappear.

Through the car windows, she looked once more around the area, then at the gray-black heap of burned wood. Already nature was beginning a reclamation. Sprouting up through the scattered charcoal were green tufts of coarse, wide-bladed grass, while around several blackened and fallen beams young vines wove yellow-green stripes. A sudden darting movement caught her eye as a small lizard scurried through a ragged patch of unswallowed sunlight, sending up puffs of ash dust behind it.

The ugly ruins would never disappear, but in time the dreadful, sooty scar would recede into the sheathing greenery, eventually blurring into no more than a memory; yet she knew the terrible, haunting mystery would remain forever.

She backed the Buick from under the peppertree, pushed the gearshift into drive, slowly inching the car down the driveway, watching the house slip past her left shoulder. She thought she could feel the silence which filled the empty rooms reaching out for her. Her fingers tightened around the rim of the steering wheel as she resisted the urge to jam her foot down hard on the accelerator, refusing, no matter how loudly her instincts screamed at her, to hurry, determined she was not going to retreat in complete fear.

But as she swung from the driveway onto the county road, she knew she would never again return alone to the house. She wasn't sure if she would allow Ned Anderson's portrait of her to remain hanging in the living room of her home. She might just donate it to the historical society. Now that Ned's mother had signed the property over to the society, the painting could be displayed in the house's parlor. After all—all of Sebastian's paintings had disappeared.

When the entrance of the driveway came into sight, the Plymouth braked to no more than a creep, then eased into the driveway to slowly roll past the house with its tires crunching on the gravel. In the area between the big, silent house and the pile of tumbled rubble, it hesitated as if deciding whether to stay or to retreat down the driveway. Finally it pulled under the bowed limbs of a peppertree. It carried a Florida license plate, but from a county sixty miles distant.

A man and a woman in their early thirties got out of the front seat, immediately followed by a seven- or eight-year-old boy from the back. For a moment, the man and the woman stood looking around while the boy ran toward the mound of blackened wood.

"This must be the place," the man said.

"Yeah." The woman nodded. "It's pretty much like it looked on TV."

The man began walking in the direction of the ruins. The woman quickly took several fast steps to place herself at his side.

"It's sure quiet around here," the man said, the first hint of a frown creasing his brow. "Kinda heavy and, well . . . private feeling. Do you feel it?"

"It's spooky, that's what it is."

"Is this where they found the bones, Daddy?" Pointing at the collapsed jumble of burned wood, the boy narrowed his eyes in the sharp light to look up at his father. "In there?"

"Yeah, that's the place, Danny. Right in that pile of burned-up wood is where the bones were found."

"A whole bunch, huh, Dad?"

"Quite a few. The police think there were at least sixteen skeletons in there, son. All of them women, but maybe one man. They can't be sure, because they say the fire burned with such heat that many of the bones were probably burned up."

"Why didn't the women get out? Didn't they have a smoke detector like we do?"

"Apparently not, Danny."

"Then why didn't the firemen rescue them?"

The woman answered. "The man on TV said there's no fire department out here, Danny. And, besides, no one knew the women were in the building. No one knew there were people who needed to be rescued."

"Oh . . ."

The boy looked from his mother to his father, then once more at the carriage house ruins before turning away to wander off in the direction of the house.

"Don't go far, Danny," his mother called. "And stay away from the house. It's probably locked anyway."

The man lost interest in the ruins, too. There was disappointment on his face. "There's not much to see, is there?"

The woman gave a final dubious glance at the charred timbers. "No. Maybe it'll be more interesting when it's fixed up. Didn't they say some local historical society just took it over and is planning to restore the house and garden?"

"I think so, but even then, I don't think it would be worth the drive. It's still going to be just another old house with a garden. We've got those at home."

They began to walk slowly to the car.

"There is that spooky feeling, though." The woman lowered her voice to little more than a whisper. "Don't you feel it? Like, maybe, something is watching us . . ."

"Holy Christ, Darlene! You're just trying to scare yourself, for God's sakes."

"Well . . ." She frowned sidewise at him. "You've got to admit, Willy, if ever a place could be haunted, this is it. That artist and his wife being mauled to death a hundred years ago, according to the newspaper story, then those mystery women burning to death in the old carriage house. And don't forget the owner and his girlfriend disappearing. It's sort of like those stories by—oh, you know, what's-his-name . . . Edgar something."

"Allan Poe."

"Yes. Isn't it?"

"I suppose so, but the place is still disappointing. Besides, the guy that owned it, and his girlfriend, maybe didn't disappear. The cops think that some of the bones that were found might be theirs."

"Oh." She shrugged, was silent for several paces, then said, "Well, at least it gave us something to do on a Sunday afternoon."

He laid a hand on the clenching sway of her hips. "I can think of other things I'd rather do."

She pushed his hand away. "Behave yourself, Willy. Remember, Danny's here."

Already bored and pouting, the boy was waiting for them beside the Plymouth, leaning with his elbows on a front fender. "Are we going now? This a real dumb place."

OCTOBER

1986

In the west, the sun was resting on the long, flat line of the horizon. From it, leading from that outer edge of the world, a path of reddish-tinted orange paved the purpling water of the Gulf of Mexico. The half a dozen or so palm trees near the water's edge stretched their slender shadows across the gradually sloping lawn in the direction of the cottage, which was half hidden among the untrimmed azaleas and schefflera.

On the small porch of the cottage, a young woman sat on the top step of the four which descended to a narrow path of shell that circled the building. Her arms hugged her drawn-up legs, and her chin rested on her knees. Half closing her eyes against the setting sun, she watched the silhouetted figure of a man standing at a portable easel near where the grass faded into the sandy ribbon of narrow beach. He was furiously daubing watercolors on a sheet in an opened artist's pad, creating a hurried sketch of the drama unfolding in the western sky.

Sweeping back along the woman's temples, forming wings over her ears, long streaks of gray showed boldly in the blue-black of her hair. The gray lent enchantment to her strong-featured face. But that face, although handsome, was the exhausted face of a person who might be recovering from the ravages of an extended illness, the gauntness slowly being filled out by healthy tissue. In her eyes, however, remnants of the sickness remained. Far back in them, deep in their blue depths behind the sunset reflections, there was a haunting. Shadows moved, dark shadows that scurried across a mind which struggled with memories that were impossible to forget, but which refused to come into focus.

She sighed and stood up, pulling at her jeans to straighten their legs. Half-submerged in the Gulf, the sun was making one last endeavor at washing the sky a fiery yellow-orange. The man had stepped away from the easel to study the color sketch while wiping his brushes on a rag. She smiled. She felt a special warmth surround her. Her smile became a silent laugh. She felt all the dull and wooden reactions of the past weeks going from her.

She walked slowly across the lawn, certain she was on the verge of returning to a living world and wanting to savor each precious second of reentry. She watched the man drop his brushes into a wooden paint box, then lay the pad on the top of it before commencing to fold the easel. In a fleeting fragment of clairvoyance, she saw the man as a future name in the world of art, and wrapped her arms around herself in a quick shiver of excitement.

He looked up, saw her and waved. She waved back. Behind him, just offshore, a single file of pelicans dipped and soared on their evening fishing flight, resembling creatures from a prehistoric past. She counted them. Twenty-one. The old tale of the number of pelicans in a flight being odd or even, corresponding to the date, was correct this time. This was Friday, the seventeenth.

Seventeen . . .

It was one more than the skeletons found in those ruins.

She shivered. The long article in the Tampa newspaper had stated that sixteen skeletons, all presumably young women, had been found in the rubble of a mysterious fire in Orange County when the carriage house on a historic estate was destroyed. The article appeared in the same issue of the paper in which they found the rental advertisement for this cottage. She did not know why, but ever since reading that article, she had felt the pressure of memory encroaching into reality. But those undefined images were all from so long ago, she felt, from another time and another life which might not really have existed, so impossibly distant they no longer held meaning to her, and always, for some remote reason, she prayed that her memory of everything which had occurred before they moved into this cottage would forever remain obscure.

She heard a rustling in a clump of foliage off to her right, a sound like a small body pushing its way through entangling twigs. She stopped to stare, feeling a coldness spreading across her shoulders and down her back, then a trembling which threatened to weaken her legs so she would crumple into a quivering heap on the warm earth. But she saw no blue eyes watching her, no impossible grin on a feline face pointed in her direction.

Dear God! What was there about watching blue eyes and a grinning cat's face? Why should she remember?

When she became certain no animal was hidden in the bushes, she felt a rush of relief that swept away the encroaching terror. She swallowed hard, drew a long breath and looked at the man.

He was holding out his arms to her, and once more she was filled with warmth and began walking rapidly toward him, already feeling the strength of his arms around her.

Over his shoulder, standing hand in hand on the beach with an orange-red nimbus flaring behind them, she saw the silhouettes of their two friends, Sabra and Sebastian, who came at times to visit them.